PENGUIN CLASSICS

FATHERS AND SONS

IVAN SERGEYEVICH TURGENEV was born in 1818 in the Province of Orel, and suffered during his childhood from a tyrannical mother. After the family had moved to Moscow in 1827 he entered Petersburg University where he studied philosophy. When he was nineteen he published his first poems and, convinced that Europe contained the source of real knowledge, went to the University of Berlin. After two years he returned to Russia and took his degree at the University of Moscow. In 1843 he fell in love with Pauline Garcia-Viardot, a young Spanish singer, who influenced the rest of his life; he followed her on her singing tours in Europe and spent long periods in the French house of herself and her husband, both of whom accepted him as a family friend. He sent his daughter by a sempstress to be brought up among the Viardot children. After 1856 he lived mostly abroad, and he became the first Russian writer to gain a wide reputation in Europe; he was a well-known figure in Parisian literary circles, where his friends included Flaubert and the Goncourt brothers, and an honorary degree was conferred on him at Oxford. His series of six novels reflect a period of Russian life from 1830s to the 1870s: they are *Rudin* (1855), *A House of Gentlefolk* (1858), *On the Eve* (1859; a Penguin Classic), *Fathers and Sons* (1861), *Smoke* (1867) and *Virgin Soil* (1876). He also wrote plays, which include the comedy *A Month in the Country*; short stories and *Sketches from a Hunter's Album* (a Penguin Classic); and literary essays and memoirs. He died in Paris in 1883 after being ill for a year, and was buried in Russia.

•

ROSEMARY EDMONDS was born in London and studied English, Russian, French, Italian and Old Church Slavonic at universities in England, France and Italy. During the war she was translator to General de Gaulle at Fighting France Headquarters in London and, after the liberation, in Paris. She went on to study Russian Orthodox Spirituality, and has translated Archimandrite Sophrony's *The Undistorted Image* (now published in two volumes as *The Monk of Mount Athos* and *The Wisdom from Mount Athos*) and *His Life is Mine*. She has also translated Tolstoy's *War and Peace*, *Anna Karenin*, *Resurrection*, *The Cossacks* and *Childhood, Boyhood, Youth*, and *The Queen of Spades* by Pushkin, Her other translations include works by Gogol and Leskov. She is at present researching into Old Church Slavonic texts.

IVAN TURGENEV

FATHERS AND SONS

TRANSLATED
BY ROSEMARY EDMONDS
WITH THE ROMANES LECTURE
'FATHERS AND CHILDREN'
BY
ISAIAH BERLIN

PENGUIN BOOKS

PENGUIN BOOKS

Published by the Penguin Group
27 Wrights Lane, London w8 5tz, England
Viking Penguin Inc., 40 West 23rd Street, New York, New York 10010, USA
Penguin Books Australia Ltd, Ringwood, Victoria, Australia
Penguin Books Canada Ltd, 2801 John Street, Markham, Ontario, Canada l3r 1b4
Penguin Books (NZ) Ltd, 182–190 Wairau Road, Auckland 10, New Zealand

Penguin Books Ltd, Registered Offices: Harmondsworth, Middlesex, England

This translation first published 1965
Reprinted with the Romanes Lecture, 1975
17 19 20 18 16

Made and printed in Great Britain by
Hazell Watson & Viney Limited
Member of BPCC plc
Aylesbury, Bucks, England
Set in Linotype Granjon

Contents

Fathers and Children

Turgenev and the Liberal Predicament

You do not, I see, quite understand the Russian public. Its character is determined by the condition of Russian society, which
contains, imprisoned within it, fresh forces seething and bursting
to break out; but crushed by heavy repression and unable to escape,
they produce gloom, bitter depression, apathy. Only in literature,
in spite of our Tartar censorship, there is still some life and forward movement. This is why the writer's calling enjoys such
respect among us, why literary success is so easy here even when
there is little talent. This is why, especially amongst us, universal
attention is paid . . . to every manifestation of any so-called liberal
trend, no matter how poor the writer's gifts. . . The public . . . sees
in Russian writers its only leaders, defenders and saviours from
dark autocracy, Orthodoxy and the national way of life . . .[1]

Vissarion Belinsky (*Open Letter to Gogol*, 15 July 1847)[2]

On 9 October 1883 Ivan Turgenev was buried, as he had
wished, in St Petersburg, near the grave of his admired friend,

1. Belinsky's words – 'autocracy, Orthodoxy and the people' – echo the
official patriotic formula invented by a Minister of Education early in
the reign of Nicolas I. The last of these words – *narodnost* – was evidently
intended as the Russian equivalent of *Volkstum*; it was used in this con-
text to contrast the traditional 'folkways' of the common people with the
imported, 'artificial' constructions of 'wiseacres' influenced by Western
Enlightenment. In practice it counted official patriotism as well as such
institutions as serfdom, the hierarchy of estates and the duty of implicit
obedience to the Emperor and his Government. Belinsky's letter is a
bitter indictment of Gogol for using his genius 'sincerely or insincerely'
to serve the cause of obscurantism and reaction. It was on the charge
of reading the letter at a secret meeting of a subversive group that Dostoyevsky was arrested and condemned to death.

2. All translations from Russian originals are the author's own; the
transliterations are the publishers'.

the critic Vissarion Belinsky. His body was brought from Paris after a brief ceremony near the Gare de l'Est, at which Ernest Renan and Edmond About delivered appropriate addresses. The burial service took place in the presence of representatives of the Imperial Government, the intelligentsia, and workers' organizations, perhaps the first and last occasion on which these groups peacefully met in Russia. The times were troubled. The wave of terrorist acts had culminated in the assassination of Alexander II two years earlier; the ringleaders of the conspiracy had been hanged or sent to Siberia, but there was still great unrest, especially among students. The Government feared that the funeral procession might turn into a political demonstration. The press received a secret circular from the Ministry of the Interior instructing it to print only official information about the funeral without disclosing that any such instructions had been received. Neither the St Petersburg municipality nor the workers' organizations were permitted to identify themselves in the inscriptions on their wreaths. A literary gathering at which Tolstoy was to have spoken about his old friend and rival was cancelled by government order. A revolutionary leaflet was distributed during the funeral procession, but no official notice of this was taken, and the occasion seems to have passed off without incident. Yet these precautions, and the uneasy atmosphere in which the funeral was conducted, may surprise those who see Turgenev as Henry James or George Moore or Maurice Baring saw him, and as most of his readers perhaps see him still: as a writer of beautiful lyrical prose, the author of nostalgic idylls of country life, the elegiac poet of the last enchantments of decaying country-houses and of their ineffective but irresistibly attractive inhabitants, the incomparable story-teller with a marvellous gift for describing nuances of mood and feeling, the poetry of nature and of love, gifts which have given him a place among the foremost writers of his time. In the French memoirs of the time he appears as *le doux géant*, as his friend Edmond de

Goncourt had called him, the good giant, gentle, charming, infinitely agreeable, an entrancing talker, known as 'The Siren' to some of his Russian companions, the admired friend of Flaubert and Daudet, George Sand and Zola and Maupassant, the most welcome and delightful of all the *habitués* of the *salon* of his intimate life-long companion, the singer Pauline Viardot. Yet the Russian Government had some grounds for its fears. They had not welcomed Turgenev's visit to Russia, more particularly his meetings with students, two years before, and had found a way of conveying this to him in unambiguous terms. Audacity was not among his attributes; he cut his visit short and returned to Paris.

The Government's nervousness is not surprising, for Turgenev was something more than a psychological observer and an exquisite stylist. Like virtually every major Russian writer of his time, he was, all his life, profoundly and painfully concerned with his country's condition and destiny. His novels constitute the best account of the social and political development of the small, but influential, *élite* of the liberal and radical Russian youth of his day – of it and of its critics. His books, from the point of view of the authorities in St Petersburg, were by no means safe. Yet, unlike his great contemporaries, Tolstoy and Dostoyevsky, he was not a preacher and did not wish to thunder at his generation. He was concerned, above all, to enter into, to understand, views, ideals, temperaments, both those which he found sympathetic and those by which he was puzzled or repelled. Turgenev possessed in a highly developed form what Keats called negative capability, an ability to enter into beliefs, feelings, and attitudes alien and at times acutely antipathetic to his own, a gift which Renan had emphasized in his eulogy;[3] indeed, some of the young Russian revolutionaries freely conceded the accuracy and justice of his portraits of them. During much of his life he was painfully preoccupied with the controversies, moral

3. For the text of the *Discours* delivered on 1 October 1883 see I. Tourguéneff, *Œuvres dernières*, 2nd edn, Paris, 1885, pp. 297–302.

and political, social and personal, which divided the educated Russians of his day; in particular, the profound and bitter conflicts between Slavophile nationalists and admirers of the West, conservatives and liberals, liberals and radicals, moderates and fanatics, realists and visionaries, above all between old and young. He tried to stand aside and see the scene objectively. He did not always succeed. But because he was an acute and responsive observer, self-critical and self-effacing both as a man and as a writer, and, above all, because he was not anxious to bind his vision upon the reader, to preach, to convert, he proved a better prophet than the two self-centred, angry literary giants with whom he is usually compared, and discerned the birth of social issues which have grown worldwide since his day. Many years after Turgenev's death the radical novelist Vladimir Korolenko, who declared himself a 'fanatical' admirer, remarked that Turgenev 'irritated ... by touching painfully the most exposed nerves of the live issues of the day'; that he excited passionate love and respect and violent criticism, and 'was a storm centre ... yet he knew the pleasures of triumph too; he understood others, and others understood him'.[4] It is with this relatively neglected aspect of Turgenev's writing, which speaks most directly to our own time, that I intend to deal.

I

By temperament Turgenev was not politically minded. Nature, personal relationships, quality of feeling – these are what he understood best, these, and their expression in art. He loved every manifestation of art and of beauty as deeply as anyone has ever done. The conscious use of art for ends extraneous to itself, ideological, didactic, or utilitarian, and especially as a deliberate weapon in the class war, as de-

4. Quoted from the article 'I. A. Goncharov and the younger generation' in the collected works of V. G. Korolenko, Petrograd, 1914, vol. ix, p. 324; see *Turgenev v russkoi kritike*, Moscow, 1953, p. 527.

manded by the radicals of the sixties, was detestable to him. He was often described as a pure aesthete and a believer in art for art's sake, and was accused of escapism and lack of civic sense, then, as now, regarded in the view of a section of Russian opinion as being a despicable form of irresponsible self-indulgence. Yet these descriptions do not fit him. His writing was not as deeply and passionately committed as that of Dostoyevsky after his Siberian exile, or of the later Tolstoy, but it was sufficiently concerned with social analysis to enable both the revolutionaries and their critics, especially the liberals among them, to draw ammunition from his novels. The Emperor Alexander II, who had once admired Turgenev's early work, ended by looking upon him as his *bête noire*. In this respect Turgenev was typical of his time and his class. More sensitive and scrupulous, less obsessed and intolerant than the great tormented moralists of his age, he reacted just as bitterly against the horrors of the Russian autocracy. In a huge and backward country, where the number of educated persons was very small and was divided by a gulf from the vast majority of their fellow-men – they could scarcely be described as citizens – living in conditions of unspeakable poverty, oppression, and ignorance, a major crisis of public conscience was bound sooner or later to arise. The facts are familiar enough: the Napoleonic wars precipitated Russia into Europe, and thereby, inevitably, into a more direct contact with Western Enlightenment than had previously been permitted. Army officers drawn from the land-owning *élite* were brought into a degree of companionship with their men, lifted as they all were by a common wave of vast patriotic emotion. This for the moment broke through the rigid stratification of Russian society. The salient features of this society included an ignorant, State-dominated, largely corrupt church; a small, semi-Westernized, ill-trained bureaucracy struggling to keep under and hold back an enormous, primitive, socially and economically undeveloped, semi-feudal, but vigorous and potentially undisciplined, population straining against its shackles; a widespread sense of inferiority, both social and intellectual, before Western civilization; a society distorted by arbitrary bullying from above and nauseating conformity and obsequiousness from below, in which men with any degree of independence or originality or character found scarcely any outlet for normal development. This is enough, perhaps, to account for the genesis, in the first half of the century, of what came to be known as the 'superfluous person', the hero of the new literature of protest, a member of the tiny minority of educated and morally sensitive men, who is unable to find a place in his native land and, driven in upon himself, is liable to escape either in fantasies and illusions, or into cynicism or despair, ending, more often than not, in self-destruction or surrender. Acute shame or furious indignation caused by the misery and degradation of a system in which human beings – serfs – were viewed as 'baptized property', together with a sense of impotence before the rule of injustice, stupidity, and corruption, tended to drive pent-up imagination and moral feeling into the only channels that the censorship had not completely shut off – literature and the arts. Hence the notorious fact that in Russia social and political thinkers turned into poets and novelists, while creative writers often became publicists. Any protest against institutions, no matter what its origin or purpose, under an absolute despotism is *eo ipso* a political act. Consequently literature became the battleground on which the central social and political issues of life were fought out. Literary or aesthetic questions which in their birthplace – in Germany or France – were confined to academic or artistic coteries, became personal and social problems that obsessed an entire generation of educated young Russians not primarily interested in literature or the arts as such. So, for example, the controversy between the supporters of the theory of pure art and those who believed that it had a social function – a dispute that preoccupied a relatively small section of French critical opinion during the July Monarchy – in Russia grew into a major moral and political issue, of progress against reaction, enlightenment versus obscurantism, moral decency, social responsibility, and human feeling against autocracy, piety, tradition, conformity, and obedience to established authority.

The most passionate and influential voice of his generation was that of the radical critic Vissarion Belinsky. Poor, consumptive, ill-born, ill-educated, a man of incorruptible sincerity and great strength of character, he became the Savonarola of his generation – a burning moralist who preached the unity of theory and practice, of literature and life. His genius as a critic and his instinctive insight into the heart of the social and moral problems that troubled the new radical youth made him its natural leader. His literary essays were to him and to his readers an unbroken, agonizing, unswerving attempt to find the truth about the ends of life, what to believe and what to do. A man of passionate and undivided personality, Belinsky went through violent changes of position, but never without having lived painfully through each of his convictions and having acted upon them with the whole force of his ardent and uncalculating nature until they failed him, one by one, and forced him, again and again, to make a new beginning, a task ended only by his early death. Literature was for him not a *métier*, nor a profession, but the artistic expression of an all-embracing outlook, an ethical and metaphysical doctrine, a view of history and of man's place in the cosmos, a vision that embraced all facts and all values. Belinsky was, first and foremost, a seeker after justice and truth, and it was as much by the example of his profoundly moving life and character as by his precepts that he bound his spell upon the young radicals. Turgenev, whose early efforts as a poet he encouraged, became his devoted and lifelong admirer. The image of Belinsky, particularly after his death, became the very embodiment of the committed man of letters; after him no Russian writer was wholly free from the belief that to write was, first and foremost, to bear witness to the truth: that the writer, of all men, had no right to avert his gaze from the central issues of his day and his society. For an artist – and particularly a writer – to try to detach himself from the deepest concerns of his nation in order to devote himself to the creation of beautiful objects or the pursuit of personal ends was condemned as self-destructive egoism and frivolity; he would only be maimed and impoverished by such betrayal of his chosen calling.

The tormented honesty and integrity of Belinsky's judgements – the tone, even more than the content – penetrated the moral consciousness of his Russian contemporaries, sometimes to be rejected, but never to be forgotten. Turgenev was by nature cautious, judicious, frightened of all extremes, liable at critical moments to take evasive action; his friend, the poet Jacob Polonsky, many years later described him to a reactionary minister as being 'kind and soft as wax ... feminine ... without character'.[5] Even if this goes too far, it is true that he was highly impressionable and liable to yield to stronger personalities all his life. Belinsky died in 1848, but his invisible presence seemed to haunt Turgenev for the rest of his life. Whenever from weakness, or love of ease, or craving for a quiet life, or sheer amiability of character, Turgenev felt tempted to abandon the struggle for individual liberty or common decency and to come to terms with the enemy, it may well have been the stern and moving image of Belinsky that, like an icon, at all times stood in his way and called him back to the sacred task. The *Sportsman's Sketches* was his first and most lasting tribute to his dying friend and mentor. To its readers this masterpiece seemed, and seems still, a marvellous description of the old and changing rural Russia, of the life of nature and of the lives of peasants, transformed into a pure vision of art. But Turgenev looked on it as his first great assault on the hated institution of serfdom, a cry of indignation designed to burn itself into the conscious-

5. See *Sbornik Pushkinskogo doma na 1923 god*, Petrograd, 1922, pp. 288–9 (Letter to K. Pobedonostsev, 1881).

ness of the ruling class. When, in 1879, he was made an Honorary Doctor of Laws by the University of Oxford in this very place,[6] James Bryce, who presented him, described him as a champion of freedom. This delighted him.

Belinsky was neither the first nor the last to exercise a dominating influence on Turgenev's life; the first, and perhaps the most destructive, was his widowed mother, a strong-willed, hysterical, brutal, bitterly frustrated woman who loved her son, and broke his spirit. She was a savage monster even by the none too exacting standards of humanity of the Russian landowners of those days. As a child Turgenev had witnessed abominable cruelties and humiliations which she inflicted upon her serfs and dependants; an episode in his story *The Brigadier* is founded on his maternal grand-mother's murder of one of her boy serfs: she struck him in a fit of rage; he fell wounded on the ground; irritated by the spectacle she smothered him with a pillow. Memories of this kind fill his stories, and it took him his entire life to work them out of his system. It was early experience of scenes of this kind on the part of men brought up at school and univer-sity to respect the values of Western civilization that was largely responsible for the lasting preoccupation with the freedom and dignity of the individual, and for the hatred of the relics of Russian feudalism, that characterized the politi-cal position of the entire Russian intelligentsia from its be-ginnings. The moral confusion was very great. 'Our time longs for convictions, it is tormented by hunger for the truth,'[7] wrote Belinsky in 1842, when Turgenev was twenty-five and had become intimate with him, 'our age is all ques-tioning, questing, searching, nostalgic longing for the truth ...'[8] Thirteen years later Turgenev echoed this: 'There are

6. The Sheldonian Theatre, Oxford, in which a shortened version of this lecture was delivered in November 1970.

7. 'Rech o kritike', *Polnoye sobraniye sochineniy*, vol. vi, Moscow, 1955, p. 267.

8. ibid., p. 269.

15

epochs when literature cannot *merely* be artistic, there are interests higher than poetry.'[9] Three years later Tolstoy, then dedicated to the ideal of pure art, suggested to him the publication of a purely literary and artistic periodical divorced from the squalid political polemics of the day. Turgenev replied that it was not 'lyrical twittering' that the times were calling for, nor 'birds singing on boughs';[10] 'you loathe this political morass; true, it is a dirty, dusty, vulgar business. But there is dirt and dust in the streets, and yet we cannot, after all, do without towns.'[11] The conventional picture of Turgenev as a pure artist drawn into political strife against his will but remaining fundamentally alien to it, drawn by critics both on the Right and on the Left (particularly by those whom his political novels irritated), is misleading. His major novels, from the middle fifties onwards, are deeply concerned with the central social and political questions that troubled the liberals of his generation. His outlook was profoundly and permanently influenced by Belinsky's indignant humanism and in particular by his furious philippics against all that was dark, corrupt, oppressive, false.[12] Two or three years earlier, at the University of Berlin, he had listened to the Hegelian sermons of the future anarchist agitator Bakunin, who was his fellow student, sat at the feet of the same Ger-

9. Letter to Vassili Botkin, 29 June 1855. I. S. Turgenev, *Polnoye sobraniye sochineniy i pisem*, Moscow/Leningrad, 1960–68, *Pisma*, vol. ii, p. 282. All references to Turgenev's letters are to this edition, unless otherwise indicated.

10. Letter to L. N. Tolstoy, 29 January 1858.

11. To Tolstoy, 8 April 1858.

12. 'Doubts tormented [Belinsky], robbed him of sleep, food, relentlessly gnawed at him, burnt him, he would not let himself sink into forgetfulness, did not know fatigue . . . his sincerity affected me too,' he wrote in his reminiscences with characteristic irony and affection, 'his fire communicated itself to me, the importance of the topic absorbed me; but after talking for two to three hours I used to weaken, the frivolity of youth would take its toll, I wanted to rest, I began to think of a walk, of dinner . . .' *Literaturnyye i zhiteiskiye vospominaniya*, Leningrad, 1934, p. 79.

man philosophical master and, as Belinsky had once done, admired Bakunin's dialectical brilliance. Five years later he met in Moscow and soon became intimate with the radical young publicist Herzen and his friends. He shared their hatred of every form of enslavement, injustice, and brutality, but unlike some among them he could not rest comfortably in any doctrine or ideological system. All that was general, abstract, absolute, repelled him: his vision remained delicate, sharp, concrete, and incurably realistic. Hegelianism, right-wing and left-wing, which he had imbibed as a student in Berlin, materialism, socialism, positivism, about which his friends ceaselessly argued, populism, collectivism, the Russian village commune idealized by those Russian socialists whom the ignominious collapse of the Left in Europe in 1848 had bitterly disappointed and disillusioned – these came to seem mere abstractions to him, substitutes for reality, in which many believed, and a few even tried to live, doctrines which life, with its uneven surface and irregular shapes of real human character and activity, would surely resist and shatter if ever a serious effort were made to translate them into practice. Bakunin was a dear friend and a delightful boon companion, but his fantasies, whether Slavophile or anarchist, left no trace on Turgenev's thought. Herzen was a different matter: he was a sharp, ironical, imaginative thinker, and in their early years they had much in common. Yet Herzen's populist socialism seemed to Turgenev a pathetic fantasy, the dream of a man whose earlier illusions were killed by the failure of the revolution in the West, but who could not live long without faith; with his old ideals, social justice, equality, liberal democracy, impotent before the forces of reaction in the West, he must find himself a new idol, not, in Turgenev's words, 'the golden calf' of acquisitive capitalism, but 'the sheepskin coat' of the Russian peasant. Turgenev understood and sympathized with his friend's cultural despair. Like Carlyle and Flaubert, like Stendhal and Nietzsche, Ibsen and Wagner, Herzen felt increasingly asphyxiated in a world in which all values had become debased. All that was free and dignified and independent and creative seemed to Herzen to have gone under beneath the wave of bourgeois philistinism, the commercialization of life by corrupt and vulgar dealers in human commodities and their mean and insolent lackeys who served the huge joint-stock companies called France, England, Germany; even Italy (he wrote), 'the most poetical country in Europe', when the 'fat, bespectacled little bourgeois of genius', Cavour, offered to keep her, could not restrain herself and, deserting both her fanatical lover Mazzini and her Herculean husband Garibaldi, gave herself to him.[13] Was it to this decaying corpse that Russia was to look as the ideal model? The time was surely ripe for some cataclysmic transformation – a barbarian invasion from the East which would clear the air like a healing storm. Against this, Herzen declared, there was only one lightning conductor – the Russian peasant commune, free from the taint of capitalism, from the greed and fear of inhumanity of destructive individualism. Upon this foundation a new society of free, self-governing human beings might yet be built. Turgenev regarded all this as a violent exaggeration, the dramatization of private despair. Of course the Germans were pompous and ridiculous; Louis Napoleon and the profiteers of Paris were odious, but the civilization of the West was not crumbling. It was the greatest achievement of mankind. It was not for Russians, who had nothing comparable to offer, to mock at it or keep it from their gates. He accused Herzen of being a tired and disillusioned man, who after 1849 was looking for a new divinity and had found it in the simple Russian peasant.[14] 'You erect an altar to this new and unknown God because almost nothing is known about him, and one can ... pray and believe and wait. This God does not begin to do what

13. A. I. Herzen, 'Kontsy i nachala' ('Ends and Beginnings'), First Letter, 1862. *Sobraniye sochineniy v tridtsati tomakh*, Moscow, 1954–65, vol. xvi, p. 138. Later references to Herzen's works are to this edition.
14. Letter to Herzen, 8 November 1862.

you expect of him; this, you say, is temporary, accidental, injected by outside forces; your God loves and adores that which you hate, hates that which you love; [he] accepts precisely what you reject on his behalf: ... you avert your eyes, you stop your ears.' [15] 'Either you must serve the revolution, and European ideals as before. Or, if you now think that there is nothing in all this, you must have the courage to look the devil in *both* eyes, plead guilty to the *whole of Europe* – to its face – and not make an open or implied exception for some coming Russian Messiah' – least of all for the Russian peasant who is, in embryo, the worst conservative of all, and cares nothing for liberal ideals.[16] Turgenev's sober realism never deserted him. He responded to the faintest tremors of Russian life; in particular, to the changes of expression on what he called 'the swiftly altering physiognomy of those who belong to the cultured section of Russian society'.[17] He claimed to do no more than to record what Shakespeare had called 'the body and pressure of time'. He faithfully described them all – the talkers, the idealists, the fighters, the cowards, the reactionaries, and the radicals, sometimes, as in *Smoke*, with biting polemical irony, but, as a rule, so scrupulously, with so much understanding for all the overlapping sides of every question, so much unruffled patience, touched only occasionally with undisguised irony or satire (without sparing his own character and views), that he angered almost everyone at some time.

Those who still think of him as an uncommitted artist, raised high above the ideological battle, may be surprised to learn that no one in the entire history of Russian literature,

15. ibid. On this topic see *Pisma K. D. Kavelina i I. S. Turgeneva k A. I. Gertsenu*, ed. M. Dragomanov, Geneva, 1892 (letters by Turgenev for 1862–3).

16. Letter to Herzen, 8 November 1862.

17. Introduction to the collected novels, 1880, *Polnoye sobraniye sochineniy i pisem*, Moscow/Leningrad, 1960–68, *Sochineniya*, vol. xii, p. 303. Later references to Turgenev's works are to this edition, unless otherwise indicated.

perhaps of literature in general, has been so ferociously and continuously attacked, both from the Right and from the Left, as Turgenev. Dostoyevsky and Tolstoy held far more violent views, but they were formidable figures, angry prophets treated with nervous respect even by their bitterest opponents. Turgenev was not in the least formidable; he was amiable, sceptical, 'kind and soft as wax',[18] too courteous and too self-distrustful to frighten anyone. He embodied no clear principles, advocated no doctrine, no panacea for the 'accursed questions', as they came to be called, personal and social. 'He felt and understood the opposite sides of life,' said Henry James of him, 'our Anglo-Saxon, Protestant, moralistic conventional standards were far away from him ... half the charm of conversation with him was that one breathed an air in which cant phrases ... simply sounded ridiculous.'[19] In a country in which readers, and especially the young, to this day look to writers for moral direction, he refused to preach. He was aware of the price he would have to pay for such reticence. He knew that the Russian reader wanted to be told what to believe and how to live, expected to be provided with clearly contrasted values, clearly distinguishable heroes and villains. When the author did not provide this, Turgenev wrote, the reader was dissatisfied and blamed the writer, since he found it difficult and irritating to have to make up his own mind, find his own way. And, indeed, it is true that Tolstoy never leaves you in doubt about whom he favours and whom he condemns; Dostoyevsky does not conceal what he regards as the path of salvation. Among these great, tormented Laocoöns Turgenev remained cautious and sceptical; the reader is left in suspense, in a state of doubt; the central problems are left unanswered.

No society demanded more of its authors than Russia, then or now. Turgenev was accused of vacillation, temporiz-

18. See above, p. 14, n. 5.
19. *Partial Portraits*, London, 1888, pp. 296-7. For James's view of Turgenev see also *The Art of Fiction*, Oxford, 1948.

ing, infirmity of purpose, of speaking with too many voices. Indeed, this very topic obsessed him. *Rudin, Asya, On the Eve*, the major works of the fifties, are preoccupied with weakness – the failure of men of generous heart, sincerely held ideals, who remain impotent and give in without a struggle to the forces of stagnation. Rudin, drawn partly from the young Bakunin, partly from himself,[20] is a man of high ideals, talks well, fascinates his listeners, expresses views which Turgenev could accept and defend. But he is made of paper. When he is faced with a genuine crisis which calls for courage and resolution, he crumples and collapses. His friend, Lezhnev, defends Rudin's memory: his ideals were noble but he had 'no blood, no character'. In the epilogue (which the author added as an afterthought to a later edition), after aimless wanderings, Rudin dies bravely but uselessly on the barricades of Paris in 1848, something of which his proto- type Bakunin was, in Turgenev's view, scarcely capable. But even this was not open to him in his native land; even if Rudin had blood and character, what could he have done in the Russian society of his time? This 'superfluous' man, the ancestor of all the sympathetic, futile, ineffective talkers in Russian literature, should he, could he, in the circumstances of his time have declared war upon the odious aristocratic lady and her world to which he capitulates? The reader is left without guidance. The heroine of *On the Eve*, Elena, who looks for a heroic personality to help her to escape from the false existence of her parents and their milieu, finds that even the best and most gifted Russians in her circle lack will- power, cannot act. She follows the fearless Bulgarian con- spirator Insarov who is thinner, drier, less civilized, more wooden than the sculptor Shubin or the historian Bersenev, but, unlike them, is possessed by a single thought – to liberate

20. His critical friend Herzen said that Turgenev created Rudin 'in biblical fashion – after his own image and likeness'. 'Rudin', he added, 'is Turgenev the Second, plus (*maslusharshiysya*) a lot of . . . Bakunin's philosophical jargon.' *Sobraniye sochineniy*, vol. xi, p. 359.

his country from the Turk, a simple dominant purpose that unites him with the last peasant and the last beggar in his land. Elena goes with him because he alone, in her world, is whole and unbroken, because his ideals are backed by indomitable moral strength.

Turgenev published *On the Eve* in the *Contemporary*, a radical journal then moving steadily and rapidly to the Left. The group of men who dominated it were as uncongenial to him as they were to Tolstoy; he thought them dull, narrow doctrinaires, devoid of all understanding of art, enemies of beauty, uninterested in personal relationships (which were everything to him), but they were bold and strong, fanatics who judged everything in the light of a single goal – the liberation of the Russian people. They rejected compromise: they were bent on a radical solution. The emancipation of the serfs, which moved Turgenev and all his liberal friends profoundly, was to these men not the beginning of a new era, but a miserable fraud: the peasants were still chained to their landlords by the new economic arrangements. Only 'the peasant's axe', a mass rising of the people in arms, would give it freedom. Dobrolyubov, the literary editor of the magazine, in his review of *On the Eve*, acclaimed the Bulgarian as a positive hero: for he was ready to give his life to drive out the Turk from his country. And we? We Russians, too (he declared), have our Turks – only they are internal: the court, the gentry, the generals, the officials, the rising bourgeoisie, oppressors and exploiters whose weapons are the ignorance of the masses and brute force. Where are *our* Insarovs? Turgenev speaks of an eve, when will the real day dawn? If it has not dawned yet, this is because the good, the enlightened young men, the Shubins and Bersenevs in Turgenev's novel, are impotent. They are paralysed, and will, for all their fine words, end by adapting themselves to the conventions of the philistine life of their society, because they are too closely connected with the prevailing order by a network of family and institutional and economic relationships which they cannot bring themselves to break entirely. 'If you sit in an empty box', said Dobrolyubov, in the final version of his article, 'and try to upset it with yourself inside it, what a fearful effort you have to make! But if you come at it from outside, one push will topple this box.'[21] Insarov stood outside his box – the box is the Turkish invader. Those who are truly serious must get out of the Russian box, break off every relationship with the entire monstrous structure, and then knock it over from outside. Herzen and Ogarev sit in London and waste their time in exposing isolated cases of injustice, corruption, or mismanagement in the Russian empire; but this, so far from weakening that empire, may even help it to eliminate such shortcomings and last longer. The real task is to destroy the whole inhuman system. Dobrolyubov's advice is clear: those who are serious must endeavour to abandon the box – remove themselves from all contact with the Russian state as it is at present, for there is no other means to acquire an Archimedean point, leverage for causing it to collapse. Insarov rightly lets private revenge – the execution of those who tortured and killed his parents – wait until the larger task is accomplished. There must be no waste of energy on piecemeal denunciations, on the rescue of individuals from cruelty or injustice. This is mere liberal fiddling, escape from the radical task. There is nothing common between 'us' and 'them'. 'They', and Turgenev with them, seek reform, accommodation. We want destruction, revolution, new foundations of life; nothing else will destroy the reign of darkness. This, for the radicals, is the clear implication of Turgenev's novel; but he and his friends are evidently too craven to draw it.

Turgenev was upset and, indeed, frightened by this interpretation of his book. He tried to get the review with-

21. This sentence does not occur in the original review of 1860, but was included in the posthumous edition of Dobrolyubov's essays two years later. See 'Kogda zhe pridet nastoyashchy den?' ('When will the real day come?'), *Sobraniye sochineniy*, vol. vi, Moscow, 1963, p. 126.

drawn. He said that if it appeared he would not know what to do or where to run. Nevertheless he was fascinated by these new men. He loathed the gloomy puritanism of these 'Daniels of the Neva' as they were called by Herzen [22] who thought them cynical and brutal and could not bear their crude anti-aesthetic utilitarianism, their fanatical rejection of all that he held dear – liberal culture, art, civilized human relationships. But they were young, brave, ready to die in the fight against the common enemy, the reactionaries, the police, the State. Turgenev wished, in spite of everything, to be liked and respected by them. He tried to flirt with Dobrolyubov, and constantly engaged him in conversation. One day, when they met in the offices of the *Contemporary*, Dobrolyubov suddenly said to him, 'Ivan Sergeyevich, do not let us go on talking to each other: it bores me,' [23] and walked away to a distant corner of the room. Turgenev did not give up immediately. He was a celebrated charmer; he did his best to find a way to woo the grim young man. It was of no use; when he saw Turgenev approach he stared at the wall or pointedly left the room. 'You can talk to Turgenev if you like,' Dobrolyubov said to his fellow editor Chernyshevsky, who at this time still looked with favour and admiration on Turgenev, and he added, characteristically, that in his view bad allies were no allies. [24] This is worthy of Lenin; Dobrolyubov had, perhaps, the most Bolshevik temperament of all the early radicals. Turgenev in the fifties and early sixties was the most famous writer in Russia, the only Russian writer with a great and growing European reputation. Nobody had ever treated him like this. He was deeply wounded. Neverthe-

22. A. I. Herzen, *Sobraniye sochineniy*, vol. xiv, p. 322.

23. N. G. Chernyshevsky's reminiscences quoted in *Turgenev v vospominaniyakh sovremennikov*, Moscow, 1969, vol. i, p. 356. This story was recorded by Chernyshevsky in 1884, many years after the event, at the request of his cousin Pypin who was collecting material about the radical movement of the sixties; there is no reason for doubting its accuracy.

24. ibid., p. 358.

less, he persisted for a while, but in the end, faced with Dobrolyubov's implacable hostility, gave up. There was an open breach. He crossed over to the conservative review edited by Mikhail Katkov, a man regarded by the left wing as their deadliest enemy.

In the meanwhile the political atmosphere grew more stormy. The terrorist Land and Liberty League was created in 1861, the very year of the great Emancipation. Violently worded manifestos calling on the peasants to revolt began to circulate. The radical leaders were charged with conspiracy, were imprisoned or exiled. Fires broke out in the capital and university students were accused of starting them; Turgenev did not come to their defence. The booing and whistling of the radicals, their brutal mockery, seemed to him mere vandalism; their revolutionary aims, dangerous utopianism. Yet he felt that something new was rising – a vast social mutation of some kind. He declared that he felt it everywhere. He was repelled and at the same time fascinated by it. A new and formidable type of adversary of the regime – and of much that he and his generation of liberals believed in – was coming into existence. Turgenev's curiosity was always stronger than his fears : he wanted, above everything, to understand the new Jacobins. These men were crude, fanatical, hostile, insulting, but they were undemoralized, self-confident, and, in some narrow but genuine sense, rational and disinterested. He could not bear to turn his back upon them. They seemed to him a new, clear-eyed generation, undeluded by the old romantic myths; above all they were the young, the future of his country lay in their hands; he did not wish to be cut off from anything that seemed to him alive, passionate, and disturbing. After all, the evils that they wished to fight were evils; their enemies were, to some degree, his enemies too; these young men were wrong-headed, barbarous, contemptuous of liberals like himself, but they were fighters and martyrs in the battle against despotism. He was intrigued, horrified, and dazzled by them. During the whole of the rest of his life he was obsessed by a desire to explain them to himself, and perhaps himself to them.

2

Young Man to Middle-Aged Man: 'You had content but no force.'
Middle-Aged Man to Young Man: 'And you have force but no content.'

From a contemporary conversation [25]

This is the topic of Turgenev's most famous, and politically most interesting, novel *Fathers and Children*. It was an attempt to give flesh and substance to his image of the new men, whose mysterious, implacable presence, he declared, he felt about him everywhere, and who inspired in him feelings that he found difficult to analyse. 'There was', he wrote many years later to a friend, ' – please don't laugh – some sort of *fatum*, something stronger than the author himself, something independent of him. I know one thing: I started with no preconceived idea, no "tendency"; I wrote naïvely, as if myself astonished at what was emerging.' [26] He said that the central figure of the novel, Bazarov, was mainly modelled on a Russian doctor whom he met in a train in Russia. But Bazarov has some of the characteristics of Belinsky too. Like him, he is the son of a poor army doctor, and he possesses some of Belinsky's brusqueness, his directness, his intolerance, his liability to explode at any sign of hypocrisy, of solemnity, of pompous conservative, or evasive liberal, cant. And there is, despite Turgenev's denials, something of the ferocious, militant, anti-aestheticism of Dobrolyubov too. The central topic of the novel is the confrontation of the old and the young, of liberals and radicals, traditional civilization and the new, harsh posi-

25. The original epigraph to *Fathers and Children* which Turgenev later discarded. See A. Mazon, *Manuscrits parisiens d'Ivan Tourguénev*, Paris, 1930, pp. 64-5.

26. From a letter to Saltykov-Shchedrin, 15 January 1876.

tivism which has no use for anything except what is needed by a rational man. Bazarov, a young medical researcher, is invited by his fellow student and disciple, Arkady Kirsanov, to stay at his father's house in the country. Nicolai Kirsanov, the father, is a gentle, kindly, modest country gentleman, who adores poetry and nature, and greets his son's brilliant friend with touching courtesy. Also in the house is Nicolai Kirsanov's brother, Paul, a retired army officer, a carefully dressed, vain, pompous, old-fashioned dandy, who had once been a minor lion in the *salons* of the capital, and is now living out his life in elegant and irritated boredom. Bazarov scents an enemy, and takes deliberate pleasure in describing himself and his allies as 'nihilists', by which he means no more than that he, and those who think like him, reject everything that cannot be established by the rational methods of natural science. Truth alone matters: what cannot be established by observation and experiment is useless or harmful ballast – 'romantic rubbish' – which an intelligent man will ruthlessly eliminate. In this heap of irrational nonsense Bazarov includes all that is impalpable, that cannot be reduced to quantitative measurement – literature and philosophy, the beauty of art and the beauty of nature, tradition and authority, religion and intuition, the uncriticized assumptions of conservatives and liberals, of populists and socialists, of landowners and serfs. He believes in strength, will-power, energy, utility, work, in ruthless criticism of all that exists. He wishes to tear off masks, blow up all revered principles and norms. Only irrefutable facts, only useful knowledge, matter. He clashes almost immediately with the touchy, conventional Paul Kirsanov: 'At present', he tells him, 'the most useful thing is to deny. So we deny.' 'Everything?' asks Paul Kirsanov. 'Everything.' 'What? Not only art, poetry . . . but even . . . too horrible to utter . . .' 'Everything.' 'So you destroy everything . . . but surely one must build, too?' 'That's not our business . . . First one must clear the ground.' The fiery revolutionary agitator Bakunin, who had just then escaped

27

from Siberia to London, was saying something of this kind: the entire rotten structure, the corrupt old world, must be razed to the ground, before something new can be built upon it; what this is to be is not for us to say; we are revolutionaries, our business is to demolish. The new men, purified from the infection of the world of idlers and exploiters and its bogus values – these men will know what to do. The French anarchist Georges Sorel once quoted Marx as saying 'Anyone who makes plans for after the revolution is a reactionary.'[27] This went beyond the position of Turgenev's radical critics of the *Contemporary Review*; they did have a programme of sorts: they were democratic populists. But faith in the people seems just as irrational to Bazarov as the rest of the 'romantic rubbish'. 'Peasants?' he says, 'They are prepared to rob themselves in order to drink themselves blind at the inn.' A man's first duty is to develop his own powers, to be strong and rational, to create a society in which other rational men can breathe and live and learn. His mild disciple Arkady suggests to him that it would be ideal if all peasants lived in a pleasant, whitewashed hut, like the head man of their village. 'I have conceived a loathing for this . . . peasant,' Bazarov says, 'I have to work the skin off my hands for him, and he won't so much as thank me for it; anyway, what do I need his thanks for? He'll go on living in his whitewashed hut, while weeds grow out of me.' Arkady is shocked by such talk; but it is the voice of the new, hard-boiled, unashamed materialism. Nevertheless Bazarov is at his ease with peasants, they are not self-conscious with him even if they think him an odd sort of member of the gentry. Bazarov spends his afternoon in dissecting frogs. 'A decent chemist', he tells his shaken host, 'is twenty times more use than any poet.' Arkady, after

27. Sorel declares that this passage occurs in a letter which, according to the economist Lujo Brentano, Marx wrote to one of his English friends, Professor Beesly (*Réfléxions sur la violence*, 7th edn, Paris, 1930, p. 199, n. 2). I have not found it in any published collection of Marx's letters.

consulting Bazarov, gently draws a volume of Pushkin out of his father's hands, and slips into them Büchner's *Kraft und Stoff*,[28] the latest popular exposition of materialism. Turgenev describes the older Kirsanov walking in his garden: 'Nikolai Petrovich dropped his head, and passed his hand over his face. "But to reject poetry," he thought again, "not to have a feeling for art, for nature ..." and he cast about him, as if trying to understand how it was possible not to have a feeling for nature.' All principles, Bazarov declares, are reducible to mere sensations. Arkady asks whether, in that case, honesty is only a sensation. 'You find this hard to swallow?' says Bazarov. 'No, friend, if you have decided to knock everything down, you must knock yourself down, too! ...' This is the voice of Bakunin and Dobrolyubov: 'one must clear the ground.' The new culture must be founded on real, that is materialist, scientific values: socialism is just as unreal and abstract as any other of the 'isms' imported from abroad. As for the old aesthetic, literary culture, it will crumble before the realists, the new, tough-minded men who can look the brutal truth in the face. 'Aristocracy, liberalism, progress, principles ... what a lot of foreign ... and useless words. A Russian would not want them as a gift.' Paul Kirsanov rejects this contemptuously; but his nephew Arkady cannot, in the end, accept it either. 'You aren't made for our harsh, bitter, solitary kind of life,' Bazarov tells him, 'you aren't insolent, you aren't nasty, all you have is the audacity, the impulsiveness of youth, and that is of no use in our business. Your type, the gentry, cannot get beyond noble humility, noble indignation, and that is nonsense. You won't, for instance, fight, and yet you think yourselves terrific. We want to fight ... Our dust will eat out your eyes, our dirt will spoil your clothes, you haven't risen to our level yet, you still can't help admiring yourselves, you like castigating yourselves, and that bores us. Hand us others – it is them we want to break. You are a good

28. Turgenev calls it *Stoff und Kraft*.

fellow, but, all the same, you are nothing but a soft, beautifully bred, liberal boy ...'

Bazarov, someone once said, is the first Bolshevik; even though he is not a socialist, there is some truth in this. He wants radical change and does not shrink from brute force. The old dandy, Paul Kirsanov, protests against this: 'Force? There is force in savage Kalmucks and Mongols, too ... What do we want it for? ... Civilization, its fruits, are dear to us. And don't tell me they are worthless. The most miserable dauber ... the pianist who taps on the keys in a restaurant ... they are more useful than you are, because they represent civilization and not brute Mongol force. You imagine that you are progressive; you should be sitting in a Kalmuck wagon !' In the end, Bazarov, against all his principles, falls in love with a cold, clever, well-born society beauty, is rejected by her, suffers deeply, and not long after dies as a result of an infection caught while dissecting a corpse in a village autopsy. He dies stoically, wondering whether his country had any real need of him and men like him; and his death is bitterly lamented by his old, humble, loving parents. Bazarov falls because he is broken by fate, not through failure of will or intellect. 'I conceived him', Turgenev later wrote to a young student, 'as a sombre figure, wild, huge, half-grown out of the soil, powerful, nasty, honest, but doomed to destruction because he still stands only in the gateway to the future ...' [29] This brutal, fanatical, dedicated figure, with his unused powers, is represented as an avenger for insulted human reason; yet, in the end, he is incurably wounded by a love, by a human passion that he suppresses and denies within himself. In the end, he is crushed by heartless nature, by what the author calls the cold-eyed goddess Isis who does not care for good or evil, or art or beauty, still less for man, the creature of an hour; he struggles to assert himself; but she is indifferent; she obeys her own inexorable laws.

Fathers and Children was published in the spring of 1862

29. Letter to Sluchevsky, 26 April 1862.

and caused the greatest storm among its Russian readers of any novel before or, indeed, since. What was Bazarov? How was he to be taken? Was he a positive or a negative figure? A hero or a devil? He is young, bold, intelligent, strong, he has thrown off the burden of the past, the melancholy impotence of the 'superfluous men' beating vainly against the bars of the prison house of Russian society. The critic Strakhov in his review spoke of him as a character conceived on a heroic scale.[30] Many years later Lunacharsky described him as the first 'positive' hero in Russian literature. Does he then symbolize progress? Freedom? Yet his hatred of art and culture, of the entire world of liberal values, his cynical asides – does the author mean to hold these up for admiration? Even before the novel was published his editor, Mikhail Katkov, protested to Turgenev. This glorification of nihilism, he complained, was nothing but grovelling at the feet of the young radicals. 'Turgenev', he said to the novelist's friend Annenkov, 'should be ashamed of lowering the flag before a radical, or saluting him as an honourable soldier.'[31] Katkov declared that he was not deceived by the author's apparent objectivity: 'There is concealed approval lurking here ... this fellow, Bazarov, definitely dominates the others and does not encounter proper resistance,' and he concluded that what Turgenev had done was politically dangerous.[32] Strakhov was more sympathetic. He wrote that Turgenev, with his devotion to timeless truth and beauty, only wanted to describe reality, not to judge it. He too, however, spoke of Bazarov as towering over the other characters, and declared that Turgenev might claim to be drawn to him by an irresistible attraction, but it would be truer to say that he feared him. Katkov echoes this: 'One gets the impression of a kind of embarrassment in the author's

30. 'Ottsy i dyeti', *Vremya*, 1862, no. 4, pp. 58–84. See also his essays on Turgenev in *Kriticheskiye stati ob I. S. Turgeneve i L. N. Tolstom* (1862–85), St Petersburg, 1885.

31. *I. S. Turgenev v vospominaniyakh sovremennikov*, vol. i, p. 343.

32. ibid, pp. 343–4.

attitude to the hero of his story ... It is as if the author didn't like him, felt lost before him, and, more than this, was terrified of him!'[33]

The attack from the Left was a good deal more virulent. Dobrolyubov's successor, Antonovich, accused Turgenev in the *Contemporary*[34] of perpetrating a hideous and disgusting caricature of the young. Bazarov was a brutish, cynical sensualist, hankering after wine and women, unconcerned with the fate of the people; his creator, whatever his views in the past, had evidently crossed over to the blackest reactionaries and oppressors. And, indeed, there were conservatives who congratulated Turgenev for exposing the horrors of the new, destructive nihilism, and thereby rendering a public service for which all men of decent feeling must be grateful. But it was the attack from the Left that hurt Turgenev most. Seven years later he wrote to a friend that 'mud and filth' had been flung at him by the young. He had been called fool, donkey, reptile, Judas, police agent.[35] And again, 'While some accused me of ... backwardness, black obscurantism, and informed me that "my photographs were being burnt amid contemptuous laughter", yet others indignantly reproached me with kowtowing to the ... young. "You are crawling at Bazarov's feet!" cried one of my correspondents. "You are only pretending to condemn him. Actually you scrape and bow to him, you wait obsequiously for the favour of a casual smile." ... A shadow has fallen upon my name.'[36] At least one of his liberal friends who had read the manuscript of *Fathers and*

33. Letter to Turgenev, quoted by him in *Literaturnyye i zhiteiskiye vospominaniya*, p. 158.

34. See *Sovremennik*, March 1862, pp. 65–114, and V. Bazanov, 'Turgenev i anti-nigilistichesky roman', *Kareliya*, Petrozavodsk, 1940, vol. iv, p. 160. Also V. Zelinsky, *Kriticheskiye razbory romana 'Ottsy i dyeti' I. S. Turgeneva*, Moscow, 1894, and V. Tukhomitsky. 'Prototipy Bazarova', *K pravde*, Moscow, 1904, pp. 227–85.

35. To L. Pietsch, 3 June 1869.

36. 'Po povodu *Ottsov i dyetei*' ('About *Fathers and Children*'), *Literaturnyye i zhiteiskiye vospominaniya*, pp. 157–9.

Children told him to burn it, since it would compromise him for ever with the progressives. Hostile caricatures appeared in the left-wing press, in which Turgenev was represented as pandering to the fathers, with Bazarov as a leering Mephistopheles, mocking his disciple Arkady's love for his father. At best, the author was drawn as a bewildered figure simultaneously attacked by frantic democrats from the Left and threatened by armed fathers from the Right, as he stood helplessly between them.[37] But the Left was not unanimous. The radical critic Pisarev came to Turgenev's aid. He boldly identified himself with Bazarov and his position. Turgenev, Pisarev wrote, might be too soft or tired to accompany us, the men of the future; but he knows that true progress is to be found not in men tied to tradition, but in active, self-emancipated, independent men, like Bazarov, free from fantasies, from romantic or religious nonsense. The author does not bully us, he does not tell us to accept the values of the 'fathers'. Bazarov is in revolt; he is the prisoner of no theory; that is his attractive strength; that is what makes for progress and freedom. Turgenev may wish to tell us that we are on a false path, but in fact he is a kind of Balaam : he has become deeply attached to the hero of his novel through the very process of creation, and pins all his hopes to him. 'Nature is a workshop, not a temple' and we are workers in it; not melancholy daydreams, but will, strength, intelligence, realism – these, Pisarev declares, speaking through Bazarov, these will find the road. Bazarov, he adds, is what parents today see emerging in their sons and daughters, sisters in their brothers. They may be frightened by it, they may be puzzled, but that is where the road to the future lies.[38]

37. e.g. in the journal *Osa* (no. 7, 1863). See M. Klevensky, 'Ivan Sergeyevich Turgenev v karikaturakh i parodiyakh', *Golos minuvshego*, Moscow, 1918, nos. 1–3, pp. 185–218, and *Dumy i pesni D. D. Minayeva*, St Petersburg, 1863.

38. D. I. Pisarev, 'Bazarov' (*Russkoe Slovo*, 1862, no. 3), *Polnoye sobraniye sochineniy*, St Petersburg, 1901, vol. ii, pp. 379–428; and 'Realisty' (1864), ibid., vol. iv, pp. 1–146.

Turgenev's familiar friend, Annenkov, to whom he submitted all his novels for criticism before he published them, saw Bazarov as a Mongol, a Genghiz Khan, a wild beast symptomatic of the savage condition of Russia, only 'thinly concealed by books from the Leipzig Fair'.[39] Was Turgenev aiming to become the leader of a political movement? 'The author himself ... does not know how to take him,' he wrote, 'as a fruitful force for the future, or as a disgusting boil on the body of a hollow civilization, to be removed as rapidly as possible.'[40] Yet he cannot be both, 'he is a Janus with two faces, each party will see only what it wants to see or can understand.'[41] Katkov, in an unsigned review in his own journal (in which the novel had appeared), went a good deal further. After mocking the confusion on the Left as a result of being unexpectedly faced with its own image in nihilism, which pleased some and horrified others, he reproaches the author for being altogether too anxious not to be unjust to Bazarov, and consequently of representing him always in the best possible light. There is such a thing, he says, as being too fair : this leads to its own brand of distortion of the truth. As for the hero, he is represented as being brutally candid : that is good, very good; he believes in telling the whole truth, however upsetting to the poor, gentle Kirsanovs, father and son, with no respect for persons or circumstances : most admirable; he attacks art, riches, luxurious living; yes, but in the name of what? Of science and knowledge? But, Katkov declares, this is simply not true. Bazarov's purpose is not the discovery of scientific truth, else he would not peddle cheap popular tracts – Büchner and the rest – which are not science at all, but journalism, materialist propaganda. Bazarov (he goes on to say) is not a scientist; this species scarcely exists

39. Letter to Turgenev, 26 September 1861. Quoted in V. Arkhipov, 'K tvorcheskoi istorii romana I. S. Turgeneva *Ottsy i dyeti*', *Russkaya literatura*, Moscow, 1958, no. 1, p. 148.

40. ibid., p. 147.

41. ibid.

in Russia in our time. Bazarov and his fellow nihilists are merely preachers: they denounce phrases, rhetoric, inflated language – Bazarov tells Arkady not to talk so 'beautifully' – but only in order to substitute for this their own political propaganda; they offer not hard scientific facts, in which they are not interested, with which, indeed, they are not acquainted, but slogans, diatribes, radical cant. Bazarov's dissection of frogs is not genuine pursuit of the truth, it is only an occasion for rejecting civilized and traditional values which Paul Kirsanov, who in a better-ordered society – say England – would have done useful work, rightly defends. Bazarov and his friends will discover nothing; they are not researchers; they are mere ranters, men who declaim in the name of a science which they do not trouble to master; in the end they are no better than the ignorant, benighted Russian priesthood from whose ranks they mostly spring, and far more dangerous.[42]

Herzen, as always, was both penetrating and amusing. 'Turgenev was more of an artist in his novel than people think, and for this reason lost his way, and, in my opinion, did very well. He wanted to go to one room, but ended up in another and a better one.'[43] The author clearly started by wanting to do something for the fathers, but they turned out to be such nonentities that he 'became carried away by Bazarov's very extremism; with the result that instead of flogging the son, he whipped the fathers.'[44] Nature sometimes follows art: Bazarov affected the young as Werther, in the previous century, influenced them, like Schiller's *The Robbers*, like Byron's Laras and Giaours and Childe Harolds in their day. Yet these new men, Herzen added in a later

42. 'Roman Turgeneva i ego kritiki', *Russky vestnik*, May 1862, pp. 393–426, and 'O nashem nigilizme. Po povodu romana Turgeneva', ibid., July 1862, pp. 402–26.

43. A. I. Herzen, 'Yeshche raz Bazarov' ('Again Bazarov'), *Sobraniye sochineniy*, vol. xx, p. 339.

44. ibid.

essay, are so dogmatic, doctrinaire, jargon-ridden, as to exhibit the least attractive aspect of the Russian character, the policeman's – the martinet's – side of it, the brutal bureaucratic jackboot; they want to break the yoke of the old despotism, but only in order to replace it with one of their own. The 'generation of the forties', his own and Turgenev's, may have been fatuous and weak, but does it follow that their successors – the brutally rude, loveless, cynical, philistine young men of the sixties, who sneer and mock and push and jostle and don't apologize – are necessarily superior beings? What new principles, what new constructive answers have they provided? Destruction is destruction. It is not creation.[45]

In the violent babel of voices aroused by the novel, at least five attitudes can be distinguished.[46] There was the angry right wing which thought that Bazarov represented the apotheosis of the new nihilists, and sprang from Turgenev's unworthy desire to flatter and be accepted by the young. There were those who congratulated him on successfully exposing barbarism and subversion. There were those who denounced him for his wicked travesty of the radicals, for providing reactionaries with ammunition and playing into the hands of the police; by them he was called renegade and traitor. Still others, like Dimitri Pisarev, proudly nailed Bazarov's colours to their mast and expressed gratitude to Turgenev for his honesty and sympathy with all that was most living and fearless in the growing party of the future. Finally there were some who detected that the author himself was not wholly sure of what he wanted to do, that his attitude was genuinely ambivalent, that he was an artist and not a pamphleteer, that he told the truth as he saw it, without a clear partisan purpose.

This controversy continued in full strength after Tur-

45. *Sobraniye sochineniy*, vol. xi, p. 351.
46. For a full analysis of the immediate reaction to the novel see 'Z' (E. Zarin), 'Ne v brov, a v glaz', *Biblioteka dlya chteniya*, 1862, no. 4, pp. 21–55.

genev's death. It says something for the vitality of his creation that the debate did not die even in the following century, neither before nor after the Russian Revolution. Indeed, as lately as ten years ago the battle was still raging amongst Soviet critics. Was Turgenev for us or against us? Was he a Hamlet blinded by the pessimism of his declining class, or did he, like Balzac or Tolstoy, see beyond it? Is Bazarov a forerunner of the politically committed, militant Soviet intellectual, or a malicious caricature of the fathers of Russian communism? The debate is not over yet.[47]

Turgenev was upset and bewildered by the reception of his book. Before sending it to the printer, he had taken his usual precaution of seeking endless advice. He read the manuscript to friends in Paris, he altered, he modified, he tried to please everyone. The figure of Bazarov suffered several transformations in successive drafts, up and down the moral scale as this or that friend or consultant reported his impressions. The attack from the Left inflicted wounds which festered for the rest of his life. Years later he wrote 'I am told that I am on the side of the "fathers" – I, who in the person of Paul Kirsanov, actually sinned against artistic truth,

47. The literature, mostly polemical, is very extensive. Among the most representative essays may be listed: V. V. Vorovsky's celebrated 'Dva nigilizma: Bazarov i Sanin' (1909), *Sochineniya*, Moscow, 1931, vol. ii, pp. 74–100; V. P. Kin in *Literatura i marksizm*, Moscow, 1929, vol. vi, pp. 71–116; L. V. Pumpyansky, '*Ottsy i dyeti*'. Istoriko-literaturny ocherk', in I. S. Turgenev, *Sochineniya*, Moscow/Leningrad, 1930, vol. vi, pp. 167–86; I. Ippolit, *Lenin o Turgeneve*, Moscow, 1934; I. I. Veksler, *I. S. Turgenev i politicheskaya borba shestidesyatykh godov*, Moscow/Leningrad, 1935; V. Arkhipov, in *Russkaya literatura*, 1958, no. 1, pp. 132–62; G. Byaly, in *Novy Mir*, Moscow, 1958, no. 8, pp. 255–9; A. I. Batyuto, in *I. S. Turgenev (1818–1883–1958)*. *Stati i materialy*, Orel, 1960, pp. 77–95; P. G. Pustovoit, *Roman I. S. Turgeneva* Ottsy i dyeti *i ideinaya borba 60kh godov XIX veka*, Moscow, 1960; N. Chernov in *Voprosy literatury*, Moscow, 1961, no. 8, pp. 188–93; William Egerton in *Russkaya literatura*, 1967, no. 1, pp. 149–54.

This represents a mere sample of the continuing controversy, in which Lenin's scathing reference to the similarity of Turgenev's views to those

went too far, exaggerated his defects to the point of travesty, and made him ridiculous!'[48] As for Bazarov, he was 'honest, truthful, a democrat to his fingertips'.[49] Many years later, Turgenev told the anarchist Kropotkin that he loved Bazarov 'very, very much ... I will show you my diaries – you will see how I wept when I ended the book with Bazarov's death.'[50] 'Tell me honestly,' he wrote to one of his most caustic critics, the satirist Saltykov (who complained that the word 'nihilist' was used by reactionaries to damn anyone they did not like), 'how could anybody be offended by being compared to Bazarov? Do you not yourself realize that he is the most sympathetic of all my characters?'[51] As for 'nihilism', that, perhaps, was a mistake. 'I am ready to admit ... that I had no right to give our reactionary scum the opportunity to seize on a name, a catchword; the writer in me should have brought the sacrifice to the citizen – I admit the justice of my rejection by the young and of all the gibes hurled at me ...

---

of German right-wing social democrats is constantly quoted both for and against the conception of Bazarov as a prototype of Bolshevik activists. There is an even more extensive mass of writing on the question of whether, and how far, Katkov managed to persuade Turgenev to amend his text in a 'moderate' direction by darkening Bazarov's image. That Turgenev did alter his text as a result of Katkov's pleading is certain; he may, however, have restored some, at any rate, of the original language when the novel was published as a book. His relations with Katkov deteriorated rapidly; Turgenev came to look on him as a vicious reactionary and refused his proffered hand at a banquet in honour of Pushkin in 1880; one of his favourite habits was to refer to the arthritis which tormented him as Katkovitis (*Katkovka*). On this see N. M. Gutyar, *Ivan Sergeyevich Turgenev*, Yurev, 1907, and V. Bazanov, *Iz literaturnoi polemiki 60kh godov*, Petrozavodsk, 1941, pp. 46–8. The list of 'corrections' in the text for which Katkov is held responsible is ritually reproduced in virtually every Soviet study of Turgenev's works.

48. *Literaturnyye i zhiteiskiye vospominaniya*, p. 155.

49. Letter to Sluchevsky, 26 April 1862.

50. *I. S. Turgenev v vospominaniyakh sovremennikov*, vol. i, p. 441.

51. Letter to Saltykov-Shchedrin, 15 January 1867.

The issue was more important than artistic truth, and I ought to have foreseen this.'[52] He claimed that he shared almost all Bazarov's views, all save those on art.[53] A lady of his acquaintance had told him that he was neither for the fathers, nor for the children, but was a nihilist himself; he thought she might be right.[54] Herzen had said that there had been something of Bazarov in them all, in himself, in Belinsky, in Bakunin, in all those who in the forties denounced the Russian kingdom of darkness in the name of the West and science and civilization.[55] Turgenev did not deny this either. He did, no doubt, adopt a different tone in writing to different correspondents. When radical Russian students in Heidelberg demanded clarification of his own position, he told them that 'if the reader does not love Bazarov, as he is – coarse, heartless, ruthlessly dry and brusque ... the fault is mine; I have not succeeded in my task. But to "melt him in syrup" (to use his own expression) – that I was not prepared to do ... I did not wish to buy popularity by this sort of concession. Better lose a battle (and I think I have lost this one), than win it by a trick.'[56] Yet to his friend the poet Fet, a conservative landowner, he wrote that he did not himself know if he loved Bazarov or hated him. Did he mean to praise or denigrate him? He did not know.[57] And this is echoed eight years later : 'My personal feelings [towards Bazarov] were confused (God only knows whether I loved him or hated him!).'[58] To the liberal Madame Filosofova he wrote, 'Bazarov is my beloved child; on his account I quarrelled with Katkov ... Bazarov, that intelligent, heroic man – a caricature? !' And he added that this was 'a senseless charge'.[59] He

52. Letter to Saltykov-Shchedrin, 15 January 1867.
53. *Literaturnyye i zhiteiskiye vospominaniya*, p. 155.
54. ibid., p. 157.
55. 'Yeshche raz Bazarov', *Sobraniye sochineniy*, vol. xx, pp. 335–50.
56. Letter to Sluchevsky, op. cit.
57. Letter of 18 April 1862.
58. Letter to I. Borisov, 4 January 1870.
59. Letter of 30 August 1874.

found the scorn of the young unjust beyond endurance. He wrote that in the summer of 1862 'despicable generals praised me, the young insulted me.' [60] The socialist leader Lavrov reports that he bitterly complained to him of the injustice of the radicals' change of attitude towards him. He returns to this in one of his late *Poems in Prose*: 'Honest souls turned away from him. Honest faces grew red with indignation at the mere mention of his name.' [61] This was not mere wounded *amour propre*. He suffered from a genuine sense of having got himself into a politically false position. All his life he wished to march with the progressives, with the party of liberty and protest. But, in the end, he could not bring himself to accept their brutal contempt for art, civilized behaviour, for everything that he held dear in European culture. He hated their dogmatism, their arrogance, their destructiveness, their appalling ignorance of life. He went abroad, lived in Germany and France, and returned to Russia only on flying visits. In the West he was universally praised and admired. But in the end it was to Russians that he wished to speak. Although his popularity with the Russian public in the sixties, and at all times, was very great, it was the radicals he most of all wanted to please. They were hostile or unresponsive.

His next novel, *Smoke*, which he began immediately after the publication of *Fathers and Children*, was a characteristic attempt to staunch his wounds, to settle his account with all his opponents. It was published five years later, in 1867, and contained a biting satire directed at both camps: at the pompous, stupid, reactionary generals and bureaucrats, and at the foolish, shallow, irresponsible left-wing talkers, equally remote from reality, equally incapable of remedying the ills of Russia. This provoked further onslaughts on him. This

60. Letter to Marko Vovchok (Mme Markovich), 27 August 1862.

61. From the prose poem 'Uslyshish sud gluptsa' ('You will hear the judgement of a fool'). Quoted by P. Lavrov in 'I. S. Turgenev i razvitiye russkogo obshchestva', *Vestnik narodnoi voli*, vol. ii, Geneva, 1884, p. 119.

time he was not surprised. 'They are all attacking me, Reds and Whites, from above and below, and from the sides, especially from the sides.'[62] The Polish rebellion of 1863 and, three years later, Karakozov's attempt to assassinate the Emperor produced great waves of patriotic feeling even within the ranks of the liberal Russian intelligentsia. Turgenev was written off by the Russian critics, of both the Right and the Left, as a disappointed man, an expatriate who no longer knew his country from the distance of Baden-Baden and Paris. Dostoyevsky denounced him as a renegade Russian and advised him to procure a telescope which might enable him to see Russia a little better.[63] In the seventies he began nervously, in constant fear of being insulted and humiliated, to rebuild his relations with the left wing. To his astonishment and relief, he was well received in Russian revolutionary circles in Paris and London; his intelligence, his goodwill, his undiminished hatred for Tsardom, his transparent honesty and fair-mindedness, his warm sympathy with individual revolutionaries, his great charm, had its effect on their leaders. Moreover, he showed courage, the courage of a naturally timorous man determined to overcome his terrors: he supported subversive publications with secret gifts of money, he took risks in openly meeting proscribed terrorists shadowed by the police in Paris or London; this melted their resistance. In 1876 he published *Virgin Soil* (which he intended as a continuation of *Fathers and Children*) in a final attempt to explain himself to the indignant young. 'The younger generation', he wrote in the following year, 'have, so far, been represented in our literature either as a gang of cheats and crooks ... or ... elevated into an ideal, which again is wrong, and, what is more, harmful. I decided to find the middle way, to come closer to the truth – to take young people, for the most part good and honest, and show that, in spite of

62. Letter to Herzen, 4 June 1867.
63. See Dostoyevsky's letter to the poet A. N. Maikov of 28 August 1867 (quoted in N. M. Gutyar, op. cit., pp. 337-40).

their honesty, their cause is so devoid of truth and life that it can only end in a total fiasco. How far I have succeeded is not for me to say. . . But they must feel my sympathy . . . if not for their goals, at least for their personalities.'[64] The hero of *Virgin Soil*, Nezhdanov, a failed revolutionary, ends by committing suicide. He does so largely because his origins and character make him incapable of adapting himself to the harsh discipline of a revolutionary organization, or to the slow and solid work of the true hero of the novel, the practical revolutionary Solomin, whose quietly ruthless labours within his own democratically organized factory will create a more just social order. Nezhdanov is too civilized, too sensitive, too weak, above all too complex, to fit into an austere, monastic, new order: he thrashes about painfully, but, in the end, fails because he 'cannot simplify himself'. Nor – and this (as Mr Irving Howe has pointed out)[65] is the central point – could Turgenev. To his friend Jacob Polonsky he wrote: 'If I was beaten with sticks for *Fathers and Children*, for *Virgin Soil* they will beat me with staves, from both sides, as usual.'[66] Three years later Katkov's newspaper again denounced him for 'performing clownish somersaults to please the young'.[67] As always, he replied at once: he had not, he said, altered his views by an iota during the last forty years. 'I am, and have always been, a "gradualist", an old-fashioned liberal in the English dynastic sense, a man expecting reform *only from above*. I oppose revolution in principle . . . I should regard it as unworthy of [our youth] and myself, to represent myself in any other light.'[68]

By the late seventies his shortcomings had been forgiven

64. Letter to Stasyulevich, 3 January 1877.

65. See the excellent essay on Turgenev in *Politics and the Novel*, London, 1961.

66. Letter of 23 November 1876.

67. See B. Markevich (under the pseudonym 'Inogorodny obyvatel'), 'S beregov Nevy', *Moskovskiye vedomosti*, 9 December 1879.

68. Letter to *Vestnik Yevropy* (*The European Herald*), 2 January 1880, *Sobraniye sochineniy*, vol. xv, p. 185.

by the Left. His moments of weakness, his constant attempts to justify himself before the Russian authorities, his disavowals of relations with the exiles in London or Paris – all these sins seem to have been all but forgotten.[69] His charm, his sympathy for the persons and convictions of individual revolutionaries, his truthfulness as a writer, won much goodwill among the exiles, even though they harboured no illusions about the extreme moderation of his views and his inveterate habit of taking cover when the battle became too hot. He went on telling the radicals that they were mistaken. When the old has lost authority and the new works badly, what is needed is something that he spoke of in the *Nest of Gentlefolk*: 'Active patience, not without some cunning and ingenuity.' When the crisis is upon us, 'when', in his telling phrase, 'the incompetent come up against the unscrupulous', what is wanted is practical good sense, not the absurd, nostalgic idyll of Herzen and the populists, with their blind, idolatrous adoration of the peasant who is the worst reactionary of the lot. He said over and over again that he loathed

69. In 1863 he was summoned back from Paris to be interrogated by a Senatorial Commission in St Petersburg about his relations with Herzen and Bakunin. How could he have plotted with these men, he protested, he who was a life-long monarchist, a butt of bitter onslaughts by the 'Reds'? After *Fathers and Children*, he assured the Senators, his relations with Herzen, which had never been very close, had been 'severed'. There was an element of truth in this. But it was not perhaps surprising that Herzen (who had not forgotten Turgenev's refusal to sign his and Ogarev's manifesto criticizing the shortcomings of the Act of Emancipation of the serfs) should, characteristically, have referred to 'a white-haired Magdalen of the male sex' who could not sleep at night for thinking that the Emperor might not have heard of her repentance. Turgenev and Herzen saw each other again in later years, but never again on the same intimate terms. In 1879 Turgenev similarly hastened to deny all connection with Lavrov and his fellow revolutionaries. Lavrov, too, forgave him. (For Turgenev's relations with Lavrov and other revolutionary *émigrés* see P. Lavrov, 'I. S. Turgenev i razvitiye russkogo obshchestva', op. cit., pp. 69–149, and Michel Delines (M. O. Ashkinazy), *Tourguéneff inconnu*, Paris, 1888, pp. 53–75.)

revolution, violence, barbarism. He believed in slow progress, made only by minorities 'if only they do not destroy each other'. As for socialism, it was a fantasy. It is characteristic of Russians, says his hero and mouthpiece, Potughin, in *Smoke*, 'to pick up an old, worn-out shoe which long, long ago fell from the foot of a Saint-Simon or a Fourier, and, placing it reverently on one's head, to treat it as a sacred object'. As for equality, to the revolutionary Hermann Lopatin he said, 'We are not, all of us, really going to walk about in identical yellow tunics *à la* Saint-Simon, all buttoned at the back?' [70] Still, they were the young, the party of freedom and generosity, the party of the have-nots, of those in pain or at least in distress; he would not refuse them his sympathy, his help, his love, even while all the time looking over his shoulder guiltily at his right-wing friends to whom he tried again and again to minimize his unceasing flirtation with the Left. On his visits to Moscow or St Petersburg he tried to arrange meetings with groups of radical students. Sometimes the conversations went well, at other times, particularly when he tried to charm them with his reminiscences of the forties, they tended to become bored, contemptuous, and resentful. Even when they liked or admired him, he felt that a gulf divided them, divided those who wanted to destroy the old world, root and branch, from those who, like him, wished to save it, because in a new world, created by fanaticism and violence, there might be too little worth living for.

It was his irony, his tolerant scepticism, his lack of passion, his 'velvet touch', above all his determination to avoid too definite a social or political commitment that, in the end, alienated both sides. Tolstoy and Dostoyevsky, despite their open opposition to 'the progressives', embodied unshakeable principles and remained proud and self-confident, and so never became targets for those who threw stones at Turgenev.

70. See Hermann Lopatin's reminiscences in *I. S. Turgenev v vospominaniyakh revolyutsionerov-semidesyatnikov*, Moscow/Leningrad, 1930, p. 124.

His very gifts, his power of minute and careful observation, his fascination with the varieties of character and situation as such, his detachment, his inveterate habit of doing justice to the full complexity and diversity of goals, attitudes, beliefs – these seemed to them morally self-indulgent and politically irresponsible. Like Montesquieu, he was accused by the radicals of too much description, too little criticism. Beyond all Russian writers, Turgenev possessed what Strakhov described as his poetic and truthful genius – a capacity for rendering the very multiplicity of inter-penetrating human perspectives that shade imperceptibly into each other, nuances of character and behaviour, motives and attitudes, undistorted by moral passion. The defence of civilization by the spoilt but intelligent Paul Kirsanov is not a caricature, and carries a kind of conviction, while the defence of what are apparently the very same values by the worthless Panshin in the *Nest of Gentlefolk* does not, and is not meant to do so; Lavretsky's Slavophile feeling is moving and sympathetic; the populism of both the radicals and the conservatives in *Smoke* is – and is intended to be – repulsive. This calm, finely discriminating, slightly ironical vision, wholly dissimilar from the obsessed genius of Dostoyevsky or Tolstoy, irritated all those who craved for primary colours, for certainty, who looked to writers for moral guidance and found none in Turgenev's scrupulous, honest, but – as it seemed to them – somewhat complacent ambivalence. He seemed to enjoy his very doubts: he would not cut too deep. Both his great rivals found this increasingly intolerable. Dostoyevsky, who began as an enthusiastic admirer, came to look on him as a smiling, shallow, cosmopolitan *poseur*, a cold-hearted traitor to Russia. Tolstoy thought him a gifted and truthful writer but a moral weakling, and hopelessly blind to the deepest and most agonizing spiritual problems of mankind. To Herzen he was an amiable old friend, a gifted artist, and a feeble ally, a reed that bent too easily before every storm, an inveterate compromiser. Turgenev could never bear his wounds in silence. He complained, he apologized, he protested. He knew that he was accused of lack of depth or seriousness or courage. The reception of *Fathers and Children* continued to prey upon him. 'Seventeen years have passed since the appearance of *Fathers and Children*,' he wrote in 1880, 'yet the attitude of the critics ... has not become stabilized. Only last year, I happened to read in a journal apropos Bazarov, that I am nothing but a Bashiboozook[71] who beats to death men wounded by others.'[72] His sympathies, he insisted again and again, were with the victims, never the oppressors – with peasants, students, artists, women, civilized minorities, not the big battalions. How could his critics be so blind? As for Bazarov, there was, of course, a great deal wrong with him, but he was a better man than his detractors; it was easy enough to depict radicals as men with rough exteriors and hearts of gold; 'the trick is to make Bazarov a wild wolf, and still manage to justify him ...'[73]

The one step Turgenev refused to take was to seek an alibi in the doctrine of art for art's sake. He did not say, as he might easily have done, 'I am an artist, not a pamphleteer; I write fiction, which must not be judged by social or political criteria; my opinions are my private affair; you don't drag Scott or Dickens or Stendhal or even Flaubert before your ideological tribunals – why don't you leave me alone?' He never seeks to deny the social responsibility of the writer; the doctrine of social commitment was instilled into him once and for all by his adored friend Belinsky, and from it he never wholly departed. This social concern colours even his most lyrical writing, and it was this that broke through the reserve of the revolutionaries he met abroad. These men knew perfectly well that Turgenev was genuinely at his ease only with old friends of his own class, men who held views that could

71. Barbarous Turkish mercenary.
72. Preface to the 1880 edition of his novels. *Sobraniye sochineniy*, vol. xii, pp. 307–8.
73. Letter to Herzen, 28 April 1862.

not conceivably be described as radical – with civilized liberals or country squires with whom he went duck shooting whenever he could. Nevertheless, the revolutionaries liked him because he liked them, because he sympathized with their indignation: 'I know I am only a stick they use to beat the Government with, but' (at this point according to the exiled revolutionary Lopatin who reports this conversation, he made an appropriate gesture) 'let them do it, I am only too glad.' [74] Above all, they felt drawn to him because he was responsive to them as individuals and did not treat them simply as representatives of parties or outlooks. This was, in a sense, paradoxical, for it was precisely individual social or moral characteristics that, in theory, these men tried to ignore; they believed in objective analysis, in judging men sociologically, in terms of the role that, whatever their conscious motives, they played (whether as individuals or as members of a social class) in promoting or obstructing desirable human ends – scientific knowledge, or the emancipation of women, or economic progress, or the revolution. This was the very attitude that Turgenev recoiled from; it was what he feared in Bazarov and the revolutionaries of *Virgin Soil*. Turgenev and liberals generally saw tendencies, political attitudes, as functions of human beings, not human beings as functions of social tendencies.[75] Acts, ideas, art, literature were expressions of individuals, not of objective forces of which the actors or thinkers were merely the embodiments. The reduction of men to the function of being primarily carriers or agents of impersonal forces was as deeply repellent to Turgenev as it had been to Herzen or, in his later phases, to his revered friend Belinsky. To be treated with so much sympathy and understanding, and indeed affection, as human beings and not primarily as spokesmen for ideologies, was a rare enough

74. H. Lopatin, op. cit., p. 126.

75. For this excellent formulation of the distinction between liberals and radicals see *The Positive Hero in Russian Literature*, by Professor Rufus Mathewson, New York, 1958.

experience, a kind of luxury, for Russian revolutionary exiles abroad. This alone goes some way to account for the fact that men like Stepniak, Lopatin, Lavrov, and Kropotkin responded warmly to so understanding, and, moreover, so delightful and so richly gifted a man as Turgenev. He gave them secret subsidies but made no intellectual concessions. He believed – this was his 'old-fashioned' liberalism of the 'English dynastic [he meant constitutional] sense' [76] – that only education, only gradual methods, 'industry, patience, self-sacrifice, without glitter, without noise, homoeopathic injections of science and culture' could improve the lives of men. He shook and shivered under the ceaseless criticisms to which he had exposed himself, but, in his own apologetic way, refused to 'simplify' himself. He went on believing – perhaps this was a relic of his Hegelian youth – that no issue was closed for ever, that every thesis must be weighed against its antithesis, that systems and absolutes of every kind – social and political no less than religious – were a form of dangerous idolatry;[77] above all, one must never go to war unless and until all that one believes in is at stake and there is literally no other way out. Some of the fanatical young men responded with genuine regard and, at times, profound admiration. A young radical wrote in 1883 'Turgenev is dead. If Shchedrin [78] should die too, then one might as well go down to the grave alive... For us these men replaced parliament, meetings, life, liberty!' [79] A hunted member of a terrorist organization, in a tribute illegally published on the day of Turgenev's funeral,

76. Letter to *Vestnik Yevropy*, see above, p. 42, n. 68. See also the letters to Stasyulevich (p. 42 above, n. 64), and to Herzen of 25 November 1862, and F. Volkhovsky's article, 'Ivan Sergeevich Turgenev', *Free Russia*, vol. ix, no. 4, London, 1898, pp. 26–9.

77. See the letters to Countess Lambert in 1864, and to the writer Milyutina in 1875, quoted with much other relevant material in V. N. Gorbacheva, *Molodyye gody Turgeneva*, Kazan, 1926.

78. The satirist Saltykov-Shchedrin.

79. *Literaturnoye Nasledstvo*, vol. lxxvi, p. 332, and *I. S. Turgenev v vospominaniyakh sovremennikov*, vol. i, Introduction, p. 36.

wrote 'A gentleman by birth, an aristocrat by upbringing and character, a gradualist by conviction, Turgenev, perhaps without knowing it himself ... sympathized and even served the Russian revolution.' [80] The special police precautions at Turgenev's funeral were clearly not wholly superfluous.

3

It is time that Saturns ceased dining off their children; time, too, that children stopped devouring their parents like the natives of Kamchatka.

Alexander Herzen [81]

Critical turning-points in history tend to occur, we are told, when a form of life and its institutions are increasingly felt to cramp and obstruct the most vigorous productive forces alive in a society – economic or social, artistic or intellectual – and it has not enough strength to resist them. Against such a social order, men and groups of very different tempers and classes and conditions unite. There is an upheaval – a revolution – which, at times, achieves a limited success. It reaches a point at which some of the demands or interests of its original promoters are satisfied to an extent which makes further fighting on their part unprofitable. They stop, or struggle uncertainly. The alliance disintegrates. The most passionate and single-minded, especially among those whose purposes or ideals are furthest from fulfilment, wish to press on. To stop half-way seems to them a betrayal. The sated groups, or the less visionary, or those who fear that the old yoke may be followed by an even more oppressive one, tend to hang back. They find themselves assailed on two sides. The conservatives look on them as, at best, knock-kneed sup-

80. The author of the pamphlet was P. F. Yakubovich (quoted in *Turgenev v russkoi kritike*, p. 401).

81. *Sobraniye sochineniy*, vol. x, p. 319.

porters, at worst as deserters and traitors. The radicals look on them as pusillanimous allies, more often as diversionists and renegades. Men of this sort need a good deal of courage to resist magnetization by either polar force and to urge moderation in a disturbed situation. Among them are those who see, and cannot help seeing, many sides of a case, as well as those who perceive that a humane cause promoted by means that are too ruthless is in danger of turning into its opposite, liberty into oppression in the name of liberty, equality into a new, self-perpetuating oligarchy to defend equality, justice into crushing of all forms of noncomformity, love of men into hatred of those who oppose brutal methods of achieving it. The middle ground is a notoriously exposed, dangerous, and ungrateful position. The complex position of those who, in the thick of the fight, wish to continue to speak to both sides is often interpreted as softness, trimming, opportunism, cowardice. Yet this description, which may apply to some men, was not true of Erasmus; it was not true of Montaigne; it was not true of Spinoza, when he agreed to talk to the French invader of Holland; it was not true of the best representatives of the Gironde, or of some among the defeated liberals in 1848, or of stout-hearted members of the European Left who did not side with the Paris Commune in 1871. It was not weakness or cowardice that prevented the Mensheviks from joining Lenin in 1917, or the unhappy German socialists from turning communist in 1932. The ambivalence of such moderates, who are not prepared to break their principles or betray the cause in which they believe, has become a common feature of political life after the last war. This stems, in part, from the historic position of nineteenth-century liberals for whom the enemy had hitherto always been on the Right – monarchists, clericals, aristocratic supporters of political or economic oligarchies, men whose rule promoted, or was indifferent to, poverty, ignorance, injustice and the exploitation and degradation of men. The natural inclination of liberals has been, and still is, towards the Left, the party of generosity and humanity, towards anything that destroys barriers between men. Even after the inevitable split they tend to be deeply reluctant to believe that there can be real enemies on the Left. They may feel morally outraged by the resort to brutal violence by some of their allies; they protest that such methods will distort or destroy the common goal. The Girondins were driven into this position in 1792; liberals like Heine or Lamartine in 1848; Mazzini, and a good many socialists, of whom Louis Blanc was the most representative, were repelled by the methods of the Paris Commune of 1871. These crises passed. Breaches were healed. Ordinary political warfare was resumed. The hopes of the moderates began to revive. The desperate dilemmas in which they found themselves could be viewed as being due to moments of sudden aberration which could not last. But in Russia, from the 1860s until the revolution of 1917, this uneasy feeling, made more painful by periods of repression and horror, became a chronic condition – a long, unceasing malaise of the entire enlightened section of society. The dilemma of the liberals became insoluble. They wished to destroy the regime which seemed to them wholly evil. They believed in reason, secularism, the rights of the individual, freedom of speech, of association, of opinion, the liberty of groups and races and nations, greater social and economic equality, above all in the rule of justice. They admired the selfless dedication, the purity of motive, the martyrdom of those, no matter how extremist, who offered their lives for the violent overthrow of the *status quo*. But they feared that the losses entailed by terrorist or Jacobin methods might be irreparable, and greater than any possible gains; they were horrified by the fanaticism and barbarism of the extreme Left, by its contempt for the only culture that they knew, by its blind faith in what seemed to them Utopian fantasies, whether anarchist or populist or Marxist. These Russians believed in European civilization as converts believe in a newly acquired faith. They could not bring themselves to contemplate, still less to sanction, the destruction of much that seemed to them of infinite value for themselves and for all men in the past, even the Tsarist past. Caught between two armies, denounced by both, they repeated their mild and rational words without much genuine hope of being heard by either side. They remained obstinately reformist and non-revolutionary. Many suffered from complex forms of guilt: they sympathized more deeply with the goals upon their Left; but, spurned by the radicals, they tended to question, like the self-critical, open-minded human beings that they were, the validity of their own positions, they doubted, they wondered, they felt tempted, from time to time, to jettison their enlightened principles and find peace by conversion to a revolutionary faith, above all by submission to the domination of the fanatics. To stretch themselves upon a comfortable bed of dogma would, after all, save them from being plagued by their own uncertainties, from the terrible suspicion that the simple solutions of the extreme Left might, in the end, be as irrational and as repressive as the nationalism, or élitism, or mysticism of the Right. Moreover, despite all its shortcomings the Left still seemed to them to stand for a more human faith than the frozen, bureaucratic, heartless Right, if only because it was always better to be with the persecuted than with the persecutors. But there was one conviction which they never abandoned: they knew that evil means destroyed good ends. They knew that to extinguish existing liberties, civilized habits, rational behaviour, to abolish them today, in the belief that, like a phoenix, they would arise in a purer and more glorious form tomorrow, was to fall into a terrible snare and delusion. Herzen told his old friend, the anarchist Bakunin, in 1869 that to order the intellect to stop because its fruits might be misused by the enemy, to arrest science, invention, the progress of reason, until men were made pure by the fires of a total revolution – until 'we are free' – was nothing but a self-destructive fallacy. 'One cannot stop intelligence', Herzen wrote in his last and magnificent essay, 'because the majority lacks understanding, while the minority makes evil use of it . . . Wild cries to close books, abandon science, and go to some senseless battle of destruction – that is the most violent and harmful kind of demagoguery. It will be followed by the eruption of the most savage passions . . . No! Great revolutions are not achieved by the unleashing of evil passions . . . I do not believe in the seriousness of men who prefer crude force and destruction to development and arriving at settlements . . .' [82] and then, in an insufficiently remembered phrase, 'One must open men's eyes, not tear them out.' [83] Bakunin had declared that one must first clear the ground: then we shall see. That savoured to Herzen of the dark ages of barbarism. In this he spoke for his entire generation in Russia. This is what Turgenev, too, felt and wrote during the last twenty years of his life. He declared that he was a European; Western culture was the only culture that he knew; this was the banner under which he had marched as a young man: it was his banner still.[84] His spokesman is Potugin in *Smoke*, when he says 'I am devoted to Europe, or to be more precise to . . . civilization . . . this word is pure and holy, while other words, "folk", for example, or . . . yes, or "glory", smell of blood . . .' His condemnation of political mysticism and irrationalism, populist and Slavophile, conservative or anarchist, remained absolute.

But short of this, these 'men of the forties' were less sure: to support the Left in its excesses went against the civilized grain; but to go against it, or even to remain indifferent to its fate, to abandon it to the forces of reaction, seemed even more unthinkable. The moderates hoped, against all evidence, that the ferocious anti-intellectualism, which, liberals in Russia told Turgenev, was spreading like an infectious disease among the young, the contempt for painting, music, books, the mounting political terrorism, were passing excesses due to

82. 'K. staromu tovarishchu' ('To an Old Comrade'), Fourth Letter, 1869, *Sobraniye sochineniy*, vol. xx, pp. 592–3.

83. ibid., p. 593.

84. Letter to Herzen of 25 November 1862.

immaturity, lack of education; they were results of a long frustration; they would disappear once the pressures that had generated them were removed. Consequently they explained away the violent language and the violent acts of the extreme Left, and continued to support the uneasy alliance.

This painful conflict, which became the permanent predicament of the Russian liberals for half a century, has now grown world-wide. We must be clear: it is not the Bazarovs who are the champions of the rebellion today. In a sense, the Bazarovs have won. The victorious advance of quantitative methods, belief in the organization of human lives by technological organization, reliance on nothing but calculation of utilitarian consequences in evaluating policies that affect vast numbers of human beings, this is Bazarov, not the Kirsanovs. The triumphs of the calm moral arithmetic of cost effectiveness which liberates decent men from qualms, because they no longer think of the entities to which they apply their scientific computations as actual human beings who live the lives and suffer the deaths of concrete individuals – this, today, is rather more typical of the establishment than of the opposition. The suspicion of all that is qualitative, impressive, unanalysable, yet precious to men, and its relegation to Bazarov's obsolete, intuitive, pre-scientific rubbish heap, has, by a strange paradox, stirred both the anti-rationalist Right and the irrationalist Left to an equally vehement opposition to the technocratic establishment in the middle. From their opposed standpoints the extreme Left and the extreme Right see such efforts to rationalize social life as a terrible threat to what both sides regard as the deepest human values. If Turgenev were living at this hour, the young radicals whom he would wish to describe, and perhaps to please, are those who wish to rescue men from the reign of those very 'sophisters, economists, and calculators' whose coming Burke lamented – those who ignore or despise what men are and what they live by. The new insurgents of our time favour – so far as they can bring themselves to be at all coherent – something like a vague species of the old, Natural law. They want to build a society in which men treat one another as human beings with unique claims to self-expression, however undisciplined and wild, not as producing or consuming units in a centralized, world-wide, self-propelling social mechanism. Bazarov's progeny has won, and it is the descendants of the defeated, despised 'superfluous men', of the Rudins and Kirsanovs and Nezhdanovs, of Chekhov's muddled, pathetic students and cynical, broken doctors, who are today preparing to man the revolutionary barricades. Yet the similarity with Turgenev's predicament does hold: the modern rebels believe, as Bazarov and Pisarev and Bakunin believed, that the first requirement is the clean sweep, the total destruction of the present system; the rest is not their business. The future must look after itself. Better anarchy than prison; there is nothing in between. This violent cry meets with a similar response in the breasts of Turgenev's liberals, our contemporary Shubins and Kirsanovs and Potughins, the small, hesitant, self-critical, not always very brave, band of men who occupy a position somewhere to the left of centre, and are morally repelled both by the hard faces to their right and the hysteria and mindless violence and demagoguery on their left. Like their forefathers and biographer Turgenev, they are at once horrified and fascinated. They are shocked by the violent irrationalism of the dervishes on the Left, yet they are not prepared to reject wholesale the position of those who claim to represent the young and the disinherited, the indignant champions of the poor and the socially deprived or repressed. This is the notoriously unsatisfactory, at times agonizing, position of the modern heirs of the liberal tradition.

'I understand the reasons for the anger which my book provoked in a certain party,' wrote Turgenev just over a hundred years ago. 'A shadow has fallen upon my name . . . But is this really of the slightest importance? Who, in twenty or thirty years time, will remember all these storms in a teacup, or indeed my name, with or without a shadow?'[85] Turgenev's name still lies under a shadow in his native land. His artistic reputation is not in question; it is as a social thinker that he is still today the subject of a continuing dispute. The situation that he diagnosed in novel after novel, the painful predicament of the believers in liberal Western values, a predicament once thought peculiarly Russian, is today familiar everywhere. So, too, is his own oscillating, uncertain position, his horror of reactionaries, his fear of the barbarous radicals, mingled with a passionate anxiety to be understood and approved of by the ardent young. Still more familiar is his inability, despite his greater sympathy for the party of protest, to cross over unreservedly to either side in the conflict of ideas, classes, and, above all, generations. The figure of the well-meaning, troubled, self-questioning liberal, witness to the complex truth, which, as a literary type, Turgenev virtually created in his own image, has today become universal. These are the men who, when the battle grows too hot, tend either to stop their ears to the terrible din, or attempt to promote armistices, save lives, avert chaos.

As for the storm in a teacup, of which Turgenev spoke, so far from being forgotten, it blows over the entire world today. If the inner life, the ideas, the moral predicament of men matter at all in explaining the course of human history, then Turgenev's novels, especially *Fathers and Children*, quite apart from their literary qualities, are as basic a document for the understanding of the Russian past and of our present as the plays of Aristophanes for the understanding of classical Athens, or Cicero's letters, or novels by Dickens or George Eliot, for the understanding of Rome and Victorian England.

Turgenev may have loved Bazarov; he certainly trembled before him. He understood, and to a degree sympathized with, the case presented by the new Jacobins, but he could not bear to think of what their feet would trample. 'We have

85. 'Po povodu *Ottsov i dyetei* (1869), *Literaturnyye i zhiteiskiye vospominaniya*, p. 159.

the same credulity', he wrote in the mid-sixties, 'and the same cruelty; the same hunger for blood, gold, filth . . . the same meaningless suffering in the name of . . . the same nonsense as that which Aristophanes mocked at two thousand years ago. . .'[86] And art? And beauty? 'Yes, these are powerful words . . . The *Venus of Milo* is less open to question than Roman Law or the principles of 1789'[87] – yet she, too, and the works of Goethe and Beethoven would perish. Cold-eyed Isis – as he calls nature – 'has no cause for haste. Soon or late, she will have the upper hand . . . she knows nothing of art or liberty, as she does not know the good . . .'[88] But why must men hurry so zealously to help her with her work of turning all to dust? Education, only education, can retard this painful process, for our civilization is far from exhausted yet.

Civilization, humane culture, meant more to the Russians, late-comers to Hegel's feast of the spirit, than to the blasé natives of the West. Turgenev clung to it more passionately, was more conscious of its precariousness, than even his friends Flaubert or Renan. But unlike them, he discerned behind the philistine bourgeoisie a far more furious opponent – the young iconoclasts bent on the total annihilation of his world in the certainty that a new and more just world would emerge. He understood the best among these Robespierres, as Tolstoy, or even Dostoyevsky, did not. He rejected their methods, he thought their goals naïve and grotesque, but his hand would not rise against them if this meant giving aid and comfort to the generals and the bureaucrats. He offered no clear way out: only gradualism and education, only reason. Chekhov once said that a writer's business was not to provide solutions, only to describe a situation so truthfully, do such justice to all sides of the question, that the reader could no longer evade it. The

86. Quoted from *Dovolno* (*Enough*), an address read by him in 1864, which was later caricatured by Dostoyevsky in *The Possessed*. See *Sobraniye sochineniy*, vol. ix, pp. 118–19.

87. ibid., p. 119.

88. ibid., p. 120.

doubts Turgenev raised have not been stilled. The dilemma of morally sensitive, honest, and intellectually responsible men at a time of acute polarization of opinion has, since his time, grown acute and world-wide. The predicament of what, for him, was only the 'educated section' of a country then scarcely regarded as fully European, has come to be that of men in every class of society in our day. He recognized it in its earlier beginnings, and described it with incomparable sharpness of vision, poetry, and truth.

Appendix

As an illustration of the political atmosphere in Russia in the seventies and eighties, especially with regard to the mounting wave of political terrorism, the account that follows of a conversation with Dostoyevsky by his editor, A. S. Suvorin, may be of interest. Both Suvorin and Dostoyevsky were loyal supporters of the autocracy and were looked upon by liberals, not without reason, as strong and irredeemable reactionaries. Suvorin's periodical, *New Times* (*Novoye Vremya*), was the best edited and most powerful extreme right-wing journal published in Russia towards the end of the nineteenth and the beginning of the twentieth century. Suvorin's political position gives particular point to this entry in his diary.[89]

On the day of the attempt by Mlodetsky[90] on Loris Melikov I was with F. M. Dostoyevsky.

He lived in a shabby little apartment. I found him sitting by a small round table in the drawing-room, he was rolling cigarettes; his face was like that of someone who had just emerged from a Russian bath, from a shelf on which he had been steaming himself . . . I probably did not manage to conceal my surprise, because he gave me a look and after greeting me, said 'I have just had an attack. I am glad, very glad, to see you' and went on rolling his cigarettes. Neither he nor I knew anything about the assassination. But our conversation presently turned to political crimes in general, and a [recent] explosion in the Winter Palace in particular. In the course of talking about this, Dostoyevsky commented

89. *Dnevnik A. S. Suvorina*, ed. M. Krichevsky, Moscow/Petrograd, 1923, pp. 15–16. This entry for 1887 is the first in the diary of Dostoyevsky's (and Chekhov's) friend and publisher.

90. Ippolit Mlodetsky made his attempt on the life of the head of the Government on 20 February 1880, some weeks after Khalturin's failure to blow up the Winter Palace. He was hanged two days later.

on the odd attitude of the public to these crimes. Society seemed to sympathize with them, or, it might be truer to say, was not too clear about how to look upon them. 'Imagine', he said, 'that you and I are standing by the window of Datsiaro's shop and looking at the pictures. A man is standing near us, and pretending to look too. He seems to be waiting for something, and keeps looking round. Suddenly another man comes up to him hurriedly and says, "The Winter Palace will be blown up very soon. I've set the machine." We hear this. You must imagine that we hear it – that these people are so excited that they pay no attention to their surroundings or how far their voices carry. How would we act? Would we go to the Winter Palace to warn them about the explosion, would we go to the police, or get the corner constable to arrest these men? Would you do this?'

'No, I would not.'

'Nor would I. Why not? After all, it is dreadful; it is a crime. We should have forestalled it.[91] This is what I had been thinking about before you came in, while I was rolling my cigarettes. I went over all the reasons that might have made me do this. Weighty, solid reasons. Then I considered the reasons that would have stopped me from doing it. They are absolutely trivial. Simply fear of being thought an informer. I imagined how I might come, the kind of look I might get from them, how I might be interrogated, perhaps confronted with someone, be offered a reward, or, maybe, suspected of complicity. The newspapers might say that "Dostoyevsky identified the criminals." Is this my affair? It is the job of the police. This is what they have to do, what they are paid for. The liberals would never forgive me. They would torment me, drive me to despair. Is this normal? Everything is abnormal in our society; that is how these things happen, and, when they do, nobody knows how to act – not only in the most difficult situations, but even in the simplest. I might write about this. I could say a great deal that might be good and bad both for society and for the Government; but it cannot be done. About the most important things we are not allowed to talk.'

He talked a great deal on this theme, and talked with inspired feeling. He added that he would write a novel, the hero of which

91. The Russian word can also mean 'give warning'.

would be Alyosha Karamazov. He wanted to take him through a monastery and make him a revolutionary; he would then commit a political crime; he would be executed. He would search for the truth, and in the course of this quest would naturally become a revolutionary . . .[92]

92. The editor of this text, which he calls a 'fragment', mentions a passage in the novel in which Ivan Karamazov speaks to his saintly brother Alyosha about the case of the general who set his dogs to hound a peasant boy to death before the eyes of his mother; he asks Alyosha whether he would want the general to be killed for this. Alyosha, after a tormented silence, says that he would. 'Bravo' says Ivan.

('Fathers and Children', the Romanes Lecture for 1970, was delivered in the Sheldonian Theatre, Oxford, on 12 November of that year)

Introduction

Fir-trees stretch monotonous like ribbons over the flat country-side. Little gullies criss-cross the dark earth (it is not yet black), with here and there an artless village or a manor-house half hidden in a clump of green. Cattle have trampled the grass round the village ponds. The wind blows. This is the province of Orel, the meeting-place of central and southern Russia, of Moscow and the steppes. Here are the wide plains where Turgenev, Tolstoy and Dostoyevsky were born.

In the year 1816 an impecunious but extraordinarily hand-some young cavalry officer – 'a mighty hunter before the Lord', as his son afterwards described him – called on the owner of a large estate in a birch-wood outside the town of Orel. He wanted to buy horses for his regiment. Set in a park and surrounded by orangeries and orchards he found what was practically a minor kingdom of five thousand serfs, ferociously ruled over by an ugly heiress six years his senior. She immediately fell in love with him, invited him to stay ... and took away his sword-belt to assist matters. They married, and within a year their first son was born; and then – as she noted in her journal – 'On Monday, the 28th day of October, 1818, at Twelve of the Clock in the Morning, son Ivan, 21 inches Tall, born in our house at Orel. Christened the 4th day of November.'

Ivan Turgenev ought to have had a golden childhood in his mother's palace of a house. There were balls and masque-rades for relays of guests. They acted plays indoors in the galleries and outside in the gardens. There was a private orchestra; an apprehensive chaplain to conduct services on feast-days; and a governess and tutors for the children. But his feudal mother believed in the rod for serfs and children alike, and she had the boys beaten – or whipped them herself – almost daily for the most trivial offences, even for nothing at all. Yet life was not only punishment and tears: in these early years Turgenev learned to appreciate Nature, to know the simple peasants who taught him old songs and tales of Russia, and to begin his intuitive listening to 'the still, sad music of humanity', which he later transcribed with such truth of insight. His wonderful thumbnail sketches of country scenes are not interruptions in his novels, nor even a poetic background, but an integral part of the narrative. As Virginia Woolf pointed out:

In Turgenev's novels the individual never dominates, many other things seem to be going on at the same time. We hear the hum of life in the fields, a horse champs his bit; a butterfly circles and settles. And as we notice, without seeming to notice, life going on, we feel more intensely for the men and women themselves because they are not the whole of life, but only a part of the whole.

In 1827 the family moved to Moscow and, for Turgenev, to a romantic period of schoolboy friendships. French was the language spoken at home, except to the servants, but the children were urged by their father to write their day-books in Russian at least twice a week. At the age of sixteen Turgenev entered Petersburg University, and three years later published his first poems and realized his dream of going abroad. Together with the more sensitive young men of his generation he was convinced that the source of real knowledge was to be found in Europe, and so he went to Berlin University and dived enthusiastically into the study of Hegel. 'We still believed,' he wrote, 'in the efficacy and importance of philosophical and metaphysical ideas.' Like their forbears, the ancient Slavs of the ninth century who sought better rulers for themselves among foreign Varengian Vikings, they were irritated that their country, although 'great and abundant', was 'devoid of order' and unstable. 'Therefore I flung myself head foremost into that German ocean required to purify and regenerate me, and when at last I emerged from its waves I found myself a *Westernizer*, and so I have always remained.' Europe had the sense of purpose which Russia lacked, a feeling for the dignity of man (in acute contrast to the despotism of his mother and her land-owning class) and a superior culture that Russia could absorb without losing her own identity.

After two years in Berlin, during which time his mother, who concentrated her emotional life on her children, on Ivan especially, when her husband died, clamoured in vain for chatty letters, Turgenev returned to Russia, an elegantly attired, brilliant young man, and took his degree at the University of Moscow. On his twenty-fifth birthday, out hunting near St Petersburg, he was introduced to the middle-aged husband of the young Spanish prima donna, Pauline Garcia-Viardot (who was the model for George Sand's heroine, Consuelo). A few days later, on the morning of 1 November 1843 – a 'sacred' day which he afterwards celebrated for many years – he met Pauline in her apartment opposite the theatre where she was singing. He became infatuated. She allowed herself to be loved – for her he was one of many. He learned Spanish and for the rest of his life followed in her wake, back to Berlin, to London, to France, the journeyings always ending in the Viardots' château at Courtavenel, not far from the small town of Rozoy in the Seine-et-Marne *département*. And when his daughter by a sempstress of his mother's reached the age of ten he had the girl sent to France to be brought up with Pauline Viardot's own children.

Incensed by his devotion to the Spanish singer, as by his decision to abandon the civil service in order to turn man of letters, Turgenev's mother cut off his allowance. This meant more than uncomfortable poverty until her death – she died a tyrant, unrepentant and unreconciled, but left Turgenev a sizeable fortune.

The fact that Pauline Viardot would accept him only as a friend of the family may have been one of the causes of

Turgenev's nostalgia, of his cult of frustration. (*Fathers and Sons* has been called 'an elegy on all human frustration'.) But there were other, deeper reasons. Although an ardent champion of liberal Europe and progress, Turgenev the artist belonged essentially to the 'nests of gentlefolk' of the past, to a social layer already doomed by history and therefore 'superfluous'. Disappointed in love and life he was glad to spend most of his time abroad, where he became a vital link between Russia and the West, himself receiving much in return. In Paris he knew George Sand, Mérimée, Chopin, Musset and others of the cultural *élite*. Flaubert was a close friend and Maupassant proudly proclaimed himself his disciple. In London, where he went to visit Herzen and the little colony of Russian exiles, he met Disraeli, Carlyle, Macaulay and Thackeray, and altogether was agreeably surprised by the English whom he found 'truly a great nation' – this eulogy was to be qualified on a succeeding occasion by the dictum that 'no Englishman has the slightest suspicion as to what art is'. A D.C.L. was conferred on him at Oxford: he had become the idol of all that was eclectic, and to acclaim his work was considered the hall-mark of good taste. And it was while he was staying in Ventnor, where he had gone in 1860 for the sake of the sea-bathing, that the idea occurred to him for his most successful work, *Fathers and Sons*.

Turgenev met the ordeal of his last years with stoic detachment. His only child had married a Frenchman who squandered her money, so that her father was obliged to sell land and personal possessions to provide for her. In the spring of the same year, 1882, he fell ill with cancer of the spinal cord which the French doctors diagnosed and treated as *angina pectoris*. Pain affected his reason and he asked to be given poison or a revolver. Shortly before the end, at Bougival, near Paris, on the 22 August 1883, he failed to recognize Madame Viardot and cried out that she was a dreadful woman who outdid Lady Macbeth in iniquity. He had loved without achieving love; but the photograph taken as he lay in his coffin shows a strength of will and purpose that he never had in life. He died in France, and Renan delivered his funeral oration (at the Gare du Nord, just before the train left Paris) but in accordance with his wishes his remains were buried in Russia.

Turgenev has been called the 'un-Russian Russian'. He was certainly the most urbanely international and highly civilized of the literary giants of nineteenth-century Russia; and the first Russian author both to win general recognition at home and to be esteemed all over Europe. George Moore, who met him in Paris, remembered how he had condemned as vicious that method which always records what a person felt rather than what he thought. In realizing his characters Turgenev's procedure was not to analyse their consciousness but to exhibit their behaviour. It is perhaps his ability to observe facts objectively and then interpret them – to give the photograph and the poem – which makes his work more accessible to Western minds. There is nothing arbitrary or didactic, no 'architecture' in his plots. He is concerned with registering the interwoven fates of three or four *dramatis personae*, and their interaction on each other. His situation unfolds of itself until we see it in the round and receive a generalized and organically blended picture of life. Turgenev is no prophet clothed with thunder: he is a seer who wants to understand, and who writes with the realism of Defoe. His intellectual honesty – and his historian's need for documentation – made him contemplative: thus in 1848, hearing that Paris was in the throes of giving birth to the Republic, he instantly rushed from Brussels – not to fight but to watch the revolution. All through his life he sought to know, to see … and in doing so he paved the way for the triumph of Russian literature as a European power.

Turgenev was a virtuoso of style. He believed that the artist can only teach 'by giving the world images of beauty'. Unlike the majority of his contemporaries he was meticulous about the artistic finish of his writings. He loved the Russian language and used it unerringly – indeed, he would even go so far as to put a word in italics to emphasize how precisely it fits. When he was doubtful or troubled over the fate of his country, the 'great, powerful, truthful, free Russian tongue' was a comfort to him, persuaded as he was that such a language 'can only have been given to a great people'.

Turgenev first made a name with his sketches, *The Papers of a Sportsman*, which appeared in collected form in 1852. These descriptions of the wretched condition of the peasants, with whom he had always sympathized, were read by all classes, including the Emperor himself, and undoubtedly speeded the work of emancipation. But nothing in his literary life caused such a commotion as his masterpiece, *Fathers and Sons*, published ten years later, in 1862. The conservative nobility saw this social-political study as a dangerous glorification of Nihilism, while radical circles reviled it as a crude caricature of progressive youth, a calumny and a libel. The storm of criticism which burst over his head made him wish to abandon writing altogether.

Fathers and Sons, as perfectly constructed as a drama of Sophocles, is a revelation of not merely Russian contemporary life but of humanity. It is a powerful picture of the universal clash between generations, in this instance localized in the hostility between the reactionary 'fathers' of the forties and the revolutionary 'sons' of the sixties, a decade of 'plebeians' who began to assert themselves not only in culture but in public life as a whole, and reflected the new realization and materialistic spirit of the age. These young Russian radicals found their spiritual home in Nihilism because Nihilism emancipated them from any allegiance to the Establishment. In Bazarov, the protagonist of *Fathers and Sons*, Turgenev, a descendant of the forties with all their abstract idealism, has portrayed 'a hero of our time' from the outside, and painted an exact, courageous and intelligent portrait of the first Bolshevik, of the original angry young man. But Bazarov is also the Lucifer figure who recurs again and again in Russian history and fiction; and Turgenev's only convincingly strong character. Bazarov is the man who 'looks at everything critically', who repudiates 'because in these days the most useful thing we can do is to repudiate', who despises aesthetic culture and scorns tradition and all social institutions. He and his fellows have 'had enough of finding fault with themselves'. They want 'fresh victims'. They must 'smash people'. And as though with his tongue in his cheek, Turgenev suddenly plunges Bazarov into the conventional world of the soporifically respectable 'fathers', where his arrogance and studied bad manners shock and repel. In a letter addressed to the Russian students at Heidelberg Turgenev wrote: 'I dreamed of a sombre, savage and great figure, only half emerged from barbarism, strong, *méchant* and honest, but nevertheless doomed to perish because always in advance of the future.' Nourished on biology and physics, Bazarov would cast away religious and metaphysical conceptions in order to reorganize society on strictly scientific and utilitarian principles.

The nihilist of Turgenev's day has turned into the beatnik of ours. There is the same uncompromising sincerity and refusal to 'trust in lying words, that cannot profit' – as Bazarov said, 'It is stupid to tell useless lies'; the same disillusion with the world – 'the world is full of things that pall on one' (Turgenev himself only just managed to overlay his own little faith by a composed despair); there are the same long-haired, 'slovenly dressed' university students – 'You look so spruce and smart . . .' is Bazarov's reproach to Arkady, his erstwhile follower; and the same urge to destroy. 'What can be broken, should be broken,' announced their spokesman, the critic Pisarev. But there is this difference. Bazarov and his fellow nihilists sought to destroy, not for the sake of destruction but in order to clear the ground for a new and better society. Their watchword was Reality, and not Negation. (In so far as our beatniks tend to stop at destruction perhaps it is they who are the real nihilists.)

Incarnating the eternal spirit of revolution, Bazarov must die prematurely because he could never go beyond the threshold of the future. On his deathbed – and this is one of the most beautifully understated death scenes in literature – it dawns on him that revolutionaries, unlike the cobbler, the tailor, or the butcher, are of no practical use to Russia or anybody else. His last desire is that the woman he has loved – and hated himself for loving – should kiss him (they have not kissed before): 'Breathe on the dying flame and let it go out . . .'

Fathers and Sons is no *roman à thèse*. Turgenev's concern is to observe and depict with impartiality so scrupulous that it is not always easy to discern where his personal sympathies lie. He seems to oscillate between dislike and admiration for Bazarov, admiring his vitality and forthright rejection of all mental, social and other taboos, but deprecating his iconoclasm and lack of humanity. The lesser characters are served with equal subtlety and truth. We *know* them all: Bazarov's friend and disciple, Arkady, very ordinary and very nice, easily influenced, trying hard to be as progressive and advanced as his mentor but quite unable to be anything more than 'a good little liberal gentleman'; Nikolai Petrovich, veritable father of his son and very human although he does not evince a single outstanding trait; the exquisite Pavel Petrovich, a dandy – but (to his own wonder, maybe) his emotions function; pretty, diffident Fenichka, collecting more admirers than the intellectual Madame Odintsov who goes to bid farewell of Bazarov when he lies dying of typhus – she probably never made nor ever will make a nobler gesture in her life. And finally Bazarov's father and mother. Could anything be more insignificant and unimportant than these old people who have outlived their day – but what depth and breadth of sentiment they show, what tolerance and breeding! Their sorrow over the loss of their son remains in the mind like an actual experience. This is portrait-painting of genius.

If the enigmatic figure of Bazarov is the pivot determining

the development of character and action, it is life itself which eventually triumphs. Bazarov is beaten, not by people and circumstances but by life. And in the end, without reproaching Bazarov, Turgenev takes his stand for the eternal values, the values for which all poets stand : for love – love of father for son, of man for woman; for friendship and devotion; for art; for religion, even; and we leave Bazarov in his grave, bathed in the tears of his faithful parents, while the sun shines and the birds sing overhead.

Rosemary Edmonds, London, 1963

The footnotes throughout the text of *Fathers and Sons* have been added by the translator.

Fathers and Sons

I

A gentleman in the early forties, wearing check trousers and a dusty overcoat, came out on to the low porch of the coaching-inn on the — highway. The date was the twentieth of May in the year 1859.

'Well, Piotr, still no sign of them?' he asked his servant, a chubby-faced young fellow with small lack-lustre eyes and a chin that was covered with very fair down.

Everything about the servant, from the single turquoise ear-ring to the dyed pomaded hair and his mincing gait, proclaimed him to be a man of the advanced modern generation. He glanced superciliously along the road before answering:

'No, sir, definitely no sign.'

'No sign?' repeated his master.

'No sign,' said the man for the second time.

The gentleman sighed, and then sat down on a little bench. While he is sitting there with his feet tucked under him and gazing pensively around let us introduce him to the reader.

His name is Nikolai Petrovich Kirsanov. Some ten miles from the coaching-inn stands a respectable little property of his consisting of a couple of hundred serfs – or five thousand acres, as he expresses it now that he has divided up his land and let it to the peasants, and started a 'farm'. His father, a general who had seen active service in 1812, a coarse, semi-illiterate but good-natured type of Russian, had been in harness all his life, first in command of a brigade and then of a division. He had always been stationed in the provinces, where his rank enabled him to wield quite considerable influence. His son, Nikolai Petrovich, like his brother Pavel (of whom we shall speak presently), was born in southern Russia and until his fourteenth year brought up at home, surrounded by ill-paid tutors, happy-go-lucky but obsequious adjutants and other such members of the regiment and staff. His mother, born a Kolyazin, was called Agatha before her marriage but as the general's wife she was addressed by her full name: Agafokleya Kuzminishna Kirsanov. She was very much the commanding officer's wife, wore splendid caps and rustling silk gowns and was always the first to go up to the cross in church. She talked volubly in a loud voice, permitted her children to kiss her hand in the morning and gave them her blessing at night – in brief, she enjoyed her life. As the son of a general Nikolai Petrovich should, like his brother Pavel, have entered the army, although he was so little distinguished for bravery that he had earned the nickname 'Funky'. But on the very day the news came that he had got his commission he broke his leg, and after spending two months in bed walked with a slight limp for the rest of his life. The general gave his son up as a bad job and resigned him to a career in the civil service. He took him to Petersburg as soon as he was seventeen and entered him in the University. At the same time Nikolai's brother Pavel was made an officer in the Guards. The two young men set up in apartments together under the distant supervision of a cousin on their mother's side, Ilya Kolyazin, who was an official of some standing. The general returned to his division and his wife, and only at rare intervals sent his sons sheets of grey foolscap written and cross-written in the bold hand of the public scribe, and signed in a laborious flourish at the bottom, 'Piotr Kirsanov, Major-General'. In 1835 Nikolai Petrovich graduated from the University and in the same year General Kirsanov was placed on the retired list after an occasion when his men had failed to pass muster on parade, and he and his wife arrived to settle in Petersburg. He was on the point of taking a house in the neighbourhood of the Tavrichesky Gardens, and had put his name down for the English Club, when suddenly he had an apoplectic stroke and died. Not long afterwards his wife followed her husband to the grave: she could not adapt herself to the dull life of the capital and fell a prey to the *ennui* of existence away from the regiment. In the meantime, while his parents were still alive and to their great chagrin, Nikolai Petrovich had contrived to fall in love with the daughter of his former landlord, a petty official by the name of Prepolovensky. She was a comely girl and, as they say, an 'intellectual' who read the serious articles in the science columns of the periodicals. He married her as soon as the term of mourning for his parents was over and, abandoning the Ministry of Land Distribution in which his father's influence had obtained him a post, was blissfully happy with his Masha. At first they lived in a country villa near the Institute of Forestry, then in town, in a pretty little apartment with a spotless staircase and a chilly drawing-room, and finally in the country where he settled down for good and where before long his son, Arkady, was born. Husband and wife lived very comfortably and quietly : they were hardly ever apart – they read together, sang and played duets together at the piano; she grew flowers and looked after the chickens, while he went hunting now and again and busied himself with the estate, and Arkady grew and grew – comfortably and quietly like his parents. Ten years passed like a dream. In 1847 Kirsanov's wife died. The blow nearly killed him and in a few weeks his hair turned grey. In the hope of somewhat distracting his thoughts he decided to go abroad ... but then came the year 1848. Reluctantly he returned to the country and after a fairly prolonged period of inactivity he set about improving the management of his estate. In 1855 Nikolai Petrovich brought his son to the University; he spent three winters with him in Petersburg, seldom going out anywhere and trying to make friends with Arkady's youthful fellow students. But this last winter he had not been able to go to Petersburg, and so we meet him, quite grey now, stoutish and a trifle bent, in this month of May 1859, waiting for the arrival of his son, who has just taken his degree as once he himself had done.

The servant, out of a sense of propriety or perhaps because he was not anxious to stay under the eye of his master, had gone to the gateway and lit a pipe. Nikolai Petrovich let his head droop as he contemplated the crumbling steps of the porch, where a large speckled hen strutted gravely about, firmly tapping her way on her sturdy yellow legs. A grimy cat sprawled affectedly on the railing, observing the hen with an unfriendly eye. The sun blazed down. A smell of warm rye bread was wafted out of the dark passage of the inn. Our Nikolai Petrovich is lost in reverie. 'My son . . . a graduate . . . my boy Arkady . . .' Again and again the words ran through his head. He tried to think of other things but back came the same thoughts. He remembered his dead wife. 'She did not live to see this day,' he murmured sadly. . . . A fat blue-grey pigeon flew down on to the road, hurrying to drink from a puddle beside the wall. Nikolai Petrovich began watching it but his ears had already caught the sound of approaching wheels.

'Looks as if they're coming, sir,' the servant reported, emerging from the gateway.

Nikolai Petrovich jumped up and strained his eyes along the road. A tarantass came into view, drawn by three post-horses harnessed abreast. Inside the carriage he caught a glimpse of a student's cap-band and the familiar outline of a much-loved face . . .

'Arkady! Arkady!' cried Kirsanov, and he ran forward waving his arms . . . A few seconds later and he was pressing his lips to the smooth, dusty, sun-tanned cheek of the young graduate.

2

'Let me shake myself first, papa,' said Arkady in a voice which, though a trifle hoarse from travelling, was yet boyish and as clear as a bell. 'I shall cover you with dust,' he added, gaily responding to his father's embraces.

'Never mind, never mind,' Nikolai Petrovich kept repeating with a tender smile, and he patted the collar of his son's greatcoat and his own coat a couple of times. 'Let me have a look at you now, let me have a look,' he continued, standing back; and then immediately hurrying off towards the yard of the posting-station he called:

'This way, this way. Quick now with the horses.'

Nikolai Petrovich appeared to be far more excited than his son. He seemed a little flurried and overcome with shyness. Arkady stopped him.

'Papa,' he cried, 'let me introduce my great friend Bazarov, whom I have so often mentioned in my letters. Very kindly he has consented to come and stay with us.'

Nikolai Petrovich spun round quickly and, going up to a tall man in a long loose-fitting coat with tassels who had just climbed out of the carriage, he warmly gripped the red, ungloved hand which his son's friend somewhat tardily offered to him.

'I am indeed glad,' he began, 'and much obliged by your kind attention in paying us this visit. I hope that – But might I inquire your name?'

'Yevgeny Vassilyich,' Bazarov replied in a lazy but virile voice, and throwing back the collar of his coat showed his full face to Nikolai Petrovich. It was a long thin face with a broad forehead, a nose flat at the top but tapering sharply, large greenish eyes and drooping, sandy whiskers – the whole animated by a tranquil smile betokening self-assurance and intelligence.

'I hope, my dear Yevgeny Vassilyich,' pursued Nikolai Petrovich, 'you won't find it dull with us.'

Bazarov's thin lips gave a slight twitch but beyond taking off his cap he made no reply. His light-brown hair, which was long and thick, failed to hide the bulging temples of his broad head.

'Well, Arkady,' Nikolai Petrovich began again, turning to his son, 'shall we have the horses brought round at once or would you like to rest?'

'We'll rest at home, papa. Tell them to harness the horses.'

'Straight away, straight away,' his father exclaimed. 'Hey, Piotr, do you hear? Get a move on, my boy. Look lively.'

Piotr, being one of the modern 'up-to-date' servants, had not approached to kiss the young master's hand but merely bowed to him from a distance, now vanished again through the gateway.

'I have my barouche here but there are three horses available for your tarantass too,' Nikolai Petrovich put in fussily, while Arkady gulped some water from an iron dipper brought him by the landlord's wife, and Bazarov lit his pipe and went up to the coachman who was taking out the horses. 'But the barouche only has room for two and I don't know how your friend . . .'

'He'll go in the tarantass,' Arkady interrupted him in an undertone. 'Please don't stand on ceremony with him. He's a grand fellow, and not a bit pretentious – you'll see.'

Nikolai Petrovich's coachman brought the horses round.

'Come, hurry up, old bushy-beard!' said Bazarov, addressing the driver.

'Did you hear that, Mitya?' chipped in another driver, standing with his hands behind him thrust into the slits of his sheepskin coat. 'Did you hear what the gentleman just called you? And a bushy-beard you are too.'

Mitya only jerked his cap and dragged the reins from the steaming shaft-horse.

'Look sharp, lads, look sharp. Lend a hand,' cried Nikolai Petrovich. 'There'll be something to drink our health with!'

In a few minutes the harnessing was completed; father and son seated themselves in the barouche; Piotr climbed on to the box; Bazarov jumped into the tarantass, leaned his head against the leather cushion – and both vehicles moved off.

3

'So here you are, a graduate now – and home again,' said Nikolai Petrovich, patting Arkady now on the shoulder, now on the knee. 'Home at last!'

'And how is Uncle Pavel? Is he keeping well?' inquired Arkady, anxious, in spite of the genuine almost childish delight filling his heart, to switch the conversation as soon as possible from an emotional to a more commonplace level.

'Yes, quite well. He wanted to come and meet you but for some reason changed his mind.'

'And did you have a long wait for me?' Arkady asked.

'Oh, about five hours.'

'Dear old papa!'

Arkady swung round to imprint a smacking kiss on his father's cheek. Nikolai Petrovich chuckled quietly.

'Just you wait and see the famous horse I've got for you,' he began. 'You'll see. And your room has had new wall-paper.'

'And is there a room ready for Bazarov?'

'We will find him one all right.'

'Please, papa, make a fuss of him. I can't tell you how much I prize his friendship.'

'You only met him recently?'

'Quite recently, yes.'

'That explains why I did not see him last winter. What is he studying?'

'Natural science is his main subject. But he knows everything. Next year he wants to take a degree in medicine.'

'Oh, so he's in the medical faculty,' remarked Nikolai Petrovich, and then paused. 'Piotr,' he went on, pointing with arm outstretched, 'aren't those our peasants driving along over there?'

Piotr glanced in the direction his master indicated. Some carts drawn by unbridled horses were rolling rapidly along a narrow side-track. In each cart there were one or two peasants with their sheepskin coats unbuttoned.

'Just so, sir,' Piotr replied.

'Where can they be going? To the town?'

'To the town, most likely. To the tavern,' he added contemptuously, and half turned towards the coachman as if calling him to witness. But the coachman remained completely aloof: he was a peasant of the old type who disapproved of the modern outlook.

'The peasants are giving me a lot of trouble this year,' Nikolai Petrovich continued, turning to his son. 'They won't pay their tithes. What would you do with them?'

'And the hired men – are you satisfied with them?'

'Yes,' Arkady's father said doggedly. 'The trouble is, they are being set against me, and there is no proper effort being made yet. They ruin the tools. However, they did manage the ploughing tolerably well. When the corn is threshed we should have enough flour. But, tell me, are you beginning to take an interest in farming?'

'It's a pity we haven't any shade,' remarked Arkady, not replying to the question.

'I've had a large awning put up on the north side, over the verandah,' observed Nikolai Petrovich. 'Now we can take our meals in the open air.'

'But won't that make the place look too like a summer villa? ... But that's not important. The air here! How wonderful it is! I do believe the air smells sweeter here than anywhere else in the world. And what skies too ...'

Arkady suddenly stopped short, cast a quick look behind him and fell silent. *check*

'Of course,' Nikolai Petrovich remarked, 'you were born here so everything is bound to strike you with a special ...'

'But papa, what difference does it make where a person was born?'

'Still –'

'No, it makes absolutely no difference.'

Nikolai Petrovich gave a sidelong glance at his son, and the barouche rolled on for another half mile before the conversation was renewed between them.

'I forget whether I wrote and told you,' Nikolai Petrovich began, 'about the death of your old nurse, Yegorovna?'

'You don't mean to say she's dead? Poor old woman! What about Prokofyich – is he still alive?'

'Yes, and he hasn't altered a scrap. Grumbles as much as ever. In fact, you won't find many changes at Maryino.'

'Have you still got the same bailiff?'

'Well, I have made a change there. I decided not to keep any of the former house-serfs about the place, once they received their freedom; or at least not to entrust them with any jobs involving responsibility.' (Arkady glanced in Piotr's direction.) '*Il est libre, en effet,*' Nikolai Petrovich said in an undertone, 'but of course he is only a valet. My new bailiff, now, is a townsman: he seems a capable fellow. I pay him two hundred and fifty roubles a year. However,' he added as he passed his hand over his forehead and eyebrows (which was always a sign of embarrassment with him) 'I told you just now that you would not find many alterations at Maryino ... That's not quite correct. I think I ought to warn you that –'

He hesitated for an instant and then went on in French.

'A stern moralist would consider my frankness improper; but in the first place the thing cannot be concealed and, secondly, as you know, I have always had my own ideas on the subject of the relations between father and son. Though naturally you would have every right to blame me. At my age ... To cut a long story short, that – that girl of whom you have probably already heard ...'

'Fenichka?' inquired Arkady casually.

Nikolai Petrovich coloured.

'Please do not say the name out loud ... Well, yes ... she is living with me now. I have taken her into the house ...

there were a couple of small rooms to spare. But of course we can change all that.'

'My goodness, papa, what for?'

'Your friend will be staying with us ... it might be awkward ...'

'Oh please don't trouble yourself about Bazarov. He's above all that.'

'Well, but there is you to consider,' said Nikolai Petrovich. 'The little side-wing is horrid, that's the trouble.'

'For goodness' sake, papa,' Arkady protested, 'it's almost as if you were apologizing – I wonder you're not ashamed?'

'Of course I ought to be ashamed,' Nikolai Petrovich replied, turning redder and redder.

'Stop, papa, stop, I implore you!' Arkady exclaimed, smiling affectionately. 'What a thing to apologize for!' he thought to himself, and his heart was filled with a feeling of indulgent tenderness for his good, kind father, though mixed with a secret sense of superiority. 'Please don't,' he repeated again, unable to resist a conscious enjoyment of his own more emancipated outlook.

Nikolai Petrovich glanced at him through the fingers of the hand with which he was still rubbing his forehead and something seemed to stab his heart ... But he immediately reproached himself for it.

'Look, here are our meadows at last,' he said after a long silence.

'And that's our forest over there, isn't it?' asked Arkady.

'Yes. But I've sold it. This year they'll cut it down for timber.'

'Why did you sell it?'

'I needed the money; besides, that land is to go to the peasants.'

'Who don't pay you their rent?'

'That can't be helped; anyhow, they will pay it one day.'

'It's a pity about the forest,' Arkady remarked, looking about him.

The country through which they were driving was not in the least picturesque. Field after field stretched away to the horizon, now sloping gently up, now dropping down again. Here and there was a copse, and winding ravines sparsely planted with low bushes, reminding one of the way in which the old maps showed them in the time of Catherine. There were little streams, too, with hollow banks and diminutive ponds with narrow dams, hamlets with squat little huts beneath blackened and often half collapsing roofs, and crooked threshing barns with wattled walls and gaping doorways opening on to abandoned threshing floors, and churches, some brick-built with the stucco peeling off in patches, others of wood with crosses awry and churchyards that had gone to wrack and ruin. Slowly Arkady's heart sank. As though to complete the pattern the peasants whom they met on the way were all in rags and mounted on the sorriest little nags; willows with broken branches and bark hanging in strips stood like tattered beggars on the roadside; emaciated and shaggy cows, gaunt with hunger, were greedily tearing up the grass along the ditches. They looked as if they had just been snatched from the murderous talons of some terrifying monster; and the pitiful sight of the sickly cattle in the setting of that lovely spring day conjured up like a white spectre the vision of an interminable comfortless winter of blizzards, frosts and snows ... 'No,' thought Arkady, 'there is no prosperity here, no sign of contentment or hard work. It just can't go on like this: this must all be transformed ... but how are we to do it, how should we begin?'

Thus Arkady. But even as he reflected spring regained its sway. All around lay a sea of golden green—everything, trees, bushes, grass, gently shone and stirred in sweeping waves under the soft warm breath of the wind; on every side larks poured out their never-ceasing trills. Plovers called as they glided above the low-lying meadows or ran noiselessly over the tufts of grass; the rooks strutted about, black and beautiful against the tender green of the low spring corn: they disappeared in the already whitening rye, and their heads only now and again peeped out from among its smoke-like waves. Arkady gazed and gazed, until his thoughts grew dim and faded away . . . He flung off his greatcoat and turned to his father with a face so bright and boyish that Nikolai Petrovich embraced him again.

'It is no distance now,' Nikolai Petrovich remarked. 'Once we reach the top of the hill the house will be in sight. And what a life we shall have together, Arkady. You shall help me with the estate – if you care to, that is. We must draw close to one another now, get to know each other properly, mustn't we?'

'Of course,' cried Arkady. 'But what a marvellous day it is!'

'To welcome you home, my dear boy. Yes, this is spring in all its glory. Though I agree with Pushkin – do you remember those lines in *Eugene Onegin*?

> To me how sad thy coming is,
> O spring, O spring, sweet time of love!
> What –'

'Arkady!' shouted Bazarov from the tarantass. 'Send over a match, will you, I've nothing to light my pipe with.'

Nikolai Petrovich fell silent while Arkady, who had been listening to him with some surprise but not without sympathy, hastened to produce a silver matchbox from his pocket and told Piotr to take it to Bazarov.

'Would you like a cigar?' Bazarov shouted again.

'Thanks,' Arkady called back.

Piotr returned to the barouche and together with the matchbox handed him a fat black cigar, which Arkady promptly began to smoke, diffusing about him such a strong and acrid smell of cheap tobacco that Nikolai Petrovich, who had never been a smoker, was forced to avert his nose (which he did as discreetly as he could, not to hurt his son's feelings).

A quarter of an hour later both vehicles drew up in front of the porch of a newly-built wooden house painted grey, with a red iron roof. This was Maryino, also known as New Wick or, as the peasants had nicknamed it, The Farm-with-out-any-land.

<h1 style="text-align:center">4</h1>

No crowd of house-servants swarmed out on to the steps to meet the gentlemen – only a girl of about twelve appeared, followed by a young lad very like Piotr, wearing a grey livery jacket with white armorial buttons, who was Pavel Petrovich Kirsanov's servant. Without speaking he opened the door of the barouche and unbuttoned the apron of the tarantass. Nikolai Petrovich with his son and Bazarov made their way through a dark, almost bare hall (behind the door of which they caught a glimpse of a young woman's face) into a drawing-room furnished in the latest style.

'Well, here we are at home,' exclaimed Nikolai Petrovich, taking off his cap and tossing back his hair. 'Now the main thing is supper and bed.'

'A meal would not come amiss, certainly,' remarked Bazarov, stretching himself and dropping down on the sofa.

'Yes, yes, let us have supper at once,' and for no apparent reason Nikolai Petrovich stamped his foot. 'Ah, here comes Prokofyich, just at the right moment.'

A man of about sixty entered, white-haired, lean and dark-complexioned, in a cinnamon-coloured coat with brass buttons, and a pink neckerchief. He grinned, went up to kiss Arkady's hand, and after bowing to the guest retreated to the door and put his hands behind his back.

'So here is the young master, Prokofyich,' began Nikolai Petrovich. 'Come back to us at last ... Well? How do you think he looks?'

'Couldn't look better, sir,' said the old man, and grinned again. Then he quickly knitted his shaggy eyebrows. 'Shall I lay the table, sir?' he inquired impressively.

'If you please, if you please. But wouldn't you like to go to your room first, Yevgeny Vassilyich?'

'No, I thank you, there is no need. But will you be so good as to have my trunk taken there, and this wrap too,' he added, taking off his loose travelling coat.

'Certainly. Prokofyich, will you see to the gentleman's greatcoat.' (Prokofyich, looking slightly puzzled, picked up Bazarov's 'wrap' with both hands and holding it high above his head went out on tiptoe.) 'What about you, Arkady, are you going to your room for a moment?'

'Yes, I must tidy myself,' Arkady replied, and was just moving towards the door when at that moment a man of medium height came into the drawing-room wearing a dark suit of English cut, a fashionable low cravat and patent-leather shoes. It was Pavel Petrovich Kirsanov. He looked about forty-five. His close-cropped grey hair had the black sheen of unpolished silver; his face, the colour of old ivory but without a wrinkle, had unusually regular and clean-cut features as though carved by a sharp and delicate chisel, and showed traces of remarkable beauty: particularly fine were his clear dark almond-shaped eyes. The whole person of Arkady's uncle, with its aristocratic elegance, had preserved a youthful shapeliness and that soaring quality, up and away from the earth, which usually disappears when a man has turned thirty.

Drawing from his trouser pocket an exquisite hand having long tapering pink nails – a hand whose beauty was further enhanced by the snowy whiteness of his cuff buttoned with a single large opal – Pavel Petrovich held it out to his nephew. After a preliminary European handshake he kissed Arkady three times in the Russian fashion, that is to say, he touched his cheeks thrice with his perfumed moustaches, and murmured 'Welcome home.'

Nikolai Petrovich introduced him to Bazarov. Pavel Petrovich responded with a slight inclination of his supple body and a slight smile but he did not offer his hand and even put it back in his pocket.

'I was beginning to think you were not coming today,' he

began in a pleasant voice, with a genial swing and shrug of the shoulders and a display of fine white teeth. 'Did anything happen on the road?'

'No, nothing,' Arkady answered, 'except that we dawdled a bit. With the result that we're now as hungry as wolves. Make Prokofyich hurry up, papa: I'll be back in a second.'

'Wait, I'll come with you,' exclaimed Bazarov, suddenly pulling himself off the sofa. The two young men went out.

'Who's that?' inquired Pavel Petrovich.

'A friend of Arkady's, and according to him a very intelligent fellow.'

'Is he staying with us?'

'Yes.'

'That long-haired creature?'

'Well, yes.'

Pavel Petrovich drummed on the table with his finger-tips. 'I find Arkady *s'est dégourdi*,' he remarked. 'I am glad he is back.'

There was little conversation at supper. Bazarov in particular hardly uttered a word though he ate heartily. Nikolai Petrovich related various incidents in what he termed his 'farming career', talked about the impending government reforms, about committees and deputations, the need for more machinery, and so on. Pavel Petrovich paced slowly up and down the dining-room (he never ate supper), taking an occasional sip from a glass of red wine and even more occasionally making some remark or, rather, some exclamation such as 'Ah! Aha! H'm!' Arkady contributed some of the latest Petersburg gossip but he was conscious of a faint feeling of embarrassment – the embarrassment which generally overcomes a young man after he has but lately been a child and returns to a place where everyone is accustomed to regard and treat him as a child. He made his sentences quite unnecessarily long, avoided saying 'papa' and even substituted the word 'father', mumbled, it is true, between his teeth; with exaggerated nonchalance he poured into his glass far more wine than he really wanted and drank it all. Prokofyich could not take his eyes off him and kept biting his lips. After supper they all separated at once.

'Your uncle's a queer fellow,' Bazarov said to Arkady as he sat in his dressing-gown by the bed, smoking a short pipe. 'All that foppery in the country – just fancy! And his nails, his nails – they ought to be shown at an exhibition!'

'Ah, but you don't know,' replied Arkady. 'Why, he was a great figure in his day. I'll tell you his story sometime. He was very handsome, you know; used to turn all the women's heads.'

'Oh, so that's it! Keeps it up for the sake of old times, does he? What a pity there's no one for him to fascinate here. I couldn't help staring at the astonishing collars he wears, they might be made of marble, and his chin so meticulously shaved. Confess, Arkady, it's ridiculous, isn't it?'

'Perhaps it is. But he's a fine person really.'

'An archaic survival! But your father's nice. He wastes his time reading poetry, and knows precious little about farming, but his heart's in the right place.'

'My father has a heart of gold.'

'Have you noticed how shy he is?'

Arkady shook his head as though he himself did not know what it was to be shy.

'They amaze me, these old romantics!' Bazarov went on. 'They stimulate their nervous systems to the point where they completely break down. However, good night. In my room there's an English washstand, but the door won't fasten. Anyhow, that's something to be encouraged – English washstands spell progress!'

Bazarov departed, and a feeling of joy swept over Arkady. It was sweet to fall asleep in his own home, in the familiar bed, under the quilt worked by loving hands – those of his old nurse, perhaps; those gentle, good and tireless hands. Arkady thought of Yegorovna, and sighed and wished her eternal peace ... For himself he said no prayer.

Both he and Bazarov soon fell asleep but others in the house were awake for a long time. His son's return had excited Nikolai Petrovich. He got into bed but did not snuff out the candle, and propping his head in his hands he brooded deeply. His brother was sitting well after midnight in his study, in a roomy armchair in front of the fireplace where a few embers glowed faintly. Pavel Petrovich had not undressed but merely changed his patent-leather shoes for a pair of heelless red Chinese slippers. In his hand he held the last number of *Galignani* but he was not reading; he gazed fixedly into the grate where a bluish flame flickered, dying down, then flaring up again ... Heaven only knows where his thoughts meandered but they were not wandering entirely in the past; there was a grim, tense expression on his face and this is not so when a man is absorbed solely by his memories. And in a small back room a young woman called Fenichka, wearing a blue wadded jacket with a white kerchief thrown over her dark hair, sat on a large chest, now listening, now dozing, now looking across at the open door through which she could see a child's cot and was able to hear the regular breathing of a sleeping infant.

5

Next morning Bazarov was the first to wake and go out of doors. 'Ugh!' he thought, looking about him. 'This isn't much of a place!' When Nikolai Petrovich had divided his estate with his peasants he had been obliged to build his new manor-house on some nine acres of entirely flat and barren land. He had built a house, offices and farm buildings, laid out a garden, dug a pond and sunk two wells; but the young trees had done badly, very little water had collected in the pond, and the well-water had a brackish taste. Only the arbour of lilac and acacia had grown properly: they sometimes drank tea or dined there. In a few minutes Bazarov had explored all the little paths in the garden, inspected the cattle-yard and the stables, come upon two farm-boys with whom he immediately made friends and set off with them to a small swamp about a mile from the house to look for frogs.

'What do you want frogs for, mister?' one of the boys asked him.

'I'll tell you,' answered Bazarov, who possessed a special faculty for winning the confidence of the lower orders, though he never pandered to them and indeed was very off-hand with them. 'I shall cut the frog open to see what goes on inside him, and then, since you and I are much the same as frogs except that we walk about on our hind legs, I shall know what's going on inside us too.'

'And what do you want to know that for?'

'So as not to make a mistake if you're taken ill and I have to treat you.'

'Are you a doctor then?'

'Yes.'

'Vasska, d'you hear that? The gentleman says you and me are the same as frogs. That's funny!'

'They scare me, them frogs,' observed Vasska, a boy of seven with flaxen hair and bare feet, dressed in a grey smock with a high collar.

'What's there to be scared of? They don't bite yer, do they?'

'Go on, into the water with you, my young philosophers!' said Bazarov.

Meanwhile Nikolai Petrovich too had woken up and gone in to see Arkady, whom he found fully dressed. Father and son went out on to the terrace under the shelter of the awning; a samovar was already boiling on the table near the balustrade, among great bunches of lilac. A little girl appeared, the same one who had been the first to meet the travellers on the steps the evening before. In a shrill voice she said:

'Fedosya Nikolayevna is not very well and can't come to breakfast; she told me to ask you, will you please to pour out for yourselves or shall she send Dunyasha?'

'I will attend to it, I'll do it,' interposed Nikolai Petrovich hurriedly. 'Arkady, how do you like your tea? With cream or with lemon?'

'With cream,' answered Arkady. Then, after a brief pause, 'Papa?' he said questioningly.

Nikolai Petrovich looked at his son with embarrassment. 'Well?' he said.

Arkady lowered his eyes.

'Forgive me, papa, if my question seems to you indiscreet,' he began, 'but you yourself, by the frank way you spoke yesterday, encourage me to be frank ... you won't be angry?'

'Go on.'

'You make me bold enough to ask you ... Is it because I am here that Fen – ... that she won't come to pour out tea?'

Nikolai Petrovich turned slightly away.

'Perhaps,' he answered at length, 'she supposes ... she feels ashamed ...'

Arkady cast a quick glance at his father.

'She has no reason to be ashamed. In the first place, you are aware of my views,' (Arkady much enjoyed saying this) 'and secondly – would I ever dream of interfering with your life and ways by so much as a hairsbreadth? Besides, I am sure you could not make a bad choice: if you have allowed her to live under the same roof with you, she must be worthy of it; in any case, it's not for a son to sit in judgment on his father – least of all for me, and least of all with a father like you, who has never restricted my freedom in any way.'

At first Arkady's voice trembled a little: he felt he was being magnanimous though at the same time he realized that he was delivering something like a lecture to his father; but the sound of his own voice affects a man strongly, and Arkady's concluding words were spoken firmly, emphatically even.

'Thank you, Arkady,' Nikolai Petrovich said thickly, and his fingers again strayed over his eyebrows and forehead. 'What you say is indeed true. Of course, if this girl hadn't deserved ... this is not just a passing fancy of mine. I feel awkward talking to you about it but you can understand that it was difficult for her to come with you here, especially the first morning after your arrival.'

'In that case I'll go to her!' exclaimed Arkady in a fresh rush of generous feeling, and he jumped up from his chair. 'I will explain to her that she has no cause to be embarrassed with me.'

Nikolai Petrovich got up too.

'Arkady,' he began, 'please ... how can ... there ... I have not told you yet ...'

But Arkady was no longer listening to his father: he had darted from the terrace. Nikolai Petrovich gazed after him and then, overcome with confusion, he sank back into a chair. His heart was pounding ... Did he realize at that moment the inevitable strangeness of his future relations with his son? Was he aware that Arkady might have shown him greater respect had he never mentioned the subject at all? Was he reproaching himself for his weakness? It is hard to say. All these feelings stirred within him or, rather, he sensed them – they were vague sensations only but the flush remained on his face and his heart beat rapidly.

There was a sound of hurrying footsteps and Arkady appeared on the terrace.

'We have introduced ourselves, father!' he cried with an expression of affectionate and good-natured triumph on his face. 'Fenichka really is not feeling too well, and she'll come out later on. But why ever didn't you tell me I had a brother? I should have given him a good kiss last night, the way I have done just now.'

Nikolai Petrovich wanted to say something, wanted to get up and open his arms wide ... Arkady flung himself on his neck.

'What's this? Embracing again?' cried Pavel Petrovich from behind them.

Father and son were equally glad to see him at that

moment; there are affecting situations from which one is anxious nevertheless to escape as quickly as possible.

'Are you surprised?' said Nikolai Petrovich gaily. 'Think what ages I've been waiting for Arkady . . . I haven't had time to get a good look at him since yesterday.'

'I am not in the least surprised,' observed Pavel Petrovich. 'I wouldn't mind embracing him myself.'

Arkady went up to his uncle and again felt the perfumed moustaches brush his cheeks. Pavel Petrovich sat down at the table. He was wearing an elegant suit cut in the English fashion, and a gay little fez graced his head. The fez and the carelessly knotted cravat carried a suggestion of the more free life in the country but the stiff collar of his shirt – not white, it is true, but striped as is correct for morning wear – stood up as inexorably as ever against his well-shaved chin.

'But where is your new friend?' he asked Arkady.

'Not in the house; he usually gets up early and goes off somewhere. The great thing is not to pay any attention to him: he can't stand ceremony.'

'Yes, that is obvious.' Taking his time, Pavel Petrovich began buttering his bread. 'Is he staying with us for long?'

'That depends. He's stopping here on his way to his father's.'

'And where does his father live?'

'In the same province as ourselves, about sixty miles from here. He owns a smallish estate. He used to be an army doctor.'

'Tut, tut, tut! Of course. I kept wondering where I had heard that name before: Bazarov? Nikolai, don't you remember, there was a surgeon called Bazarov in our father's division?'

'I believe there was.'

'Yes, yes, to be sure. So that surgeon will be this fellow's father. H'm!' Pavel Petrovich pulled his moustaches. 'Well, and this Monsieur Bazarov, what is he exactly?' he inquired with deliberation.

'What is Bazarov?' Arkady smiled. 'Would you like me to tell you, uncle, what he is exactly?'

'Please do, nephew.'

'He is a nihilist!'

'A what?' asked Nikolai Petrovich, while his brother lifted his knife in the air with a small piece of butter on the tip and remained motionless.

'He is a nihilist,' repeated Arkady.

'A nihilist,' said Nikolai Petrovich. 'That comes from the Latin *nihil – nothing*, I imagine; the term must signify a man who . . . who recognizes nothing?'

'Say – who respects nothing,' put in Pavel Petrovich, and set to work with the butter again.

'Who looks at everything critically,' observed Arkady.

'Isn't that exactly the same thing?' asked Pavel Petrovich.

'No, it's not the same thing. A nihilist is a person who does not take any principle for granted, however much that principle may be revered.'

'Well, and is that a good thing?' interrupted Pavel Petrovich.

'It depends on the individual, my dear uncle. It's good in some cases and very bad in others.'

'Indeed. Well, I can see this is not our cup of tea. We of the older generation think that without principles' (Pavel Petrovich pronounced the word as if it were French, whereas Arkady put the stress on the first syllable) – 'without principles taken as you say on trust one cannot move an inch or draw a single breath. *Vous avez changé tout cela*, may God grant you health and a general's rank, but we shall be content to look on and admire *Messieurs les* . . . what was it?'

'Nihilists,' said Arkady, speaking very distinctly.

'Yes. It used to be Hegelians, and now there are nihilists. We shall see how you manage to exist in a void, in an airless vacuum; and now please ring the bell, brother Nikolai, it is time for me to drink my cocoa.'

Nikolai Petrovich rang the bell and called 'Dunyasha!'

But instead of Dunyasha, Fenichka herself appeared on the terrace. She was a young woman of about three and twenty with a soft white skin, dark hair and eyes, red childishly-pouting lips and small delicate hands. She wore a neat print dress; a new pale blue kerchief lay lightly on her soft shoulders. She carried a large cup of cocoa and, setting it down in front of Pavel Petrovich, she was suddenly overcome with confusion: the hot blood spread in a wave of crimson beneath the delicate skin of her pretty face. She lowered her eyes and stood by the table, leaning on it lightly with the tips of her fingers. She looked as if she were ashamed to have come in, yet at the same time somehow felt that she had a right to come.

Pavel Petrovich knitted his brows severely while Nikolai Petrovich looked embarrassed.

'Good morning, Fenichka,' he muttered through his teeth.

'Good morning,' she replied in a voice that carried without being too loud, and with a sidelong glance at Arkady, who gave her a friendly smile, she quietly retired. There was a trace of a waddle in her walk but that, too, suited her.

For some minutes silence reigned on the terrace. Pavel Petrovich sipped his cocoa and suddenly raised his head. 'Here is Monsieur Nihilist about to give us the pleasure of his company,' he said in an undertone.

Bazarov was in fact approaching through the garden, striding over the flower-beds. His linen coat and trousers were bespattered with mud; a clinging marsh-plant had twined itself round the crown of his old round hat; in his right hand he held a small sack; in the sack something alive was wriggling. He walked quickly up to the terrace and said with a nod, 'Good morning, gentlemen. Sorry I'm late for tea: I'll be back in a moment – I must just stow these prisoners away.'

'What have you got there, leeches?' asked Pavel Petrovich.

'No, frogs.'

'Do you eat them or breed them?'

'They're for experiments,' Bazarov replied indifferently, and went into the house.

'So he's going to cut them up,' observed Pavel Petrovich. 'He has no faith in principles, only in frogs.'

Arkady looked with pity at his uncle, and Nikolai Petrovich half shrugged his shoulders. Pavel Petrovich himself felt that his *bon mot* had fallen flat and began to talk about farming and the new bailiff who had come to him the day before with a complaint about Foma, a farm-hand who kept slinking off and was quite unmanageable. 'A regular Aesop, that Foma,' the steward had added. 'Shown himself all round to be a worthless fellow; but he'll live and learn, and shake off his stupid ways.'

6

Bazarov came back, sat down at the table and began hurriedly to drink his tea. The brothers watched him in silence, while Arkady glanced covertly from his father to his uncle.

'Did you go far?' at length Nikolai Petrovich inquired.

'To where you've got a little marsh near an aspen wood. I flushed half a dozen snipe : you might bag them, Arkady.'

'So you don't shoot?'

'No.'

'Physics is your special subject, is it not?' asked Pavel Petrovich in his turn.

'Physics, yes; and natural science in general.'

'I am told the Teutons have made great strides in that department lately.'

'Yes, the Germans are our masters there,' Bazarov answered casually.

Pavel Petrovich had used the word 'Teutons' instead of 'Germans' with ironical intent, which, however, no one noticed.

'Have you such a high opinion of Germans?' Pavel Petrovich spoke with studious politeness. He was secretly beginning to feel irritated. Bazarov's complete indifference exasperated his aristocratic nature. This son of a medico was not only self-assured : he actually returned abrupt and reluctant answers, and there was a churlish, almost insolent note in his voice.

'Their scientists know their business.'

'I see, I see. And your opinion of Russian scientists is, I dare say, less flattering.'

'I'm afraid so.'

'That is a very laudable piece of modesty on your part,' Pavel Petrovich remarked, drawing himself up and throwing back his head. 'But how is it that Arkady was telling us just now that you acknowledge no authorities whatsoever? Have you no belief in them?'

'Why should I? And what am I to believe? If they talk sense, I agree with them. That's all there is to it.'

'And do all Germans talk sense?' said Pavel Petrovich, and his face assumed a distant, aloof expression, as if he had withdrawn into the clouds.

'Not all,' Bazarov replied with a stifled yawn, obviously not wanting to continue the wrangle.

Pavel Petrovich glanced at Arkady as if to say, 'You must admit your friend is very civil !'

'For my part,' he began again, not without a certain effort, 'I plead guilty to holding no brief for Germans. As for Russian Germans, I do not need to mention them – we all know what sort of creatures they are. But German Germans do not appeal to me either. Once upon a time there were a few Germans here and there – well, Schiller, for instance, Goethe ... my brother is particularly partial to them ... but nowadays they only seem to churn out chemists and materialists.'

'A decent chemist is twenty times more useful than any poet,' interrupted Bazarov.

'Oh, indeed,' commented Pavel Petrovich, raising his eyebrows slightly, as though he had come near to falling asleep. 'I take it, you do not acknowledge art, then?'

'The art of making money or of advertising pills for piles!' exclaimed Bazarov with a contemptuous laugh.

'Quite so, sir, quite so. You will have your joke, I see. So you reject all that? Very well. So you only believe in science?'

'I have already explained to you that I don't believe in anything: and what is science – science in the abstract? There are sciences, as there are trades and professions, but abstract science just doesn't exist.'

'Very good. Well now as regards the other socially accepted conventions – do you maintain the same negative attitude towards them?'

'What is this, a cross-examination?' asked Bazarov.

Pavel Petrovich turned slightly pale ... Nikolai Petrovich thought it time to intervene in the conversation.

'Some day we must discuss this matter with you in more detail, my dear Yevgeny Vassilyich; we will hear your views and express our own. I must say I personally am very glad you are studying the natural sciences. I have heard that Liebig* has made some astonishing discoveries to do with improving the soil. You may be able to help me in my agricultural labours: you can give me some useful advice.'

'I'm at your service, Nikolai Petrovich; but Liebig is miles above our heads! One must learn the alphabet before beginning to read, and we don't know the first letter yet.'

'You are a nihilist all right,' thought Nikolai Petrovich, and added aloud: 'All the same, I hope you will let me apply to you on occasion. And now, brother, I fancy it is time for us to go and have our talk with the bailiff.'

Pavel Petrovich rose from his chair.

'Yes,' he said, without looking at anyone, 'what a calamity it is to have spent five years in the country like this, far from mighty intellects! One becomes a complete fool. You struggle not to forget what you have learned – and then one fine day it turns out to be all rubbish, and they tell you that sensible

* Justus Freiherr von Liebig (1803–73), German chemist and founder of agricultural chemistry.

men no longer have anything to do with such nonsense, and that you, if you please, are an antiquated old fogey. What is to be done? Obviously the younger generation are more intelligent than we are.'

Pavel Petrovich turned slowly on his heels and slowly walked away. Nikolai Petrovich followed him.

'Is he always like that?' Bazarov coolly inquired of Arkady as soon as the door had closed behind the two brothers.

'I must say, Yevgeny, you were a bit curt with him,' Arkady remarked. 'You hurt his feelings.'

'Do you think I'm going to pander to these provincial aristocrats! Why, it's all personal vanity with them, the habit of being top dog and showing off. He should have continued his career in Petersburg, if that's the way he's made. But enough of him! I've found rather a rare specimen of water-beetle, *Dytiscus marginatus* – do you know it? I'll show you.'

'I promised to tell you his story . . .' Arkady began.

'Whose story? The water-beetle's?'

'No, stop it, Yevgeny. My uncle's story. You'll see he's not the kind of man you imagine. He deserves pity rather than ridicule.'

'I don't dispute it. But why are you so taken up with him?'

'One must be fair, Yevgeny.'

'What makes you say that?'

'No, listen . . .'

And Arkady proceeded to relate his uncle's story. Which the reader will find in the following chapter.

7

Like his younger brother Nikolai, Pavel Petrovich Kirsanov had, to begin with, been brought up at home, and then enrolled in the Corps of Pages. Distinguished from childhood for his remarkable good looks, he was in addition self-confident, somewhat quizzical, and had a biting sense of humour – he could not fail to please people. Directly he obtained his commission as an officer he began to be seen everywhere. The darling of society, he indulged in every kind of whim and folly, and gave himself airs, but all this only added to his appeal. Women lost their heads over him, and men dubbed him a fop but were secretly envious. As we have already said, he shared an apartment with his brother, whom he genuinely loved though he was not at all like him. Nikolai Petrovich was slightly lame, had small pleasing features of a rather melancholy cast, little black eyes and soft thin hair; he enjoyed being lazy but he liked reading and was shy in society. Pavel Petrovich never spent an evening at home, prided himself on his courage and agility (he had practically set the fashion for gymnastics among the gilded youth of his day) and had read at most half a dozen French novels. At twenty-seven he was already a captain; a brilliant career lay before him. Suddenly everything was changed.

At that time there used to appear occasionally in Petersburg society a woman who is still remembered even now – Princess R. She had a well-bred and respectable, albeit somewhat stupid, husband and no children. It was her custom to make sudden visits abroad, then as suddenly to return to Russia, and in general lead an eccentric life. She had the reputation of being a frivolous coquette, she abandoned herself eagerly to every kind of pleasure, danced till she dropped, roared with laughter and jested with the young men whom she used to receive before dinner in a dimly-lit drawing-room, but at night she wept and prayed, finding no peace in anything, and would often pace her room till dawn, wringing her hands in anguish, or sit, pale and cold, over a psalter. The coming of day transformed her into a lady of fashion again, driving out to pay her calls, laughing, chatting and literally flinging herself into any activity that might afford her the slightest distraction. She had a wonderful figure; her hair, the colour of gold and as heavy as gold, fell below her knees, yet no one would have called her a beauty: the only good feature in her whole face was her eyes – and not even her eyes, they were small and grey, but the expression in them, which was swift and penetrating, carefree to the point of audacity and thoughtful to the verge of melancholy : an enigmatic expression. Even when her tongue was engaged in lisping the most fatuous nonsense something extraordinary shone in those eyes. She dressed exquisitely. Pavel Petrovich met her at a ball, danced a mazurka with her, in the course of which she did not utter one single sensible word, and fell passionately in love with her. Accustomed to making conquests, he soon succeeded with her too; but the easy triumph did not cool his ardour. On the contrary, he found himself still more painfully attached to this woman in whom, even when she surrendered herself without reserve, something always seemed to remain that was hidden and unattainable, beyond the power of human penetration. What resided in that soul – only God knows! She seemed to be in the grip of mysterious forces, unknown even to herself, which played with her at will, her limited intelligence being unable to cope with their caprices. Her whole behaviour was a maze of inconsistencies; the only letters which might justly have excited her husband's suspicions she wrote to a man she hardly knew, and her love had an element of sadness; she no longer laughed and joked with her heart's choice but would listen to him and gaze at him in bewilderment. Sometimes, usually quite suddenly, this bewilderment would change to a chill horror; her face took on a wild, death-like expression; she would lock herself in her bedroom, and her maid, putting her ear to the keyhole, would hear her smothered sobbing. More than once, returning home from a tender meeting with her, Kirsanov felt his heart overcome by the devastating bitter vexation of spirit which follows the consciousness of total failure. 'What more do I want?' he would ask himself, while his heart ached. One day he gave her a ring with a sphinx engraved on the stone.

'What is this?' she asked. 'A sphinx?'

'Yes,' he answered, 'and that sphinx is – you.'

'Me?' she asked, and slowly raised her enigmatic eyes to

him. 'Do you know, that is very flattering?' she added with a meaningless smile, while her eyes still kept the same strange look.

Pavel Petrovich suffered torments even when Princess R. reciprocated his love, but when she lost interest in him, which happened fairly soon, he almost went out of his mind. He suffered tortures, he was jealous and gave her no peace but dogged her footsteps. Weary of such persistent pursuit, she went abroad. In spite of the entreaties of his friends and the advice of his superiors he resigned his commission to follow the princess; some four years he spent in foreign lands, now chasing after her, now trying to lose sight of her. He felt ashamed of himself, angry at his own lack of spirit ... but nothing helped. Her image – that baffling, almost vacant but fascinating image – had bitten too deeply into his soul. In Baden the pair somehow came together again and resumed their old relationship; to all appearances she had never loved him so passionately ... but within a month it was all over: the fire blazed for the last time and went out for ever. Foreseeing the inevitable break, he was anxious at least to remain her friend, as if friendship with such a woman were possible. ... She left Baden secretly and thereafter consistently avoided him. He returned to Russia and tried to take up his former life but could not get back into the old groove. Like a man with a poisoned system he wandered from place to place; he still went into society and retained the habits of a man about town; he could boast of two or three fresh conquests; but he no longer expected anything much of himself or of others, and he undertook nothing new. He aged and his hair turned grey; to spend all his evenings at the club, embittered and bored and arguing in bachelor company, became a necessity for him – and that is a bad sign, as we all know. Needless to say, he entertained no thought of marriage. Ten years passed in this wise, drab, fruitless years, but they sped by terribly quickly. Nowhere does time fly as it does in Russia; in prison, they say, it flies even faster. One day when he was dining at the club Pavel Petrovich heard that Princess R. was dead. She had died in Paris in a state bordering on insanity. He rose from the table and for a long while paced about the rooms of the club, occasionally halting like one transfixed behind some card-player; but he returned home no earlier than usual. A few weeks later he received a package on which his name was written: it contained the ring which he had given to the princess. She had scratched lines in the shape of a cross over the sphinx and sent him a message that the solution of the enigma was the cross.

This took place at the beginning of the year 1848, at the same time as Nikolai Petrovich arrived in Petersburg after the death of his wife. Pavel Petrovich had hardly seen his brother since the latter had settled in the country: Nikolai Petrovich's marriage had coincided with the early days of Pavel Petrovich's acquaintance with the princess. On his return from abroad Pavel Petrovich had gone to his brother's with the intention of spending a couple of months with him and enjoying the sight of his happiness, but he could only stand it for a week. The difference in the positions of the two brothers was too great. By 1848 this difference had narrowed. Nikolai Petrovich had lost his wife, Pavel Petrovich had abandoned his memories (after the death of the princess he tried not to think about her). But Nikolai could look back on a well-spent life and had a son growing up under his eyes; whereas Pavel, the lonely bachelor, was just entering on that indefinite twilight period of regrets that are akin to hopes, and hopes which are akin to regrets, when youth is over and old age has not yet come.

This period was harder for Pavel Petrovich than for other people, for in losing his past he lost everything he had.

'I won't ask you to Maryino now,' Nikolai Petrovich said to him one day (he had called his village by that name in honour of his wife). 'You found it tedious enough even when my dear wife was alive and now, I fear, you would be bored to extinction.'

'I was stupid and restless in those days,' Pavel Petrovich replied. 'I may not have grown any wiser but I have calmed down since then. So now, if you will let me, I am ready to come and make my home with you for good.'

Instead of answering, Nikolai Petrovich embraced him; but a year and a half elapsed after this conversation before Pavel Petrovich finally decided to carry out his intention. Once he was established in the country, however, he would not leave it, even during those three winters which Nikolai Petrovich spent in Petersburg with his son. He began to read, chiefly English books; indeed he ordered his whole life on the English pattern, rarely seeing his neighbours and visiting the town only to attend elections, and then he was usually silent, though he occasionally teased and alarmed landowners of the old school by his liberal sallies. At the same time he kept members of the new generation at a distance. Both parties regarded him as 'stuck up', and both respected him for his perfect aristocratic manners, for his reputation as a lady-killer, for the fact that he dressed superbly and always stayed in the best room in the best hotel; for the fact that he was knowledgeable about food and had once even dined with Louis-Philippe together with the Duke of Wellington; for the fact that wherever he went he took with him a real silver dressing-case and a portable bath; for the fact that he always smelt of some unusual and strikingly 'distinguished' scent; for the fact that he played a masterly game of whist and invariably lost; and finally they respected him for his incorruptible honesty. The ladies found him enchantingly romantic, but he did not cultivate the society of ladies . . .

'So you see, Yevgeny,' observed Arkady as he finished his story, 'how unfair you were about my uncle. Not to mention that he has more than once helped my father out of financial troubles, given him all his money – perhaps you don't know, the property was never divided between them – he's ready to help anyone and, incidentally, he's always standing up for the peasants; it's true, when he talks to them he screws up his face and sniffs eau-de-cologne . . .'

'Obviously a nervous case,' interrupted Bazarov.

'Perhaps so; but his heart is very much in the right place. And he's far from being a fool. What a lot of useful advice he has given me . . . especially . . . especially as regards relations with women.'

'Aha! Messes up his own life and gives advice to others! We know all about that!'

'Well, in short,' Arkady went on, 'he's profoundly unhappy, believe me – it's a crime to despise him.'

'And who is despising him?' retorted Bazarov. 'Still, I must say that a fellow who has staked his whole life on the one card of a woman's love, and when that card fails, turns sour and lets himself go till he's fit for nothing, is not a man, is not a male creature. You say he's unhappy: you know him better than I do; but he certainly hasn't got free of all his old nonsense. I'm sure he imagines himself in all seriousness a man of action because he reads that wretched *Galignani* and once a month saves a peasant from being flogged.'

'But remember the sort of education he had, the period in which he grew up,' Arkady rejoined.

'The sort of education he had!' Bazarov exclaimed. 'Everyone ought to educate himself – as I've done, for instance . . . And as to the times we live in, why should I depend upon them? Much better they should depend upon me. No, my dear fellow, all that is just empty thinking! And what are these mysterious relations between a man and a woman? We physiologists know what they are. You study the anatomy of the eye; and where does that enigmatic look you talk about come in? That's all romantic rot, mouldy aesthetics. We had much better go and inspect that beetle.'

And the two friends sauntered off to Bazarov's room, which was already pervaded by a sort of medico-surgical smell, mixed with the reek of cheap tobacco.

8

Pavel Petrovich did not stay long at his brother's interview with the bailiff, a tall thin man with the soft voice of the consumptive and shifty eyes, who to all Nikolai Petrovich's remarks answered, 'Yes, sir, to be sure, that goes without saying, sir,' and tried to make out that all the peasants were drunkards and thieves. The estate had only recently been put on to the new system, whose mechanism still creaked like an ungreased wheel, and cracked in places like home-made furniture of unseasoned wood. Nikolai Petrovich did not despair but he often sighed and felt discouraged: he saw that things could not improve without more money, and his money had almost all gone. Arkady had spoken the truth: Pavel Petrovich had helped his brother more than once. On more than one occasion, seeing him perplexed, racking his brains, not knowing which way to turn, Pavel Petrovich had walked slowly up to the window and with his hands thrust into his pockets had muttered between his teeth, *'Mais je puis vous donner de l'argent,'* and had given him money; but on this particular day he had none left himself and he preferred to go away. The petty troubles of estate management depressed him; besides, he could not help feeling that Nikolai Petrovich, for all his enthusiasm and hard work, did not set about things in the right way, although he could not have pointed out exactly where his brother went wrong. 'My brother is not practical enough,' he would argue to himself. 'They cheat him.' Nikolai Petrovich, on the other hand, had the highest opinion of Pavel's practical ability and was always asking his advice. 'I'm too mild and easy-going,' he would say. 'I've spent my whole life buried in the depths of the country. But you haven't seen so much of the world for nothing : you understand people. You see through them with the eye of an eagle.' To this Pavel Petrovich would make no reply but merely turn away without attempting to disillusion his brother.

Leaving Nikolai Petrovich in the study, he walked down the corridor which separated the front part of the house from the back; on reaching a low door he stopped and hesitated for a moment; then, pulling at his moustaches, he knocked.

'Who is it? Come in,' called Fenichka's voice.

'It is I,' said Pavel Petrovich, opening the door.

Fenichka jumped up from the chair where she was sitting with her baby, and handing the child over to a girl, who at once carried him out of the room, she hastily straightened her kerchief.

'Excuse me for disturbing you,' Pavel Petrovich began without looking at her. 'I only wanted to ask you ... as they are sending into town today ... will you get them to buy me some green tea?'

'Certainly,' Fenichka replied. 'How much would you like?'

'Oh, half a pound will do, I should think. I perceive you have made some changes here,' he added, casting a rapid look around which also took in Fenichka's face. 'The curtains, I mean,' he explained, seeing that she did not understand him.

'Oh yes, the curtains. Nikolai Petrovich kindly gave them to me; but they've been up a long time now.'

'Yes, it is quite a while since I have been to see you. The room looks very cosy now.'

'Thanks to Nikolai Petrovich's kindness,' murmured Fenichka.

'You are more comfortable here than in the little side-wing where you used to be?' Pavel Petrovich inquired politely, but without any trace of a smile.

'Of course, it's much nicer.'

'Who has been put in your old quarters?'

'The laundry-maids are there now.'

'Ah!'

Pavel Petrovich was silent. 'He'll go away now,' thought Fenichka; but he made no move and she stood in front of him as though rooted to the spot, nervously twisting her fingers.

'Why did you send the little one away?' said Pavel Petrovich at last. 'I like children: do let me have a look at him.'

Fenichka blushed all over with confusion and delight. She was afraid of Pavel Petrovich, who hardly ever spoke to her.

'Dunyasha,' she called. 'Will you bring Mitya, please?' (Fenichka was polite to every member of the household.) 'But wait a moment: we must put his frock on first.' And Fenichka made for the door.

'That does not matter,' remarked Pavel Petrovich.

'I shall be back in a second,' Fenichka replied, quickly going out.

Pavel Petrovich was left alone and this time he looked around him with singular attention. The small low room in which he found himself was very clean and snug. There was a smell of paint from the freshly painted floor and of camomile and lemon-balm. Against the walls stood a set of chairs with lyre-shaped backs which had been bought by the late General Kirsanov in Poland, during the campaign;* in one corner next to a chest with iron clamps and a curved lid was a little bedstead under a muslin canopy. In the opposite corner a lamp glowed in front of a large dark ikon of St Nikolas the Miracle-Worker; a tiny china Easter-egg hung down over the saint's breast suspended by a red ribbon from his metal halo; on the window-sills stood greenish jars filled with last year's jam tied up with meticulous care; on the paper covers Fenichka had herself written in large letters 'Gooseberry'; it was Nikolai Petrovich's favourite jam. A cage with a short-tailed goldfinch in it hung on a long cord from the ceiling; the bird was perpetually chirping and hopping about, and the cage kept swinging and rocking, while hemp seeds fell with a light tap on the floor. On the wall between the windows and just above a small chest of drawers hung some rather bad photo-

* The reference is to the 1812 campaign against the French.

graphs of Nikolai Petrovich taken in various poses by a travelling photographer; there was also a hopelessly poor photograph of Fenichka herself: it showed a sort of eyeless face straining to smile from a dark frame – that was all that could be distinguished – and above Fenichka, General Yermolov, in a Caucasian cloak, glowered menacingly at distant Caucasian mountains, from under a little silk shoe for pins which fell right over his forehead.

Five minutes passed; whispering and rustling could be heard in the next room. Pavel Petrovich picked up from the chest of drawers a greasy tattered book, an odd volume of Masalsky's *The Streltsy** and turned over a few pages ... The door opened and Fenichka came in with Mitya in her arms. She had dressed him in a little red shirt with an embroidered collar, combed his hair and wiped his face; he was breathing heavily, and wriggling his whole body about and waving his little arms, the way all healthy infants do; but his smart shirt obviously impressed him and his plump little person radiated delight. Fenichka had tidied her own hair too and rearranged her kerchief; but she might well have stayed as she was. Is there anything in the world more captivating than a beautiful young mother with a healthy child in her arms?

'What a chubby little fellow,' exclaimed Pavel Petrovich benevolently, tickling Mitya's double chin with the tapering nail of his forefinger; the baby stared up at the goldfinch and chuckled.

'That's our uncle,' said Fenichka, bending her face down to him and giving him a little shake, while Dunyasha quietly placed a fumigating pastille on the window-sill, with a brass coin under it.

'How old do you say he is?' asked Pavel Petrovich.

'Six months; it will soon be seven, on the eleventh of this month.'

'Isn't it eight, Fedosya Nikolayevna?' Dunyasha put in shyly.

* A novel by K. P. Masalsky, 1802–61.

'No, seven; of course!'

The baby chuckled again, stared at the chest in the corner and suddenly caught hold of his mother's nose and lips with all five fingers of one hand.

'You little rogue!' said Fenichka, without drawing her face away.

'He is very like my brother,' commented Pavel Petrovich.

'Who else should he be like?' thought Fenichka.

'Yes,' Pavel Petrovich continued as though talking to himself, 'the likeness is unmistakable.' He looked attentively, almost sadly, at Fenichka.

'That's our uncle,' she repeated, but this time in a whisper.

'Ah, Pavel, so this is where you are!' Nikolai Petrovich's voice suddenly cried behind them.

Pavel Petrovich hastily turned round, a frown on his face; but his brother looked at him with such delight, such gratitude, that he could not help responding to his smile.

'A fine little fellow you've got,' he said, looking at his watch. 'I came in here to ask about some tea ...'

And assuming an air of indifference, Pavel Petrovich at once left the room.

'Did he come of his own accord?' Nikolai Petrovich asked Fenichka.

'Yes; he just knocked and walked in.'

'And what about Arkady – has he been to see you again?'

'No. Hadn't I better move back into the rooms in the wing, Nikolai Petrovich?'

'Why should you?'

'I wonder if it wouldn't be better for a time at the beginning?'

'N-no,' Nikolai Petrovich replied hesitantly, and rubbed his forehead. 'We ought to have done it before ... Hullo, my piccaninny,' he said, suddenly brightening, and going up to the child he kissed him on the cheek; then he bent down and pressed his lips to Fenichka's hand, which lay white as milk on Mitya's little red shirt.

'Nikolai Petrovich, what are you doing?' she murmured, lowering her eyes, then softly looking up again ... Her expression was lovely as she peeped from under her eyelids and laughed tenderly and a little foolishly.

Nikolai Petrovich had become acquainted with Fenichka in the following way. Three years ago he had happened to stay the night at an inn in a remote provincial town. He was agreeably struck by the cleanliness of the room assigned to him and the freshness of the bed linen. 'Surely the woman of the house must be a German?' he thought to himself. But the landlady turned out to be a Russian, a woman of about fifty, neatly dressed, with a good-looking sensible face and a grave manner of speech. He got into conversation with her while he was having tea and liked her very much. Nikolai Petrovich at that time had only just moved into his new home and, loath to employ any of his former serfs, was looking for wage-servants; for her part the woman of the inn complained of the small number of travellers who passed through the town and of hard times; he suggested that she should come to him and be his housekeeper, and she agreed. Her husband had died long before, leaving her with an only daughter, Fenichka. Within a fortnight or so Arina Savishna (such was the new housekeeper's name) arrived with her daughter at Maryino and was installed in the side-wing. Nikolai Petrovich's choice proved a happy one. Arina brought order into the household. No one said anything about Fenichka, who was then turned seventeen, and few saw her: she stayed quietly out of sight and it was only on Sundays that Nikolai Petrovich would notice the delicate profile of her pale face somewhere in the corner of the parish church. More than a year passed thus.

One morning Arina came into his study and, after bowing low as usual, asked him if he could help her daughter, who had got a spark from the stove in her eye. Like all home-loving country people Nikolai Petrovich had studied simple remedies and had even procured a homoeopathic medicine chest. He at once told Arina to bring the patient to him. Fenichka was much perturbed when she heard that the master had sent for her but she followed her mother. Nikolai Petrovich led her to the window and took her head between his hands. After thoroughly examining her red and swollen eye he prescribed an eyewash, made up the lotion there and then, and tearing his handkerchief in strips showed her how to bathe the eye. Fenichka listened to all he said and turned to go. 'Kiss the master's hand, now, you silly girl,' Arina said to her. Nikolai Petrovich did not hold out his hand and in some confusion kissed her bent head on the parting of the hair. Fenichka's eye was soon well again but the impression she had made on Nikolai Petrovich did not fade so quickly. He kept picturing that pure, gentle, timidly upturned face; he could feel that soft hair under the palms of his hands, and see those innocent, slightly parted lips through which pearly teeth gleamed with moist brilliance in the sunshine. He began to watch her intently in church, and tried to engage her in conversation. At first she was very shy with him, and once, meeting him towards evening on a narrow footpath through a rye field, she plunged into the tall thick rye, overgrown with cornflowers and wormwood, to avoid coming face to face with him. He caught sight of her little head through the golden network of ears of rye, from which she was peering out like a small wild animal, and called to her in a friendly tone:

'Good evening, Fenichka, I don't bite!'

'Good evening,' she murmured back, without emerging from her hiding-place.

By degrees she began to be more at ease with him but was still shy in his presence, when suddenly her mother, Arina, died of cholera. What was to become of Fenichka? She had inherited her mother's love of order, her common sense and dependability; but she was so young, so alone; Nikolai Petrovich was so genuinely kind and considerate.... There is no need to describe what followed....

'So my brother dropped in to see you after all?' Nikolai Petrovich asked her. 'He just knocked and came in?'

'Yes.'

'Well, that's a good thing. Let me give Mitya a swing.'

And Nikolai Petrovich began to toss him almost to the ceiling, to the vast delight of the baby, and to the considerable anxiety of the mother, who each time he flew upwards stretched her arms up towards his little bare legs.

Pavel Petrovich meanwhile had gone back to his elegant study. Its walls were covered with greyish wall-paper and hung with an assortment of weapons on a many-hued Persian tapestry. The walnut furniture was upholstered in dark green velvet. There was a Renaissance bookcase of old black oak, bronze statuettes on the magnificent writing-table, an open hearth ... He threw himself on the sofa, clasped his hands behind his head and remained motionless, staring at the ceiling with an expression verging on despair. Perhaps because he wanted to hide from the very walls what was reflected in his face, or for some other reason – anyway, he got up, unfastened the heavy window curtains and threw himself back again on the sofa.

Reminded of the funeral of the one loved

9

On that same day Bazarov met Fenichka. He was strolling in the garden with Arkady and explaining to him why some of the trees, the oaks in particular, were not doing well.

'You ought to plant the place with silver poplars, and spruce firs and perhaps limes, giving them some rich black soil. Now this arbour here is flourishing,' he added, 'because acacias and lilacs are sturdy fellows, they don't require looking after. But there's someone in there.'

Fenichka was sitting in the arbour with Dunyasha and Mitya. Bazarov stopped and Arkady nodded to Fenichka like an old friend.

'Who's that?' Bazarov inquired directly they had gone past. 'What a pretty girl!'

'Who do you mean?'

'You know who I meant: only one of them was pretty.'

Arkady, not without embarrassment, explained to him briefly who Fenichka was.

'Aha!' remarked Bazarov. 'That shows your father's got good taste. I like your father, I really do. He's a fine chap. But I must be introduced,' he added, and turned back towards the arbour.

'Yevgeny!' Arkady shouted after him in alarm. 'Mind what you do, for mercy's sake.'

'Don't worry yourself,' said Bazarov. 'I'm an old hand, not a country bumpkin.'

Going up to Fenichka, he took off his cap. 'May I introduce myself,' he began, making a polite bow. 'I'm a friend of Arkady Nikolayevich's and a harmless person.'

Fenichka got up from the garden seat and looked at him without speaking.

'What a wonderful baby,' continued Bazarov. 'Don't be uneasy, I haven't cast a spell on anyone yet. Why are his cheeks so flushed? Is he cutting his teeth?'

'Yes,' murmured Fenichka; 'he has cut four teeth already and now the gums are swollen again.'

'Show me . . . and don't be afraid, I'm a doctor.'

Bazarov took the baby in his arms, and to both Fenichka's and Dunyasha's surprise the child made no resistance and showed no fear.

'I see, I see . . . It's nothing, everything's as it should be – he'll have a good set of teeth. If you have any trouble, just let me know. And are you quite well yourself?'

'Quite, thanks be.'

'Yes, thanks be – that's the great thing. And what about you?' he added, turning to Dunyasha.

Dunyasha, who behaved very primly in the house and was a tomboy out of doors, only giggled in reply.

'Well, that's all right. Here's your little Hercules.'

Fenichka took the baby back in her arms.

'How quiet he was with you,' she said in an undertone.

'All children are good with me,' answered Bazarov. 'I have a way with them.'

'Children know when people are fond of them,' Dunyasha remarked.

'They certainly do,' Fenichka confirmed. 'Why Mitya won't let some people touch him, not for anything.'

'Will he come to me?' asked Arkady, who after standing at a distance for a while had come up to the arbour.

He tried to entice Mitya into his arms but Mitya threw his head back and screamed, much to Fenichka's embarrassment.

'Another day, when he's had time to get used to me,' said Arkady indulgently, and the two friends walked away.

'What did you say her name was?' asked Bazarov.

'Fenichka ... Fedosya,' Arkady replied.

'And her patronymic? One must know that too.'

'Nikolayevna.'

'*Bene*. What I like about her is that she's not too shy and awkward. Some people, I suppose, might think ill of her on that account. But what rubbish! Why should she be embarrassed? She's a mother and she's quite right.'

'She's right enough,' observed Arkady, 'but my father now ...'

'He's right too,' interrupted Bazarov.

'Well, no, I don't think so.'

'I suppose an extra little heir is not to your liking?'

'You ought to be ashamed to impute such ideas to me!' Arkady retorted hotly. 'I don't consider my father wrong from that point of view; as I see it, he ought to marry her.'

'Well, well,' said Bazarov calmly. 'What noble-minded fellows we are! So you still attach importance to marriage: I didn't expect that from you.'

The friends walked on a few steps in silence.

'I've been all round your father's establishment,' Bazarov

began again. 'The cattle are inferior, the horses mere hacks. The buildings aren't up to much and the labourers look like a set of inveterate loafers; as for the bailiff, he's either a fool or a knave, I haven't yet found out which.'

'You are pretty censorious today, Yevgeny Vassilyich.'

'And there's no doubt these good peasants are taking your father in properly: you know the saying – "the Russian peasant will get the better of God himself".'

'I begin to agree with my uncle,' remarked Arkady. 'You certainly have a poor opinion of Russians.'

'As if that mattered! The only good thing about a Russian is the poor opinion he has of himself. What is important is that two and two make four, and the rest is just trivial.'

'And is nature trivial?' said Arkady, staring thoughtfully at the parti-coloured fields in the distance, beautiful in the soft light of the setting sun.

'Nature, too, is trivial, in the sense you give to it. Nature is not a temple, but a workshop, and man's the workman in it.'

Just then the long-drawn notes of a 'cello floated out to them from the house. Someone was playing Schubert's *Expectation* with feeling, though in an amateurish manner, and the melody flowed sweet as honey through the air.

'What's that?' cried Bazarov in amazement.

'It's my father.'

'Your father plays the 'cello?'

'Yes.'

'And how old is your father?'

'Forty-four.'

Bazarov suddenly roared with laughter.

'What are you laughing at?'

'My goodness! A man of forty-four, a *pater familias*, in this out-of-the-way province, playing the 'cello!'

Bazarov went on laughing; but, much as he revered his mentor, this time Arkady did not even smile.

10

About a fortnight passed. Life at Maryino pursued its normal course: Arkady gave himself up to luxurious living and Bazarov worked. Everyone in the house had got used to him, to his casual ways, to his curt and abrupt manner of speech. Fenichka, in particular, felt so much at ease with him that one night she even sent to wake him up: Mitya was having convulsions; and Bazarov had come along and, as usual half joking, half yawning, had stayed a couple of hours with her and got the child better. On the other hand Pavel Petrovich detested Bazarov with every fibre of his being: he regarded him as an arrogant, impudent fellow, a cynic and a vulgarian. He suspected that Bazarov had little esteem for him, that he all but despised him – him, Pavel Petrovich Kirsanov! Nikolai Petrovich was slightly apprehensive of the young 'nihilist', and was doubtful whether his influence on Arkady was desirable; but he listened to him willingly enough and assisted just as willingly at his experiments in physics and chemistry. Bazarov had brought a microscope with him and pored over it for hours on end. The servants, too, had taken to him, although he made fun of them: they felt he was one of themselves, and not gentry. Dunyasha was always ready for a giggle with him and would cast meaning sidelong glances in his direction as she skipped flirtatiously by. Piotr, who was utterly vain and stupid, with a perpetual forced frown on his brow, a man whose only merit consisted in the fact that he looked respectful, could spell out syllable by syllable and often brushed his coat – even he smirked and brightened up as soon as Bazarov paid him any attention; as for the servant lads, they followed 'the doctor' about like puppies. Old Prokofyich was the only one to dislike him, looking sour when he served him at table, calling him a 'butcher' and a 'humbug' and declaring that with his side-whiskers he was a regular pig in a poke. Prokofyich in his own way was quite as much of an aristocrat as Pavel Petrovich.

The best time of the year had come – the first days of June. The weather was lovely. True, there were remote threats of cholera again but the inhabitants of the province had grown accustomed to its visitations. Bazarov used to get up very early and tramp for a mile or two, not for the sake of walking, which he could not bear without an object – but to collect grasses and insects. Sometimes he took Arkady with him. On the way home they generally got into an argument in which Arkady was usually worsted, although he was more eloquent than his companion.

One morning they were out longer than was their habit. Nikolai Petrovich had strolled into the garden to meet them. Just as he reached the arbour he suddenly heard the quick steps and voices of the two young men. They were walking along on the other side of the arbour and could not see him.

'You don't know my father well enough,' Arkady was saying.

Nikolai Petrovich kept quiet.

'Your father's a good man,' said Bazarov, 'but he's old-fashioned, he's had his day.'

Nikolai Petrovich strained his ears ... Arkady made no reply.

The man who was 'old-fashioned' stood still for a minute or two – then trailed slowly back to the house.

'A couple of days ago I noticed that he was reading Pushkin,' Bazarov went on meanwhile. 'You ought to explain to him that he won't get anywhere that way. After all, he's not a boy, it's time he got rid of such rubbish. And what an idea to be a romantic in these days! Give him something sensible to read.'

'For instance?' asked Arkady.

'Oh I should think Büchner's *Stoff und Kraft** would do for a start.'

* Ludwig Büchner, 1824–99, German materialist philosopher.

'I think so too,' remarked Arkady approvingly. '*Stoff und Kraft* is written in popular language.'

'So it seems that you and I are old-fashioned, over and done with,' said Nikolai Petrovich to his brother that same day as they sat in his study after dinner. 'Well, well. Maybe Bazarov is right; but one thing, I confess, does hurt me: I was so hoping that now was the time for me to get on to really close and friendly terms with Arkady, but it turns out that I have been left standing while he has forged ahead, and now we cannot understand one another.'

'And why should he have forged ahead? And in what way is he so different from us?' Pavel Petrovich exclaimed impatiently. 'It's that *signor* of a nihilist has crammed all that into his head. I detest that doctor fellow; in my opinion he's just a quack; I am positive that for all his frogs he hasn't got very far even with physics.'

'No, Pavel, don't say that. Bazarov is clever and knowledgeable.'

'And his conceit is quite revolting,' Pavel Petrovich broke in again.

'Yes,' observed Nikolai Petrovich, 'he is conceited. But evidently one cannot succeed without conceit; only there is one thing I cannot make out. I thought I was doing everything to keep up with the times: I have done well by the peasants, set up a model farm, so that all over the province I am known as a *radical*. I read, I study, I try in every way to keep abreast with the requirements of the age – and yet here they are saying I'm over and done with. And, Pavel, I really begin to think they are right.'

'Why do you think that?'

'I will tell you why. Today I was sitting reading Pushkin – I remember, it happened to be *The Gypsies*. . . . Suddenly Arkady comes up to me and without a word, as gently as if I were a child, with an affectionate look of pity on his face, took away my book and put another before me, a German book. ... Then he gave me a smile and went out, carrying Pushkin off with him.'

'Upon my word! What book did he give you?'

'This.'

And Nikolai Petrovich pulled out of the back pocket of his frock-coat a copy of the ninth edition of Büchner's celebrated treatise.

Pavel Petrovich turned it over in his hands.

'H'm!' he growled. 'So Arkady is seeing to your education. Well, have you tried to read it?'

'Yes, I've tried.'

'And what do you make of it?'

'Either I am stupid or it is all rubbish. I suppose I must be stupid.'

'I suppose you haven't forgotten your German?' inquired Pavel Petrovich.

'Oh, I understand the language all right.'

Pavel Petrovich again turned the book over in his hands and glanced distrustfully at his brother. Both were silent.

'Oh, by the way,' began Nikolai Petrovich, obviously anxious to change the subject, 'I have had a letter from Kolyazin.'

'From Matvei Ilyich?'

'Yes. He has arrived in town to inspect the province. He is quite a bigwig now and writes to say that as a relative of ours he would like to see us, and invites you and me and Arkady to go and stay with him.'

'Are you going?' asked Pavel Petrovich.

'No; will you?'

'No, nor me either. Where's the sense of dragging oneself thirty miles for nothing? *Matthieu* wants to display himself in all his glory. Let him go to the devil! He will have the whole province kow-towing to him, he can get along without us. And it is not as though a privy councillor were such a big fish! If I had stayed in the Service, drudging on in that dreary routine, I would have been an adjutant-general by now. Anyway, you and I are back numbers, you know.'

'Yes, Pavel. It seems the time has come to order our coffins and cross our hands upon our breasts,' Nikolai Petrovich remarked with a sigh.

'Well, I shall not give up quite so quickly,' muttered his brother. 'I have got a skirmish with that doctor fellow before me, I feel sure of that.'

The skirmish took place that very day, at tea-time. Pavel Petrovich came down to the sitting-room, irritable and determined, prepared to do battle. He was only waiting for a pretext to rush upon the enemy but the pretext was a long time presenting itself. Bazarov never said much in the presence of the 'old Kirsanovs' (that was how he spoke of the brothers), and that evening he felt out of sorts as he sipped one cup of tea after another in silence. Pavel Petrovich was consumed with impatience; at last his wish was granted.

The conversation turned to one of the neighbouring landowners. 'A complete rotter, a third-rate aristocrat,' Bazarov, who had met him in Petersburg, remarked dispassionately.

'Permit me to inquire,' began Pavel Petrovich, his lips trembling, 'in your opinion are the words "rotter" and "aristocrat" synonymous?'

'I said "third-rate aristocrat",' replied Bazarov, lazily taking a sip of tea.

'Precisely; but I imagine you hold the same opinion of true aristocrats as you do of third-rate ones. I think it my duty to tell you that I do not share that opinion. I venture to assert that everyone knows I am a man of liberal views and devoted to progress; but for that very reason I respect aristocrats – genuine ones. Kindly remember, sir' (at these words Bazarov raised his eyes to Pavel Petrovich) – 'kindly remember, sir,' he repeated with acrimony, 'the English aristocracy. They never yield one iota of their rights, and for that reason they respect the rights of others; they demand the fulfilment of obligations due to them, and therefore they fulfil their own obligations to others. The aristocracy has given England her freedom and maintains it for her.'

'You're harping on an old tune,' Bazarov retorted, 'but what are you trying to prove by it?'

'*Phthis*, my dear sir.' (When Pavel Petrovich was angry he would deliberately say 'phthis' and 'phthat', though he knew perfectly well that the dictionary allowed of no such words. This odd habit was a legacy from the period of Alexander I. The exquisites of those days, on the rare occasions when they spoke their own language, said 'phthis' and 'phthat', as much as to say, 'We, of course, are Russian born, at the same time we are important personages who can dispense with grammatical rules.') 'I am seeking to prove *phthis* – without a sense of proper pride, without a sense of self-respect – and these feelings are highly developed in the aristocrat – there can be no firm foundation for the social ... *bien public* ... the social fabric. It is personal character that matters, my dear sir: a man's personal character must be as strong as a rock, since everything else is built up on it. I am very well aware, for instance, that you are pleased to ridicule my habits, my way of dressing, my punctiliousness, in fact. But those very things proceed from a sense of self-respect, from a sense of duty – yes, sir, of duty. I may live in the country, in the wilds of the country, but I do not let myself go, I respect myself as a human being.'

'Allow me, Pavel Petrovich,' Bazarov put in, 'you say you respect yourself and you sit with your arms folded : what sort of benefit does that do the *bien public*? If you didn't respect yourself, you'd do just the same.'

Pavel Petrovich turned pale.

'That is quite another matter. I am not under the slightest obligation to explain to you why I sit with folded arms, as you are pleased to put it. I merely wish to say that aristocratism is a principle, and only immoral or silly people can live in our age without principles. I said as much to Arkady the day after he came home, and I repeat it to you now. Isn't that so, Nikolai?'

Nikolai Petrovich nodded assent, while Bazarov exclaimed: *Westernizers?*

'Aristocratism, liberalism, progress, principles – think of it, what a lot of foreign . . . and useless words! To a Russian they're not worth a straw.'

'What, in your opinion, does he need? To hear you talk we might all be living outside human society, beyond its laws. Doesn't the logic of history demand. . . .'

'What has that logic to do with us? We can get on without that too.'

'What do you mean?'

'Just that. You don't need logic, I suppose, to put a piece of bread in your mouth when you're hungry? We've no time for such abstractions!'

Pavel Petrovich threw up his hands.

'After that I fail to understand you. You insult the Russian people. How you can decline to recognize principles and precepts passes my comprehension. What other basis for conduct in life have we got?'

'I've told you already, uncle, that we don't recognize any authorities,' Arkady interposed.

'We base our conduct on what we recognize as useful,' Bazarov went on. 'In these days the most useful thing we can do is to repudiate – and so we repudiate.'

'Everything?'

'Everything.'

'What? Not only art, poetry . . . but also . . . I am afraid to say it . . .'

'Everything,' Bazarov repeated with indescribable composure.

Pavel Petrovich stared at him. He had not expected this; while Arkady positively glowed with satisfaction.

'However, if I may say so,' began Nikolai Petrovich, 'you repudiate everything, or, to put it more precisely, you are destroying everything. . . . But one must construct too, you know.'

'That is not our affair. . . . The ground must be cleared first.'

'The present condition of the people requires it,' added Arkady pompously. 'We are bound to carry out these requirements, we have no right to indulge in the gratification of our personal egoism.'

This last sentence obviously did not please Bazarov: it smacked of philosophy, that is, of romanticism, for Bazarov considered philosophy synonymous with romanticism; but he did not judge it necessary to contradict his young disciple.

'No, no!' Pavel Petrovich cried with sudden vehemence. 'I cannot believe that you two really know the Russian people, that you represent their needs and aspirations! No, the Russians are not what you imagine them to be. They hold tradition sacred, they are a patriarchal people – they cannot live without faith . . .'

'I am not going to dispute that,' Bazarov interrupted. 'I'm even ready to agree that there you are right.'

'But if I am right . . .'

'It still proves nothing.'

'Exactly, it proves nothing,' echoed Arkady with the assurance of a practised chess-player who has anticipated an apparently dangerous move on the part of his opponent, and so is not in the least disconcerted.

'What do you mean – it proves nothing?' muttered Pavel Petrovich, dumbfounded. 'You must be going against your own people then?'

'And what if we are?' shouted Bazarov. 'The people believe that when it thunders the prophet Elijah is riding across the sky in his chariot. Well? Am I to agree with them? Besides, if they are Russian, so am I.'

'No, you are no Russian after what you have just said! I must decline to recognize you as a Russian.'

'My grandfather tilled the soil,' answered Bazarov with

supercilious pride. 'Ask any of your peasants which of us – you or me – he would more readily acknowledge as a fellow-countryman. You don't even know how to talk to them.'

'While you talk to them and despise them at the same time.'

'Why not, if they deserve to be despised. You find fault with my attitude, but who told you I stumbled on it by chance – that it was not the product of that very national spirit which you are so anxious to defend?'

'What an idea! A fat lot of use nihilists are!'

'Of use or not, it's not for us to decide. After all, you consider yourself of some use in the world.'

'Gentlemen, gentlemen, no personalities, please!' cried Nikolai Petrovich, getting up.

Pavel Petrovich smiled, and laying his hand on his brother's shoulder made him sit down again.

'Do not worry,' he said. 'I shall not forget myself, thanks to that very sense of dignity which is so savagely assailed by Mr – by Dr Bazarov. If you will allow me,' he continued, turning to Bazarov again, 'perhaps you think your doctrine is a novelty? That is quite a mistake. The materialism you preach has gained currency more than once and has always proved bankrupt . . .'

'Another foreign term!' Bazarov interrupted him. He was beginning to lose his temper, and his face had gone a coarse coppery colour. 'In the first place, we preach nothing: that's not our way . . .'

'What do you do, then?'

'This is what we do. Not so very long ago we were saying that our officials took bribes, that we had no roads, no trade, no impartial courts of justice . . .'

'Oh, I see, you are accusers – that, I think, is the right name. Well, I too should agree with many of your criticisms, but . . .'

'Then we realized that just to keep on and on talking about our social diseases was a waste of time, and merely led to a trivial doctrinaire attitude. We saw that our clever men, our so-called progressives and reformers never accomplished anything, that we were concerning ourselves with a lot of non-sense, discussing art, unconscious creative work, parliamentarianism, the bar, and the devil knows what, while all the time the real question was getting daily bread to eat, when the most vulgar superstitions are stifling us, when our industrial enterprises come to grief solely for want of honest men at the top, when even the emancipation of the serfs – the emancipation the government is making such a fuss about – is not likely to be to our advantage, since those peasants of ours are only too glad to rob even themselves to drink themselves silly at the gin-shop.'

'So,' Pavel Petrovich interrupted him – 'so you were convinced of all this and decided not to do anything serious yourselves.'

'And decided not to do anything serious,' Bazarov repeated grimly. He suddenly felt vexed with himself for having spoken so freely in front of this member of the upper class.

'But to confine yourselves to abuse?'

'To confine ourselves to abuse.'

'And that is called nihilism?'

'And that is called nihilism,' Bazarov repeated again, this time with marked insolence.

Pavel Petrovich screwed up his eyes slightly.

'So that's it,' he muttered in a voice that was curiously calm. 'Nihilism's a panacea for every ill, and you – you are our saviours and heroes. Very well. But why do you abuse other people, even other accusers like yourselves? Aren't you just talking like all the rest?'

'We may have our faults but we are not guilty of that one,' muttered Bazarov through his teeth.

'What then? Are you doing anything? Are you preparing for action?'

Bazarov did not answer. Pavel Petrovich quivered but at once regained control of himself.

'H'm! ... Action, destruction ...' he went on. 'But how can you destroy without even knowing why?'

'We destroy because we are a force,' remarked Arkady. Pavel Petrovich looked at his nephew and laughed.

'Yes, a force, and therefore not accountable to anyone,' said Arkady, drawing himself up.

'Wretched boy!' groaned Pavel Petrovich, now no longer in a state to restrain himself. 'Can't you realize the kind of thing you are encouraging in Russia with your miserable creed? No, it's enough to try the patience of an angel! A force! You might as well say that the wild Kalmuck and the Mongolian represent a force – but what is that to us? Civilization is what we value, yes, yes, my good sir: its fruits are precious to us. And don't tell me those fruits are of no importance: the meanest penny-a-liner – *un barbouilleur*, a piano-player who makes five farthings an evening – even they are of more use than you, because they stand for civilization and not crude Mongolian force! You fancy yourselves advanced, but your proper home is a Kalmuck tent! A force! And finally, my forceful gentlemen, remember this: there are only four men and a half of you, whereas the others number millions who won't let you trample their most sacred beliefs underfoot – it is they who will crush you!'

'If they do crush us, it will serve us right,' observed Bazarov. 'But we shall see what we shall see. We're not so few as you suppose.'

'What? Do you seriously think you can take on the whole nation?'

'A penny candle, you know, set Moscow on fire,' Bazarov responded.

'I see. First an almost Satanic pride, then gibes – so that is what attracts the young, that is what wins the inexperienced hearts of boys! Look, there is one sitting beside you, ready to worship the ground beneath your feet. Look at him.' (Arkady turned away and scowled.) 'And this plague has already spread far and wide. I am told that in Rome our artists never set foot in the Vatican. Raphael they practically regard as a fool because, if you please, he is an authority. Yet they themselves are so impotent and sterile that their imagination cannot rise above *Girl at the Fountain*, try as they may. And the girl is abominably drawn. They are fine fellows to your mind, are they not?'

'To my mind,' retorted Bazarov, 'Raphael's not worth a brass farthing; and they are no better.'

'Bravo! Bravo! Do you hear, Arkady . . . that is how young men of today should express themselves! And if you come to think of it, how could they fail to follow you! In the old days young people had to study. If they did not want to be thought ignorant they had to work hard whether they liked it or not. But now they need only say, "Everything in the world is rubbish!" – and the trick's done. The young men are simply delighted. Whereas they were only sheep's heads before, now they have suddenly blossomed out as nihilists!'

'Your vaunted sense of your own dignity has let you down,' Bazarov remarked phlegmatically, while Arkady went hot all over and his eyes flashed. 'Our argument has gone too far . . . we'd better stop. I shall be prepared to agree with you,' he added, getting up, 'when you can show me a single institution of contemporary life, private or public, which does not call for absolute and ruthless repudiation.'

'I can confront you with a million such,' cried Pavel Petrovich. 'A million! Now take the Peasant Commune, for example.'

A cold sneer twisted Bazarov's face.

'Well, so far as the commune is concerned,' he said, 'you had better discuss that with your brother. I should think he has seen by now what the commune is like in reality – its mutual responsibility, sobriety and the like.'

'Take the family, then – the family as it exists among our peasants!' shouted Pavel Petrovich.

'I suggest you had better not investigate that too closely either. You have, I suppose, heard of the way the head of the family can select his daughters-in-law? Listen to me, Pavel Petrovich, give yourself a couple of days to think it over – you're not likely to come on anything straight away. Go through the various classes of society and scrutinize them carefully, and in the meantime Arkady and I will –'

'Jeer at everything,' broke in Pavel Petrovich.

'No, go and dissect frogs. Come along, Arkady. Good-bye for the present, gentlemen!'

The two friends went out, leaving the brothers alone, speechless and just looking at each other.

'So that,' began Pavel Petrovich at last, 'so that's the youth of this generation. There are our heirs!'

'Our heirs,' repeated Nikolai with a despondent sigh. He had been on thorns all through the argument, and only from time to time cast a surreptitious, rueful glance at Arkady. 'Do you know what all this reminded me of, Pavel? Once I quarrelled with our late mamma: she stormed and would not listen to me ... At last I said to her, "Of course, you cannot understand me: we belong to two different generations," I said. She was dreadfully offended but I thought to myself, "It can't be helped. It is a bitter pill but she must swallow it." You see, now our turn has come, and our successors say to us, "You are not of our generation: swallow your pill".'

'You are much too good-natured and modest,' Pavel Petrovich expostulated. 'I am convinced, on the contrary, that you and I are far more in the right than these young gentlemen, although perhaps we express ourselves in somewhat old-fashioned, *vieilli* language and are not so insolently conceited. ... And the airs these young people give themselves nowadays! Ask one of them, "Will you drink red or white wine?" – "I am in the habit of preferring red," he replies in a deep voice and with a face as solemn as if the whole universe had its eyes on him at that instant ...'

'Would you like some more tea?' asked Fenichka, putting her head in at the door: she had hesitated to come into the sitting-room while she could hear voices raised in argument.

'No, you can tell them to take away the samovar,' Nikolai Petrovich answered, getting up to meet her. With a brusque '*Bonsoir*' to him Pavel Petrovich retired to his study.

II

Half an hour later Nikolai Petrovich went into the garden to his favourite arbour. He was filled with melancholy thoughts. For the first time he realized clearly the distance separating him from his son and he foresaw that the gap would grow wider day by day. In vain, then, those winters in Petersburg poring over the latest books; in vain the hours spent listening to the young men talk; in vain his delight when he succeeded in slipping a word or two of his own into their heated discussions.

'My brother says we are right,' he reflected, 'and laying aside all personal vanity I do think myself that they are farther from the truth than we are, and yet all the same I cannot help feeling that they have something we lack, something which gives them an advantage over us. . . . Is it youth? No, it can't be only a question of youth. Perhaps their advantage lies in their having fewer traces of the serf-owning mentality than we have?'

Nikolai Petrovich's head sank despondently and he passed his hand over his face.

'But to reject poetry, to have no feeling for art, for nature? . . .'

And he looked round, as though trying to understand how it was possible to have no feeling for nature. The evening was beginning to close in; the sun was hidden behind a small grove of aspen-trees which lay about a quarter of a mile from the garden; its shadow stretched indefinitely across the still fields. A peasant on a white pony was riding at a trot along the dark narrow path that skirted the grove: the whole figure was clearly visible even to the patch on his shoulders, although he was in the shade; the pony's hooves flashed up and down with pleasing precision. The rays of the sun on the farther side fell full on the clump of trees and, piercing their foliage, threw such a warm light on the aspen trunks that they looked like pines and their leaves were almost dark blue, while above them rose an azure sky, tinged by the red glow of sunset. Swallows flew high; the wind had quite died down; a few late-homing bees hummed lazily and drowsily among the lilac; swarms of midges hung like a cloud over a single far-projecting branch. 'O Lord, how beautiful it is!' thought Nikolai Petrovich, and his favourite verses almost rose to his lips when he remembered Arkady's *Stoff und Kraft* – and he restrained himself; but he still sat there, surrendering himself to the mournful consolation of solitary thought. He was fond of dreaming and life in the country had developed the tendency. How short a time ago he had been dreaming like this while waiting for his son at the posting-station, and what a change since then : their relations, then undefined, had now become defined – and how defined! His dead wife came into his mind again but not as he had known her through their many years together, not as a good thrifty housewife but as a young girl with a slim waist, innocently inquiring eyes and a plait of hair knotted tightly on her childish neck. He remembered their first meeting. He was still a student then. They had met on the staircase of his lodgings, and bumping into her by accident he had wanted to apologize but had only succeeded in muttering *'Pardon, Monsieur!'* while she had nodded, smiled, then suddenly taken fright as it were and fled; but at the bend of the staircase she had glanced quickly round at him, assumed a serious air and blushed. Afterwards – the first timid visits, the half-expressed phrases, the bashful smiles and embarrassed silences; the fits of depression, the transports of emotion and at last the breathless happiness. . . . Whither had it all vanished? She had become his wife, he had been happy as few on earth are happy. . . . 'But,' he mused, 'why could not one live those first sweet moments deathlessly for ever?'

He did not try to make his thought clear to himself but he felt that he longed to hold on to that blissful time by something stronger than memory: he yearned to have his Masha near him again, to sense her warmth and her breathing, and already it seemed to him that there, just above him. . . .

'Nikolai Petrovich,' came the sound of Fenichka's voice close by. 'Where are you?'

He started. He felt no remorse, no shame. He never admitted even the possibility of comparison between his wife and Fenichka, but he was sorry she had taken it into her head to come and look for him. Her voice was an immediate reminder of his grey hairs, his age, his life now. . . .

The enchanted world which he was on the point of entering and which was just rising out of the dim mists of the past wavered – and vanished.

'I am here,' he answered. 'I am coming. You run along.' ('There they are – those traces of the serf-owner,' flashed through his mind as he said this.) Fenichka peeped into the arbour at him without speaking and was gone; and he noticed with surprise that night had fallen while he was dreaming. Everything around was dark and hushed, and Fenichka's face had glimmered before him so pale and slight. He got up and was about to make for the house but the emotions stirring his heart could not be calmed so soon and he began to pace slowly up and down the garden, now staring thoughtfully at the ground at his feet, now raising his eyes to the sky where multitudes of stars were twinkling. He continued walking about until he was almost worn out but the restlessness within him, a vague probing melancholy yearning, was still not appeased. Oh, how Bazarov would have laughed if he had known what was happening to him then! Even Arkady would have condemned him. Here he was, at forty-four, a gentleman farmer and landowner, shedding tears, uncalled-for tears: it was a hundred times worse than playing the 'cello.

Nikolai Petrovich continued on, unable to make up his mind to go into the house, into the cosy peaceful nest which looked out at him so hospitably from all its lighted windows: he had not the strength to tear himself away from the darkness, the garden, the feel of the fresh air on his face, and that sad restless excitement.

At a turn in the path he met Pavel Petrovich.

'What is the matter with you?' Pavel Petrovich asked. 'You look as white as a ghost. You aren't well. Why don't you lie down?'

Nikolai Petrovich briefly explained his state of mind and moved away. Pavel Petrovich strolled to the end of the garden, and he too grew pensive and likewise raised his eyes to the sky. But his fine large eyes reflected only the light of the stars. He was not a born romantic, and his fastidiously dry though passionate soul, with its tinge of French cynicism, was not capable of reverie.

'Do you know what?' Bazarov said to Arkady that same night. 'I've had a splendid idea. Your father was saying today that he had received an invitation from that illustrious relative of yours. Your father doesn't want to go, but why shouldn't we be off to — since the gentleman in question has invited you too? You see how lovely the weather has turned: we could drive over and look at the town. Let's have a jaunt for five or six days, no more.'

'And you'll come back here afterwards?'

'No, I must go on to my father's. You know he lives about twenty miles from —. I've not seen him or my mother for a long while: I must cheer the old folk up. They're nice parents, especially my father: he's a most amusing person. I'm the only child.'

'Will you stay long with them?'

'I don't think so. It's sure to be dull.'

'And you'll come to us again on your way back?'

'I don't know ... I'll see. Well, what do you say? Shall we go?'

'If you like,' observed Arkady languidly.

In his heart of hearts he was highly delighted with his friend's suggestion but thought it a duty to conceal his feelings. He was not a nihilist for nothing!

The following day he set off with Bazarov for —. The younger folk at Maryino regretted their departure; Dunyasha even shed a tear or two ... but the older men breathed a sigh of relief.

12

The town of — to which our friends set off was under the jurisdiction of a governor who was still a young man – a man who, as is often the case in Russia, was at once progressive and despotic. Before the end of his first year in office he had managed to quarrel not only with the marshal of nobility, a retired cavalry officer of the Guards, who ran a stud farm and kept open house, but even with his own subordinates. The resulting feuds at length assumed such proportions that the ministry in Petersburg found it necessary to send down a trusted official to investigate everything on the spot. The choice of the authorities fell on Matvei Ilyich Kolyazin, son of the Kolyazin who had once upon a time acted as guardian to the two Kirsanov brothers. He too was one of the 'younger men' – that is to say, he had just turned forty, but he was well on the way to becoming a statesman and already wore two stars on his breast – admittedly one of them was a foreign decoration not of the first magnitude. Like the governor upon whom he had come to pass judgment, he was considered a 'progressive' and though he was already a bigwig he was not like the majority of bigwigs. He had the highest opinion of himself: his vanity knew no bounds but his manner was simple, he had an affable expression, he listened indulgently and laughed so good-naturedly

134

that on first acquaintance he might even have been taken for 'a jolly good fellow'. On important occasions, however, he knew, so to speak, how to make his weight felt. 'Energy is essential,' he used to say then. '*L'énergie est la première qualité d'un homme d'état.*' Yet for all that he was always being made a fool of, and any moderately experienced official could twist him round his finger. Matvei Ilyich used to speak with great respect about Guizot,* and tried to suggest to all and sundry that he himself did not belong to the category of routine officials and old-fashioned bureaucrats, that not a single phenomenon of social life escaped his attention.... He was thoroughly familiar with expressions of the kind. He even followed (with a certain casual condescension, it is true) the development of contemporary literature – in the way a grown-up man who meets a procession of street-urchins will sometimes join them. In reality, Matvei Ilyich had not advanced much beyond those politicians of the days of Alexander I who used to prepare for an evening party at Madame Svyetchin's,† then resident in Petersburg, by reading a page of Condillac;‡ only his methods were different, more modern. He was a skilful courtier, extremely sly, and that was all; he had no aptitude for handling public affairs, and no intelligence – though he knew how to manage his own business successfully: no one could get the better of him in this domain, and of course that is what really matters.

Matvei Ilyich greeted Arkady with all the *bonhomie* – or should we say waggishness – characteristic of the enlightened higher official. He was amazed, however, when he heard that the cousins he had invited had preferred to remain at home in

* François Pierre Guillaume Guizot, 1787–1874, French statesman, *littérateur* and educationalist.

† Sophia Yuryevna Svyetchin, 1782–1859, fashionable writer on mysticism. Wife of the Russian General Svyetchin. For over forty years she maintained a famous salon.

‡ Etienne Bonnot Condillac, 1715–80, French writer on logic, psychology and economic science.

the country. 'Your father always was a queer fish,' he re-marked, playing with the tassels of his sumptuous velvet dressing-gown, and turning suddenly to a young official in a punctiliously buttoned-up undress uniform he exclaimed with an air of concentrated attention: 'What?' The young man whose lips were almost glued together from prolonged silence, leapt up and looked at his chief in perplexity. . . . But having nonplussed his subordinate Matvei Ilyich paid him no further attention. Our higher officials in general are fond of startling their subordinates, and employ quite a variety of means to achieve this end. Among others the following method is in great vogue – 'is quite a favourite', as the English say: a high official will suddenly cease to understand the simplest words and pretend to be deaf. He will ask, for in-stance, what day of the week it is.

He is respectfully informed, 'Today's Friday, your Ex-len-cy.'

'Eh, what? What's that? What do you say?' the great man repeats with strained attention.

'Today is Friday, your Ex-len-cy.'

'Eh? What? What's Friday? Which Friday?'

'Friday, your Ex-ccc-len-cccy, the day of the week.'

'Well, I. . . . Are you presuming to teach me something?'

Matvei Ilyich was first and foremost a higher official, though he was reputed to be a liberal.

'I advise you, my dear boy, to go and call on the governor,' he said to Arkady. 'You understand, I do not advise you to do so because of any old-fashioned ideas about the necessity of paying respect to the authorities but simply because the gov-ernor is a decent fellow; besides, you would probably like to get to know the society here. . . . You are not a country bumpkin, I hope? And he's giving a large ball the day after tomorrow.'

'Will you be at the ball?' inquired Arkady.

'He gives it in my honour,' Matvei Ilyich replied, almost pityingly. 'Do you dance?'

'Yes, but not well.'

'That is unfortunate. There are pretty women here and it's a disgrace for a young man not to dance. Again, I do not say this out of convention: I would never suggest that a man's wit should lie in his feet but Byronism is ridiculous now – *il a fait son temps*.'

'But, uncle, Byronism has nothing to do with my not . . .'

'I'll introduce you to some of the local ladies, I am taking you under my wing,' interrupted Matvei Ilyich, laughing complacently. 'You will be in luck, won't you?'

A servant entered and announced the arrival of the superintendent of the Provincial Treasury, a mild-eyed old man with wrinkled lips, who was a great lover of nature, especially on summer days when, to use his own words, 'Every wee busy bee takes a wee bribe from every wee flower. . . .' Arkady withdrew.

He found Bazarov at the inn where they were staying and was a long while persuading him to accompany him to the governor's.

'Well, there's no help for it,' said Bazarov at last. 'It's no good doing things by halves. We came to look at the local gentry, so let's look at them!'

The governor received the young men affably but did not ask them to sit down, nor did he sit down himself. He was in an everlasting fuss and hurry: in the morning he donned his tight-fitting undress uniform and an excessively stiff cravat; he never found time to finish a single meal, and was constantly issuing orders. As a result he was known throughout the province as 'Bourdaloue' – not after the well-known French preacher* but after a fermented liquor called 'bourda'. He invited Kirsanov and Bazarov to his ball, and a couple of minutes later invited them again, taking them for brothers and addressing them as the Messieurs Kaisarov.

* Louis Bourdaloue, 1632–1704, orator and professor at the Jesuit College of Bourges.

As they were walking back from the governor's a short man in a Hungarian jacket much favoured by the Slavophils jumped out of a passing carriage and with a shout of 'Yevgeny Vassilyich!' dashed up to Bazarov.

'Ah, it's you, Herr Sitnikov,' remarked Bazarov, still walking along the pavement. 'What chance brings you here?'

'Just fancy, quite by accident,' the other replied, and turning round to the carriage he waved his arms four or five times and shouted, 'Follow us, follow! ... My father had business here,' he went on, jumping across the gutter, 'and so he asked me ... Today I heard of your arrival and have already been to see you. ...' (The friends did, in fact, on returning to their room, find a visiting card with the corners bent, bearing the name Sitnikov in French on one side and Slavonic characters on the other.) 'I hope you are not coming from the governor's?'

'Don't hope. We've come straight from him.'

'Ah, in that case I will call on him too ... Yevgeny Vassilyich, introduce me to your ... to the ...'

'Sitnikov – Kirsanov,' growled Bazarov without halting.

'Delighted!' Sitnikov began, walking sideways, smirking and hurriedly pulling off his over-elegant gloves. 'I have heard so much ... I am an old friend of Yevgeny Vassilyich's and I may say – his disciple. I am indebted to him for my regeneration ...'

Arkady looked at Bazarov's disciple. There was an anxious expression of vacant tension on the small but pleasant features of his well-groomed face; his smallish eyes, which suggested that he was permanently astonished, had a staring uneasy look, and his laugh, too, was uneasy – a sort of abrupt, wooden laugh.

'Would you believe it,' he went on, 'when I heard Yevgeny Vassilyich say for the first time that we should not accept any species of authority I was bowled over with enthusiasm ... my eyes were opened! Here, I thought, at last I have found my man! By the way, Yevgeny Vassilyich, you simply must get to know a lady here, who is really capable of understanding you and for whom your visit would be a positive red-letter event: you may have heard of her?'

'Who is she?' Bazarov brought out unwillingly.

'Madame Kukshin, *Eudoxie*, Yevdoxia Kukshin. She's a remarkable nature, *émancipée* in the true sense of the word, an advanced woman. Do you know what? Let's go and see her, all three of us together, now. She lives only two steps from here. . . . We will have lunch there. You haven't lunched yet, have you?'

'No, not yet.'

'Well, that's capital. She has separated from her husband, you understand, and is quite independent.'

'Is she pretty?' Bazarov put in.

'N-no, one couldn't say that.'

'Then why the devil are you asking us to call on her?'

'Ah-ha! You will have your little joke. . . . She's sure to offer us a bottle of champagne.'

'So that's it! The practical man shows himself at once. By the way, is your father still in the liquor business?'

'He is,' said Sitnikov hurriedly, and burst into a shrill laugh. 'Well now, shall we go?'

'I really don't know.'

'You wanted to meet people, go along,' Arkady interjected in an undertone.

'And what about you, Monsieur Kirsanov?' Sitnikov put in. 'You must come too – we can't go without you.'

'But how can we all descend upon her at once?'

'Never mind about that. Madame Kukshin's a marvellous person.'

'There will be a bottle of champagne?' queried Bazarov.

'Three!' cried Sitnikov. 'I'll answer for that!'

'What with?'

'My own head.'

'Your father's money-bags would be better. However, let's go.'

13

The small detached villa in the Moscow style where Avdotya (otherwise Yevdoxia) Kukshin lived stood in one of those streets of — recently destroyed by fire. (It is well known that every fifth year sees our provincial towns burnt to the ground.) At the door, above a visiting card pinned on askew, there was a bell-handle, and in the hall the visitors were met by someone, not exactly a servant, not exactly a companion, in a cap – unmistakable signs of the progressive tendencies of the lady of the house. Sitnikov inquired whether Avdotya Nikitishna was at home.

'Is that you, Victor?' a shrill voice called from an adjoining room. 'Come in.'

The woman in the cap disappeared at once.

'I am not alone,' said Sitnikov, casting a keen look at Arkady and Bazarov as he briskly pulled off his Hungarian jacket, beneath which appeared something in the nature of a long jerkin.

'Never mind,' the voice replied. *'Entrez!'*

The young men went in. The room in which they found themselves was more like a working study than a drawing-room. Papers, letters, fat numbers of Russian periodicals, for the most part uncut, lay strewn about on dusty tables; white cigarette-ends were scattered all over the place. On a leather couch a lady, still young, half reclined; her blonde hair was rather dishevelled and she was wearing a crumpled silk dress, with heavy bracelets on her short arms and a lace kerchief on her head. She rose from the sofa and, carelessly drawing over her shoulders a velvet cape lined with yellowish ermine, she said languidly, 'Good morning, Victor,' and held out her hand to Sitnikov.

'Bazarov, Kirsanov,' he announced curtly after the manner of Bazarov.

'Welcome!' responded Madame Kukshin, and fixing on Bazarov a pair of round eyes, between which appeared a forlorn little turned-up nose, 'I know you,' she added, and held out her hand to him too.

Bazarov frowned. There was nothing definitely ugly in the small plain figure of the emancipated woman; but the expression of her face produced an uncomfortable effect on the spectator. One found oneself longing to ask her 'What's the matter? Are you hungry? Or bored? Or shy? Why are you so fidgety?' Like Sitnikov she seemed perpetually on edge. She spoke and moved in a free and easy yet at the same time awkward manner; she evidently regarded herself as a good-natured, simple creature, and all the while, whatever she did, it always struck one that it was the opposite of what she wanted to do; everything with her seemed done on purpose, as children say – in other words, nothing was simple and spontaneous.

'Yes, yes, I know you, Bazarov,' she repeated. (Like many provincial and Moscow ladies she had adopted the habit of calling men by their surnames alone from the moment she met them.) 'Will you have a cigar?'

'A cigar's all very well,' interjected Sitnikov, who was already lolling in an armchair with one of his legs in the air, 'but do give us some lunch. We're frightfully hungry; and tell them to bring up a nice bottle of champagne.'

'You sybarite!' exclaimed Yevdoxia with a laugh. (When she laughed the gums showed above her top teeth.) 'He's a sybarite, isn't he, Bazarov?'

'I appreciate the comforts of life,' Sitnikov pronounced pompously. 'But that doesn't prevent me from being a liberal.'

'Yes, it does, it does!' cried Yevdoxia. However, she gave instructions to her maid to see to both the lunch and the champagne. 'Now what do you think?' she added, turning to Bazarov. 'I am sure you share my opinion.'

'Well, no,' retorted Bazarov. 'A slice of meat is better than a piece of bread, even from the point of view of chemistry.'

'Are you interested in chemistry? That is my passion. I have even invented a new sort of mastic myself.'

'A new mastic? You?'

'Yes. And do you know what it is for? To make dolls' heads so that they can't break. You see that, like yourself, I am of a practical turn of mind. But it's not quite ready yet. I have still got to read Liebig. By the way, have you seen Kislyakov's article on female labour in the *Moscow News*? Do read it. You are interested in the question of women's emancipation, I suppose? And in the schools problem too? What does your friend do? What is his name?'

Madame Kukshin poured out her questions one after another with feminine insouciance, without waiting for answers, in the way spoilt children talk to their nannies.

'My name is Arkady Nikolayevich Kirsanov,' Arkady informed her, 'and I don't do anything.'

Yevdoxia burst into a laugh.

'Oh, how delightful! Why, don't you smoke? Victor, you know I am very angry with you.'

'What for?'

'They tell me you've begun singing the praises of George Sand again, that out-of-date woman. How can she be compared with Emerson? She hasn't a single idea about education or physiology or anything. I am convinced she's never even heard of embryology, and in these days – how can one get on without that?' (Yevdoxia actually threw up her hands.) 'Oh, but what a splendid article Yelisevich has written on the subject! He's a gentleman of genius.' (Yevdoxia constantly used the word 'gentleman' instead of 'man'.) 'Bazarov, sit by me on the sofa. You may not know it but I'm awfully afraid of you.'

'Why is that? May I have the curiosity to inquire?'

'You're a dangerous gentleman, you're such a critic. Heavens, how absurd! I'm talking like any staid lady of the manor. I really am a provincial, though. I manage my estate myself, and just fancy, I have a bailiff, Yerofey, who's a wonderful type – just like Fenimore Cooper's Pathfinder: there's something so spontaneous about him! I have now definitely settled here: it's quite unbearable, this town, isn't it? But what is one to do?'

'The town's like any other town,' Bazarov remarked indifferently.

'All its interests are so petty, that's what is so awful! I used to spend the winter in Moscow ... but now my worthy spouse, Monsieur Kukshin, resides there. And besides, Moscow nowadays – I don't know, it's not what it was. I am thinking of going abroad – I almost went last year.'

'To Paris, I suppose?' queried Bazarov.

'To Paris and to Heidelberg.'

'Why Heidelberg?'

'How can you ask? Bunsen lives there!'

To this Bazarov could find no reply.

'Pierre Sapozhnikov ... do you know him?'

'No, I don't.'

'Not know Pierre Sapozhnikov! ... He's always at Lydia Khostatov's.'

'I don't know her either.'

'Well, he's taken it upon himself to escort me. Thank God, I'm independent, I've no children.... Did I say "Thank God"? – not that it matters anyway.'

Yevdoxia rolled a cigarette between her fingers which were brown with tobacco stains, put it to her tongue, licked it up and started to smoke. The maid came in with a tray.

'Ah, here's lunch! Will you have an appetizer first? Victor, open the bottle: that's in your line.'

'It is, it is,' Sitnikov mumbled, and gave vent to another shrill laugh.

'Are there any pretty women here?' asked Bazarov as he drank off a third glass.

'Yes, there are,' answered Yevdoxia, 'but they're all such

empty-headed creatures. *Mon amie*, Odintsov, for instance, is nice-looking. It's a pity her reputation's. . . . However, that wouldn't matter so much but she has no independence of outlook, no breadth, nothing . . . of that kind. Our whole system of education needs changing. I've thought a lot about it : our women are very badly educated.'

'You won't do anything with them,' put in Sitnikov. 'The only thing is to despise them, and I do despise them, utterly and completely!' (To Sitnikov the chance to be scathing and express contempt was the most agreeable of sensations; he used to attack women in particular, never suspecting that before many months were over he would be grovelling at the feet of his wife merely because she was born a Princess Durdoleosov.) 'Not one of them would be capable of understanding our conversation; not one of them deserves to be mentioned by serious-minded men like ourselves!'

'But there is no need whatsoever for them to understand our conversation,' observed Bazarov.

'Whom do you mean?' put in Yevdoxia.

'Pretty women.'

'What? Do you then share the ideas of Proudhon?'*

Bazarov drew himself up haughtily.

'I share no one's ideas : I have my own.'

'Damn all authorities!' shouted Sitnikov, delighted to have an opportunity of expressing himself boldly in front of the man he slavishly admired.

'But even Macaulay . . .' Madame Kukshin was beginning.

'Damn Macaulay!' thundered Sitnikov. 'Are you going to stand up for those silly females?'

'Not for silly females, no, but for the rights of women which I have sworn to defend to the last drop of my blood.'

'Down with . . .' but here Sitnikov stopped. 'But I don't deny you that,' he said.

'I can see you're a Slavophil.'

* Pierre-Joseph Proudhon, 1809–65, French doctrinaire who taught that anarchy is the goal of the free development of society.

144

'No, I'm not a Slavophil, though of course . . .'

'Yes, yes, yes. You are a Slavophil. You're a supporter of patriarchal despotism. You want to go about with the whip in your hand!'

'A whip is an excellent thing,' said Bazarov, 'but we've got to the last drop . . .'

'Of what?' interrupted Yevdoxia.

'Of champagne, most respected Avdotya Nikitishna, of champagne – not of your blood.'

'I can never listen calmly when women are attacked,' Yevdoxia went on. 'It's terrible, simply terrible. Instead of black-guarding them you would do better to read Michelet's *De l'Amour*. It's a marvellous work. Gentlemen, let us talk about love,' added Yevdoxia, letting her arm fall languidly on the crumpled sofa cushion.

A sudden silence followed.

'No, why should we talk of love?' said Bazarov; 'but you mentioned just now a Madame Odintsov. . . . That was the name, I think? Who is the lady?'

'She's charming – charming!' squeaked Sitnikov. 'I'll introduce you. Clever, rich, a widow. Unfortunately she's not sufficiently advanced yet: she ought to see more of our Yevdoxia. I drink to your health, *Eudoxie*! Let us clink glasses! *Et toc, et toc, et tin-tin-tin! Et toc, et toc, et tin-tin-tin!*'

'Victor, you're a wretch!'

The lunch continued for a long time. The first bottle of champagne was followed by another, by a third and even a fourth. . . . Yevdoxia chattered away without ceasing; Sitnikov echoed her. They had much to say about the nature of marriage – was it prejudice or crime? – and whether men were born equal or not, and what precisely was the essence of individuality. The proceedings ultimately reached a stage when Yevdoxia, flushed with the wine she had drunk, began tapping with her splay finger-tips on the keys of a discordant piano, and singing in a husky voice, first gipsy songs, then

Seymour Schiff's ballad *Granada lies slumbering*, while Sitnikov tied a scarf round his head to represent the dying lover in the passage:

> In burning kiss
> Your lips meet mine ...

Arkady could stand no more. 'Gentlemen, this is approaching Bedlam,' he exclaimed aloud.

Bazarov, who had merely every now and then dropped a sarcastic word or two into the conversation – his attention being more devoted to the champagne – yawned noisily, got up and, without taking leave of their hostess, he walked off with Arkady. Sitnikov jumped to his feet and followed them.

'Well, what do you think of her?' he asked, skipping obsequiously from right to left of them. 'Didn't I tell you she was a remarkable personality? If only we had more women like her! She is, in her own way, a highly moral phenomenon.'

'And is that establishment of your dear papa's also a moral phenomenon?' muttered Bazarov, pointing to a vodka-shop which they were passing at that moment.

Sitnikov went off into another shrill laugh. He was greatly ashamed of his origins and did not know whether to feel flattered or offended by Bazarov's unexpected familiarity.

14

A few days later the governor's ball took place. Matvei Ilyich was indeed the hero of the occasion. The marshal of nobility declared to all and sundry that he had come only out of respect for him; and the governor, even while the ball was in full swing, even while he himself was standing still, continued to issue orders. Matvei Ilyich's suavity of demeanour was equalled only by his stately manner. He had a gracious word for everyone – with an added shade of disgust in some cases and deference in others; he was gallant, *un vrai chevalier français*, to all the ladies, and was continually bursting into hearty resounding laughter, in which no one else took part, as befits a high official. He patted Arkady on the back and addressed him loudly as 'young nephew'; bestowed on Bazarov – who was attired in a shabby dress-coat – an absent-minded but condescending glance in passing, and a vague but friendly grunt in which nothing could be distinguished save the words 'I' and ' 'xtremely'; held out a finger to Sitnikov, and gave him a smile – though with his head already turned away to greet someone else; even to Madame Kukshin, who appeared at the ball without a crinoline, wearing soiled gloves and a bird of paradise in her hair, he vouchsafed an *'enchanté'*. There were crowds of people and no lack of men for dancing-partners; the civilians tended to bunch together along the walls but the officers danced assiduously, especially one who had spent six weeks in Paris, where he had mastered various daring exclamations such as *'zut'* – *'Ah fichtrre!'* – *'pst, pst, mon bibi'*. He pronounced them to perfection with genuine Parisian *chic* but at the same time he said *'si j'aurais'* instead of *'si j'avais'* and *'absolument'* when he meant 'certainly' – expressed himself, in fact, in that Greater-Russo-French jargon which affords the French such amusement when there is no necessity for them to assure us that we speak their language like angels – *'comme des anges'*.

Arkady was a poor dancer, as we already know, and Bazarov did not dance at all: they both took up their position in a corner, where Sitnikov joined them. With a mocking expression on his face, and letting fall one spiteful remark after another, he looked insolently about him and appeared to be thoroughly enjoying himself. Suddenly his face changed and turning to Arkady he said in a rather embarrassed tone: 'Madame Odintsov has arrived'.

Arkady glanced round and saw a tall woman in a black dress standing near the door. He was struck by the dignity of her carriage. Her bare arms hung gracefully beside her slim waist; light sprays of fuchsia trailed prettily from her shining hair upon her sloping shoulders; her clear eyes looked out from under a rather prominent white forehead with a tranquil and intelligent expression – tranquil but not pensive – and a scarcely perceptible smile played on her lips. A sort of affectionate and gentle strength radiated from her face.

'Do you know her?' Arkady asked Sitnikov.

'Very well. Would you like me to introduce you?'

'Please ... after this quadrille.'

Bazarov also noticed Madame Odintsov.

'What a striking figure,' he said. 'Not a bit like the other females.'

When the quadrille was over Sitnikov led Arkady up to Madame Odintsov, but he hardly seemed to know her at all: he stuttered and hesitated, while she gazed at him with a shade of astonishment. But her face brightened when she heard Arkady's name and she asked him whether he was not the son of Nikolai Petrovich.

'Yes, indeed!'

'I have met your father twice and heard a lot about him,' she went on. 'I am very glad to meet you.'

At that moment an aide-de-camp flew up and begged her for a quadrille. She accepted.

'Do you dance then?' asked Arkady respectfully.

'Yes, I dance. But why should you think I didn't? Do I appear to you to be too old?'

'I beg your pardon, I didn't intend ... But in that case may I ask you for the mazurka?'

Madame Odintsov smiled graciously.

'Certainly,' she said, and looked at Arkady, not exactly patronizingly but in the way married sisters look at very young brothers.

Madame Odintsov was a little older than Arkady – she was twenty-nine – but in her presence he felt like a schoolboy, a young student, as though the difference in their ages was much greater. Matvei Ilyich approached her with a majestic air and ingratiating speeches. Arkady moved away but he still watched her: he could not take his eyes off her even during the quadrille. She talked to her partner as easily as she had to the grand official, slightly turning her head and eyes, and twice she laughed softly. Her nose – like most Russian noses – was a trifle thick and her complexion was not translucently clear; but Arkady decided that he had never yet met such a fascinating woman. The sound of her voice haunted his ears; the very folds of her dress seemed to fall differently – more gracefully and amply than on other women – and her every movement was wonderfully flowing and natural.

Arkady felt a certain diffidence when at the first sounds of the mazurka he and his partner began to sit it out together; he wanted to engage her in conversation but he could only pass his hand over his hair, and found not a single thing to say. But his shyness and agitation were short-lived: Madame Odintsov's tranquillity communicated itself to him and within a quarter of an hour he was talking away and telling her about his father, his uncle, his life in Petersburg and in the country. Madame Odintsov listened with courteous interest, opening and shutting her fan a little as she did so. His chatter was interrupted whenever a new partner claimed her for a dance; Sitnikov, among others, asked her to dance twice. She came back, sat down again, and took up her fan, without appearing to breathe any faster; while Arkady started talking again, full of happiness at being near her, talking to her, gazing into her eyes, at her lovely forehead, at her whole charming, dignified, intelligent face. She herself said little but her words showed an understanding of life: from some of her observations Arkady came to the conclusion that this young woman had already experienced and pondered much. . . .

'Who was the man you were standing with?' she asked him, 'when Monsieur Sitnikov brought you over to me?'

'So you noticed him?' Arkady inquired in his turn. 'He has a wonderful face, hasn't he? That's my friend, Bazarov.'

Arkady launched into a description of 'his friend'.

He spoke of him in such detail and with so much enthusiasm that Madame Odintsov turned round and looked at him attentively. Meanwhile the mazurka was drawing to a close. Arkady felt sorry to lose his partner; he had spent nearly an hour with her so happily! True, he had felt the whole time as though she were condescending to him, as though he ought to be grateful to her ... but young hearts are not weighed down by feelings of that sort.

The music stopped.

'*Merci*,' Madame Odintsov murmured, getting up. 'You have promised to come and see me: bring your friend with you. I am very curious to meet a man who has the courage not to believe in anything.'

The governor came up to Madame Odintsov, announced that supper was ready and with a worried look offered her his arm. As she went out she turned to give a last smile and nod to Arkady. He bowed and followed her with his eyes (how graceful her figure seemed to him, sheathed in the greyish lustre of black silk!). 'By now she's already forgotten my existence,' he thought – and was conscious of an exquisite humility flooding his soul.

'Well?' Bazarov asked, as soon as Arkady returned to him in the corner. 'Did you enjoy yourself? A certain gentleman was just telling me that your lady is – *Oo là là*!; but the fellow is probably a fool. What do *you* think of her? Is she –?'

'I don't understand what you mean,' replied Arkady.

'Oh my! What innocence!'

'At all events I don't understand your informant's meaning. Madame Odintsov is very charming – there is no doubt about that – but so cold and reserved that ...'

'Still waters ... you know,' put in Bazarov. 'You say she is cold; that just adds to the flavour. You like ice-cream, don't you?'

'Maybe,' muttered Arkady. 'I'm no judge of such matters. She wants to meet you and asked me to bring you along when I call.'

'I can imagine how you described me! Never mind, you did well. Take me along. Whoever she is – a provincial lioness or an "*émancipée*" like Madame Kukshin – anyhow she's got a pair of shoulders the like of which I haven't set eyes on for a long while.'

Bazarov's cynicism jarred on Arkady but – as often happens – the reproach he levelled against his friend did not tally exactly with what he really had against him. . . .

'Why are you unwilling to allow that women are capable of independence of thought?' he asked in a low voice.

'Because, my boy, my observations lead me to conclude that free-thinking women are monstrosities.'

And here the conversation ended. Both young men left immediately after supper. They were pursued by a nervously spiteful but somewhat faint-hearted laugh from Madame Kukshin, whose vanity had been deeply wounded by the fact that neither of them had paid the smallest attention to her. She stayed later than anyone else at the ball, and at four o'clock in the morning was dancing a polka-mazurka in Parisian style with Sitnikov. This edifying spectacle brought the governor's festivities to an end.

15

'Let us see to what species of mammal this specimen belongs,' Bazarov said to Arkady the following day as they mounted the staircase of the hotel where Madame Odintsov was staying. 'I can smell something not quite right here.'

'You surprise me,' cried Arkady. 'What? You – you of all people – Bazarov, clinging to the narrow morality which . . .'

'What an odd chap you are!' Bazarov interrupted him carelessly. 'Don't you know that in our phraseology and for our sort of people "not quite right" means "quite all right"? It's all the better for me, of course. Didn't you tell me yourself this morning that she had made a strange marriage, though to my mind to marry a rich old man is by no means a strange thing to do but, on the contrary, very sensible. I don't believe the gossip of the town but I should like to think, as our enlightened governor says, that it has a basis of fact.'

Arkady made no answer, and knocked at the door of the apartment. A young servant in livery ushered the two friends into a large room, hideously furnished like all Russian hotel rooms but filled with flowers. Presently Madame Odintsov appeared in a simple morning dress. The spring sunshine made her look younger than ever. Arkady introduced Bazarov and noted with secret astonishment that he seemed uncomfortable, whereas Madame Odintsov remained as self-possessed as she had been on the previous day. Bazarov was himself conscious of a feeling of embarrassment and was annoyed about it. 'What an idea – frightened of a petticoat,' he thought and, lolling in an armchair, quite like Sitnikov, he began to hold forth in an exaggeratedly free and easy manner, while Madame Odintsov kept her clear eyes fixed on him.

Anna Sergeyevna Odintsov was the daughter of Sergei Nikolayevich Loktev, who had been well known for his handsome looks, his speculations and his gambling propensities. After fifteen years of staying the course and cutting a figure in Petersburg and Moscow he had ended up by completely ruining himself at cards and being obliged to retire to the country, where soon afterwards he died, leaving a tiny income to his two daughters – Anna, a girl of twenty, and Katya, a child of twelve. Their mother, who came of an impoverished line of princes, had died in Petersburg while her husband was still in his heyday. After her father's death Anna found herself in a very difficult situation. The brilliant education she had received in Petersburg had not fitted her for the cares of domestic life and the management of an estate – nor for an obscure existence in the depths of the country. She did not know a soul in the whole neighbourhood and there was no one whose advice she could ask. Her father had done his best to avoid all contact with his neighbours : he looked down on them in his way and they looked down on him in theirs. However, she did not lose her head and promptly wrote off to a sister of her mother's, Princess Avdotya Stepanovna X., a spiteful, arrogant old lady who came and installed herself in her niece's house, appropriated all the best rooms for herself, grumbled and scolded from morning till night and refused to walk a step, even in the garden, without being attended by her one and only retainer, a surly footman in threadbare pea-green livery trimmed with pale-blue braid and a three-cornered hat. Anna patiently put up with all her aunt's caprices, gradually took on her sister's education and, it seemed, was already reconciled to the idea of wasting her life in the wilds. . . . But fate had decreed otherwise. She happened to meet a certain Odintsov, a very wealthy man of about forty-six, an eccentric hypochondriac, bloated, ponderous and sour but neither stupid nor ill-natured. He fell in love with her and offered her his hand. She consented to become his wife and they lived together for six years before he died, leaving her all his property. Anna Sergeyevna remained in the country for nearly a year after his death; then she went abroad with her sister, but only as far as Germany. Becoming homesick, they returned to live at their beloved Nikolskoye, some thirty miles from the provincial town of —. There Anna Sergeyevna kept up a sumptuous, luxuriously furnished house and a beautiful garden with a range of conservatories : her late husband had spared no expense to gratify his fancies. She rarely visited the town and as a rule only on business; even then she did not stay long. She was not popular in the province : there had been a fearful outcry when she married Odintsov and all sorts of impossible stories were invented about her : it was asserted that she had helped her father in his gambling escapades, that she had gone abroad for excellent reasons and that it had been necessary to conceal certain unfortunate consequences. . . . 'You understand?' the indignant gossips would wind up. 'There's nothing she doesn't know,' they said of her, to which a noted provincial wit usually added, 'Fire, water and all the other element.' All this gossip reached her but she turned a deaf ear: she had an independent and pretty determined character.

Madame Odintsov sat leaning back in her armchair, her hands clasped, and listened to Bazarov. Contrary to his habit, he was talking a good deal and obviously trying to interest her – which again surprised Arkady. He could not make up his mind whether Bazarov was succeeding in his purpose. It was difficult to tell from Anna Sergeyevna's face what impression he was making on her: the keen, friendly expression did not vary and her beautiful eyes shone with attention but it was a serene attention. At first Bazarov's affected manners had impressed her disagreeably, like a bad smell or a discordant sound, but she quickly realized that he was ill at ease and that flattered her. Only the commonplace was repulsive to her, and no one would have accused Bazarov of being commonplace. Wonders were not to cease for Arkady that day. He had expected Bazarov would talk to an intelligent woman like Madame Odintsov about his convictions and views, seeing that she had herself expressed a desire to hear a man 'who dares to have no belief in anything'; but instead of that Bazarov talked about medicine, about homoeopathy and about botany. It turned out that Madame Odintsov had not wasted her time in solitude: she had read a number of excellent books and could express herself in faultless Russian. She brought the conversation round to music but perceiving that Bazarov had no appreciation of art quietly returned to botany, although Arkady was just launching into a discourse upon the significance of folk melodies. Madame Odintsov continued to treat him like a younger brother: she seemed to value his good nature and youthful simplicity – and that was all. A lively conversation lasted for more than three hours, ranging freely over a variety of subjects.

At length the friends got up and began to take their leave. With a kindly glance Anna Sergeyevna held out her beautiful white hand to each in turn and, reflecting for a moment, said with a diffident but delightful smile:

'If you are not afraid of being bored, gentlemen, come and visit me at Nikolskoye.'

'How can you say that!' exclaimed Arkady. 'It would be the greatest pleasure . . .'

'And you, Monsieur Bazarov?'

Bazarov merely bowed – and a final surprise for Arkady: he noticed that his friend was blushing.

'Well?' he said to him when they were out in the street. 'Do you still think she's – *oo là là?*'

'Who can tell? Look what an icicle she has made of herself,' retorted Bazarov, and after a brief pause he added, 'A regular grand-duchess, a commanding sort of person. She only needs a train behind her and a crown on her head.'

'Our grand-duchesses can't speak Russian like that,' remarked Arkady.

'She's been through the mill, my lad: she's known what it is to be hard up.'

'Anyhow, she's delightful,' said Arkady.

'What a magnificent body!' Bazarov pursued. 'Shouldn't I like to see it on the dissecting-table!'

'Stop, for heaven's sake, Yevgeny. That's going too far.'

'Well don't upset yourself, softie. I meant – it's first-class. We must go and pay her a visit.'

'When?'

'What about the day after tomorrow? What is there to do here? Drink champagne with Madame Kukshin? Listen to the harangues of your kinsman, the liberal bigwig? . . . Let's be off the day after tomorrow. By the way – my father's little place is not far from there. This Nikolskoye's on the — road, isn't it?'

'Yes.'

'*Optime.* Why dawdle then? Only fools procrastinate – and intellectuals. I say, what a splendid body!'

Three days later the two friends were on the road to Nikolskoye. It was sunny without being too hot and the sleek post-horses trotted smartly along, flicking their tied and plaited tails. Arkady stared at the road and without knowing why smiled to himself.

'Wish me many happy returns,' Bazarov suddenly exclaimed. 'Today's the twenty-second of June, my name day. We'll see how my patron saint will watch over me. They are expecting me home today,' he added, lowering his voice. 'Well, they can wait – what does it matter!'

16

Anna Sergeyevna's country house stood on the slope of a bare hill not far from a yellow stone church with a green roof, white columns, and a fresco over the main entrance representing the Resurrection of Christ in the 'Italian' style. Sprawling in the foreground of the picture was a swarthy warrior in a helmet, especially remarkable for his voluminous contours. Behind the church a village stretched in a double row of houses, with chimneys peeping out here and there over thatched roofs. The manor-house was built in the same style as the church, the style we know in Russia as Alexandrine. The house, too, was painted yellow and had a green roof and white columns and a pediment with a coat-of-arms. The architect of the province had erected both buildings according to the instructions of the late Odintsov, who could not endure 'pointless and arbitrary innovations', as he expressed it. The house was flanked on either side by the sombre trees of an old garden; an avenue of clipped pines led up to the front door.

Our friends were met in the hall by two tall footmen in livery; one of them at once ran for the butler. The butler, a stout man in a black tail-coat, immediately appeared and led the visitors up a carpeted staircase to a specially prepared room which already contained two bedsteads and every kind of toilet accessory. Evidently the house was very well managed:

everything was spick and span, everywhere there was an odour of respectability, after the manner of ministerial reception rooms.

'Madame will be glad to see you in half an hour,' the butler announced. 'Have you any orders to give meanwhile?'

'No, worthy one,' replied Bazarov. 'Except that you might deign to bring a glass of vodka.'

'Certainly, sir,' said the butler, looking somewhat puzzled, and he withdrew, his boots creaking as he walked.

'What *grand genre*,' remarked Bazarov. 'That's what you call it in your set, I think? A grand-duchess, and no mistake.'

'A nice grand-duchess,' Arkady retorted, 'to invite at first sight two such obvious aristocrats as you and me to stay with her.'

'Me in particular, a country doctor in the making, and a doctor's son, and grandson of the village sexton ... You knew, didn't you, that I was the grandson of a sexton? Like the great Speransky,'* Bazarov added after a short pause, pursing his lips. 'Anyhow, she gives herself the best of everything, this pampered lady! Oughtn't we to don our dress clothes?'

Arkady only shrugged his shoulders ... but he, too, felt a certain constraint.

Half an hour later Bazarov and Arkady made their way together into the drawing-room. It was a spacious, lofty room, furnished fairly luxuriously but without any particular taste. Heavy expensive furniture stood in a conventional stiff arrangement along the walls, which were papered with a buff wall-paper with golden arabesques; the late Odintsov had ordered the furnishings from Moscow through an agent friend of his who was a wine merchant. Over a sofa in the centre of one wall hung a portrait of a flabby fair-haired man – he seemed to stare disapprovingly at the visitors. 'It must be the late lamented,' Bazarov whispered to Arkady and, wrink-

* M. Speransky, 1772–1839, Russian statesman of westernizing and reformist tendencies.

ling up his nose, 'Shall we make a bolt for it?' But at that instant the lady of the house entered. She wore a light muslin dress; her hair, smoothly combed back behind her ears, gave a girlish expression to her pure fresh face.

'Thank you for keeping your promise,' she began. 'You must stay a little while : it's really not so bad here. I will introduce you to my sister; she plays the piano well. That is of no interest to you, Monsieur Bazarov; but I believe that Monsieur Kirsanov is fond of music. Besides my sister I have an old aunt living with me, and one of our neighbours drives over sometimes to play cards. That makes up our whole circle. And now let us sit down.'

Madame Odintsov delivered all this little speech very precisely, as though she had learnt it by heart; then she turned to Arkady. It transpired that her mother had known Arkady's mother and had even been her confidante when the latter had fallen in love with Nikolai Petrovich. Arkady began to speak with great feeling about his dead mother, while Bazarov sat and looked through some albums. 'What a tame cat I've become,' he thought to himself.

A beautiful white borzoi with a pale blue collar ran into the drawing-room, the nails on its paws tapping on the floor; it was followed by a girl of eighteen with black hair, an olive complexion, a rather round but pleasing face and small dark eyes. In her hands she held a basket full of flowers. 'This is my Katya,' said Madame Odintsov, nodding in her direction.

Katya made a slight curtsy, sat down beside her sister and began to sort out the flowers. The borzoi, whose name was Fifi, went up to both the visitors in turn, wagging her tail and thrusting her cold nose into their hands.

'Did you pick them all yourself?' asked Madame Odintsov.

'Yes,' answered Katya.

'Is auntie coming down for tea?'

'Yes.'

When Katya spoke she had a charming smile, at once bashful and candid, and she looked up from under her eyebrows with a sort of humorous severity. Everything about her was still innocently fresh : her voice, the downy bloom on her face, the rose-pink hands with their white palms, and the rather narrow shoulders . . .

She was constantly blushing and apt to catch her breath.

Madame Odintsov turned to Bazarov.

'You are only looking at those pictures out of politeness, Monsieur Bazarov,' she began. 'They don't really interest you. You had better come and join us and then we can start an argument about something.'

Bazarov moved nearer.

'What shall we discuss?' he inquired.

'Anything you like. I warn you, I am dreadfully argumentative.'

'You?'

'Yes. That seems to surprise you. Why?'

'Because, so far as I can judge, you have a calm cool temperament, and to be argumentative one has to be excitable.'

'How have you managed to sum me up so quickly? In the first place, I am impatient and obstinate – you should ask Katya; and secondly, I am very easily carried away.'

Bazarov looked at Anna Sergeyevna.

'Perhaps; you know best. So you would like us to have an argument – all right then. I was looking at the views of German Switzerland in your album, and you remarked that they couldn't interest me. You said that, because you assume that I have no feeling for art – and it is true, I haven't. But those views might interest me from a geological standpoint, for studying the formation of mountains, for instance.'

'If I may say so, as a geologist you would do better to consult a text-book, some special work on the subject, rather than a drawing.'

'A drawing shows me at one glance something that takes ten pages of text to describe.'

Anna Sergeyevna was silent for a moment or two.

'And so you have no feeling whatsoever for art?' she said, leaning her elbow on the table, a movement which brought her face closer to Bazarov. 'How can you get on without it?'

'Why, what is it needed for, may I ask?'

'Well, at least to help one to know and understand people.'

Bazarov smiled.

'In the first place, experience of life does that, and in the second, I assure you the study of separate individuals is not worth the trouble it involves. All men are similar, in soul as well as in body. Each of us has a brain, spleen, heart and lungs of similar construction; and the so-called moral qualities are the same in all of us – the slight variations are of no importance. It is enough to have one single human specimen in order to judge all the others. People are like trees in a forest: no botanist would dream of studying each individual birch-tree.'

Katya, who was arranging the flowers one by one in a leisurely way, lifted her eyes to Bazarov with a puzzled look, and meeting his quick casual glance she blushed to her ears. Anna Sergeyevna shook her head.

'The trees in a forest,' she repeated. 'According to you, then, there is no difference between a stupid and an intelligent person, or between a good and a bad one?'

'Oh yes, there is: it's like the difference between the sick and the healthy. The lungs of the consumptive are not in the same condition as yours and mine, though they are constructed on the same lines. We know more or less what causes physical ailments; and moral diseases are caused by the wrong sort of education, by all the rubbish people's heads are stuffed with from childhood onwards, in short by the disordered state of society. Reform society and there will be no diseases.'

Bazarov said all this looking as though he were thinking aloud to himself: 'Believe me or not as you like, it makes no odds to me!' He slowly passed his long fingers over his side-whiskers, while his eyes strayed round the room.

'And you suppose,' said Anna Sergeyevna, 'that when

society is reformed there will no longer be any stupid or wicked people?'

'At any rate, in a properly organized society it won't matter a jot whether a man is stupid or clever, bad or good.'

'Yes, I see. They will all have identical spleens.'

'Precisely, madame.'

Anna Sergeyevna turned to Arkady. 'And what is your opinion, Monsieur Kirsanov?'

'I agree with Yevgeny,' he answered.

Katya looked at him from under her eyelids.

'You amaze me, gentlemen,' commented Madame Odintsov, 'but we will talk about this again. Now I hear my aunt coming down for tea: we must spare her.'

Anna Sergeyevna's aunt, Princess ——, a small shrivelled woman with a clenched fist of a face and glaring spiteful eyes under a grey wig, came in and, scarcely bowing to the guests, sank into a wide velvet-covered armchair which no one but herself was privileged to use. Katya placed a hassock under her feet; the old lady did not thank her or even look at her, but chafed her hands under the yellow shawl which covered almost the whole of her decrepit body. The princess was fond of yellow: even her cap had bright yellow ribbons.

'How did you sleep, auntie?' Madame Odintsov inquired, raising her voice.

'That dog in here again,' the old lady muttered in reply, and seeing Fifi making a couple of hesitant steps in her direction she cried 'Shoo! Shoo!'

Katya called Fifi and opened the door.

Fifi rushed out delighted, expecting to be taken for a walk, but when she found herself left alone outside the door she began to scratch and whine. The princess frowned. Katya rose to go out. . . .

'I think tea is ready,' said Madame Odintsov. 'Come, gentlemen. Auntie, please come and have some tea.'

The princess silently got up from her armchair and was the first to leave the drawing-room. They all followed her into the dining-room. A little Cossack page-boy in livery noisily pulled back from the table another sacred armchair, laden with cushions, into which the princess lowered herself; Katya, who was pouring out the tea, served her first with a cup emblazoned with a coat of arms. The old lady put some honey in her cup (she considered it both sinful and extravagant to drink tea with sugar in it, although she never spent a penny of her own on anything), and suddenly asked in a hoarse voice, 'And what does *Preence* Ivan write?'

No one answered. Bazarov and Arkady soon realized that, though they were respectful, they paid no attention to her. 'They put up with her because she comes of a noble tribe – because she's a princess,' thought Bazarov. After tea Anna Sergeyevna suggested a stroll but it began to rain a little and the whole party, with the exception of the princess, returned to the drawing-room. The neighbour arrived, the devoted card-player; his name was Porfiry Platonych, a stoutish grizzled man with short spindly legs, very courteous and jocular. Anna Sergeyevna, who still talked mainly to Bazarov, asked him whether he would like to pit himself against them in an old-fashioned game of preference. Bazarov accepted, saying that it behoved him to train in advance for the duties in store for him as a country doctor.

'You must be careful,' observed Anna Sergeyevna. 'Porfiry Platonych and I will beat you. And you, Katya,' she added, 'play something to Arkady Nikolayevich; he's fond of music and we shall enjoy listening too.'

Katya went reluctantly to the piano; and, though he genuinely was fond of music, Arkady followed her as reluctantly: it seemed to him that Madame Odintsov was getting rid of him – and already, like most young men of his age, he felt that vague, oppressive excitement in the heart which is the foretaste of love. Katya lifted the lid of the piano and not looking at Arkady asked in an undertone:

'What shall I play for you?'

'Anything you like,' Arkady replied indifferently.

'What sort of music do you like best?' went on Katya, without making any move.

'Classical,' Arkady replied in the same tone of voice.

'Do you like Mozart?'

'Yes, I like Mozart.'

Katya brought out Mozart's Sonata Fantasia in C minor. She played very well, although a trifle too mechanically and drily. She sat upright and motionless without taking her eyes off the music, her lips tightly compressed, and only towards the end of the sonata did her face begin to glow, her hair loosened and a little lock fell over her dark brow.

Arkady was particularly struck by the last part of the sonata, the part where the bewitching gaiety of the careless melody is suddenly invaded by gusts of such mournful, almost tragic grief ... but the reflections inspired in him by the music of Mozart had nothing to do with Katya. Looking at her, he merely thought: 'Well, the young lady doesn't play at all badly, and she's not bad-looking either.'

When she had come to the end of the sonata Katya, without taking her hands off the keys, inquired: 'Is that enough?' Arkady declared that he would not venture to impose on her any further, and began talking about Mozart; he asked if she had chosen that sonata herself or had anyone recommended it to her. But Katya answered him in monosyllables: she had gone into hiding and retired into herself. Whenever this happened it took her a long while to emerge again: on such occasions her face assumed a stubborn almost stupid expression. She was not exactly shy, but diffident and slightly overawed by her sister who had brought her up – a fact which the other had no suspicion of. Arkady was finally reduced to calling Fifi, now back in the room again, over to him and, with a benevolent smile, stroking her head, to give himself an appearance of being at ease. Katya returned to work on her flowers.

Meanwhile Bazarov was losing one hand after another. Anna Sergeyevna was an expert player; Porfiry Platonych, too, knew how to hold his own. Bazarov ended up by losing a sum which, though by no means considerable in itself, was none too pleasant for him. At supper Anna Sergeyevna again turned the conversation to botany.

'Let us go for a walk tomorrow morning,' she said to him. 'I want you to teach me the Latin names of our field flowers and their characteristics.'

'What do you want with Latin names?' Bazarov asked.

'System is needed in everything,' she replied.

'What a wonderful woman Anna Sergeyevna is!' exclaimed Arkady as soon as he was alone with his friend in their room.

'Yes,' answered Bazarov, 'a female with brains. And she's seen life too!'

'In what sense do you mean that, Yevgeny Vassilyich?'

'In the right sense, in the right sense, my worthy Arkady Nikolayevich! I'm sure she manages her estate very efficiently too. But it's not her but her sister who's wonderful.'

'What? That sallow little thing?'

'Yes, that little dark creature. Now she's fresh and untouched and shy and silent and anything else you like. One could make something of her. But the other – she's an old stager.'

Arkady did not answer, and each got into bed, pondering his own thoughts.

Anna Sergeyevna was also thinking about her guests that evening. She liked Bazarov – his total lack of affectation and the downright severity of his views appealed to her. She found something new in him which she had never encountered before, and she was curious.

Anna Sergeyevna was a rather strange person. Having no prejudices of any kind, and no strong convictions even, she was not put off by obstacles and she had no goal in life. She had clear ideas about many things and a variety of interests, but nothing ever completely satisfied her; indeed, she did not really seek satisfaction. Her mind was at once probing and indifferent; any doubts she entertained were never soothed into oblivion, nor ever swelled into unrest. If she had not been rich and independent she might perhaps have thrown herself into the struggle and experienced passion. ... But life was easy for her, though tedious at times, and she continued to pursue her daily round without haste and rarely upsetting herself about anything. Rainbow-coloured dreams occasionally danced before even *her* eyes, but she breathed more freely when they faded away, and did not regret them. Her imagination certainly ranged beyond the bounds of what is considered permissible by conventional morality; but even then her blood flowed as quietly as ever in her fascinatingly graceful, tranquil body. Sometimes, emerging all warm and languorous from a fragrant bath, she would fall to musing on the futility of life, its sorrow and toil and cruelty. ... Her soul would be filled with sudden daring and begin to seethe with noble aspirations; but then a draught would blow from a half-open window and Anna Sergeyevna would shrink back into herself, feel plaintive and almost angry, and at that instant the one thing she cared for beyond all others was to get away from that abominable draught.

Like all women who have not succeeded in falling in love she hankered after something without knowing what it was. In reality there was nothing she wanted, though it seemed to her that she wanted everything. She could hardly endure her late husband (she had married him for practical reasons, although she probably would not have consented to become his wife if she had not regarded him as a kindly man) and had conceived a secret repugnance for all men, whom she could only think of as slovenly, clumsy, dull, feebly irritating creatures. Once, somewhere abroad, she had met a handsome young Swede with a chivalrous expression and a pair of honest blue eyes under an open brow; he had made a strong impression on her but that had not prevented her from returning to Russia.

'A strange man, that medico,' she thought as she lay in her luxurious bed, on lace pillows and beneath a light silk coverlet. ... Anna Sergeyevna had inherited from her father a little of his propensity for luxury. She had been very fond of her reprobate but good-natured father, and he had idolized her, cracked jokes with her as with a friend and equal, confided in her and sought her advice. Her mother she scarcely remembered.

'The medico's a strange man,' she repeated. Stretching herself, she smiled, clasped her hands behind her head and then, after letting her eyes stray over a couple of pages of a silly French novel, dropped the book and fell asleep, all pure and cold in her pure and fragrant linen.

Next morning, directly after breakfast, Anna Odintsov set off on a botany expedition with Bazarov and came back just before dinner. Arkady stayed indoors and spent about an hour with Katya. He was not bored in her company and she offered of her own accord to play the Mozart sonata again; but when Madame Odintsov returned at last and he caught sight of her he felt an instantaneous pang in his heart. ... She came through the garden with a rather tired step, her cheeks glowed and her eyes shone more brightly than usual under her round straw hat. She was twirling in her fingers the slender stalk of some wild flower, her light shawl had slipped down to her elbows, and the wide grey ribbons of her hat clung to her bosom. Bazarov strode beside her, self-confident and casual as ever, but Arkady did not care for the expression on his face, although it was cheerful and even tender. With a muttered 'Hullo, how are you?' Bazarov betook himself to his room, while Madame Odintsov absent-mindedly pressed Arkady's hand and also walked past him.

'Why "how are you?" ... ?' thought Arkady. 'As if we had not seen each other already today!'

17

Time (as we all know) sometimes flies like a bird and some-times crawls like a snail; but man is happiest when he does not even notice whether time is passing quickly or slowly. It was in this condition that Arkady and Bazarov spent about a fortnight at Madame Odintsov's. The good order she had established in her house and her daily life was partly respon-sible for this. She adhered strictly to her régime and obliged others to submit to it as well. Everything throughout the day was done at a fixed time. In the morning, punctually at eight o'clock, the company would assemble for breakfast; from then until luncheon everyone did what he liked while the hostess herself was engaged with her bailiff (the estate was run on the tithes system), her butler and her head housekeeper. Before dinner the party met again for conversation or reading aloud; the evening was devoted to walks, card-games and music; at half past ten Anna Sergeyevna would retire to her own room, give her orders for the following day and go to bed. Bazarov did not care for this measured, somewhat ostentatious form-ality in daily life, like 'gliding along rails', he called it; the footmen in livery, the decorous butlers and servants offended his democratic instinct. He declared that if one went that far one might as well dine in the English style outright – in tail-coats and white ties. One day he spoke out on the subject to Anna Sergeyevna. Her manner was such that no one hesitated to say what they thought in front of her. She heard him out and then remarked, 'From your point of view you are right – and perhaps in that respect I am too much of a fine lady; but in the country one must lead an orderly life, otherwise one would die of *ennui*' – and she continued to go her own way. Bazarov grumbled, but the very reason both he and Arkady found life so easy at Madame Odintsov's was because every-thing in the house did run 'on rails'. For all that, a change had taken place in both the young men since the first days of their stay at Nikolskoye. Bazarov, for whom Anna Sergeyevna obviously had a soft spot though she seldom saw eye to eye with him, began to show quite unprecedented signs of emo-tional disturbance: he was easily irritated, reluctant to talk, glared about him and, as if driven by some hidden unrest, could hardly sit still for a moment; while Arkady, who had quite made up his mind that he was in love with Madame Odintsov, started to abandon himself to a gentle melancholy. This melancholy, however, did not prevent him from making friends with Katya: it even helped him to develop a cordial, affectionate relationship with her. '*She* does not appreciate me!' he thought. 'All right . . . but here is a good-hearted creature who does not give me the cold shoulder'; and his heart again knew the sweet satisfaction of feeling magnanimous. Katya vaguely realized that he was seeking some sort of consolation in her company, and did not deny him or herself the innocent pleasure of a half-diffident, half-intimate friendship. They did not talk to each other in Anna Sergeyevna's presence: Katya always shrank into herself under her sister's probing eye; while Arkady, as befits a young man in love, had no other thought in his mind when near the object of his passion; but he felt happy with Katya when he was alone with her. He knew that it was beyond his power to interest Madame Odint-sov; he was shy and at a loss when left in her company, and she had no idea what to say to him: he was too young for her. With Katya, on the other hand, Arkady felt at home; he treated her indulgently, let her talk about the effect music had on her, and the novels she read, and verses and other such 'trifles', without noticing or being aware that these trifles interested him too. Katya for her part did not inter-fere with his melancholy. Arkady was happy with Katya, Madame Odintsov with Bazarov, so it usually happened that after the two couples had been together for a while they went off in their separate directions, especially when they were out walking. Katya *adored* nature, and so did Arkady, though he did not dare to admit it; Madame Odintsov, like Bazarov, was rather indifferent to the beauties of nature. The fact that they were almost continuously separated from one another was not without its consequence for our two friends: their relationship underwent a change. Bazarov gave up talking to Arkady about Madame Odintsov: he even stopped railing at her 'aristocratic ways'; true, he sang Katya's praises as before, and only advised Arkady to restrain her sentimental tendencies, but his praises were hurried, his counsels dry, and in general he talked to Arkady far less than formerly . . . he seemed to avoid him, to be uncomfortable with him. . . .

Arkady observed all this but kept his observations to himself.

The real cause of all this change was the feeling inspired in Bazarov by Madame Odintsov, a feeling which at once tortured and maddened him, and which he would promptly have denied with scornful laughter and cynical abuse, if anyone had even remotely hinted at the possibility of what was taking place within him. Bazarov was a great devotee of women and of feminine beauty, but love in the ideal – or, as he would have expressed it, the romantic – sense he called tomfoolery, unpardonable imbecility; he regarded chivalrous feelings as a sort of aberration or disease, and had more than once declared his astonishment that Toggenburg and all the Minnesingers and troubadours had not been clapped into a lunatic asylum. 'If a woman takes your fancy,' he would say, 'try to gain your end; and if you don't succeed – well, don't bother, turn your back on her: there are plenty more good fish in the sea.' Madame Odintsov appealed to him; the rumours about her, the freedom and independence of her ideas, her unmistakable liking for him – all seemed to be in his favour; but he soon discovered that with her he would not 'gain his end', and as for turning his back on her, he found, to his own bewilderment, that it was more than he could do. His blood took fire the moment he thought of her; he could easily have mastered his blood but something else was taking possession of him, something he had never allowed, at which he had always scoffed, at which all his pride revolted. In his conversations with Anna Sergeyevna he went out of his way to pour quiet scorn on everything which savoured of the 'romantic'; but when he was alone he recognized with indignation a romantic strain in himself. Then he would go off into the forest, and stride about smashing the twigs that barred his path and cursing under his breath both her and himself; or he would climb into the hayloft in the barn and, stubbornly shutting his eyes, try to force himself to sleep, in which of course he did not always succeed. Suddenly he would imagine those arms that were so chaste one day twining themselves round his neck, those proud lips responding to his kisses, those intelligent eyes gazing lovingly – yes, lovingly – into his own; and his head would swirl and for a moment he would be lost in reverie, till indignation boiled up in him again. He caught himself indulging in all sorts of 'shameful' thoughts, as though a devil were mocking him. At times it seemed to him that a change was taking place in Madame Odintsov too, that there were signs of something special in the expression of her face, that perhaps. ... But at that point he would generally stamp his feet or grind his teeth and shake his fist at himself.

Meanwhile Bazarov was not entirely mistaken. He had excited Madame Odintsov's imagination; he interested her, she thought a great deal about him. In his absence she did not miss him, and was not impatient for him to come, but immediately he appeared she became more animated; she enjoyed their *tête-à-têtes* and she liked talking to him, even when he annoyed her or offended her taste and her refined habits. She was, as it were, eager both to sound him and to analyse herself.

One day as they were strolling together in the garden he

abruptly announced in a surly voice that he intended to leave very soon to go to his father's place. . . . She went white as though something had pricked her heart, and pricked it so painfully that she was astonished and for a long time afterwards pondered what it could mean. Bazarov had told her of his intended departure without any idea of testing her with the news: he never 'schemed'. Earlier that morning he had seen his father's bailiff, Timofeich, who had looked after him when he was a child. This Timofeich, a decrepit, astute old man with faded yellow hair, a red weather-beaten face and tiny tear-drops in his sunken eyes, had unexpectedly presented himself before Bazarov, wearing a short coat of stout grey-blue cloth, leather girdle and tarred boots.

'Hullo, old man, how are you?' Bazarov had exclaimed.

'Good-day to you, Yevgeny Vassilyich, sir,' began the little old man, and he smiled with such delight that his whole face was suddenly covered with wrinkles.

'What have you come here for? Sent to fetch me, eh?'

'Upon my word, sir, how could that be!' mumbled Timofeich (he remembered the strict injunctions received before he left). 'I was on the way to town on the master's business when I chanced to hear of your honour's being here, so I turned aside from the main road, that is to say – to have a peep at your honour . . . no, not to disturb you at all – oh dear no!'

'Now then, no fibbing,' Bazarov interrupted him. 'Do you mean to tell me this is on the road to the town?'

Timofeich looked sheepish and said nothing.

'Is my father well?'

'Yes, sir, praise be.'

'And my mother?'

'Arina Vlassyevna's very well too, glory be to God!'

'They're expecting me, I suppose?'

The old man hung his small head on one side.

'Ah, your honour, expecting and expecting. It makes your heart ache to see them, really and truly it does.'

'All right, all right! Don't pile on the agony. Tell them I'll be coming soon.'

'Yes, sir,' Timofeich had replied with a sigh.

As he went out of the house he had pulled his cap down over his eyes with both hands, clambered into a rickety racing carriage, which he had left at the gate, and went off at a trot, but not in the direction of the town.

That evening Madame Odintsov sat in her own sitting-room with Bazarov, while Arkady walked up and down the music-room listening to Katya playing the piano. The princess had retired upstairs to her apartments; she could not abide the presence of visitors in general, and 'these new young imbeciles', as she called them, in particular. In the drawing-room she merely sulked but in her own quarters she made up for it by breaking out into such torrents of abuse before her maid that the cap danced on her head, wig and all. Anna Serge-yevna was well aware of this.

'How is it you are proposing to leave us?' she began. 'What about your promise?'

Bazarov started.

'What promise?'

'Have you forgotten? You were going to give me some chemistry lessons.'

'It can't be helped! My father is expecting me: I can't hang about any longer. Besides, you can read Pelouse and Frémy, *Notions générales de Chimie*: it's a good book and clearly written. You will find in it all you need.'

'But don't you remember, you told me that a book can't take the place of ... I forget how you put it but you know what I mean ... don't you remember?'

'It can't be helped,' repeated Bazarov.

'Why must you go?' asked Madame Odintsov, lowering her voice.

He glanced at her. Her head had fallen back against the easy chair, and her arms, bare to the elbow, were folded over her bosom. She looked paler in the light of the single lamp with its perforated paper shade. The soft folds of a voluminous white dress swathed her completely; only the tips of her feet, crossed like her arms, were visible.

'And why should I stay?' responded Bazarov.

Madame Odintsov turned her head slightly.

'You ask why? Have you not enjoyed yourself here? Or do you suppose that no one will miss you when you are gone?'

'I am sure of that.'

Madame Odintsov was silent for a moment.

'You are wrong if you think that. But I don't believe you do. You can't be serious.' Bazarov did not move. 'Yevgeny Vassilyich, why don't you speak?'

'And what am I to say to you? There is no point in missing people – and that applies to me even more than to most.'

'Why?'

'I'm a staid, uninteresting individual. I'm no conversationalist.'

'You are fishing for compliments, Yevgeny Vassilyich.'

'That is no habit of mine. Don't you know yourself that the elegancies of life, which you set so much store on, are beyond me?'

Madame Odintsov bit the corner of her handkerchief.

'You may think what you like but I shall find time hang heavy when you are gone.'

'Arkady will stay on,' remarked Bazarov.

Madame Odintsov gave a slight shrug of her shoulders.

'I shall miss you,' she repeated.

'Really? In any case you won't miss me for long.'

'What makes you think that?'

'Because you told me yourself that you only feel bored when your orderly routine is upset. You have organized your existence with such unimpeachable regularity that there can't be any place left in it for boredom or melancholy . . . or any disturbing emotions.'

'And do you consider that I am so faultless. . . . I mean, that I have ordered my life too regularly ever to err?'

'I should say so! For example: in five minutes the clock will strike ten, and I know beforehand that you will turn me out of the room.'

'No, I won't turn you out, Yevgeny Vassilyich. You may stay. Will you open the window . . . I feel half stifled.'

Bazarov got up and pushed at the window. It flew open at once with a crash . . . He had not expected it to open so easily; also, his hands were trembling. The mild dark night looked into the room with its almost black sky, its faintly rustling trees and the fresh fragrance of the pure untrammelled air.

'Draw the blind and sit down,' said Madame Odintsov. 'I want to have a talk with you before you depart. Tell me something about yourself: you never talk of yourself.'

'I try to converse with you about useful subjects, Anna Sergeyevna.'

'You are very modest. . . . But I should like to know something about you, about your family, your father for whom you are forsaking us.'

'Why is she talking like this?' thought Bazarov.

'None of that is the least bit interesting,' he said aloud, 'especially for you. We are little people . . .'

'While you regard me as an aristocrat?'

Bazarov lifted his eyes and looked at Madame Odintsov.

'Yes,' he said with exaggerated harshness.

She smiled.

'I see you know me very little, though of course you do maintain that all people are alike and not worth individual study. . . . Some day I will tell you the story of my life . . . but first you must tell me yours.'

'I know very little,' repeated Bazarov. 'Perhaps you are right; possibly every human being is an enigma. You, for instance: you shun society, you find people tedious – and yet you invite a couple of students to come and stay with you.

What makes you, with your intellect, with your beauty, live in the country?'

'What? What did you say?' Madame Odintsov interposed eagerly. 'With my ... beauty?'

Bazarov scowled.

'Never mind about that,' he muttered. 'I was saying that I don't exactly understand why you have settled in the country.'

'You don't understand it. . . . But you explain it to yourself in some way or other?'

'Yes ... I suppose you prefer to remain in one place because you are spoilt, because you are too fond of comfort and ease, and very indifferent to everything else.'

Madame Odintsov smiled again.

'You are determined to believe that I am incapable of being carried away by anything?'

Bazarov glanced at her from under his brows.

'Out of curiosity, maybe; but not otherwise.'

'Really? Well, now I understand why you and I get on together: you are just like me, you see.'

'Get on together . . .' echoed Bazarov in a hollow voice.

'Yes! ... But I'd forgotten that you want to go away.'

Bazarov got up. The lamp burned dimly in the darkening, fragrant, isolated room; now and again the blind swayed, letting in the pungent freshness of the night and its mysterious whisperings. Madame Odintsov did not stir; but a hidden agitation gradually took possession of her. . . . It communicated itself to Bazarov. He suddenly realized that he was alone with a young and beautiful woman.

'Why are you going?' she said slowly.

Without replying he sank back into his chair.

'So you regard me as a placid, pampered, self-indulgent creature,' she went on in the same tone, without taking her eyes off the window. 'Yet I know this much about myself, that I am very unhappy.'

'You unhappy? What for? Surely you don't attach any importance to idle gossip?'

Madame Odintsov frowned. It was annoying to have her words interpreted in that way.

'Such tittle-tattle does not even touch me, Yevgeny Vassilyich, and I am too proud to allow it to disturb me. I am unhappy because ... I have no desire, no longing for life. You look at me incredulously; you think those are the words of an aristocrat covered in lace and sitting in a velvet armchair. I don't deny for a moment that I like what you call comfort, but at the same time I have very little desire to live. Reconcile that contradiction as best you can. Of course all this is sheer romanticism in your eyes.'

Bazarov shook his head.

'You are healthy, independent, well-off – what more do you need? What is it you want?'

'What do I want?' Madame Odintsov repeated, and she sighed. 'I feel very tired and old; I seem to have lived a long, long time. Yes, I am old,' she added, softly drawing the end of her mantilla over her bare arms. Her eyes met Bazarov's and she flushed slightly. 'So many memories lie behind me: my life in Petersburg, wealth, then poverty, my father's death, my marriage, the inevitable tour of the Continent. ... So many memories and so little worth remembering, and in front of me, ahead, a long, long road without a goal. ... I have no wish to go on.'

'Are you so disillusioned?' asked Bazarov.

'No,' Madame Odintsov replied, speaking with deliberation. 'But I am unsatisfied. I think if I could get really attached to something ...'

'You are longing to fall in love,' Bazarov interrupted her, 'but you can't. That's the reason for your unhappiness.'

Madame Odintsov began to examine the mantilla over her sleeve.

'Am I incapable of love?' she murmured.

'Probably. Only I was wrong to call it an unhappiness. On the contrary, the person most to be pitied is the one who meets with that experience.'

'What experience do you mean?'

'Falling in love.'

'And how do you come to know that?'

'By hearsay,' Bazarov retorted angrily. 'You're playing the coquette,' he thought to himself. 'You are bored, and teasing me for want of something better to do, while I ...' And indeed he felt his heart bursting.

'Besides, you may be too demanding,' he said, leaning his whole body forward and playing with the fringe of his chair.

'Possibly I am. I want everything or nothing. A life for a life. If you take mine, give me yours. And no regrets or turning back. Otherwise better have nothing!'

'Well,' observed Bazarov, 'those are fair terms, and I am surprised that so far you ... haven't found what you want.'

'And do you think it would be easy to surrender oneself completely to whatever it might be?'

'Not easy, if you start deliberating, biding your time, putting a price on yourself, taking care of yourself, I mean; but to give oneself recklessly is very easy.'

'But how can one help valuing oneself? If I have no value, who would want my devotion?'

'That's not my affair: it's for the other person to discover my value. What matters is to know how to give oneself.'

Madame Odintsov leaned forward from the back of her chair.

'You speak as if you had experienced it all,' she said.

'No, words, idle words arising out of our conversation: as you know, all that is not in my line.'

'But would you be capable of surrendering yourself unreservedly?'

'I don't know. I shouldn't like to boast.'

Madame Odintsov said nothing and Bazarov fell silent. From the drawing-room the notes of the piano floated up to them.

'How is it Katya is playing so late tonight?' Madame Odintsov remarked.

Bazarov got up.

'Yes, it is quite late now, time for you to go to bed.'

'Wait a moment. Why should you hurry away? ... I want to say a word to you.'

'What is it?'

'Wait a little,' Madame Odintsov whispered. Her eyes rested on Bazarov: she seemed to be scrutinizing him intently.

He took a turn about the room, then suddenly came up to her and hastily said 'Good-bye', squeezing her hand so that she almost screamed, and was gone. She raised her crushed fingers to her lips, breathed on them, then rose impulsively from her armchair and moved rapidly towards the door, as though intending to call Bazarov back ... A maid came into the room with a decanter on a silver tray, Madame Odintsov stopped short, told the maid she could go, and sat down again, deep in thought. Her hair slipped loose and fell in a dark coil over her shoulders. The lamp went on burning for a long while in her room while she still sat there motionless, only from time to time chafing her hands which were now beginning to feel the chill of the night air.

As for Bazarov, he returned to his bedroom some two hours later, his boots wet with dew, looking dishevelled and morose. He found Arkady sitting at the writing-desk with a book in his hands, his coat buttoned up to the neck.

'Not in bed yet?' Bazarov exclaimed with what sounded like annoyance.

'You were a long time with Anna Sergeyevna tonight,' Arkady said, not answering him.

'Yes, I was with her all the time you and Katya were playing the piano.'

'I was not playing ...' Arkady began, and stopped. He felt tears welling to his eyes and he did not want to weep in front of his sarcastic friend.

18

When Madame Odintsov appeared at morning tea next day Bazarov sat for a long time hunched over his cup and then suddenly glanced up at her. .... She turned towards him as though he had touched her, and he fancied that her face was paler since the night before. She soon retired to her own room where she stayed till lunch-time. It had been drizzling since early morning and to go walking was out of the question. The whole party gathered in the drawing-room. Arkady picked up the latest number of some journal and began to read aloud from it. The princess, as usual, had reacted by looking amazed at first, as though Arkady were guilty of some indecency, then she had fixed him with a baleful stare; but he paid no attention to her.

'Yevgeny Vassilyich,' said Anna Sergeyevna at last, 'let us go to my room. I want to ask you ... you mentioned a text-book yesterday. ...'

She got up and went to the door. The princess glanced round her as much as to say: 'Well, well, just look at that, I am struck dumb!' and glared again at Arkady; but he raised his voice, and exchanging glances with Katya, who was sitting beside him, he went on reading.

Madame Odintsov walked quickly to her boudoir. Bazarov followed her promptly, not lifting his eyes, and only listening to the delicate swish and rustle of her silk gown gliding ahead of him. Madame Odintsov sank into the same easy-chair in which she had sat the evening before, and Bazarov took up his same position.

'What was the title of that book now?' she began after a brief silence.

'Pelouse and Frémy, *Notions générales* ...' answered Bazarov. 'However, I can also recommend Ganot, *Traité élémentaire de Physique expérimentale*. The diagrams are clearer, and on the whole the manual is. . . .'

Madame Odintsov held out her hand.

'Yevgeny Vassilyich, you must forgive me, but I didn't invite you here to discuss text-books. I wanted to continue our conversation of last night. You went away so suddenly ... I hope that I shall not weary you?'

'I am at your service, Anna Sergeyevna. But what was it, now, that we were talking about last night?'

Madame Odintsov flung a sidelong glance at Bazarov.

'We were discussing happiness, I believe. I was telling you about myself. Incidentally, I just used the word "happiness". Tell me, why is it that even when we are enjoying music, for instance, or a beautiful evening, or a conversation in agreeable company, it all seems no more than a hint of some infinite felicity existing apart somewhere, rather than actual happiness – such, I mean, as we ourselves can really possess? Why is it? Or perhaps you never felt like that?'

'You know the saying, "Happiness is where we are not"?' Bazarov retorted. 'Besides, you yourself told me yesterday that you felt unsatisfied. As for me, you are quite right, such thoughts never occur to me.'

'Perhaps they seem ridiculous to you?'

'No, they just don't enter my head.'

'Really? Do you know, I should very much like to know what you do think about?'

'What do you mean? I don't understand you.'

'Listen. For a long time I've been wanting to have a frank talk with you. There is no need to tell you – you know it yourself – that you are not an ordinary person; you are still young – all life is before you. For what are you preparing yourself? What future awaits you? I mean to say – what is the goal you are aiming for? Where are you going? What is the purpose animating you? In short, who are you? What are you?'

'You amaze me, Anna Sergeyevna. You know quite well I am studying natural science, and as for who I am ...'

'Yes, who are you?'

'I have already told you – a country doctor in the making.' Anna Sergeyevna made an impatient gesture.

'Why tell me that? You don't believe it yourself. Arkady might answer me in that way, but not you.'

'How does Arkady come in?'

'Do please stop talking like that! Do you mean to tell me you could be content with such a humble career? And aren't you always maintaining that you don't believe in medicine? You – with your ambition – a country doctor! You answer me like that to put me off because you have no confidence in me. But you know, Yevgeny Vassilyich, I *am* capable of understanding you: once I was poor and ambitious like you; it may be I have gone through the same difficulties.'

'That's all very well, Anna Sergeyevna, but you must excuse me ... I am not in the habit of talking about myself; and between you and me there is such a gulf ...'

'What gulf? Are you going to tell me again that I am an aristocrat? Enough of that, Yevgeny Vassilyich! I thought I had convinced you ...'

'And besides,' broke in Bazarov, 'why this eagerness to talk and think about the future, which for the most part does not depend on us? If an opportunity turns up of doing something – so much the better; and if it doesn't – at least one should be content with not chattering about it in advance.'

'You call a friendly conversation "chatter" ... Or perhaps you consider me, as a woman, unworthy of your confidence? You must really despise the lot of us!'

'I don't despise you, Anna Sergeyevna, and you know that.'

'No, I don't know anything ... but let us suppose I do understand your reluctance to speak of your future; but we could discuss what is happening in you now ...'

'Happening!' repeated Bazarov. 'As though I were some kind of government or society! In any case, it is utterly uninteresting; and besides, can a man always speak out loud of everything that "happens" in him?'

'But I don't see why it should be impossible to express what is in one's heart.'

'Can *you*?' asked Bazarov.

'I can,' answered Anna Sergeyevna after a moment of hesitation.

Bazarov bowed his head. 'You are more fortunate than I,' he said.

Anna Sergeyevna looked at him questioningly.

'As you please,' she went on, 'but still something tells me that we did not meet for nothing and that we shall become good friends. I am convinced that this – how shall I call it? – this constraint of yours, this reserve, will disappear eventually.'

'So you have noticed reserve in me ... and, how did you put it? – constraint?'

'Yes.'

Bazarov got up and went to the window.

'And you would like to know the reason for this reserve? You would like to know what is "happening" inside me?'

'Yes,' repeated Madame Odintsov with a sort of apprehension for which she could not so far account.

'And you will not be angry?'

'No.'

'No?' Bazarov was standing with his back to her. 'Let me tell you then that I love you idiotically, madly. . . . There, you have forced that out of me.'

Madame Odintsov held out both her hands before her, while Bazarov pressed his forehead against the window-pane. He was breathing heavily; his whole body trembled. But it was not the trembling of youthful timidity, not the sweet alarm of the first declaration that possessed him: it was passion struggling in him, violent and painful – passion not unlike fury and perhaps akin to it. . . . Madame Odintsov was filled with fear and at the same time felt sorry for him.

'Yevgeny Vassilyich,' she murmured, and there was a ring of unconscious tenderness in her voice.

He turned quickly, threw a devouring look at her – and, seizing both her hands, suddenly drew her to him.

She did not free herself from his embrace immediately; but an instant later she was looking at Bazarov from a corner of the room.

'You have misunderstood me,' she whispered in hasty alarm. Had he taken another step it seemed she might have screamed ... Bazarov bit his lips and strode out of the room.

Half an hour later a maid brought Anna Sergeyevna a note from Bazarov; it consisted of a single line : 'Am I to go today, or may I stop till tomorrow?'

'Why should you leave? I did not understand you – you did not understand me,' Anna Sergeyevna answered him, while to herself she thought: 'I did not understand myself either.'

She did not appear till dinner-time, and spent the hours pacing up and down in her room, hands clasped behind her back, stopping every now and then in front of the window or the looking-glass, and slowly rubbing her handkerchief over her neck, on which a spot still seemed to be burning. She kept asking herself what had impelled her to 'force' him, as Bazarov put it, into being frank with her. Had she not really had an inkling of something? ... 'I am to blame,' she decided aloud, 'but I could not have foreseen this.' She kept going over it all and blushed each time she thought of Bazarov's almost animal expression when he rushed at her.

'Or is it that ... ?' she exclaimed suddenly, and she stopped short and shook back her curls. She had caught sight of herself in the glass; the image of her head thrown back, with a mysterious smile on the half-closed eyes, half-parted lips, told her, it seemed, in a flash something at which she herself felt confused ...

'No,' she decided at last. 'God alone knows what it might have led to; this was not something to trifle with. After all, a quiet life is better than anything else in the world.'

Her peace of mind was not deeply disturbed; but she felt sad and once even burst into tears, though she could not have said why – certainly not because she had been outraged. She did not feel that she had been outraged: on the contrary, she had a feeling of guilt. The pressure of various vague emotions – the sense of life passing by, a longing for novelty – had forced her to a certain limit, forced her to look behind her – and there she had seen not even an abyss but only a void ... chaos without shape.

19

For all her self-possession and freedom from the conventions Madame Odintsov felt distinctly ill at ease when she entered the dining-room for dinner. The meal passed off fairly happily, however. Porfiry Platonych turned up and recounted various anecdotes: he had just come back from town. Among other things he related that Governor Bourdaloue ordered that his secretaries engaged on special missions should wear spurs in case he might want to send them off somewhere urgently on horseback. Arkady talked in an undertone to Katya, and was diplomatically attentive to the princess. Bazarov maintained a grim and obstinate silence. Madame Odintsov glanced at him two or three times – not covertly but straight in the face, which looked stern and forbidding. His eyes were downcast; there was contemptuous determination stamped on every feature; and she thought, 'No ... no ... no ...'. After dinner she strolled out with the whole company into the garden and, seeing that Bazarov wanted to speak to her, she took a few steps to one side and stopped. He went up to her but even then he did not raise his eyes and said in a hollow voice:

'I have to apologize to you, Anna Sergeyevna. You must be very angry with me.'

'No, I'm not angry with you, Yevgeny Vassilyich, but I am grieved.'

'That is even worse. In any case I am punished enough. I find myself, as I am sure you will agree, in a very foolish position. You wrote in your message, "Why go away?" But I can't stay, nor do I want to. By tomorrow I shall be gone.'

'Yevgeny Vassilyich, why are you ...'

'Why am I going?'

'No, that wasn't what I meant.'

'One can't put the clock back, Anna Sergeyevna ... and sooner or later this was bound to happen. Therefore I must go; I can only conceive of one condition which might have enabled me to stay; but that condition will never be. For you don't love me – forgive my impertinence – and you never will?'

Bazarov's eyes glittered for an instant under his dark brows. Anna Sergeyevna did not answer him. 'I am afraid of this man,' flashed through her mind.

'Good-bye then,' murmured Bazarov, as if he guessed her thought, and he turned back towards the house.

Anna Sergeyevna walked slowly after him, and calling Katya to her took her by the arm. She kept Katya by her side for the rest of the afternoon. She did not join in the card-playing and frequently laughed to herself, which contrasted strangely with her pale and worried face. Arkady was puzzled, and watched her as young people do, constantly wondering what it all meant. Bazarov had shut himself up in his room, but he did put in an appearance for tea. Anna Sergeyevna wanted to say something kind to him but was at a loss how to approach him....

An unexpected incident saved the situation: the butler announced the arrival of Sitnikov.

Words fail to describe the strange figure cut by the young apostle of progress as he fluttered into the room. Having decided with characteristic impudence to repair to the country to pay a visit to a lady with whom he was barely acquainted and who had never invited him, but at whose house, as he had ascertained, such talented and intimate friends of his were staying, he was nevertheless scared out of his wits, and instead of offering the apologies and compliments he had prepared in advance he mumbled some nonsense about Yevdoxia Kukshin having sent him to inquire after Anna Sergeyevna's health and that Arkady had always spoken to him in terms of the highest praise. . . . At this point he faltered and got so flustered that he sat down on his hat. However, since no one turned him out, and Anna Sergeyevna even presented him to her aunt and sister, he soon recovered himself and began to chatter volubly. The introduction of the commonplace often serves a useful purpose in life: it lowers the temperature and moderates emotions which are over-confident or too self-sacrificing by reminding one how akin they are to banality. With Sitnikov's arrival everything became somehow less significant, emptier – and easier; they all even enjoyed their supper with a better appetite and retired to their rooms half an hour earlier than usual.

'I can now repeat to you,' said Arkady, lying on his bed, to Bazarov who had also undressed, 'what you once said to me: "Why are you so melancholy? You look as if you had just fulfilled some sacred duty?" '

For some time past a sort of artificial free and easy banter – always an unmistakable sign of secret dissatisfaction or suppressed suspicions – had become the habit between the two young men.

'I'm off to my father's tomorrow,' said Bazarov.

Arkady raised himself and leaned on his elbow. He felt surprised and also for some reason pleased.

'Ah!' he commented. 'And is that why you are depressed?'

Bazarov yawned. 'Too much knowledge, and your hair will go grey.'

'And Anna Sergeyevna?' Arkady persisted.

'What about Anna Sergeyevna?'

'I mean, will she let you go?'

'I'm not her hireling.'

Arkady relapsed into thought, while Bazarov stretched himself out and turned his face to the wall.

Silence reigned for several minutes.

'Yevgeny!' Arkady suddenly exclaimed.

'Well?'

'I'm leaving with you tomorrow too.'

Bazarov made no reply.

'Only I shall go home,' continued Arkady. 'We might bear one another company as far as the new Khokhlovsky village, and there you can get a relay of horses at Fiodr's. It would give me great pleasure to meet your people but I'm afraid of being in their way and yours. But you'll come and stay with us again, won't you?'

'I've left all my things at your house,' Bazarov said, without turning round.

'Why doesn't he ask me why I'm leaving? And just as suddenly as he is?' thought Arkady. 'Why is either of us going, for that matter?' he pursued his reflections. He could find no satisfactory answer to his question and he was conscious of a sort of ache in his heart. He felt he would find it hard to break with this life to which he had grown so accustomed, but for him to stay on alone would be rather odd. 'Something has happened between them,' he told himself. 'What excuse could I offer for hanging around her after he has gone? I should bore her stiff and lose my last chance.' He began to conjure up a picture of Anna Sergeyevna: then other features gradually eclipsed the lovely image of the young widow.

'I shall miss Katya too!' Arkady whispered into his pillow, on which a tear had already fallen.... All at once he shook back his hair and said aloud: 'What the devil made that idiotic Sitnikov turn up here?'

Bazarov at first stirred in his bed, then he made the following observation:

'I can see you're still a fool, my boy. The Sitnikovs of this world are essential to us. I – I would have you understand – I need such louts. It is not for the gods to have to bake bricks! ...'

'Oho!' thought Arkady, and only then in a flash did all the fathomless depths of Bazarov's conceit dawn upon him. 'So you and I are gods, are we? Or rather, you are a god while I'm one of the louts, I suppose?'

'Yes,' repeated Bazarov gloomily, 'you're still a fool.'

Madame Odintsov expressed no particular surprise when Arkady told her the next day that he was going with Bazarov; she seemed preoccupied and weary. Katya gazed at him in silent gravity; the princess went so far as to cross herself under her shawl so that he could not help noticing it; but Sitnikov, on the other hand, was quite disconcerted. He had just come down for breakfast in a modish new costume, this time not of 'Slavophil' cut; the previous evening he had astonished the valet placed at his disposal by the quantity of linen he had brought with him, and now all of a sudden his friends were deserting him. He took a few mincing steps, doubled back like a hunted hare at the edge of a covert – and abruptly, almost panic-stricken, almost with a wail, announced that he too proposed to leave. Madame Odintsov did not attempt to detain him.

'I have a very comfortable carriage,' added the luckless young man, turning to Arkady. 'I can give you a lift while Yevgeny Vassilyich takes your tarantass. That will suit even better.'

'But really, it's quite off your road, and it's a long way to where I live.'

'Never mind, that's nothing. I have plenty of time, besides I have business in that direction.'

'Farm commerce?' Arkady inquired, a shade too contemptuously.

But Sitnikov was in such a state of desperation that he forebore to giggle in his usual fashion.

'I assure you, my carriage is exceedingly comfortable,' he muttered; 'and there will be room for everyone.'

'Don't wound Monsieur Sitnikov by refusing ...' murmured Anna Sergeyevna.

Arkady glanced at her and bowed significantly.

The visitors left after breakfast. As she said good-bye to Bazarov Madame Odintsov held out her hand to him and asked: 'We shall meet again, shall we not?'

'As you command,' answered Bazarov.

'In that case, we shall.'

Arkady was the first to go down the steps and clamber into Sitnikov's barouche. With equal readiness he could gladly have struck the servant who tucked him in obsequiously, or burst into tears. Bazarov seated himself in the tarantass. On reaching Khokhlovsky Arkady waited while Fiodr, the keeper of the posting-station, harnessed a fresh team of horses, then going up to the tarantass he said to Bazarov with his old smile: 'Yevgeny, take me with you, I want to come to your place.'

'Get in,' Bazarov growled between his teeth.

Sitnikov, who had been walking up and down and whistling cheerfully by the wheels of his carriage, could only open his mouth and gape when he heard these words and saw Arkady coolly retrieve his belongings, get in beside Bazarov and with a polite bow to his former travelling companion shout 'Drive off!' The tarantass rolled away and was soon out of sight. . . . Finally taken aback, Sitnikov looked at his coachman but the latter was flicking his whip round the tail of the off-side horse. Then Sitnikov jumped into his carriage – and shouting at two peasants who happened to be passing, 'Put on your caps, you idiots!' he dragged himself off to the town, where he arrived very late and where the following day, at Madame Kukshin's, he spoke roundly of a couple of 'nasty, stuck-up, ignorant fellows'.

When he was seated in the tarantass beside Bazarov Arkady pressed his friend's hand warmly, and for a long while said nothing. Bazarov seemed to understand and appreciate both the gesture and the silence. He had not slept at all the whole of the night before, neither had he smoked, and for several days he had scarcely eaten anything. His gaunt profile stood out, grim and sharp, from under his cap, which was pulled down over his eyes.

'Well, brother,' he said at last, 'give me a cigar. And by the way, is my tongue all coated?'

'Yes, it is,' answered Arkady.

'I thought so.... And the cigar tastes horrid. The works have broken down.'

'You certainly have changed lately,' Arkady remarked.

'Never mind! We shall recover. Only one thing bothers me – my mother fusses so. If you don't grow a pot-belly and have a dozen meals a day she worries herself to death. My father, now, is all right: he's knocked about the world and knows the ups and downs of life. No, I can't smoke,' he added, and flung the cigar away into the dusty road.

'It must be another sixteen miles or so to your place, I suppose?' asked Arkady.

'Yes. But inquire of this sage here.' He indicated the peasant in the driver's seat, one of Fiodr's men.

But the sage only answered, 'Who's to know – the miles ain't bin measured out in these parts,' and went on swearing under his breath at the shaft horse for 'kicking with her head-piece' – by which he meant jerking her head.

'Yes, indeed,' Bazarov began, 'let this be a lesson to you, my young friend, an instructive example set before you. God knows, all is vanity in this world! Everyone hangs by a thread, at any moment the abyss may open beneath our feet, and yet we go out of our way to invent all sorts of trouble for ourselves to spoil our lives.'

'What are you driving at?' asked Arkady.

'I'm not driving at anything. I am saying straight out that we've both of us behaved like fools. What's the use of talking about it! But I noticed when I was working in hospital – the patient who's furious at his illness is sure to get over it.'

'I don't quite understand you,' remarked Arkady. 'I should have thought you had nothing to complain of.'

'If you don't quite follow me, let me tell you this: to my

mind it's better to break stones on the road than to allow a woman to obtain a hold over even so much as the tip of your little finger. That's all . . .' Bazarov was on the point of uttering his favourite word, 'romanticism', but he checked himself and said 'rubbish. You won't believe me now but I tell you: you and I have been in feminine society, and very nice we found it; but to throw off that society – it's like taking a dip in cold water on a hot day. A man has no time for such trifling; as an excellent Spanish proverb says, "A man ought not to be tame". Now you, my clever fellow,' he went on, addressing the peasant on the box, 'have you a wife?'

The peasant turned his dull bleary-eyed face towards the two young friends.

'A wife, you say? Aye. Every man has a wife, don't they?'

'Do you beat her?'

'My wife? Acourse I might. If she give me good cause for it.'

'That's excellent. Well, and does she beat you?'

The peasant gave his reins a jerk. 'What a thing to say, sir. You like your joke.' He was obviously offended.

'You hear, Arkady? But you and I have taken a proper beating. . . . That's what comes of being educated people.'

Arkady laughed a forced laugh, while Bazarov turned away and did not open his mouth again for the rest of the journey.

The sixteen miles seemed to Arkady quite forty. But at last, on the slope of some gently rising ground, the little village came into sight where Bazarov's parents lived. Near by, in a young birch copse, stood a small house with a thatched roof. Two peasants with their caps on stood outside the first of the cottages, swearing at each other. 'You're a hulking swine,' one of them was saying, 'and that is worse'n being a little 'un.' – 'An' your wife's a witch,' retorted the other.

'By their free and easy ways,' Bazarov remarked, 'and their lively turns of speech you can guess that my father's peasants are not too ground down. But there he is himself, coming out on the steps of the house. He must have heard the bells.

It's him all right – I recognize his figure. But how grey he's
grown, poor old chap!'

20

Bazarov leaned out of the tarantass while Arkady, peering
over his friend's shoulder, caught sight of a tall thinnish
man with tousled hair and a sharp aquiline nose standing on
the steps of a small house, dressed in an old military jacket,
not buttoned up. He stood there with his legs apart, smoking
a long pipe and screwing up his eyes against the sun.

The horses stopped.

'So you have come at last!' exclaimed Bazarov's father,
still continuing to smoke though the pipe was fairly jumping
up and down between his fingers. 'Come, get out, get out,
let me hug you.'

He began embracing his son ... 'My little Yevgeny, my
baby,' cried a woman's quavering voice. The door flew open
and a plump little old woman in a white cap and a short
striped jacket came running down the steps. She gave a moan,
staggered and would certainly have fallen had not Bazarov
supported her. Her plump little hands immediately clasped
him round the neck, her head was pressed to his chest, and
there was a complete hush, interrupted only by the sound of
her convulsive sobs.

Old Bazarov breathed hard and screwed up his eyes more
than ever.

'There, that's enough, that's enough, Arina! Stop it now,'
he said, exchanging a glance with Arkady, who remained
standing motionless by the tarantass; even the peasant-driver
on the box-seat had turned his head away. 'This is quite
unnecessary! Do stop, please.'

'Ah, Vassily Ivanych,' faltered the old woman, 'such ages
it is since I saw my Yevgeny, my own, my darling boy ...'
and still keeping her arms clasped round him she drew back
her wrinkled face, wet with tears and working with emotion,

and gazed at him with blissful and yet somehow comic eyes, and then again fell on his neck.

'Well, yes, of course, it's all very natural,' commented Vassily Ivanych, 'only we had better come indoors. Yevgeny's brought a visitor with him. You must excuse this,' he added, turning to Arkady and slightly scraping the ground with his foot, 'you understand, a woman's weaknesses, and, well, a mother's heart . . .'

But his own lips and eyebrows were twitching too, and his chin trembled . . . though he was obviously trying to master his feelings and appear almost indifferent. Arkady bowed.

'Let's go in, mother, really,' said Bazarov, and he led the enfeebled old woman into the house. Putting her in a comfortable armchair, he once more hurriedly embraced his father and then presented Arkady.

'Heartily glad to make your acquaintance,' said Vassily Ivanych, 'but you mustn't expect too much : we live a simple soldierly life here. Arina, my dear, pray oblige us and calm yourself. Oh, fie, to give way like that ! What will our visitor think of you !'

'My dear,' said the old woman through her tears, 'I do not know the gentleman's name . . .'

'Arkady Nikolayevich,' her husband prompted ceremoniously in a low voice.

'You must forgive a foolish old woman,' and she blew her nose, and bending her head from left to right carefully wiped one eye after the other. 'Pray excuse me. You see, I thought I should die – that I should never live to see my da . . . arling again.'

'Well, we have lived to see him again, madam,' put in Vassily Ivanych. 'Tanya,' he said, turning to a bare-legged girl of about thirteen in a bright red cotton dress, who was timidly peeping in at the door, 'bring your mistress a glass of water – on a tray, do you hear? – and you, gentlemen,' he added with a kind of old-fashioned sprightliness, 'allow me to invite you into the study of a retired old veteran.'

'Just one more little kiss first,' Arina Vlassyevna cried to her son. Bazarov bent down to her. 'Gracious, how handsome you've grown!'

'Well, I don't know about being handsome,' remarked Vassily Ivanych, 'but he's a man, as the saying goes – *ommfey*.* And now, I hope, Arina Vlassyevna, now that you have satisfied your maternal heart you will turn your thoughts to satisfying the appetites of our dear guests, because, as you know, a hungry belly has no ears.'

The old lady got up from her armchair.

'This very minute, Vassily Ivanych, the table shall be laid. I will run along to the kitchen myself and order the samovar to be got ready. Everything shall be done, everything. Why, I haven't set eyes on him, haven't given him food or drink for three whole years – do you call that nothing?'

'Well, you see to things, my little housewife. Bustle about now, and don't disgrace us; and you, gentlemen, I beg you to come with me. Ah, here is Timofeich to pay his respects to you, Yevgeny. He's delighted, too, I daresay, the old rascal. Eh, you're glad, aren't you, you old rascal? Now pray follow me.'

And Vassily Ivanych fussily led the way, shuffling and flapping along in his down-at-heel slippers.

His whole house consisted of six tiny rooms. One of these – the room into which he conducted our friends – was called the study. A thick-legged table, littered with papers black with the accumulation of ancient dust and looking as if they had been smoked, occupied the entire space between the two windows; on the walls hung Turkish firearms, whips, a sabre, two maps, some anatomical diagrams, a portrait of Hufeland,† a monogram woven out of hair in a blackened frame

* *homme fait.*

† Christoph Wilhelm Hufeland, 1762–1836, German physicist whose best known treatise, *Makrobiotik, or The Art of Prolonging Life*, has been widely translated.

and a diploma under glass; a leather sofa, torn and worn hollow in places, stood between two enormous cupboards of Karelian birch; the shelves were packed with a jumble of books, little boxes, stuffed birds, jars and phials; in one corner lay a broken electric battery.

'I warned you, my dear Arkady Nikolayevich, that we live here, as it were, in camp . . .'

'Do stop apologizing all the time,' Bazarov interrupted him. 'Kirsanov knows very well that you and I are not Croesus and that you don't own a palace. Where shall we put him, that's the question?'

'For pity's sake, Yevgeny, there's a splendid room in the little wing: he will be very comfortable there.'

'So you've had a new wing built on?'

'To be sure, sir, where the bath-house is, sir,' put in Timofeich.

'That is to say, next to the bath-house,' the father hastened to explain. 'It's summer now . . . I will run over and see that everything is in order; meanwhile you, Timofeich, bring in their luggage. And, of course, I shall turn my study over to you, Yevgeny. *Suum cuique.*'*

'There you have him! A comical old chap with a heart of gold,' remarked Bazarov as soon as Vassily Ivanych had gone. 'Just as queer a fish as your father, only in a different way. Never stops talking.'

'And your mother seems a wonderful woman,' Arkady observed.

'Yes, there's no humbug about her. You just see what a dinner she'll give us.'

'We weren't expecting you today, sir; they've not brought any beef,' said Timofeich, who had just dragged in Bazarov's trunk.

'We can manage without beef. One can't do the impossible. Poverty, they say, is no crime.'

'How many serfs has your father?' Arkady asked suddenly.

* To each his own.

195

'The property is not his but mother's; there are fifteen serfs, if I remember rightly.'

'All of twenty-two,' Timofeich remarked with displeasure.

There was a sound of shuffling slippers and Vassily Ivanych reappeared.

'In a few minutes your room will be ready to receive you,' he exclaimed triumphantly, 'Arkady ... Nikolayevich? That's right, isn't it? And here is your valet,' he added, indicating a boy with close-cropped hair who had come in with him, wearing a long blue kaftan with holes in the elbows and a pair of boots which did not belong to him. 'His name is Fedka, and for all my son's injunctions I must ask you again not to expect too much. The lad knows how to fill a pipe, though. You smoke, of course?'

'I generally smoke cigars,' answered Arkady.

'And you're quite right there. I give my preference to cigars too, but they're extremely difficult to get in these remote parts.'

'There, that's enough of the poor-man stuff,' Bazarov interrupted him again. 'You had better sit down on the sofa here and let me have a look at you.'

Vassily Ivanych laughed and sat down. He was very much like his son in face, only the forehead was lower and narrower and his mouth rather wider, and he was never still – either shrugging his shoulder as though his coat cut him under the armpits, or blinking his eyes, clearing his throat and gesticulating with his fingers, while his son was distinguished by a certain detached immobility.

'Poor-man stuff!' Vassily Ivanych echoed. 'You must not imagine, Yevgeny, that I wish, as it were, to excite our guest's sympathies by complaining that we live out in the wilds. On the contrary, I maintain that for a thinking man there is no such thing as a wilderness. At least, I do my best, so far as I can, not to let myself get overgrown with moss, and to keep up with the times.'

Vassily Ivanych pulled a new yellow silk handkerchief

from his pocket, which he had found time to snatch up on the way to Arkady's room, and flourishing it in the air he went on: 'I am not now alluding to the fact that, for instance, at the cost of some considerable sacrifice to myself, I have put my peasants on the rent system and given up my land to them in return for half the crops. I regarded that as my duty; common sense itself enjoins such a proceeding, although other landowners in the neighbourhood do not even dream of doing so. No, I am speaking now of the sciences, of education.'

'Yes, I see you have here *The Friend of Health* for 1855,' remarked Bazarov.

'An old comrade of mine sends them to me for old times' sake,' Vassily Ivanych replied hastily. 'But we have, for instance, even some idea of phrenology,' he added, addressing himself principally to Arkady and pointing to a small plaster head divided into numbered squares, which stood on top of the cupboard. 'Yes indeed – nor are we ignorant of Schönlein* and Rademacher.'

'Why, do people still believe in Rademacher in this province?' asked Bazarov.

Vassily Ivanych cleared his throat.

'In the province ... Of course, you know better, gentlemen; how could we keep up with you? You are here to take our places. When we were young there was a so-called *humoralist* – one Hoffmann – and a certain Brown with his *vitalism*. They seemed quite ridiculous to us but they had great reputations in their day. Now with you someone new has taken the place of Rademacher, and you bow down to him, but in another twenty years no doubt it will be his turn to be laughed at.'

'Let me tell you by way of consolation,' said Bazarov, 'that nowadays we laugh at medicine in general, and worship no one.'

---

* Johann Lukas Schönlein, 1793–1864, German physician noted for his discoveries in parasitic diseases.

'How can that be? Why, you intend to become a doctor, don't you?'

'I do, but the one doesn't rule out the other.'

Vassily Ivanych poked his middle finger into his pipe, where a little smouldering ash was still left.

'Perhaps so, perhaps so, I won't argue the point. For who am I? A retired army doctor, *volla-too*,* who happens to have taken up farming. I served in your grandfather's brigade,' he said, speaking to Arkady again. 'Yes, oh yes, many's the sight I've seen in my time. And I was thrown into all kinds of society, brought into contact with all sorts of important people! I myself, the man you see before you now, have felt the pulse of Prince Wittgenstein, and Zhukovsky's too! They were with the Southern Army of 1814, you understand' (and here Vassily Ivanych pursed his lips significantly). 'I knew every one of them. But of course my department was separate from theirs: my business was the lancet, and no more. Your grandfather, now, was a very fine man, a real soldier.'

'Confess now, he was a real old dunderhead,' remarked Bazarov lazily.

'Ah, Yevgeny, how can you say such things! Do consider.... Of course, General Kirsanov was not one of the ...'

'Well, never mind him,' Bazarov interrupted. 'I was pleased to see your birch copse as we were driving along here: it has shot up splendidly.'

Vassily Ivanych brightened. 'And you must see the little garden I've got now. I planted every tree in it myself. I've got fruit-trees, raspberry canes and all kinds of medicinal herbs. Ah, my young sirs, however wise you may be in your generation, old Paracelsus† put his finger on the truth: *in herbis, verbis et lapidibus* ... I've retired from practice, as

---

* *voilà tout.*

† Theophrastus Bombast von Hohenheim, c. 1490–1541, Swiss physician, chemist and natural philosopher, who styled himself Philippus Aureolus Paracelsus.

you know, but at least once or twice a week I am obliged to revert to my old pastime. They will come for advice – I can't drive them away. It may be some poor person needs help. There are no doctors in the locality. One of the neighbours here, a retired major, just imagine it, does some doctoring too. I made some inquiries – had he studied medicine? and was told, "No, he hasn't ever studied, he does it more out of philanthropy" ... Ha, ha, ha – out of philanthropy! What do you think of that? Ha, ha, ha!'

'Fedka, fill me a pipe,' said Bazarov curtly.

'And there was another doctor who came to visit a patient here,' Vassily Ivanych continued in a kind of desperation, 'but the patient had already gone *ad patres*. The servant wouldn't let the doctor in, "No need for you now," he tells him. The doctor did not expect this: he gets taken aback and asks, "Tell me, did your master hiccup before he died?" – "Yes, sir, he did." – "A lot?" – "A lot." – "Ah well, that's all right," and off he went home again. Ha, ha, ha!'

The old man was the only one to laugh. Arkady forced a smile. Bazarov merely puffed at his pipe. The conversation continued in this wise for about an hour; Arkady managed to slip away for a moment to his room, which turned out to be the vestibule to the bath-house, but was very snug and clean. At last Tanya came in to announce that dinner was ready.

Vassily Ivanych was the first to get up. 'Come along, gentlemen. You must be magnanimous and pardon me if I have bored you. I daresay my good wife will give you better satisfaction.'

The dinner, though prepared in haste, turned out to be very good, even sumptuous; only the wine was not quite up to the mark, as they say: the almost black sherry, which Timofeich had procured from a wine merchant of his acquaintance, tasted slightly of copper or resin; and the flies were a nuisance too. On ordinary days a serf-boy used to keep them off with a big leafy branch; but on this occasion Vassily Ivanych had sent him away for fear of adverse comment from the younger generation. The mistress of the house had changed her dress and was wearing a high cap with silk ribbons, and a pale-blue embroidered shawl. She broke down again when she saw her little Yevgeny but her husband had no need to admonish her, for she was quick to dry her tears lest they should stain her shawl. Only the young men ate: the old folk had dined long ago. Fedka waited at table, obviously encumbered by his unfamiliar boots; he was assisted by a young woman of masculine looks and one eye, who went by the name of Anfisushka and performed the duties of housekeeper, poultry-woman and laundress. Throughout the meal Vassily Ivanych marched up and down the room, and with a completely happy, positively blissful countenance talked about the grave anxieties roused in him by Napoleon III's policy and the complications of the Italian question. His wife paid no attention to Arkady, she did not even press him to eat; propping her round face on her little fist – her full cherry-coloured lips and the moles on her cheeks and over her eyebrows gave her a most benign expression – she never took her eyes off her son and kept sighing; she was dying to find out how long he intended to stay but was afraid to ask him. 'What if he should say – for two days?' she thought to herself, and her heart would stop beating. After the roast Vassily Ivanych disappeared for a moment and returned with an opened half-bottle of champagne.

'Here,' he exclaimed, 'though we do live in the wilds, we have something to make merry with on festive occasions!' He filled three champagne-glasses and a wine-glass, proposed a toast to 'our inestimable guests' and at once tossed off his glass in military fashion and made his wife drain her wineglass to the last drop. When the time came for the preserves Arkady, who could not bear anything sweet, deemed it his duty, however, to taste four different kinds which had been freshly made – all the more so since Bazarov flatly refused them and immediately lit a cigar. Afterwards tea was served with cream, butter and cracknel-biscuits; then Vassily Ivanych took them all out into the garden to admire the beauty of the evening. As they passed a certain bench he whispered to Arkady: 'This is where I love to sit and meditate as I watch the sunset: it is just the spot for a hermit like me. And over there I have planted some of the trees beloved of Horace.'

'What trees are they?' asked Bazarov, overhearing.

'Why . . . acacias.'

Bazarov began to yawn.

'I suppose it is time for our travellers to fall into the arms of Morpheus,' observed Vassily Ivanych.

'You mean it's time for bed,' Bazarov put in. 'An opinion which is quite correct. It certainly is high time.'

Bidding his mother good night, he kissed her on the forehead while she embraced him and stealthily, behind his back, made the sign of the cross three times in blessing. Vassily Ivanych conducted Arkady to his room and wished him 'such sweet repose as I myself enjoyed when I was your happy age'. And Arkady did, in fact, sleep extremely well in the annexe to the bath-house: it smelt of mint, and two crickets behind the stove vied with each other in drowsy chirping. After leaving Arkady Vassily Ivanych repaired to his study, where he settled himself on the sofa at his son's feet, looking forward to having a chat with him; but Bazarov sent him away at once, saying that he felt sleepy, though actually he did not fall asleep till morning. With wide-open eyes he stared angrily into the darkness; memories of childhood had no power over him, and besides, he had not yet succeeded in shaking off the bitter impression of his recent experiences. As for his mother, she first poured out her heart in prayer and then indulged in a long, long conversation with Anfisushka, who stood stock-still before her mistress and, fixing her solitary eye upon her, communicated in a mysterious whisper all her observations and conjectures regarding the young master. The old lady's head was giddy with happiness, wine and tobacco-smoke; her husband tried to talk to her but gave it up as a bad job.

Arina Vlassyevna was a true Russian gentlewoman of the old school; she ought to have lived a couple of centuries earlier, in the days of Muscovy. Very devout and emotional, she believed in fortune-telling, charms, dreams and omens of every conceivable kind; she believed in half-crazy visionaries, in house-spirits, in wood-sprites, in unlucky encounters, in the evil eye, in folk remedies, in salt prepared on Maundy Thursday, and the imminent end of the world; she believed that if the candles carried in procession during the Easter night service did not go out there would be a good crop of buckwheat, and that a mushroom will stop growing if a human eye has looked on it; she believed that the devil likes to be where there is water, and that every Jew has a blood-red mark on his breast; she was afraid of mice, adders, frogs, sparrows, leeches, thunder, of cold water, draughts, of horses, goats, red-haired people and black cats; she regarded crickets and dogs as unclean creatures; she never ate veal, pigeon, crayfish, cheese, asparagus, Jerusalem artichokes, hares or water-melons because a sliced water-melon suggested the head of John the Baptist; the mere mention of oysters made her shudder; she loved food – but fasted strictly; she slept ten hours out of the twenty-four – but never went to bed at all if her husband had so much as a headache; she never read a single book except *Alexis, or The Cottage in the Forest*; she wrote one, or at the most two letters in a year, but she was an expert housewife and knew all about preserving and jam-making though she did not touch a thing with her own hands and was generally reluctant to move from her chair. Arina Vlassyevna was very kindhearted, and in her way far from stupid. She knew that the world is divided into the gentry who were there to give orders and the common people whose duty it was to serve – and so she felt no repugnance against servile behaviour and obsequiousness; but she was always gentle and considerate with subordinates, never let a single beggar go away empty-handed, and though she gossiped at times she never criticized anyone. In her youth she had been very comely, had played the clavichord and spoken French a little; but in the course of many years of wandering with her husband, to whom she had been married against her will, she had grown stout and forgotten both her music and her French. Her son she loved and feared to an inexpressible degree; she let her husband manage her property and no longer took any part in it, groaning, waving her handkerchief about and raising her eyebrows higher and higher in horror directly he broached the subject of impending land reforms and his own plans. She was apprehensive, always expecting some disaster, and would burst into tears whenever she remembered anything sad ... Nowadays such women as she have ceased to exist. Heaven only knows whether this should be a matter for rejoicing!

21

Getting out of bed in the morning, Arkady flung the window open, and the first object which met his eye was Vassily Ivanych. In a Turkish dressing-gown, tied round the waist with a pocket-handkerchief, the old man was digging away in his kitchen garden. Seeing his young visitor and leaning on his spade, he called out: 'Good morning to you! How did you sleep?'

'Splendidly,' answered Arkady.

'And here am I, as you can see, like some Cincinnatus, marking out a bed for late turnips. The time has come now – and thank God for it! – when each one of us must secure his sustenance by the work of his own hands; it is no use relying on others – one must labour oneself. Thus Jean-Jacques Rousseau is right. Half an hour ago, my dear sir, you might have seen me in a very different rôle. One peasant-woman came complaining of the "gripes", as they call it – dysentery is

our term – and there was I ... how can I put it best? ...
There was I pumping opium into her; while another wanted
a tooth extracted. I offered her an anaesthetic ... but she
wouldn't hear of it. I do all that gratis – *anamatyor*.* However, I'm used to it; you see, I'm a plebeian, *homo novus* –
I am not of ancient lineage like my dear spouse ... Wouldn't
you like to come out here in the shade and breathe the morning freshness before having tea?'

Arkady joined him.

'Welcome once again!' said Vassily Ivanych, raising his
hand in a military salute to the greasy skull-cap which covered
his head. 'You, I know, are accustomed to luxury and enjoyment, but even the great ones of this world would not disdain
to spend a short time under a cottage roof.'

'Good heavens,' protested Arkady, 'as though I were one of
the great ones of this world! And I'm not accustomed to
luxury either.'

'Pardon me, pardon me,' Vassily Ivanych retorted with a
polite simper. 'Though I'm a back number now, I have
knocked about the place in my time – I know a bird by its
flight. I am something of a psychologist, too, in my own
fashion, and a physiognomist. If I had not possessed that gift,
as I venture to call it, I should have come to grief long ago, I
should have been jostled out of the way, an unimportant
little man like me. I tell you without flattery, I am truly delighted by the friendship I observe between you and my son.
Only this morning I was speaking to him : he got up very
early as he usually does – no doubt you know that habit of
his – and went careering off round the countryside. Might
I be so curious as to inquire – have you known my son
long?'

'Since last winter.'

'Indeed. And permit me to question you further – but why
shouldn't we sit down? Permit me as a father to ask you
frankly – what is your opinion of my Yevgeny?'

* *en amateur.*

'Your son is one of the most remarkable men I have ever met,' Arkady replied with animation.

Vassily Ivanych's eyes suddenly opened wide and a faint flush suffused his cheeks. The spade dropped from his hand.

'And so you expect . . .' he began.

'I'm convinced,' Arkady took him up, 'that your son has a great future before him; that he will do honour to your name. I've felt sure of that ever since I first met him.'

'How – how did that happen?' articulated Vassily Ivanych with some effort. A rapturous smile had parted his broad lips and would not leave them.

'Would you like me to tell you how we met?'

'Yes . . . and altogether . . .'

Arkady launched forth and spoke of Bazarov with even greater warmth and enthusiasm than he had on the evening when he danced a mazurka with Madame Odintsov.

Vassily Ivanych listened and listened, blew his nose, rolled his handkerchief up into a ball with both hands, cleared his throat, ruffled his hair – until, unable to contain himself any longer, he bent down and kissed Arkady on the shoulder.

'You have made me utterly and completely happy,' he said, still smiling all the while. 'I ought to tell you, I . . . worship my son! I won't even speak of my good wife – we all know what mothers are! – but I dare not show my feelings in front of him, because he doesn't like it. He is against every kind of demonstration of feeling; many people even find fault with him for such strength of character, and take it for a sign of arrogance or lack of sensibility; but men like him ought not to be judged by any ordinary standards, ought they? For example, others in his place would have been a constant drag on their parents; but he – would you believe it? – from the day he was born he has never taken a penny more than he could help, that is God's truth!'

'He's a sincere, single-minded man,' observed Arkady.

'Exactly so. And I not only worship him, Arkady Nikolaye-vich, I am proud of him, and the height of my ambition is that some day the following lines will appear in his biography: "The son of an ordinary army-doctor, who was able, however, to recognize his talents early in life and spared no pains for his education ..." ' The old man's voice broke.

Arkady pressed his hand.

'What do you think now?' Vassily Ivanych asked after a short silence. 'Surely the field of medicine will not bring him the fame you anticipate for him?'

'Of course, not in medicine, though even in that department he will be one of the leading scientific men.'

'In what field then, Arkady Nikolayevich?'

'It would be hard to say now, but he is bound to be famous.'

'Bound to be famous!' the old man repeated, and then relapsed into thought.

'The mistress sent me to call you in to tea,' announced Anfisushka, walking by with a huge dish of ripe raspberries.

Vassily Ivanych started. 'And will there be any cold cream with the raspberries?'

'Yes, sir.'

'Cold now, mind! Don't stand on ceremony, Arkady Nikolayevich, but help yourself. I wonder why Yevgeny doesn't come back?'

'I'm here,' called Bazarov's voice from Arkady's room.

His father turned round quickly.

'Aha, you wanted to pay a visit to your friend; but you were too late, *amice*, and he and I have already had a long chat together. Now we must go in to breakfast, mother is calling us. Incidentally, I must have a word with you.'

'What about?'

'There's a peasant here; he's suffering from icterus. I have prescribed centaury and St John's wort, told him to eat carrots and given him soda; but all these are merely palliative measures; we need more radical treatment. Though you laugh at medicine I'm sure you can give me some practical advice. But we will talk of that later. Now let us go in and drink some tea.'

He jumped up briskly from the garden seat and burst into an air from *Robert le Diable* : *

> 'A rule, a rule, let us set ourselves
> To live, to live for our own delight!'

'Astonishing vitality!' observed Bazarov, moving away from the window.

Midday came. A scorching sun shone through a diaphanous veil of whitish clouds. Everything was still: only the cocks in the village crowed lustily, producing a curious drowsy lethargy in all who heard them; and somewhere high up in the tree-tops a young hawk repeated its incessant, querulous cheep. Arkady and Bazarov lay in the shade of a small hay-stack: they had made pillows for themselves of two armfuls of grass which rustled drily though it was still green and fragrant.

'That poplar-tree,' Bazarov remarked, 'reminds me of my childhood: it grows on the edge of the pit where the brick kiln used to be, and in those days I firmly believed that the clay-pit and the poplar constituted a special talisman: I never found time hang heavy on my hands when I was near them. I did not understand then that the reason time did not hang heavy was because I was a young boy. Well, now I'm grown up, the talisman no longer works.'

'How long did you live here altogether?' asked Arkady.

'A couple of years on end; then we travelled about. We led a vagabond life, traipsing from town to town for the most part.'

'And has this house been standing long?'

'Yes, quite a time. My grandfather built it – my mother's father.'

'Who was he, your grandfather?'

* French opera by Meyerbeer, 1791–1863.

'The devil knows – an army major of some sort. He served under Suvorov* and was always telling us how they crossed the Alps – made it up probably.'

'I noticed you have a portrait of Suvorov hanging in the sitting-room. I like little houses like yours: they're cosy and old-fashioned; and they always seem to have a smell of their own somehow.'

'A smell of lamp oil and clover,' Bazarov replied with a yawn. 'But the flies in these dear little houses – ugh!'

'Tell me,' Arkady resumed after a short pause, 'were they strict with you as a child?'

'You can see what my parents are like. They're not the severe sort.'

'Are you fond of them, Yevgeny?'

'I am, Arkady.'

'They adore you!'

Bazarov was silent for a while. 'Do you know what I'm thinking?' he said at last, clasping his hands behind his head.

'No. What?'

'I'm thinking what a happy life my parents lead! At the age of sixty my father can still find plenty to do, talks about "palliative measures", treats patients, plays the bountiful lord of the manor with the peasants – has a gay time of it in fact; and my mother's happy too: her days are so chockful of all sorts of occupations, sighs and groans, that she doesn't know where she is; while I . . .'

'While you?'

'While I think: here I lie under a haystack. . . . The tiny bit of space I occupy is so minute in comparison with the rest of the universe, where I am not and which is not concerned with me; and the period of time in which it is my lot to live is so infinitesimal compared with the eternity in which I have

* Prince Alexander Suvorov, 1729–1800, Russian generalissimo who, after defeating Napoleon in Italy, wanted to invade France but was obliged to retreat to southern Germany through the Swiss Alps. This retreat has been considered one of the great feats of military history.

not been and shall not be ... And yet here, in this atom which is myself, in this mathematical point, blood circulates, the brain operates and aspires to something too ... What a monstrous business! What futility!'

'Allow me to point out that what you are saying applies generally to everyone ...'

'You are right,' Bazarov took him up. 'I wanted to say that they, my parents, I mean, are so busy, they don't worry about their own insignificance. It doesn't stick in their throat ... whereas I ... I feel nothing but depression and rancour.'

'Rancour? Why rancour?'

'Why? How can you ask why? Have you forgotten?'

'I remember everything but I still can't allow that you have any right to be vexed and angry. You're unhappy, I agree, but ...'

'Ugh! I can see, Arkady Nikolayevich, that your idea of love is the same as that of all the other young men of this new generation. "Cluck, cluck, cluck," you call to the hen, and the moment the hen comes anywhere near you, you run for your life! I am different. But that's enough of that. What can't be cured must be endured.' He turned over on his side. 'Aha! there goes a valiant ant dragging off a half-dead fly. Take her away, brother, take her away! Never mind her resistance: avail yourself of your animal right to feel no compassion – not like us poor self-destructive brethren!'

'You shouldn't say that, Yevgeny! When have you destroyed yourself?'

Bazarov raised his head.

'That's the only thing I'm proud of. I have not destroyed myself, and no female shall break me. Amen! That's the end of it. You won't hear another word from me on the subject.'

The two friends lay for a while in silence.

'Yes,' Bazarov began, 'man is a strange creature. Contemplating from a distance the God-forsaken life our old folk lead here, one thinks: what could be better? You eat and drink, and you know you always do the right thing in the right way. But not a bit of it, you die of boredom. One needs people, even if it's only to have someone to swear at.'

'One ought to arrange one's life so that every moment of it is important,' remarked Arkady thoughtfully.

'I dare say! The significant is sweet, however deceptive. But one can also come to terms with the insignificant. . . . But petty troubles, petty troubles . . . that's what's unbearable.'

'Petty troubles don't exist for the man who refuses to recognize them as such.'

'H'm . . . what you've just said is a platitude turned upside down.'

'A what? What do you mean by that?'

'I'll tell you: to say, for instance, that education is beneficial is a platitude; but to say that education is injurious is an inverted platitude. It's got more dash to it but fundamentally it's the same thing.'

'And the truth is where, on which side?'

'Where? Like an echo I answer "Where?"'

'You're in a melancholy mood today, Yevgeny.'

'Am I? The sun must have softened my brain, and I ought not to have eaten so many raspberries either.'

'In that case it wouldn't be a bad idea to have a nap,' observed Arkady.

'Maybe; only don't look at me: everyone looks silly when they're asleep.'

'Surely it's all the same to you, what people think of you?'

'I don't quite know how to answer that. A proper man ought not to care: a proper man is one people don't have opinions about, he is either obeyed or detested.'

'It's odd, I don't detest anyone,' Arkady remarked after a moment's reflection.

'And I hate lots of people. You're a soft-hearted mawkish individual, how could you hate anyone? . . . You're timid, you've no confidence in yourself . . .'

'And you,' Arkady interrupted him, 'have you confidence in yourself? Have you a high opinion of yourself?'

Bazarov was silent.

'When I meet a man who can hold his own with me,' he said with slow deliberation, 'then I'll change my opinion of myself. Hatred! Here's an example for you – this morning as we were walking past the cottage of our bailiff, Philip – the one that's so clean and tidy – you said, "Only when the poorest peasant has a house like that will Russia achieve perfection, and we must all of us work to that end ..." But I've developed a hatred for that "poorest peasant" of yours, that Philip or Sidor for whose sake I'm to be ready to sacrifice my skin and who won't even thank me for it ... and anyway, what do I want with his thanks? Well, suppose he lives in a cottage with a chimney, while burdock grows out of me – so what then?'

'Stop it, Yevgeny ... to hear you today, one can't help agreeing with those who reproach us for having no principles.'

'You talk like your uncle. As a matter of fact principles don't exist – you haven't tumbled to that even yet – there are feelings. Everything depends on them.'

'How's that?'

'Well, take me for instance: I adopt a negative attitude by virtue of something I feel. I like to reject, my brain's made that way, and there's no more to it. Why does chemistry interest me? Why are you fond of apples? It's also a matter of feeling. It's the same thing. Deeper than that men will never penetrate. Not every one will tell you so, and another time I shan't tell you so myself.'

'What about integrity – is that a matter of feeling?'

'Of course!'

'Oh Yevgeny!' Arkady exclaimed sorrowfully.

'Well? What? Not to your taste, eh?' Bazarov broke in. 'No, brother. Once you've made up your mind about something, you must go the whole hog. But we've philosophized enough. "Nature wafts upon us the silence of sleep," said Pushkin.'

'He never said anything of the sort,' protested Arkady.

'Well, if he didn't, as a poet he might have and should have. Incidentally, he must have served in the army.'

'Pushkin was never in the army!'

'Why, on every page one reads "To arms! To arms! For the honour of Russia!"'

'That's pure invention on your part! It's downright calumny.'

'Calumny? There's a weighty matter for you! Thought up a word to frighten me with, didn't you? Slander a man as much as we like, and he will still deserve twenty times worse in reality.'

'We'd better have a snooze,' said Arkady in a tone of vexation.

'With the greatest of pleasure,' Bazarov replied. But neither of them felt like sleep. Both young men were in the grip of something that was almost hostility. After five minutes they opened their eyes and glanced at one another in silence.

'Look,' Arkady suddenly exclaimed, 'a withered maple leaf has come off and is fluttering to the ground: its movements are exactly like a butterfly in flight. Isn't it strange that something so mournful and dead should be like a creature so gay and full of life?'

'Oh come, friend Arkady Nikolayevich,' cried Bazarov, 'one thing I implore of you – no fine talk.'

'I talk the way I know ... And besides, that's absolute tyranny. An idea comes into my head – why shouldn't I express it?'

'All right; but why shouldn't I be allowed to say what I think? I think that sort of fine talk's positively indecent.'

'And what is decent? Abusing people?'

'Aha, so I perceive you really are determined to follow in your worthy uncle's footsteps. How that idiot would rejoice if he heard you!'

'What did you call Uncle Pavel?'

'I merely called him what he is – an idiot.'

'Really, this is intolerable,' cried Arkady.

'Oho, there speaks family feeling,' remarked Bazarov coolly. 'I've noticed how obstinately it sticks to people. A man's ready to abjure everything else, break with every prejudice, but to admit, for instance, that his brother who pinches other chap's handkerchiefs is a thief – that's too much for him. And let's face it: that one's brother – that *my* brother – shouldn't be a genius ... isn't that more than any of us can swallow?'

'I spoke from a sense of justice and out of no family feeling,' Arkady retorted hotly. 'But since you don't know what a sense of justice is, since you lack that sense, you are not in a position to pass judgment on it.'

'In other words, Arkady Kirsanov is too exalted for my understanding. I bend the knee and say no more.'

'Stop it, Yevgeny, please; we shall end by quarrelling.'

'Ah, Arkady, do me a favour, let's quarrel properly for once – go the whole hog.'

'But then we might finish up by ...'

'Tearing one another to pieces?' Bazarov broke in. 'What of it? Here in the hay, in these idyllic surroundings, far from the madding crowd and out of sight, it wouldn't matter. But you'll be no match for me. I'll get you by the throat at once ...'

Bazarov stretched out his long sinewy fingers. Arkady turned round and prepared, as though in fun, to defend himself. ... But the look on his friend's face was so sinister – there seemed to be such real menace in the smile that distorted his lips and in his glinting eyes that he instinctively quailed. ...

'So this is where you have got to!' Vassily Ivanych's voice rang out at that instant, and the old army doctor appeared before the young men, clad in a home-made linen jacket, with a straw hat, also home-made, on his head. 'I've been hunting for you all over the place. ... But you have picked on an excellent spot, and you're giving yourselves up to a fine occupation. Lying on the "earth", gazing at the "heavens".... Do you know – there is an especial significance in that?'

'I only gaze up to heaven when I want to sneeze,' Bazarov growled and, turning to Arkady, he added in an undertone: 'A pity he interrupted us.'

'Shut up,' Arkady whispered back, and he covertly squeezed his friend's hand. But no friendship can bear such strain for long.

'When I look at you, my youthful friends,' Vassily Ivanych was saying, shaking his head and leaning forward with hands clasped on a cunningly twisted stick, which he had made himself with the figure of a Turk carved on it by way of a knob, 'when I look at you, I cannot help marvelling. The physical strength you have, such youth and bloom, such abilities, such talents! Castor and Pollux in person!'

'Get along with you – shooting off into mythology again!' said Bazarov. 'One can tell at once that you were a Latin scholar in your day. Why, if I remember rightly, you won the silver medal for Latin composition, didn't you?'

'The Dioscuri, the Dioscuri themselves!' the old man repeated.

'Enough, father: don't get foolishly sentimental.'

'Just once in a way, surely I may be allowed to,' the old man murmured. 'However, gentlemen, I did not seek you out in order to pay you compliments but with the object, in the first place, of announcing to you that dinner will soon be ready, and, secondly, I wanted to warn you, Yevgeny ... you are a sensible man, you know the world and you know what women are, and therefore you will make allowances.... Your mother decided to have a thanksgiving service on the occasion of your arrival. Don't imagine that I am asking you to attend the service ... it's already over, but Father Alexei ...'

'The village parson?'

'Yes, the priest; he is – to dine with us... I did not expect this and even advised against it ... but somehow or other that's the way it is ... he didn't get me.... Well, and there was your mother too.... Besides, he's a very good worthy man.'

'He won't devour my portion of the food, I suppose?' inquired Bazarov.

The old man laughed. 'The things you say!'

'That's all I ask. I'm ready to sit at table with anyone.'

Vassily Ivanych set his hat straight.

'I was certain before I spoke,' he said, 'that you were above all superstition. And here am I, an old man of sixty-two, and I haven't any superstitious feeling either.' (Vassily Ivanych did not dare to confess that he had himself desired the thanksgiving service. He was no less devout than his wife.) 'And Father Alexei very much wanted to make your acquaintance. You will like him, you'll see. He is not against playing a game of cards either, and he will even ... but this is between ourselves – smoke a pipe.'

'All right then. After dinner we'll settle down to a round of whist, and I'll give him a trouncing.'

'He! he! he! We shall see! We shall see what we shall see.'

'Are you thinking of the old days?' said Bazarov with a peculiar emphasis.

Vassily Ivanych's bronzed cheeks were suffused with an uneasy flush.

'For shame, Yevgeny.... Let bygones be bygones. Well, I am quite ready to confess in front of your friend that I knew that passion in my youth – indeed, I did; and how I paid for it too! ... But how hot it is. May I sit down with you? I shan't be in your way, shall I?'

'Not in the least,' answered Arkady.

With a grunt Vassily Ivanych lowered himself into the hay.

'Your present billet, my dear sirs,' he began, 'reminds me of my camping days in the army, with the field hospital pitched somewhere like this near a hayrick, and that was something to be thankful for.' He sighed. 'I have seen a lot of experience in my time, I have. Now, for example, let me tell you a curious episode about the plague in Bessarabia.'

'For which they awarded you the Vladimir cross?' interrupted Bazarov. 'We know, we know.... By the way, why aren't you wearing it?'

'Why, I told you that I am not one for the conventions,' muttered Vassily Ivanych (only the evening before he had had the red ribbon unpicked from his jacket) and he proceeded to relate his episode of the plague. 'Why, he has fallen asleep,' he whispered suddenly to Arkady, pointing to Yevgeny, with a kindly wink. 'Yevgeny, get up!' he added loudly. 'Let us go and have dinner ...'

Father Alexei, a stout and imposing figure with thick, carefully combed hair and an embroidered sash round his mauve silk cassock, turned out to be a very clever man with a ready wit. He took the initiative and held out his hand to Arkady and Bazarov the moment he saw them, as though realizing in advance that they felt no need of his blessing, and in general bore himself with a complete absence of restraint. He neither belittled himself nor trod on other people's corns; at the right moment he made a joke about Latin as taught in the seminaries and stood up for his bishop; he drank two glasses of wine but declined a third; he accepted a cigar from Arkady but did not smoke it, saying he would take it home with him. The only not altogether agreeable thing about him was his habit of every now and then slowly and carefully raising his hand to catch the flies on his face, and sometimes managing to squash them. He took his seat at the card-table with a moderated show of pleasure and ended by winning from Bazarov two and a half roubles in paper money: in Arina Vlassyevna's house they had no idea of how to reckon in silver.... She sat as before close to her son (she never played cards), and as before she leaned her cheek on her little clenched fist, only getting up when it was necessary to order some fresh delicacy to be brought in. She was afraid to fondle Bazarov, who gave her no encouragement and did not invite her caresses; in addition to which Vassily Ivanych had advised her not to 'worry' him too much. 'Young men don't like that sort of thing,' he kept telling her. (There is no need to enlarge on the dinner that was served that day: Timofeich in person had galloped off at dawn to procure some extra special Circassian beef; the bailiff had gone in another direction for turbot, perch and crayfish; while a sum of forty-two kopecks had been paid to peasant women for mushrooms alone.) But Arina Vlassyevna's eyes, which never left Bazarov, expressed more than tenderness and devotion: there was sadness in them too, mingled with curiosity and awe, and a sort of humble reproach.

Bazarov, however, was in no mood to probe the significance of his mother's expression; he addressed her but rarely, and then only to ask some brief question. Once he asked her for her hand 'for luck'; quietly she laid her soft little hand on his rough broad palm.

'Well,' she inquired after a while, 'did it help?'

'I had worse luck than ever,' he replied with a careless smile.

'He plays too rashly,' pronounced Father Alexei, in a tone of feigned regret, and stroked his handsome beard.

'That was Napoleon's principle, Father, Napoleon's principle,' put in Vassily Ivanych, slamming down an ace.

'And it brought him to St Helena,' observed Father Alexei, and he trumped the ace.

'Wouldn't you like some blackcurrant tea, Yevgeny?' Arina Vlassyevna asked her son.

Bazarov merely shrugged his shoulders.

'No,' he said to Arkady the next day. 'I'm leaving this place tomorrow. I'm bored; I feel like working but I can't work here. I will come to your place again: I left all my apparatus there. In your house one can at least shut oneself in. But here my father keeps on repeating to me: "My study is at your disposal – nobody will disturb you," and all the time he himself is never more than a yard away. And for that matter it gives me an uneasy conscience somehow to shut myself away from him. It's the same with my mother. I can hear her sighing on the other side of the wall, and I go out to her – and find I have nothing to say.'

'She will be very much upset,' observed Arkady, 'and so will he.'

'I shall come back to them.'

'When?'

'Oh, on my way to Petersburg.'

'I feel particularly sorry for your mother.'

'Why? Has she won your heart with her strawberries and blackcurrants?'

Arkady looked down at his feet.

'You don't understand your mother, Yevgeny. She's not only a fine woman, she's very clever really. This morning she talked to me for half an hour, and everything she said was so to the point and interesting.'

'I suppose she was expatiating upon me all the time?'

'We didn't talk only about you.'

'Maybe as a detached observer you can see more clearly than I do. If a woman can keep up a conversation for half an hour, it's already a good sign. But I'm going all the same.'

'It won't be easy for you to break the news to them. They are making plans for us for a fortnight ahead.'

'No, it won't be easy. Some devil prompted me to tease my father this morning: he had one of his rent-paying peasants flogged the other day – and quite rightly too: yes, yes, don't look at me in such horror. He did right because the man in question is a frightful thief and drunkard; only father did not expect that I should become cognisant, as they say, of the facts. He was very much embarrassed, and now I shall have to upset him again . . . Never mind. He'll get over it.'

Bazarov said 'Never mind' but the whole day passed before he could bring himself to acquaint Vassily Ivanych with his intention. At last, when he was just saying good night to him in the study, he remarked with a drawn-out yawn: 'Oh yes ... I almost forgot to tell you ... have our horses sent forward to Fedot's tomorrow.'

Vassily Ivanych was thunderstruck.

'Is Monsieur Kirsanov leaving us then?'

'Yes, and I'm going with him.'

The old man reeled.

'You are going away?'

'Yes ... I must go. See about the horses, will you, please.'

'Very well ...' faltered the old man. 'To the posting-station ... very well ... only ... only.... Why must you?'

'I have to go and stay with him for a short time. Afterwards I will come back here again.'

'Ah! For a short time ... Very well.' Vassily Ivanych pulled out his pocket handkerchief and as he blew his nose doubled up almost to the floor. 'Well, well. It ... it will all be done. I thought you would stay with us ... a little longer. Three days ... after three years ... it's rather little; rather little, Yevgeny.'

'But I tell you, I'm coming back directly. I have to go.'

'You have to.... Oh well. Duty comes before everything.... So you want the horses sent? Very well. Of course your mother and I did not expect this. She has just begged some flowers from a neighbour, to make your room look bright.' (Vassily Ivanych did not mention that both mornings, the moment it was light, standing barefoot in his slippers, he had consulted with Timofeich and, with trembling fingers pulling out one crumpled banknote after another, had charged him with various purchases, particularly of good things to eat and the red wine which, so far as he could see, the young men were very fond of.) 'Freedom's the important thing. That has always been my principle ... one must not get in the way ... not ...'

Suddenly he stopped talking and made for the door.

'We shall soon see each other again, father, really.'

But Vassily Ivanych, without turning round, only waved

his hand and was gone. Back in the bedroom with his wife he found her in bed, and began to say his prayers in a whisper so as not to wake her. However, she did wake.

'Is that you, Vassily Ivanych?' she asked.

'Yes, mother.'

'Have you come from Yevgeny? Do you know, I'm afraid he may not be comfortable on that sofa. I told Anfisushka to put out your camp mattress and the new pillows. I would have given him our feather bed but I seem to remember he doesn't like a soft bed.'

'Never mind, my dear, don't worry now. He's all right. Lord have mercy upon us sinners,' he continued his prayers in a low voice. He felt sorry for his old wife; he did not want to tell her overnight of the grief that was in store for her.

Bazarov and Arkady departed next day. From early morning the house was filled with depression; the plates fell out of Anfisushka's hands; even Fedka did not know what he was doing and ended by taking off his boots. Vassily Ivanych bustled about more than ever: he was obviously trying to make a brave show, talked loudly and stamped his feet on the floor as he walked; but his face was drawn and he studiously avoided looking at his son. Arina Vlassyevna wept quietly: she would have broken down altogether and lost control of herself had not her husband spent two whole hours early in the morning exhorting her. But when Bazarov, after repeated promises to come back within a month at the latest, at last tore himself from their clinging embraces and took his seat in the tarantass; when the horses moved off, the bells tinkled, and the wheels spun round – when there was nothing left to gaze after, the dust had settled and Timofeich, all bent and tottering, had crept back to his tiny room; when the two old people found themselves alone in the house, which suddenly seemed as shrunken and decrepit as they – then Vassily Ivanych, who a few moments before had been vigorously waving his handkerchief on the steps, slumped into a chair and let his head drop on his chest.

'He has gone, left us!' he faltered. 'Gone, because he found it dull here with us. I'm a lonely man now, lonely as this finger,'* he repeated again and again, and each time he thrust out his hand with his forefinger pointing away from the rest. Then Arina Vlassyevna came to his side and pressing her grey head to his grey head she said: 'It can't be helped, Vasya. A son is an independent person. He's like a falcon that comes when he wills and flies off when he lists; but you and I are like the funguses growing in a hollow tree: here we sit side by side, not budging an inch. It is only I who will stay with you always, faithful for ever, just as you will stay with me.'

Vassily Ivanych took his hands from his face and clasped his wife, his friend, more warmly than he had ever done before, even in their youth: she had consoled him in his grief.

22

In silence, exchanging only a few trivial remarks now and then, our friends travelled as far as Fedot's. Bazarov was not altogether pleased with himself, Arkady was anything but pleased with him. His heart was heavy, too, in the grip of that depression which only the very young know and which has no apparent reason. The coachman changed the horses and then, clambering up on to the box, inquired: 'Right, or left, is it?'

Arkady started. The road to the right led to the town, and from there home to his father's; the road to the left led to Madame Odintsov's house.

He looked at Bazarov.

'Yevgeny,' he asked, 'shall we go left?'

Bazarov looked away. 'What folly is this?' he muttered.

'I know it's foolish,' answered Arkady. 'But what does it matter? It's not for the first time.'

* Twenty-two years after writing *Fathers and Sons*, when he was slowly dying of cancer in France, Turgenev used the same simile, saying (in Old Church Slavonic, not Russian) that he was lonely 'as a finger' – *yako pyerst*.

Bazarov pulled his cap down over his eyes.

'As you like,' he said at last.

'Turn left,' Arkady shouted.

The tarantass rolled off in the direction of Nikolskoye. But having resolved on the *folly* the friends maintained an even more obstinate silence than before and seemed positively bad-tempered.

The manner in which the butler received them on the steps of Madame Odintsov's house was enough to tell the friends that they had acted injudiciously in giving way to a sudden passing fancy. They were obviously not expected. Looking sheepish, they sat waiting for a long time in the drawing-room. At length Madame Odintsov came to them. She greeted them with her usual courtesy but showed surprise at their speedy return and, judging by her half-hearted gestures and speech, she was not over-pleased about it. They made haste to explain that they had only dropped in on their way and within four hours must continue their journey to the town. She confined herself to a mild exclamation, asked Arkady to remember her to his father, and sent for her aunt. The princess appeared looking half asleep, which gave her wrinkled old face an even more spiteful expression. Katya, who was not feeling well, stayed in her room. Arkady suddenly realized that he was quite as anxious to see Katya as to see Anna Sergeyevna herself, if not more so. They spent the four hours in desultory conversation about this and that; Anna Sergeyevna listened and talked but never smiled. Only when they were actually saying good-bye did her former friendliness come to life in her.

'I am suffering from a fit of depression today,' she said, 'but don't pay any attention to that, and come again – I mean this for both of you – before long.'

Arkady and Bazarov responded with silent bows, took their seats in the carriage and without stopping again anywhere drove straight home to Maryino, where they arrived safely on the following evening. During the whole course of the journey neither of them so much as mentioned Madame Odintsov's name; Bazarov, in particular, scarcely opened his mouth and kept staring sideways away from the road with a kind of sour intensity.

At Maryino everyone was overjoyed to see them. The prolonged absence of his son had begun to worry Nikolai Petrovich; he uttered a shout and bounced up and down on the sofa, dangling his legs, when Fenichka ran in to him with sparkling eyes to announce the arrival of the 'young gentlemen'; even Pavel Petrovich experienced a certain degree of pleasurable excitement and smiled condescendingly as he shook hands with the returning wanderers. They all began to talk and ask questions. Arkady chattered most, especially at supper, which lasted till well past midnight. Nikolai Petrovich ordered up some bottles of porter just arrived from Moscow, and set the pace so fast that his cheeks flushed crimson and he fell to laughing a half-childish, half-nervous laugh. The general gaiety spread to the servants' quarters too. Dunyasha ran to and fro like a mad-woman, and kept banging the doors; while at three o'clock in the morning Piotr was still trying to play a Cossack waltz on the guitar. The notes sounded sweet and plaintive in the still air; but with the exception of a few short preliminary flourishes nothing came of the enlightened valet's efforts: nature had endowed him with no more talent for music than for anything else.

But meanwhile things had not been going too well at Maryino, and poor Nikolai Petrovich was having a bad time of it. Every day difficulties arose on the farm – dreary, futile difficulties. His troubles with the hired labourers had become intolerable. Some gave notice or asked for higher wages, while others walked off with wages they had received in advance; the horses fell sick; the harness was damaged as though it had been burnt; work was done carelessly; a threshing-machine ordered from Moscow turned out to be useless because it was too heavy; another winnowing-machine was ruined the first time it was used; half the cattle-sheds were burned to the ground because a short-sighted old woman on the farm had gone with a blazing firebrand on a windy day to fumigate her cow ... true, the old woman maintained that the whole mishap was due to the master's taking it into his head to start manufacturing new-fangled cheeses and dairy produce. The bailiff suddenly turned lazy and began to grow fat as every Russian will grow fat when he can live 'scot-free'. Whenever he caught sight of Nikolai Petrovich in the distance he would try to give evidence of his zeal by throwing a stick at a passing pig, or threatening some half-naked urchin, but for the rest of the time he was generally asleep. The peasants who were now supposed to pay rent were late with their dues and filched their landlord's timber; almost every night the watchmen caught peasants' horses in the farm meadows and sometimes impounded them after a scrimmage. Nikolai Petrovich attempted to institute a system of fines for the damage thus caused but the matter usually ended by the master feeding the horses for a couple of days at his own expense and then restoring them to their owners. To crown all, the peasants started quarrelling among themselves: brothers demanded that their holdings should be divided up between them, and their wives refused to live together under the same roof. Suddenly fighting would break out and all at once, as though at a given signal, the whole crowd of them would spring to their feet and go running to the estate-office steps, bursting in on the master, often in a drunken state and with bruised and battered faces, clamouring for him to dispense justice and retribution; uproar and wailing would follow, the shrill screeching of the women mingling with the raucous swearing of the men. The contending parties had to be sorted out, and Kirsanov would shout himself hoarse, knowing all the time that in any case it was impossible to arrive at a just settlement. There was a shortage of labour for harvesting; a neighbouring freeholder, who seemed a very decent fellow, contracted to provide reapers for a commission of two roubles an acre – and had then cheated him in the most shameless fashion; his own peasant women began to demand unheard-of wages, and in the meantime the corn was rotting in the fields; they were behind with the mowing but at the same time the local council was issuing threats and demanding immediate payment in full of interest due . . .

'I simply can't manage it!' Nikolai Petrovich had exclaimed despairingly more than once. 'I can't fight them myself and my principles forbid me to send for the police; yet without the fear of punishment you can do nothing with them!'

'*Du calme, du calme,*' Pavel Petrovich would remark on these occasions, while he hummed to himself, frowned and tugged at his moustaches.

Bazarov held aloof from these 'petty unpleasantnesses', nor was it his business as a guest to interfere in matters which did not concern him. The day after his arrival at Maryino he applied himself to frogs, his infusoria and his chemical experiments, and spent all his time over them. Arkady, on the other hand, considered it his duty, if not to help his father, at all events to create an impression of being ready to help him. He listened to him patiently and on one occasion tendered his advice, not with any thought of its being acted upon but to show his interest. Farming was not distasteful to him : he could even find pleasure in thinking of agriculture as a possible occupation for himself, but at this time his mind was swarming with other ideas. To his own amazement Arkady found himself constantly thinking of Nikolskoye; formerly he would merely have shrugged his shoulders if anyone had told him that he could ever feel bored under the same roof as Bazarov – least of all when that roof was his father's – but now he found time hang heavy on his hands and longed to get away. He tried walking till he was tired out, but that did not help either. One day, talking to his father, he discovered that Nikolai Petrovich had in his possession a number of letters of some interest, written by Madame Odint-sov's mother to his wife, and Arkady gave him no peace until he got hold of the letters, for which Nikolai Petrovich had to rummage through twenty different drawers and boxes. With these half mouldy bits of paper in his hand Arkady seemed to calm down, as though he now saw before him the goal he must make for. 'I mean this for both of you,' he kept repeating to himself under his breath. 'She added that herself. I'll go, yes I will, and devil take the consequences!' But he remembered the recent visit, the chilly reception and the embarrassment he had felt, and shyness got the better of him. The derring-do of youth, the secret desire to try his luck, to prove his powers all by himself, without anyone else's pro-tection, prevailed in the end. Within ten days of his return to Maryino, on the pretext of studying the working of Sunday schools he was off at a gallop again to town, and from there on to Nikolskoye. Relentlessly urging the driver forward, he rushed to his destination like a young subaltern riding into battle; he felt at once terrified and light-hearted, and breath-less with impatience. 'The main thing is not to think,' he kept saying to himself. His driver happened to be a dashing fel-low, who pulled up at every inn, each time saying: 'A drink?' or 'Shall we have one?', but once having 'had one' he did not spare the horses. Then, at last, the high roof of the familiar house came into sight. . . . 'What am I doing?' the thought suddenly flashed through Arkady's head. 'Well, there's no turning back now!' The three horses sped smoothly on, the driver whooping and whistling at them. Already the bridge was echoing under the wheels and the horses' hooves, and the avenue of clipped fir-trees was running forward to meet them . . . He glimpsed a woman's pink dress against the dark foliage, a young face peeped out from under the light fringe of a parasol. He recognized Katya, and she recognized him. Arkady ordered the driver to stop the galloping horses and, jumping out of the carriage, went up to her. 'It's you!' she cried, a blush gradually suffusing her whole face and neck.

'Let us go and find my sister, she's here in the garden; she will be pleased to see you.'

Katya led Arkady into the garden. His meeting with her struck him as a particularly happy omen; he was so delighted to see her that she might have been someone close to his heart. Everything had happened so fortunately: no formalities, no butler to announce him. At a turn in the path he caught sight of Anna Sergeyevna. She was standing with her back to him. Hearing footsteps, she slowly faced round.

Arkady was on the point of feeling embarrassed again but the first words she uttered immediately set him at ease. 'Welcome, you runaway!' she said in her even caressing voice, and came forward to meet him, smiling and screwing up her eyes from the sun and the breeze. 'Where did you find him, Katya?'

'I have brought you something, Anna Sergeyevna,' he began. 'Something you certainly didn't expect.'

'You have brought yourself; that's better than anything else.'

23

Having seen Arkady off with ironical sympathy, and given him to understand that he was not in the least deceived as to the real purpose of his journey, Bazarov shut himself up in complete solitude; a perfect fever for work had come upon him. No longer did he argue with Pavel Petrovich, particularly as the latter now assumed an excessively aristocratic manner in his presence and expressed his opinions more in inarticulate sounds than in words. Once, and once only, did Pavel Petrovich allow himself to engage in a controversy with the *Nihilist* on the then much discussed question of the rights of the Baltic barons, but he quickly stopped himself, observing with frigid politeness: 'But what's the use? We cannot understand one another; or, at least, I have not the honour of understanding you.'

'Of course not!' exclaimed Bazarov. 'Man is capable of

understanding everything – the vibration of ether and what's going on in the sun; but why another person should blow his nose differently from him – that, he's incapable of understanding.'

'What, is that supposed to be witty?' Pavel Petrovich remarked in a questioning tone and walked away.

However, there were occasions when he asked permission to be present at Bazarov's experiments, and once even placed his perfumed face, cleansed with the finest of soaps, to the microscope in order to see a transparent infusorian swallow a green speck of dust and busily chew it with two very adroit fist-like organs which grew in its throat. Nikolai Petrovich dropped in to see Bazarov far more frequently than his brother; he would have come every day, to 'study', as he put it, if the management of his estate had not made such great demands on his time. He did not disturb the young naturalist: he would sit down somewhere in a corner and watch attentively, now and again venturing a cautious question. At dinner and at supper he always tried to turn the conversation to physics, geology or chemistry, since every other topic, even farming, to say nothing of politics, might lead to a clash if not to mutual displeasure. Nikolai Petrovich surmised that his brother's dislike of Bazarov had in no way diminished. A trifling incident, one of many, confirmed this. Here and there in the neighbourhood cholera had broken out and had even 'carried off' a couple of victims from Maryino itself. One night Pavel Petrovich felt violently ill. He was in torment until the morning but he did not have recourse to Bazarov's skill – and when he met him the following day, in reply to his question why he had not sent for him, he retorted, still very pale but perfectly brushed and shaved, 'Surely I remember your saying yourself you have no faith in medicine'. So the days passed. Bazarov went on obstinately and grimly working . . . and meanwhile there was one person in Nikolai Petrovich's house to whom, if he did not open his heart, he was at least glad to talk. . . . That person was Fenichka.

He used to meet her for the most part early in the morning, in the garden or the courtyard; he never went to see her in her room and she had only once come to his door to inquire – should she give Mitya his bath or not? She not only had confidence in him and was not afraid of him but she felt freer and more at ease with him than with Nikolai Petrovich himself. It is hard to say how this came about; perhaps because unconsciously she was aware of the absence in Bazarov of the aristocratic element, of all that superiority which at once attracts and intimidates. In her eyes he was both an excellent doctor and an ordinary man. She nursed her baby in his presence without feeling at all shy, and on one occasion when she was suddenly attacked with giddiness and headache she accepted a spoonful of medicine from his hands. When Nikolai Petrovich was about she seemed to keep out of Bazarov's way – she did this not out of duplicity but out of a sense of decency. More than ever she was apprehensive of Pavel Petrovich; of late he had begun to keep an eye on her and would suddenly appear as though he had sprung out of the earth behind her back, in his English-cut suit, his face red and suspicious and his hands in his pockets. 'It's like having a bucket of cold water thrown over me,' Fenichka complained to Dunyasha, who sighed in response and thought of another 'unfeeling' individual. Without having the faintest suspicion of it Bazarov had become the *cruel tyrant* of her heart.

Fenichka liked Bazarov; but he liked her too. Even his face changed when he talked to her: it took on an open, almost kindly expression, and his habitual nonchalance was tempered by a kind of playful solicitude. Fenichka grew prettier every day. There is a season in the lives of young women when they suddenly begin to unfold and bloom like summer roses; such a time had come for Fenichka. Everything contributed to it, even the sultry heat of July which was then at its height. Wearing a flimsy white dress, she looked even whiter and more diaphanous than it; the sun had not tanned her skin but the heat, from which she could not shield herself, spread a slight flush over her cheeks and ears and a soft indolence through her whole body which was reflected in the dreamy languor of her beautiful eyes. She could hardly get on with her work, her hands kept slipping to her lap. She could scarcely take a step, and kept sighing and complaining with comic helplessness.

'You should go oftener to bathe,' Nikolai Petrovich told her. He had rigged up a large bathing-tent over one of the ponds which had not yet completely dried up.

'Oh, Nikolai Petrovich! But I'd die before I ever got there, and I'd die again on the way back. There's not a bit of shade in the garden.'

'That's true, there is no shade,' Nikolai Petrovich would reply, mopping his forehead.

One day as Bazarov was returning from a stroll at about seven o'clock in the morning he came across Fenichka in the lilac arbour, which had stopped flowering long ago but was still thick with green. She was sitting on a bench and as usual she had a white kerchief thrown over her head; beside her lay a large bunch of red and white roses still wet with dew. He said good morning to her.

'Ah, Monsieur Bazarov,' she exclaimed, and lifted the edge of her kerchief a little in order to see him – a movement which bared her arm to the elbow.

'What are you doing here?' said Bazarov, sitting down beside her. 'Are you making a bouquet?'

'Yes, for the breakfast table. Nikolai Petrovich likes flowers.'

'But it's still a long time till breakfast. What a heap of flowers!'

'I picked them now, before it gets too hot to go out. Now is the only time you can breathe. I feel quite weak with this heat. I'm really afraid of falling ill.'

'What an idea! Let me feel your pulse.' Bazarov took her

hand, found her evenly beating pulse and did not even bother to count the beats. 'You'll live to be a hundred,' he said, letting go her hand.

'Ah, God forbid!' she exclaimed.

'Why not? Don't you want to live a long life?'

'Yes, but not a hundred years! We had a granny of eighty-five – and what a martyr she was! Skin all gone dark, deaf and bent, coughing all the time, she was only a burden to herself. What sort of a life is that?'

'So it's better to be young?'

'Well, isn't it?'

'Why should it be better? Tell me!'

'What do you mean – why? Here am I now, I'm young, I can do anything – I can come and go and carry things, and I don't have to be dependent on anyone. . . . What could be better?'

'Well, I don't mind whether I am young or old.'

'How can you say that – that you don't mind? It's not possible, what you say.'

'Well, judge for yourself. What good is my youth to me? I live a lonely life, all by myself . . .'

'That all depends on yourself.'

'No, it doesn't all depend on me! If only I could find someone to take pity on me.'

Fenichka looked sideways at Bazarov but said nothing. 'What's that book you have?' she asked after a short pause.

'This? It's about science, a very learned book.'

'And are you still studying? Don't you get tired of it? I should think you must know everything by now.'

'Evidently not. You try reading a few lines.'

'Why, I shouldn't understand a thing. Is it in Russian?' Fenichka asked, picking up the heavily bound volume in both hands. 'What an enormous book!'

'Yes, it's in Russian.'

'All the same, I shan't understand anything.'

'I didn't give it to you for you to understand it. I want to look at you while you read. When you read, the tip of your nose twitches so endearingly.'

Fenichka, who was about to spell out in a low voice an article on 'Creosote', burst out laughing and threw the book down ... it slipped from the bench and fell to the ground.

'I like it too when you laugh,' observed Bazarov.

'You stop it.'

'I like it when you talk. It's like a little brook babbling.'

Fenichka turned her head away.

'What a one you are!' she murmured, fingering the flowers. 'And how can you like listening to me? You have had such clever ladies talking to you.'

'Ah, Fenichka, believe me: all the clever ladies in the world aren't worth your little elbow.'

'There now, whatever will you think of next!' whispered Fenichka, clasping her hands together.

Bazarov picked the book up from the ground.

'That's a medical book: why do you throw it away?'

'A medical book?' Fenichka repeated, turning to him. 'Do you know, ever since you gave me those drops for Mitya – do you remember? – he sleeps so sound. I really don't know how to thank you: you are so good and kind, really you are.'

'Doctors usually have to be paid, don't they,' observed Bazarov with a smile. 'You know yourself, doctors are a greedy lot.'

Fenichka raised her eyes, which looked still darker in the dazzling light on the upper part of her face. She was not sure if he were joking or not.

'If you like, we'll be pleased.... I shall have to ask Nikolai Petrovich ...'

'What, do you think I want money?' Bazarov interrupted her. 'No, it's not money I need from you.'

'What is it then?' Fenichka asked.

'What?' Bazarov repeated. 'Try and guess.'

'I can't.'

'I'll tell you then. I want ... one of those roses.'

Fenichka laughed again and even threw up her hands, so funny did Bazarov's request seem to her. She laughed and at the same time felt flattered. Bazarov eyed her intently.

'Oh yes, oh yes,' she brought out at length, and bending over the bench she began picking out the roses. 'Which will you have – a red or a white one?'

'A red one, and not too large.'

She straightened herself.

'Have this one,' she said, but then immediately drew back her outstretched hand and, biting her lips, looked towards the entrance of the arbour, straining her ears.

'What's the matter?' asked Bazarov. 'Is it Nikolai Petrovich?'

'No ... he's gone to the fields ... and anyhow I'm not afraid of him ... but Pavel Petrovich ... I fancied ...'

'What?'

'I thought he was over there. No ... it was no one. Take it.' Fenichka gave Bazarov the rose.

'What makes you afraid of Pavel Petrovich?'

'I'm always scared of him. It's not that he says anything – he doesn't, he just looks at me in a meaning sort of way. And you don't like him either. You remember, you were always arguing with him. I don't know what it was all about but I could see you twisting him this way and that. . . .'

Fenichka illustrated with her hands what she thought Bazarov did with Pavel Petrovich.

Bazarov smiled.

'And if he had started getting the better of me,' he asked, 'would you have stood up for me?'

'How could I have? Besides, no one could get the better of you.'

'You think so? But I know a little finger that could topple me over like a feather if it wanted to.'

'What finger?'

'Why, don't you know? Smell how lovely this rose is that you gave me.'

Fenichka stretched her slender neck forward and put her face close to the flower.... The kerchief slipped from her head on to her shoulders, revealing a soft mass of shining black, slightly ruffled hair.

'Wait a minute, I want to smell it with you,' said Bazarov, and he bent down and kissed her vigorously on her parted lips.

She started back, pressing both her hands against his chest, but she pushed feebly and he renewed and prolonged the kiss.

A dry cough was heard beside the lilac bushes. Fenichka instantly moved away to the other end of the bench. Pavel Petrovich showed himself, made a slight bow and said with a sort of malicious melancholy, 'It is you, then!' and walked away. Fenichka at once gathered up all the roses and ran from the arbour.

'How could you, Monsieur Bazarov!' she whispered as she went. There was a note of genuine reproach in her whisper.

Bazarov recalled another scene in which he had recently taken part, and he felt a sense of shame and contemptuous annoyance. But he immediately shook his head, congratulated himself sardonically on his 'formal' entry into the ranks of the gay Lotharios, and started back to his room.

Meanwhile Pavel Petrovich had left the garden and walked with slow steps as far as the copse. He remained there for quite a long time, and when he returned for breakfast his face had such a dark expression that Nikolai Petrovich asked him anxiously if he was all right.

'You know I sometimes suffer from bilious attacks,' was Pavel Petrovich's calm reply.

24

Two hours later he knocked at Bazarov's door.

'I must apologize for interrupting you in your scientific researches,' he began, seating himself on a chair by the window and leaning with both hands on a handsome cane with an ivory knob (he did not usually carry a stick), 'but I am compelled to request you to spare me five minutes of your time ... no more.'

'All my time is at your disposal,' replied Bazarov, whose face had twitched directly Pavel Petrovich entered the room.

'Five minutes will suffice me. I have come to put just one question to you.'

'A question? What about?'

'I shall explain if you will be good enough to listen. When you first came to stay in my brother's house, and before I denied myself the pleasure of conversing with you, I had occasion to hear you express opinions on many subjects; but, so far as my memory serves, neither in conversation with me nor in my presence was any reference ever made to the subject of single combat or duelling in general. May I inquire what your views are on this subject?'

Bazarov, who had risen to receive Pavel Petrovich, sat down on the edge of the table and folded his arms.

'My views are as follows,' he replied. 'From the theoretical standpoint, duelling is absurd; but from the practical standpoint – well, that's another matter altogether.'

'That is, you mean to say, if I understand you correctly, that whatever your theoretical view of duelling you would not in practice suffer yourself to be insulted without demanding satisfaction?'

'You have grasped my meaning exactly.'

'Very good, sir. I am pleased to hear you say so. Your words deliver me from a state of uncertainty ...'

'Of indecision, you mean.'

'As you like. I am trying to express myself in a way you will understand; I ... I am not one of your college phrasemongers. Your words have saved me from a rather grievous necessity. I have decided to fight you.'

Bazarov opened his eyes wide.

'Me?'

'Precisely.'

'But what for, pray?'

'I could explain the reason to you,' began Pavel Petrovich, 'but I prefer to keep silent about it. To my way of thinking you are not wanted here; I cannot endure you; I despise you; and if that is not enough for you ...'

Pavel Petrovich's eyes flashed ... Bazarov's glinted too.

'Very well, then,' he articulated slowly. 'Further explanations are unnecessary. You have taken it into your head to test your chivalrous spirit on me. I could refuse you this satisfaction but – so be it!'

'Very much obliged to you,' answered Pavel Petrovich. 'And now may I hope that you will accept my challenge without compelling me to resort to violent measures.'

'That means, in plain language, to that cane?' Bazarov remarked coolly. 'You are quite right. There is no need for you to insult me. Nor would that have been without some peril to yourself. You can remain the gentleman ... I accept your challenge, also like a gentleman.'

'Excellent,' observed Pavel Petrovich, putting his cane in the corner. 'Now we can discuss briefly the conditions of the duel; but first of all I should like to know whether you consider it necessary for us to have recourse to the formality of a slight dispute which might serve as a pretext for my challenge?'

'No, we had better dispense with the formalities.'

'I think so myself. I also suggest that it would be out of place to probe into the true reason for our passage of arms. We cannot endure one another. What more is necessary?'

'What more is necessary!' Bazarov echoed him ironically.

'As regards the actual conditions of the duel, since we shall have no seconds ... for where could we get them? ...'

'Exactly, where could we get them?'

'... I have the honour to suggest the following: let us fight early tomorrow morning, at six, shall we say, behind the copse, with pistols, at a distance of ten paces ...'

'At ten paces? That will do; we can detest one another at that distance.'

'We could make it eight,' remarked Pavel Petrovich.

'We could: why not?'

'We shall fire two shots and, as a precaution, let each of us put a letter in his pocket, holding himself responsible for his own demise.'

'Now I don't altogether agree with that,' said Bazarov. 'It smacks too much of a French novel, it's a bit unlikely.'

'Perhaps. You will concur, however, that it would be unpleasant to be suspected of murder?'

'I agree. But there is a way of avoiding that painful accusation. We shall have no seconds, but we could have a witness.'

'And who, may I ask?'

'Why, Piotr.'

'Which Piotr?'

'Your brother's man. He's the acme of contemporary culture and would perform his rôle with all the *comme il faut* required on such occasions.'

'I think you must be joking, my dear sir.'

'Not at all. If you think over my suggestion, you will come to the conclusion that it is charged with simple good sense. Murder will out, but I will undertake to prepare Piotr in a suitable manner and bring him to the field of battle.'

'You persist in joking,' said Pavel Petrovich, rising from his chair. 'But after the amiable readiness you have displayed I have no right to insist further.... So everything is arranged.... By the way, I don't suppose you have pistols?'

'How should I have pistols? I am not a fighting man.'

'In that case I offer you mine. You may rest assured that I have not shot with them these five years.'

'That is very comforting news.'

Pavel Petrovich picked up his cane.... 'And now, my dear sir, it only remains for me to thank you and leave you to resume your studies. I have the honour to bid you good-day.'

'Until we have the pleasure of meeting again, my dear sir,' said Bazarov, escorting his visitor to the door.

Pavel Petrovich went out; Bazarov stood for a moment at the door, then suddenly exclaimed: 'Well I'm dashed! How fine and how stupid! What a farce we've been acting! Like performing dogs dancing on their hind legs. But it was out of the question to refuse: I really believe he would have struck me, and then ...' (Bazarov paled at the very thought: all his pride reared up within him.) 'Then I should have had to strangle him like a kitten.' He went back to his microscope but his heart was beating and the composure essential for accurate observation was gone. 'He must have seen us today,' he thought; 'but would he really behave like this on his brother's account? And is a kiss so very important? There must be something else in the background. Bah! Perhaps he is in love with her himself? Of course he's in love with her: it's as clear as daylight. What a mess, just imagine! ... Yes, it's a bad business,' he decided at last. 'A bad business from whatever angle one looks at it. Firstly I risk having my brains blown out, and in any case I shall have to go away from here; and then there's Arkady ... and that old heifer Nikolai Petrovich. It's a bad business, a bad business.'

The day passed quietly in a peculiar kind of languor. Fenichka gave no sign of life; she kept to her little room like a mouse in its hole. Nikolai Petrovich looked worried. He had just heard that brand was affecting his wheat crop on which he had set high hopes. Pavel Petrovich's icy politeness crushed everyone, including even Prokofyich. Bazarov began a letter to his father but tore it up and threw it under the table. 'If I die,' he thought, 'they will hear of it; but I'm not going to die. No, I shall be about in this world for a long time yet.' He gave Piotr orders to come to him on a matter of importance next morning as soon as it was light; Piotr imagined that Bazarov wanted to take him to Petersburg with him. Bazarov went late to bed and all night long was a prey to confused dreams.... Madame Odintsov kept appearing in them; now she was his mother, she was followed by a kitten with black whiskers and the kitten was Fenichka; then he saw Pavel Petrovich before him, like a huge forest which, for all that, he had to fight. At four o'clock Piotr woke him; he dressed at once and went out with him.

It was a glorious fresh morning; tiny mottled cloudlets hovered overhead like fleecy lambs in the clear blue sky; fine beads of dew lay on the leaves and grass, and sparkled like silver on the spiders' webs; the moist dark earth still seemed to glow with the rosy tints of dawn; in every quarter of the heavens the larks poured out their song. Bazarov walked as far as the copse, sat down in the shade at its edge and only then disclosed to Piotr the nature of the service he expected of him. The enlightened valet was scared to death; but Bazarov calmed his fears by assuring him that he would have nothing to do except stand at a distance and look on, and that he would not incur any sort of responsibility. 'And just think,' he added, 'what an important part you have to play.' Piotr threw up his hands, stared at his feet and, green with fright, leaned against a birch-tree for support.

The road from Maryino skirted the copse; a light dust lay on it, untouched by wheel or foot since the previous day. Bazarov could not help looking along the road, plucking as he did so blades of grass and chewing them, while he kept repeating to himself: 'What a piece of idiocy!' More than once the chilly morning air made him shiver.... Piotr glanced at him dejectedly but Bazarov only grinned back; he was not afraid.

The clatter of hooves was heard along the road.... From behind a tree a peasant came into sight. He was driving before him two horses hobbled together and as he passed Bazarov he stared at him rather strangely, without doffing his cap, a circumstance which it was easy to see disturbed Piotr as a bad omen. 'Here's someone else up early,' thought Bazarov, 'but he at least is up on business, while we ...?'

'I fancy the gentleman's coming,' Piotr whispered of a sudden.

Bazarov raised his head and saw Pavel Petrovich. Wearing a light check jacket and snow-white trousers, he was striding down the road; under his arm he carried a box wrapped in green baize.

'I beg your pardon, I think I have kept you waiting,' he said, bowing first to Bazarov and then to Piotr, who commanded his respect at that moment as something in the nature of a second. 'I did not want to wake my man.'

'It doesn't matter,' Bazarov replied. 'We have only just arrived ourselves.'

'Ah! So much the better.' Pavel Petrovich looked round him. 'There is no one about, no one to interfere with us. . . . Shall we proceed?'

'By all means.'

'You do not, I presume, require any further discussion?'

'I do not.'

'Would you care to load?' inquired Pavel Petrovich, taking the pistols out of the box.

'No, you load while I measure out the paces. My legs are longer than yours,' Bazarov added with a smile. 'One, two, three . . .'

'Please sir,' Piotr faltered with an effort (he was trembling as if he had fever) 'say what you like, but I am going farther off.'

'Four . . . five . . . all right, move away, my good fellow, move away; you may even stand behind a tree and stop up your ears, only don't shut your eyes; and if one of us falls, run and help him up. Six . . . seven . . . eight . . .' Bazarov halted. 'Is that enough?' he asked, turning to Pavel Petrovich. 'Or shall I throw in a couple of paces?'

'As you like,' the other replied, ramming in the second bullet.

'All right, we'll make it two more,' Bazarov drew a line

on the ground with the toe of his boot. 'There's the barrier. By the way, how many paces may each of us go back from the barrier? That's an important question too. We did not discuss that yesterday.'

'Ten, I suppose,' replied Pavel Petrovich, handing both pistols to Bazarov. 'Will you deign to make your choice?'

'I will deign. But you must admit, Pavel Petrovich, that our duel is unusual to the point of absurdity? Just look at our second's countenance.'

'You are still bent on joking,' Pavel Petrovich replied. 'I do not deny the strange circumstances of our duel but I consider it my duty to warn you that I intend to fight you in grim earnest. *A bon entendeur, salut!*'*

'Oh, I don't doubt that we are both resolved to annihilate each other, but why shouldn't we laugh too, and combine *utile dulci*.† There: you speak to me in French and I reply in Latin.'

'I am going to fight in earnest,' Pavel Petrovich repeated, and he moved to his place. Bazarov, for his part, counted off ten paces from the barrier and stood still.

'Are you ready?' asked Pavel Petrovich.

'Perfectly.'

'Let us begin.'

Bazarov moved slowly forward and Pavel advanced towards him, his left hand thrust in his pocket and his right gradually raising the muzzle of the pistol.... 'He's aiming straight for my nose,' Bazarov thought to himself, 'and how assiduously he screws up his eyes, the bandit! This is not a pleasant sensation though. I'm going to fix my eyes on his watch-chain ...' Something hissed close to Bazarov's ear and at that very instant a shot rang out. 'I heard it, so I must be all right then.' The thought had just time to flash through his head. He took one more step, and without aiming pressed the trigger.

* he that hath an ear let him hear.
† the practical with the agreeable.

Pavel Petrovich gave a slight start and clutched at his thigh. Blood trickled down his white trousers.

Bazarov threw away his pistol and went up to his adversary. 'Are you wounded?' he asked.

'You had the right to summon me to the barrier,' said Pavel Petrovich. 'This is only a scratch. According to our agreement each of us has the right to one more shot.'

'You must excuse me, that will have to wait until another time,' answered Bazarov, putting his arm round Pavel Petrovich, who was beginning to turn pale. 'Now I am no longer the duellist but a doctor, and first of all I must examine your wound. Piotr! Come here, Piotr! Where have you got to?'

'This is nonsense . . . I don't need any help,' Pavel Petrovich declared jerkily, 'and . . . we must . . . again . . .' He tried to pull at his moustaches but his arm sagged, his eyes rolled back, and he lost consciousness.

'Here's a pretty pass! A fainting-fit! What next!' Bazarov involuntarily exclaimed, lowering Pavel Petrovich on to the grass. 'Let's see the damage.' He pulled out a handkerchief, wiped away the blood and began to feel round the wound . . . 'The bone is intact,' he muttered through his teeth. 'The bullet didn't go deep; only one muscle, the *vastus externus*, grazed. You'll be hopping about again in three weeks' time, my boy! But fainting! Ugh, these hysterical people! My word, what a delicate skin.'

'Is he killed?' Piotr's quaking voice whispered behind his back.

Bazarov looked round.

'Go along quickly and fetch some water, my good fellow; as for him, he'll outlive us both.'

But the 'enlightened' servant seemed not to understand his words and remained rooted to the spot. Pavel Petrovich slowly opened his eyes.

'He's dying,' murmured Piotr and started crossing himself.

'You are right. . . . What an idiotic countenance!' remarked the wounded gentleman with a forced smile.

'Go and fetch some water, damn you!' Bazarov shouted.

'No need.... It was only a momentary vertigo.... Help me to sit up ... there, that's right.... This scratch merely requires a bit of bandaging and I shall be able to walk home, or else you can send a droshky for me. If you are agreeable we will not resume the duel. You have conducted yourself honourably ... today – today, note.'

'There is no point in dwelling on the past,' Bazarov replied, 'and as for the future, it's not worth your troubling your head about that either, seeing that I intend to make my departure from here at once. Let me bind up your leg now; your wound is not dangerous, but it is always advisable to stop the bleeding. But first of all we must revive this poor mortal.'

Bazarov shook Piotr by the collar and sent him off to fetch a droshky.

'Take care and don't alarm my brother,' Pavel Petrovich enjoined him. 'You are not to breathe a word of what has happened.'

Piotr set off at full speed; and while he was running for a droshky the two adversaries sat on the ground and said nothing. Pavel Petrovich tried to avoid looking at Bazarov; he still did not want to make it up with him; he was ashamed of his own arrogance, of his failure; he was ashamed of the whole affair he had started, even though he felt that the incident could not have had a more favourable ending. 'At least he will not stick round here any longer,' he consoled himself by reflecting, 'and that is something to be thankful for.' The silence between them continued, heavy and awkward. Both were ill at ease. Each was aware that the other had taken his measure. Such mutual recognition is agreeable between friends but most disagreeable between enemies, especially where it is impossible for them either to thrash things out or to part company.

'I hope I haven't bandaged your leg too tightly?' Bazarov inquired at last.

'No, it is all right, it is fine,' answered Pavel Petrovich, adding after a pause, 'You can't hoodwink my brother: we shall have to tell him that we fell out over politics.'

'Capital,' Bazarov agreed. 'You can say that I started abusing all Anglomaniacs.'

'Excellent. What do you suppose that fellow is thinking about us now?' Pavel Petrovich went on, pointing to the peasant who had driven his hobbled horses past Bazarov a few minutes before the duel and who, now trudging back along the road, played up at the sight of the 'gentry', and doffed his cap.

'Who can tell!' answered Bazarov. 'Very likely he is not thinking at all. The Russian peasant is the mysterious Unknown that Mrs Radcliffe* used to talk about so much. Does anyone understand him? He does not even understand himself.'

'Ah, so that is what you –' Pavel Petrovich began, and then suddenly exclaimed: 'Look what that idiot Piotr has done! Here's my brother galloping towards us!'

Bazarov turned round and saw Nikolai Petrovich sitting pale-faced in the droshky. Before it had time to pull up he leaped out and rushed towards his brother.

'What is this?' he cried in an agitated voice. 'Monsieur Bazarov, I beg of you, what does this mean?'

'It is nothing,' Pavel Petrovich replied. 'They have alarmed you quite unnecessarily. Monsieur Bazarov and I had a slight altercation, and I have had to pay a slight penalty for it.'

'But what was it all about, for heaven's sake?'

'How shall I explain? Monsieur Bazarov alluded disrespectfully to Sir Robert Peel. I would hasten to add that I alone am to blame in all this, and Monsieur Bazarov has conducted himself admirably. It was I who challenged him.'

'But goodness, there's blood on you!'

'And did you suppose I had water in my veins? But as a

* Anna Ward Radcliffe, 1764–1823, an English novelist who wrote *The Mysteries of Udolpho* and other romances.

matter of fact this blood-letting will do me good. Is not that so, doctor? Now help me into the droshky, and don't give way to gloomy thoughts. I shall be quite well by tomorrow. That's the way, fine. Off we go, coachman!'

Nikolai Petrovich followed the droshky on foot; Bazarov would have stayed where he was. . . .

'I must ask you to attend to my brother,' Nikolai Petrovich said to him, 'until we fetch another doctor from town.'

Bazarov nodded his head without speaking.

An hour later Pavel Petrovich was reposing in bed with a skilfully bandaged leg. The whole house was in a turmoil. Fenichka came over faint. Nikolai Petrovich wrung his hands in silence while Pavel Petrovich continued to laugh and joke, especially with Bazarov; he had donned a fine cambric shirt, an elegant morning jacket and a fez; he would not allow the blinds to be pulled down and made humorous protests at having to abstain from food.

Towards night, however, he developed a temperature and his head ached. The doctor arrived from the town. (Nikolai Petrovich had paid no heed to his brother, nor had Bazarov wanted him to; the latter had sat about in his room all day, looking bilious and angry, and making only the briefest of visits to the wounded man; twice he happened to run into Fenichka but she recoiled from him in horror.) The new doctor recommended a cooling draught and, incidentally, confirmed Bazarov's diagnosis that there was no danger of complications. Nikolai Petrovich told him that his brother had wounded himself through carelessness, to which the doctor replied: 'H'm!' but on having twenty-five roubles in silver slipped into his hand he exclaimed: 'You don't say so! Of course things of this kind often occur.'

No one in the house went to bed or undressed. Nikolai Petrovich kept tiptoeing into his brother's room and tiptoeing out again; Pavel Petrovich would doze off, groan gently or say to him in French: 'Couchez-vous,' and ask for something to drink. Once Nikolai Petrovich made Fenichka take him in a glass of lemonade; Pavel Petrovich eyed her fixedly as he drained the glass to the last drop. Towards morning the fever increased somewhat and a slight delirium set in. At first Pavel Petrovich uttered incoherent words; then he suddenly opened his eyes and, seeing his brother at the bedside anxiously leaning over him, he murmured,

'Don't you think, Nikolai, that Fenichka has something in common with Nellie?'

'What Nellie, Pavel?'

'How can you ask? With Princess R., of course. The upper part of the face especially. *C'est de la même famille.*'

Nikolai Petrovich made no reply but inwardly he marvelled at the persistent vitality of old passions in a man. 'So this is what lies below the surface!' he thought.

'Ah, how I love that worthless creature!' moaned Pavel Petrovich, clasping his hands dejectedly behind his head. 'I will suffer no insolent upstart to dare to lay a finger ...' he muttered a few moments later.

Nikolai Petrovich only sighed; he had no suspicion to whom these words might refer.

Bazarov came to see him next morning at about eight o'clock. He had now packed his belongings and set free all his frogs, insects and birds.

'You have come to say good-bye?' Nikolai Petrovich asked, rising to meet him.

'Exactly.'

'I understand your feelings, and I fully commend them. My poor brother, of course, is to blame; and he is punished for it. He told me himself that he made it impossible for you to act otherwise. I am ready to believe that you could not avoid this duel, which ... which in some considerable measure the persistent antagonism between your respective views is enough to explain.' (Nikolai Petrovich was getting entangled in his words.) 'My brother is a man of the old school, quick-tempered and obstinate. ... Thank God, the matter ended no worse. I have taken all the necessary steps to avoid publicity. ...'

'I will leave my address with you in case there is any trouble,' said Bazarov casually.

'I hope there will be no trouble, Yevgeny Vassilyich. ... I am very sorry that your stay in my house should have terminated so ... in such a fashion. And I am the more grieved in that Arkady ...'

'No doubt I shall be seeing him,' interrupted Bazarov, whom every sort of 'explanation' and 'protestation' invariably roused to irritation. 'If I don't, will you say good-bye to him for me, and accept this expression of my regret.'

'And I beg you ...' Nikolai Petrovich responded with a bow. But Bazarov, without waiting for him to finish, was gone from the room.

On learning that Bazarov was about to depart Pavel Petrovich asked to see him, and shook hands with him. But even now Bazarov remained as cold as ice; he realized that Pavel Petrovich wanted to play the magnanimous. He found no opportunity of saying good-bye to Fenichka; he was only able to exchange glances with her from the window. He thought her face looked sad. 'She's wasting her life, I am afraid,' he said to himself. 'Yet perhaps she'll manage somehow!' Piotr, however, was so overcome that he wept on his shoulder until Bazarov moderated his transports by inquiring if he were a cry-baby, while Dunyasha was obliged to run away into the copse to hide her emotion. The cause of all this woe clambered into a wagon, lit a cigar, and when three miles farther on at a bend in the road he saw for the last time the Kirsanovs' farmstead and the new manor-house standing in a line together he merely spat out a shred of tobacco and muttered, wrapping his greatcoat more closely about him, 'These damned little gentry!'

Pavel Petrovich was soon feeling better; but he had to lie in bed for another week. He bore his 'captivity', as he called it, fairly patiently, though he fussed greatly over his toilet and insisted on having pastilles of eau-de-cologne burned in the room. Nikolai Petrovich read the newspapers to him; Fenichka waited on him as before, bringing him chicken broth, lemonade, soft-boiled eggs and tea; but a secret terror gripped her every time she entered his room. Pavel Petrovich's unexpected action had alarmed all in the house, and her more than anyone; only Prokofyich remained calm, explaining that in his day gentlemen used to fight duels with other gentlemen – 'but only proper gentlemen among themselves: the likes of them scoundrels they had horsewhipped in the stables for their insolence.'

Fenichka's conscience reproached her hardly at all; but she was worried at times when she thought of the real cause of the quarrel; besides, Pavel Petrovich looked at her so strangely, so that even when her back was turned to him she could feel his eyes upon her. She grew thin from constant inward agitation and, as always happens, she looked even prettier.

One day – it was in the morning – Pavel Petrovich felt much better and moved from his bed to the sofa, while Nikolai Petrovich, having inquired how he was, went off to the threshing floor. Fenichka brought in a cup of tea and setting it down on a little table was about to withdraw. Pavel Petrovich detained her.

'Why are you in such a hurry?' he began. 'Are you so busy?'

'No – yes. What I mean is, I have to go and pour out the tea for them.'

'Dunyasha can do that without you; come and sit for a while with a poor invalid. By the way, I should like to have a chat with you.'

Fenichka silently seated herself on the edge of an armchair.

'Listen,' Pavel Petrovich said, pulling at his moustaches. 'I have wanted to ask you for a long time: you seem somehow to be afraid of me?'

'I?'

'Yes, you. You never look straight at me. In fact, one would think your conscience was not clear.'

Fenichka crimsoned but she glanced up at Pavel Petrovich. He seemed somehow so strange to her, and her heart began to throb quietly.

'But your conscience is clear?' he asked her.

'Why shouldn't it be?' she whispered.

'Why indeed! Besides, whom could you have wronged? Me? That is unlikely. Any other people living in the house? That, too, is scarcely probable. Can it be my brother? But you love him, do you not?'

'Yes, I do.'

'With all your soul, with all your heart?'

'I love Nikolai Petrovich with all my heart.'

'You really mean it? Look at me, Fenichka.' (It was the first time he had called her that.) . . . 'You know, it is a great sin to tell lies.'

'I am not telling lies. If I did not love Nikolai Petrovich I would have nothing to live for.'

'And you would never give him up for anyone else?'

'Who would I give him up for?'

'One never knows. For the gentleman who has just left, for example.'

Fenichka got to her feet.

'Merciful heavens, why do you torment me? What have I done to you? How can you say such things? . . .'

'Fenichka,' said Pavel Petrovich in a sad voice, 'you know I saw . . .'

'What did you see?'

'Why there . . . in the summer-house.'

Fenichka flushed crimson to the roots of her hair and the tips of her ears.

'But how was I to blame?' she said with an effort.

Pavel Petrovich sat up.

'You were not to blame? No? Not at all?'

'Nikolai Petrovich is the only person I love in the whole wide world and I always shall!' she cried with sudden force, while sobs rose in her throat. 'And as to what you saw, on the Day of Judgment I shall say I am not to blame, and wasn't to blame for it, and I would rather die at once if people can suspect me of such a thing behind my benefactor's back ...'

Here her voice failed her and at the same moment she felt Pavel Petrovich's hand seize and grip hers. ... She looked at him and turned to stone. He had gone even paler than before, his eyes glittered and – most astonishing of all – one large solitary tear was rolling down his cheek.

'Fenichka,' he said in a sort of strange whisper, 'love him, do love my brother! He is such a good, kind man. Don't betray him for anyone in the world. Don't heed anyone else! Think – what could be more terrible than to love and not be loved in return! Never forsake my poor dear Nikolai!'

Fenichka's eyes were dry now and her fear had passed, so great was her amazement. But what were her feelings when Pavel Petrovich – Pavel Petrovich of all people – pressed her hand hard to his lips, but without kissing it and only heaving convulsive sighs from time to time ...

'Merciful heavens!' she thought. 'Can it be that he is having a fit? ...'

At that moment the whole of his wasted life stirred within him.

The stairs creaked beneath rapid footsteps. ... He pushed her away and let his head fall back on the pillow. The door opened and Nikolai Petrovich, cheerful, fresh and ruddy-cheeked, appeared. Mitya, just as fresh and rosy as his father, wearing nothing but his little shirt, was jumping up and down in his arms, bare toes clinging to the buttons of his rough country coat.

Fenichka threw herself at Nikolai Petrovich and, clasping him and her son together in her arms, dropped her head on his shoulder. Nikolai Petrovich was surprised: Fenichka, so shy and modest, never showed her affection for him in front of a third person.

'Is anything the matter?' he said, and glancing at his brother handed Mitya over to her. 'You're not feeling worse, are you?' he asked, going up to Pavel Petrovich.

The latter buried his face in a cambric handkerchief.

'No. . . . Not at all . . . it's nothing . . . On the contrary, I am much better.'

'You shouldn't have been in such a hurry to move to the sofa. Where are you going?' Nikolai Petrovich added, turning to Fenichka, but she had gone, abruptly closing the door behind her. 'I was bringing my young hero in to show you; he has been pining for his uncle. Why did she take him away? What's wrong with you, though? Has anything happened between you?'

'Brother,' Pavel Petrovich said gravely.

Nikolai Petrovich started. He felt dismayed, he could not have said why.

'Brother,' repeated Pavel Petrovich, 'give me your word that you will carry out my one request.'

'What request? Tell me.'

'A most important one. As I see it, your entire happiness depends upon it. I have pondered deeply all this time on what I am now going to say to you. . . . Brother, you must do your duty, the duty of an honest and upright man: put an end to the scandal, to the bad example you are setting – you, the best of men!'

'What are you trying to say, Pavel?'

'Marry Fenichka. . . . She loves you: she is the mother of your son.'

Nikolai Petrovich stepped back a pace and threw up his hands.

'You say that, Pavel? You, whom I always regarded as the most relentless opponent of such marriages! You say that! But don't you realize, it was only out of respect for yourself that I have not fulfilled what you so rightly call my duty!'

'Your respect for me was mistaken in this instance,' Pavel Petrovich rejoined with a wan smile. 'I am beginning to think that Bazarov was right after all in accusing me of being a snob. No, my dear brother, enough of worrying about appearances and what people think: we are quiet, elderly folk now; it's high time we laid aside the vanity of this world. So be it, as you say, let us fulfil our duty; and, you will see, we shall get happiness that way into the bargain.'

Nikolai Petrovich rushed over to embrace his brother.

'You have really opened my eyes,' he exclaimed. 'I wasn't wrong in always maintaining that you were the kindest and wisest of men; and now I see you are just as sensible as you are noble-hearted.'

'Gently, gently,' Pavel Petrovich interrupted him. 'Don't hurt the leg of your common-sensible brother who at close on fifty fought a duel like any young ensign. So then, the matter is settled. Fenichka is to be my ... *belle soeur*.'

'My dear Pavel! But what will Arkady say?'

'Arkady? Why, he'll be simply delighted! Marriage is not a principle he upholds, but at least his sense of social equality will be gratified. And, after all, what is the point of class distinctions *au dix-neuvième siècle*?'

'Ah, Pavel, Pavel! Let me embrace you again. Don't be alarmed for your leg, I shall be very careful.'

And the brothers embraced.

'What do you think – shouldn't you tell her straight away of your intention?' Pavel Petrovich asked.

'Why hurry?' objected Nikolai Petrovich. 'Have you already discussed it with her?'

'Discussed it with her! *Quelle idée*!'

'Well, that's all right then. First you must get better; and meanwhile there's plenty of time. We must think it over carefully, consider ...'

'But you have already made up your mind, haven't you?'

'Of course I have, and I thank you from the bottom of my heart. Now I will leave you; you must rest; all this excitement is bad for you. . . . But we will talk it over again. Go to sleep, dearest of brothers, and may God restore you to health!'

'Why does he thank me like that?' thought Pavel Petrovich when he was left alone. 'Does it not depend entirely on him? As for myself, I shall go somewhere far away, as soon as he gets married, Dresden or Florence, and live there till I die.'

Pavel Petrovich moistened his forehead with eau-de-cologne and closed his eyes. In the glaring daylight his handsome emaciated head lay on the white pillow like the head of a dead man ... And, indeed, to all intents and purposes, so he was.

25

At Nikolskoye Katya and Arkady were sitting in the garden on a turf seat in the shade of a tall ash-tree. Fifi lay on the ground beside them, having arranged her elongated body in the graceful curve known to dog-fanciers as the 'hare's bend'. Both Arkady and Katya were silent; he held a half-open book in his hands, while she was engaged in picking crumbs from the bottom of her basket and throwing them to a small family of sparrows who, with the timid temerity of their tribe, were hopping about and chirping at her very feet. A faint breeze rustled the foliage of the ash-tree and shifting circles of pale gold sunlight gently dappled the dark line of the pathway and Fifi's tawny back. Arkady and Katya sat in a patch of unrelieved shadow: only now and then did a bright shaft of sunshine light up her hair. They were both silent; but the way in which they were silent, the way in which they were sitting together, spoke eloquently of the trustful intimacy between them: each seemed unmindful of the other and yet full of an inward joy at being together. The expression of their faces, too, had changed since last we saw them: Arkady looked happier, Katya more animated and self-confident.

'Don't you think,' Arkady began, 'that our Russian name, *yasen*, for the ash-tree is a very good one? *Yasen* – lucent. No other tree is so light and translucent against the sky.'

Katya looked up and murmured, 'Yes,' and Arkady

thought, 'She at least doesn't reproach me for indulging in fine talk.'

'I don't care for Heine,' said Katya, glancing at the book in Arkady's hand, 'either when he's sarcastic or plaintive. I only like him when his mood is pensive and melancholy.'

'And I like him when he gibes,' Arkady remarked.

'That's an old mark of your satirical turn of mind ...'

'Old mark!' thought Arkady. 'If Bazarov heard that!'

'You just wait,' Katya went on, 'we shall transform you.'

'Who will transform me? You?'

'Who? My sister, and Porfiry Platonych, whom you've stopped arguing with, and auntie, whom you escorted to church the day before yesterday.'

'I couldn't very well refuse! And as for your sister, you remember she agreed with Yevgeny in a great many things.'

'My sister was under his influence then, just as you were.'

'As I *was*! Why, have you noticed any signs of my breaking away from his influence?'

Katya made no reply.

'I know,' continued Arkady, 'you never took to him.'

'I am not in a position to judge him.'

'Do you know what, Katerina Sergeyevna, whenever I hear that answer I don't believe it. ... There is no man living who cannot be judged by any one of us! It's just an excuse.'

'Well, I'll tell you then, he is ... it's not that I don't like him, but I feel I have no contact with him and I'm a stranger to him ... just as you haven't anything in common with him either.'

'Why do you think that?'

'How can I explain? ... He's a wild beast, while you and I are domestic animals.'

'Am I a domestic animal?'

Katya nodded her head.

Arkady scratched his ear. 'Listen, Katerina Sergeyevna, that's really a hurtful thing to say.'

'Why, would you rather be a wild beast?'

'Not wild, but strong and energetic.'

'It's no good wishing to be like that ... your friend does not *wish* for it, he *is* like that.'

'H'm. So you think he had a great influence on Anna Sergeyevna?'

'Yes. But no one can dominate her for long,' Katya added in a low voice.

'Why do you think that?'

'She is very proud ... I don't mean that ... I mean, she sets great store by her independence.'

'Who doesn't?' queried Arkady, while the thought flashed through his mind, 'Why are we talking about her?' And the same thought occurred to Katya – 'Why are we talking about her?' Young people who are friends and often together constantly find themselves thinking the same thoughts.

Arkady smiled and edging nearer to Katya he said in a whisper: 'Confess now, you are a little afraid of her.'

'Of whom?'

'Of *her*,' Arkady repeated significantly.

'And you?' Katya asked him in her turn.

'I am too; observe, I said, I am *too*.'

Katya wagged a finger at him.

'I am surprised at that,' she began. 'My sister has never felt so friendly towards you as just now – much more so than when you first came here.'

'You don't mean it!'

'Haven't you noticed? And aren't you pleased?'

Arkady reflected for a moment.

'What have I done to win Anna Sergeyevna's favour? Could it be because I brought her your mother's letters?'

'That's one reason, but there are others which I shan't tell you.'

'Why?'

'I'm not going to.'

'Oh, I know: you're very obstinate.'

'Yes, I am.'

'And observant.'

Katya cast a sidelong glance at Arkady. 'Perhaps that makes you cross? What are you thinking about?'

'I'm wondering how it is you have come to be as observant as you undoubtedly are. You are so shy and distrustful; you keep everybody at a distance ...'

'I have lived so much alone; that in itself leads to thoughtfulness. But do I really keep everyone at a distance?'

Arkady flung a grateful glance at Katya.

'That's all very well,' he went on, 'but people in your position, I mean with your fortune, don't often have that facility; it is as hard for them as it is for emperors to get at the truth.'

'But *I* am not wealthy.'

Arkady was taken aback and at first did not understand Katya. Then it dawned on him – 'Why, of course, the estate all belongs to her sister,' he thought, and he did not find the idea unpleasing.

'How prettily you said that!' he exclaimed.

'Said what?'

'You said it nicely; simply, without feeling mortified or making much of it. Incidentally, I always imagine there must be something special, a certain sort of vanity, in a person who realizes and acknowledges that he is poor.'

'Thanks to my sister, I have never had any experience of poverty. I only referred to my circumstances because it happened to come up in our conversation.'

'Quite so. But you must admit that even you harbour a grain of the vanity I spoke of just now.'

'For instance?'

'For instance – excuse me for asking – but you would not marry a rich man, I fancy, would you?'

'If I loved him very much. ... No, probably even then I wouldn't marry him.'

'There, you see!' cried Arkady, and after a moment's pause he added: 'And why wouldn't you marry him?'

'Because even ballads sing about poor girls marrying rich men.'

'Perhaps you want to dominate or . . .'

'Oh no! What's the good of that? On the contrary, I am ready to obey, only inequality is difficult. But to respect oneself and obey – that I can understand; that is happiness; but a mere subordinate existence. . . . No, I've had enough of that as it is.'

'Enough of that as it is,' Arkady repeated after Katya. 'Yes, yes,' he went on, 'you're not Anna Sergeyevna's sister for nothing; you are just as independent as she is; but you're more reserved. I am sure you would never be the first to express your feelings, however strong or sacred they might be . . .'

'How could it be otherwise?'

'You are as intelligent as she is; you have as much if not more character . . .'

'Don't compare me with my sister, please,' interrupted Katya hurriedly. 'It's too much to my disadvantage. You seem to forget that my sister is beautiful as well as being clever, and . . . you in particular, Arkady Nikolayevich, ought not to say such things, and with such a serious face too.'

'What do you mean, me in particular? And why do you suppose that I'm not serious?'

'Of course you are not serious.'

'You think so? And what if I believe in what I am saying? If I feel that I have not even expressed myself forcibly enough?'

'I don't understand you.'

'Really? Well, now I see that I certainly took you to be more observant than you are.'

'How is that?'

Arkady made no answer and turned away, while Katya searched for a few more crumbs in the basket and began throwing them to the sparrows; but she moved her arm too jerkily and the birds flew away without stopping to pick up the bread.

'Katerina Sergeyevna!' began Arkady suddenly. 'It may be all the same to you but I should like you to know that I wouldn't exchange you for your sister or for any one else in the world either.'

He got up and walked quickly away as though in sudden alarm at the words which had burst from his lips.

Katya let her two hands drop with the basket on to her lap and for a long time she sat, her head bent, staring after Arkady. Gradually a faint scarlet crept into her cheeks; but her lips remained unsmiling and her dark eyes held a look of perplexity and some other feeling that she could not yet define.

'Are you alone?' said Anna Sergeyevna's voice close by. 'I thought you came into the garden with Arkady.'

Katya slowly raised her eyes to her sister (elegantly, almost elaborately dressed, she was standing on the path and tickling Fifi's ears with the tip of her open parasol) and slowly replied: 'I am alone.'

'So I see,' the other replied with a laugh. 'I suppose he has gone indoors to his room?'

'Yes.'

'Were you reading together?'

'Yes.'

Anna Sergeyevna took Katya under the chin and raised her face.

'You have not quarrelled, I hope?'

'No,' said Katya, gently removing her sister's hand.

'How solemnly you answer: I thought I should find him here and was going to suggest we had a walk together. He is always asking me to go for a walk with him. Your new boots have just arrived from town, go and try them on: I noticed yesterday that your old pair are quite worn out. Really you don't pay enough attention to these things, and you've got such pretty little feet still! Your hands are nice too ... only they are too big; so you must make the most of your feet. But I couldn't say you were vain.'

Anna Sergeyevna walked on down the path, her beautiful gown rustling slightly as she moved. Katya rose from the bench and picking up the volume of Heine went her way too – but not to try on the boots.

'Pretty little feet,' she thought as she slowly and lightly mounted the stone steps of the terrace which were scorching in the sun. 'Pretty little feet, you say ... Well, before long he shall be kneeling at them.'

But immediately a feeling of shame came over her and she ran swiftly up the remaining steps.

As Arkady went along the passage to his room the butler caught up with him and announced that Monsieur Bazarov was waiting for him.

'Yevgeny!' muttered Arkady almost apprehensively. 'Has he been here long?'

'He arrived this minute, sir, and instructed me not to announce him to Madame but to show him straight to your room.'

'Can anything have happened at home?' was Arkady's first thought as he ran hurriedly upstairs and flung open the door of his room. The sight of Bazarov immediately reassured him, though a more experienced eye would probably have discerned signs of inward disturbance in the sunken but always energetic face of the unexpected visitor. He was sitting on the window-sill, a dusty cloak over his shoulders and a cap pulled over his eyes; he did not get up even when Arkady threw himself with loud exclamations on his neck.

'This is a surprise! What fate brings you here?' he kept repeating, fussing about the room like someone who both imagines and wants to show that he is delighted. 'Everything's all right at home, I suppose? They're all in good health, aren't they?'

'Everything is all right there, but not everyone is in good health,' said Bazarov. 'But stop chattering, and get them to bring me a drink of rye-beer. Sit down and listen to what I have to tell you, in a few but, I hope, fairly potent sentences.'

Arkady was quiet, and Bazarov told him about his duel with Pavel Petrovich. Arkady felt greatly surprised and even upset but he did not think it necessary to reveal this; he only asked whether his uncle's wound was really not serious; and on receiving the reply that it was most interesting in every respect save from the medical point of view he forced a smile but at heart he felt secretly hurt and somehow ashamed. Bazarov seemed to have an inkling of this.

'Yes, my dear fellow,' he said, 'you see what comes of living with these feudal barons. You become a feudal personage yourself and find yourself taking part in knightly tourneys. Well, so I set off for "the home of my fathers",' Bazarov concluded, 'and on the way I turned in here . . . to tell you all this, I might have said if I didn't think it stupid to tell useless lies. No, I turned in here – the devil knows why. Do you see, it's sometimes a good thing for a man to take himself by the scruff of the neck and pull himself up like pulling a radish out of its bed. That's what I've been doing these last few days. . . . But I was overcome with a desire to take one more look at what I've parted company with – at the bed in which I was rooted.'

'I hope these words don't apply to me,' Arkady protested anxiously. 'I hope you aren't thinking of parting with *me*?'

Bazarov looked at him intently; his eyes were almost piercing.

'Would that upset you so much? It strikes me that you have parted from me already. You look so spruce and smart . . . your *affaire* with Anna Sergeyevna must be progressing excellently!'

'What do you mean, my *affaire* with Anna Sergeyevna?'

'Wasn't it on account of her that you left town and came here, my little nestling? By the way, how are those Sunday schools getting on? Do you mean to tell me you aren't in love with her? Or have you already reached the stage of being bashful about it?'

'Yevgeny, you know I have always been frank with you; I can assure you, I swear to you, you are mistaken.'

'H'm! That's new,' Bazarov remarked under his breath. 'But you needn't excite yourself, I don't care a jot. A romantic would say, "I feel our paths are beginning to diverge," but I will simply say that we are tired of each other.'

'Oh Yevgeny . . .'

'Dear lad, that's no misfortune; the world is full of things that pall on one. And now I suppose we had better say good-bye, hadn't we? Ever since I arrived here I have been feeling so uncomfortable, as though after a surfeit of Gogol's letters to the wife of the Governor of Kaluga. In fact, I didn't tell them to unharness the horses.'

'But look here, this is impossible!'

'Why, may I ask?'

'Quite apart from me, it would be the height of discourtesy to Anna Sergeyevna. I know she would like to see you.'

'Well, you're mistaken there.'

'On the contrary, I'm convinced that I'm right,' protested Arkady. 'And why do you pretend? If it comes to that, aren't you here on her account yourself?'

'That might even be true, but you are mistaken all the same.'

But Arkady was right. Anna Sergeyevna did want to see Bazarov and sent a summons to him by the butler. Bazarov changed his clothes before going to her: it turned out that he had packed his new suit in such a way as to have it handy.

Madame Odintsov received him, not in the room where he had so unexpectedly declared his love for her but in the drawing-room. She graciously extended the tips of her fingers to him but her face showed signs of uncontrollable tension.

'Anna Sergeyevna,' Bazarov hastened to say, 'I must begin by setting your mind at rest. You see before you a poor mortal who came to his senses long ago and who hopes that other people too have forgotten his foolishness. I am now going away for a considerable period and though, as you will agree, I am not given to sentiment, I should be sorry to carry away with me the idea that you think of me with repugnance.'

Anna Sergeyevna gave a deep sigh, such as a climber might utter on reaching the summit of a lofty mountain, and her face lit up with a smile. She held out her hand to Bazarov a second time and responded to his pressure.

'Let bygones be bygones,' she said, 'especially as, to be quite frank, I was also to blame, if not by being coquettish, then in some other fashion. In short, let us be friends as we were before. The other was a dream, was it not? And who ever remembers dreams?'

'Who indeed? And besides, love ... is a purely imaginary feeling.'

'Really? I am very glad to hear you say that.'

So spoke Anna Sergeyevna, and so spoke Bazarov, and they both believed they were speaking the truth. Was the truth, the whole truth, to be found in their words? They themselves did not know, and still less does the author. But in the conversation that followed each appeared to have complete faith in the other.

In the course of it Anna Sergeyevna asked Bazarov what he had been doing at the Kirsanovs'. He was on the point of telling her about his duel with Pavel Petrovich but he checked himself with the thought that she might imagine that he was trying to make himself interesting, and answered that he had been working all the time.

'And I went through a fit of depression at first, heaven knows why,' observed Anna Sergeyevna. 'I even made plans to go abroad. Fancy! ... Then that passed off, your friend, Arkady, arrived and I settled down again to play my proper part.'

'And what is that, may I ask?'

'The part of aunt, guardian, mother – call it what you like. By the way, do you know, I used not to understand your close friendship with Arkady: I thought him rather insignificant. But now I have got to know him better and I recognize his intelligence. . . . But above all, he's young, young . . . not like you and me, Yevgeny Vassilyich.'

'Is he still as shy as ever in your company?' Bazarov asked.

'Why, was he . . .' Anna Sergeyevna began but after reflecting for a moment she went on: 'He has gained more confidence now; he talks to me. He used to avoid me before. Though, as a matter of fact, I did not seek his company either. He is more Katya's friend.'

Bazarov was put out. 'Women can't help dissembling,' he thought.

'You say that he used to avoid you,' he remarked aloud with a chilly smile, 'but probably it is no secret to you that he was in love with you?'

'What? He too?' burst from Anna Sergeyevna's lips.

'He too,' repeated Bazarov with a humble bow. 'I can't believe you didn't know, that I've told you something new?'

Anna Sergeyevna lowered her eyes. 'You are mistaken, Yevgeny Vassilyich.'

'I don't think so. But perhaps I oughtn't to have mentioned it.' ('And don't you try to fool me any more,' he added to himself.)

'Why shouldn't you mention it? But I think that in this, too, you are attaching overmuch significance to a fleeting impression. I begin to suspect that you are inclined to exaggerate.'

'Let us change the subject, Anna Sergeyevna.'

'Why should we?' she retorted, but at the same time diverting the conversation into another channel. She still felt ill at ease with Bazarov though she had both told him and assured herself that the past was forgotten. Exchanging the simplest remarks – and even when she joked – with him, she was conscious of a constraint, of a faint feeling of fear. Thus people on a steamer at sea talk and laugh light-heartedly, for all the world as if they were on dry land; but let the smallest hitch occur, at the faintest hint of something unusual, and their faces instantly express a peculiar anxiety, betraying their unceasing awareness of unceasing danger.

Anna Sergeyevna's talk with Bazarov did not last very long. She began to be absorbed in her own thoughts, to answer absentmindedly, and ended by suggesting that they should go into the drawing-room, where they found the princess and Katya. 'But where is Arkady Nikolayevich?' inquired the hostess and, on learning that he had not been seen for over an hour, she sent a servant to look for him. He was not found at once: he had hidden himself in the remotest corner of the garden and with his chin propped on his fists sat plunged in thought. His reflections were profound and grave but not despondent. He knew that Anna Sergeyevna was closeted alone with Bazarov but he felt none of his old jealousy; on the contrary, his face slowly brightened; he seemed to be at once marvelling at something, and rejoicing, and reaching a decision.

26

Madame Odintsov's late husband had disliked innovations but had tolerated a 'certain display of refined taste' and consequently had erected, in a space between the hothouse and the lake, a building in the style of a Greek portico, made of Russian brick. Along the back dead wall of this portico or gallery six niches had been prepared for statues which Odintsov had intended to order from abroad. These statues were to represent Solitude, Silence, Meditation, Melancholy, Modesty and Sensibility. One of them, the Goddess of Silence, with a finger on her lips, had actually been delivered and put in position; but on the very same day some of the farm boys knocked off her nose, and although the local plasterer undertook to make her nose 'twice as good as the old one' Odintsov had ordered her to be taken away, and the goddess found herself relegated to a corner of the threshing-barn, where she remained for many years, a source of superstitious terror to the peasant women. The façade part of the portico had long been overgrown with thick shrubbery; only the capitals of the columns could be seen above the dense green. Inside the portico itself it was airy even at midday. Ever since she had seen grass-snakes there Anna Sergeyevna had not cared to go into the place; but Katya often came and sat on a big stone bench under one of the niches. Here, in the cool shade, she read and did her embroidery, or abandoned herself to that sensation of absolute peace with which we are probably all familiar and the charm of which lies in a half-conscious, hushed contemplation of the vast current of life that is for ever swirling in and around us.

On the day after Bazarov's arrival Katya was sitting on her favourite bench, and Arkady was sitting beside her again. He had begged her to come with him to the 'portico'.

It was about an hour before lunch-time; the dewy morning had already surrendered to the heat of day. Arkady's face wore the same expression as on the day before; Katya looked preoccupied. Immediately after morning tea her sister had called her into the study and, after some preliminary display of affection – which always rather alarmed Katya – had counselled her to be more guarded in her behaviour with Arkady and, in particular, to avoid those solitary talks with him which, she said, had already been remarked on by her aunt and everyone else in the house. Moreover, Anna Sergeyevna had been in a bad mood the evening before; and also Katya herself felt uncomfortable, as though she had done something wrong. Thus, when she yielded to Arkady's request, she said to herself that it was for the last time.

'Katerina Sergeyevna,' he began with a sort of bashful nonchalance, 'ever since it has been my good fortune for us to be under the same roof I have discussed a great many things with you, and yet there is one very important ... question – for me – which so far I have not touched upon. You said yesterday that I had altered since my stay here,' he went on, catching but at the same time avoiding the inquiring look that Katya had fixed upon him. 'I have indeed altered in a great many respects, and you know that better than anyone else – you know it, for in reality I owe this transformation to you.'

'I? . . . To me? . . .' Katya stammered.

'I am now no longer the conceited boy I was when I first arrived here,' Arkady continued. 'I have not reached the age of twenty-two for nothing; I still have every wish to lead a useful life, I still want to devote all my energies to the pursuit of truth; but I can no longer seek my ideal where I did before; I perceive it now . . . much closer to hand. Up till now I did not understand myself, I set myself tasks beyond my capacity. . . . My eyes have recently been opened, thanks to a certain emotion. . . . I am not expressing myself very clearly but I hope you will understand me . . .'

Katya made no reply but she stopped looking at Arkady.

'I believe,' he began again, this time in a more agitated voice, while above his head a chaffinch poured out its song unheeding among the leaves of the birch-tree, 'I believe it is the duty of every honest man to be absolutely frank with those . . . with those who . . . in a word, with those who are dear to him, and so I . . . I intend . . .'

But at this point Arkady's eloquence deserted him; he lost his thread, stammered and was obliged to stop for a while. Katya still kept her eyes lowered. She seemed not to understand what he was leading up to with all this, and yet to be expecting something.

'I can see that I am going to surprise you,' Arkady resumed, having pulled himself together again, 'all the more so, since this emotion of mine is connected in a certain way – in a certain way, notice – with you. I seem to remember your reproaching me yesterday for a lack of seriousness,' Arkady pursued with the air of a man who has walked into a swamp and feels himself sinking deeper and deeper with every step, and yet hurries on in the hope of getting across more quickly. 'That reproach is often levelled at . . . often falls on . . . young men when they cease to deserve it; and if I had more self-confidence . . .' ('Help me now, why don't you help me!' Arkady was thinking in desperation but Katya kept her head averted as before.) 'If I might hope . . .'

'If I could feel sure of what you say,' Anna Sergeyevna's clear voice rang out at that moment.

Arkady fell silent at once and Katya turned pale. A path ran past the shrubbery which concealed the portico. Anna Sergeyevna was strolling along it accompanied by Bazarov. Katya and Arkady could not see them but they heard every word, the rustle of their clothes, even the sound of their breathing. They advanced a few more steps and then, as though deliberately, stood still right in front of the portico.

'It is like this,' Anna Sergeyevna continued, 'we both made a mistake; we are both past our first youth, I particularly so; we have seen life, we are tired; we are both of us – why pretend otherwise? – intelligent; we became interested in each other, our curiosity was roused . . . and then . . .'

'And then my interest petered out,' put in Bazarov.

'You know very well that was not why we fell out. But whatever the cause, we felt no compelling need of one another, that was the main reason. We were – how shall I put it? – we were too much alike. We did not realize that at first. Now Arkady, on the other hand . . .'

'Do you feel a "compelling need" of him?' asked Bazarov.

'Stop, Yevgeny Vassilyich. You say he is not indifferent to me, and it always seemed to me that he liked me. I know that I am old enough to be his aunt but I won't conceal from you that I have begun to think about him more often. I find a sort of charm in his fresh youthful sentiments . . .'

' "Fascination" is the word more generally used in such circumstances,' Bazarov interrupted her; spite and anger were in the steady but hollow tone of his voice. 'Yesterday Arkady was secretive with me about something, and he did not mention either you or your sister . . . a revealing sign, that.'

'He is just like a brother with Katya,' Anna Sergeyevna

said; 'and I like that about him, though perhaps I ought not to have let them become such close friends.'

'Is that the ... sister speaking?' drawled Bazarov.

'Of course ... but why are we standing here? Let us walk on. What a strange conversation we are having, don't you think? I could never have believed I should be talking to you like this. You know, I am afraid of you ... and at the same time I trust you, because fundamentally you are a good man.'

'In the first place, I am far from good; and in the second, I don't mean anything to you now, and that's why you think me good. .... It's like laying a wreath of flowers at a corpse's head.'

'Yevgeny Vassilyich, it isn't in our power ...' began Anna Sergeyevna; but a gust of wind set the leaves rustling and carried her words away.

'Of course, you are free,' Bazarov was heard to say after a pause. But the rest was lost; the steps retreated ... and silence supervened.

Arkady turned to face Katya. She was sitting in the same position as before, only her head was bent still lower.

'Katerina Sergeyevna,' he said in a trembling voice, and clenching his fists, 'I love you for ever, irrevocably, and I love only you. I have been trying to tell you this, to find out what you think, and to ask you to marry me because though I am not rich I am prepared to make every sacrifice ... You don't answer? You don't believe me? You think I am speaking lightly? But remember these last few days! Surely you must be convinced by now that everything else – you understand me – absolutely everything else has long ago melted into thin air without a trace? Look at me, say one word to me ... I love ... I love you ... Do believe me!'

Katya looked up at Arkady with grave and radiant eyes, and after a long reflective pause she murmured with the faintest smile, 'Yes.'

Arkady leaped up from the bench.

'Yes! You said "Yes", Katerina Sergeyevna. But what does it mean? That I love you? That you believe me? ... Or ... or ... I dare not go on ...'

'Yes,' repeated Katya, and this time he understood her. He seized her large beautiful hands and, breathless with joy, pressed them to his heart. He could hardly stand on his feet and kept repeating, 'Katya, Katya ...', while she began to weep guilelessly, smiling gently at her own tears. No one who has not seen such tears in the eyes of his beloved knows the degree of happiness attainable on this earth, as the heart swoons with thankfulness and awe.

Early next morning Anna Sergeyevna sent a message asking Bazarov to come to her study, where with a strained laugh she handed him a folded sheet of writing-paper. It was a letter from Arkady; in it he asked for her sister's hand in marriage.

Bazarov skimmed through the letter and made an effort to control himself and hide the malicious pleasure which instantly flared in his breast.

'So that's how it is,' he commented. 'And only yesterday you were saying, were you not, that his affection for Katerina Sergeyevna was that of a brother. What do you intend to do now?'

'What do you advise me?' asked Anna Sergeyevna, continuing to laugh.

'Well, I suppose,' answered Bazarov, also with a laugh, though he felt anything but gay and no more wanted to laugh than she did, 'I suppose you ought to give the young couple your blessing. It's a good match from every point of view: Kirsanov is tolerably well off, the boy's the only son, and his father is a nice fellow – he won't raise any objections.'

Anna Sergeyevna paced up and down the room, her face alternately flushing red and turning pale.

'You think so?' she said. 'Well, why not, I see no difficulties.... I am glad for Katya ... and for Arkady Nikolaye-vich. Of course, I shall wait for the father's response. I will send Arkady in person to him. So it appears I was right yesterday when I told you that you and I are old people now. . . . How was it I noticed nothing? That surprises me!'

Anna Sergeyevna laughed again, and quickly turned away her head.

'Young folk are very artful these days,' remarked Bazarov, and he also gave a short laugh. 'Good-bye,' he started to say after a brief silence. 'I hope you will bring this affair to a very happy conclusion; I shall rejoice from afar.'

Madame Odintsov swung round to face him.

'You are not going? Why can't you stay *now*? Do stay . . . you are such an amusing conversationalist. . . . Talking to you is like walking on the edge of a precipice. At first one is frightened, then one picks up courage. Do stay.'

'Thank you for suggesting it, Anna Sergeyevna, and for your flattering opinion of my conversational talent. But I find I have tarried overlong in a sphere which is alien to me. Flying-fish can stay in the air for a while but soon they must dive back into the water; with your permission I, too, must flop back into my natural element.'

Madame Odintsov looked at Bazarov. A bitter smile twisted his pale face. 'This man loved me!' she thought – and she felt sorry for him and held out her hand with sympathy.

But he understood her too.

'No!' he said, stepping back a pace. 'I may be poor but I have never accepted charity so far. *Adieu*, now, and good-bye.'

'I am certain we are not seeing each other for the last time,' declared Anna Sergeyevna with an involuntary gesture.

'Anything can happen in this world,' answered Bazarov, and he bowed and left the room.

'So you are planning to build yourself a nest?' he said the same day to Arkady as he squatted on the floor packing his trunk. 'Why not, it's a good thing. Only you needn't have been such a humbug about it. I expected you to go in quite another quarter. Or, maybe, you yourself were taken unawares?'

'I certainly didn't expect this when I left you at Maryino,' Arkady replied, 'but why are you being a humbug yourself and calling it "a good thing", as if I didn't know your opinion of marriage?'

'Ah, my dear friend, the way you express yourself!' Bazarov exclaimed. 'You see what I'm doing: there happened to be an empty space in my trunk, and I'm stuffing it with hay; it's the same with the trunk which is our life: we fill it with anything that comes to hand rather than leave a void. Don't be offended, please; you remember, no doubt, the opinion I have always held of Katerina Sergeyevna. Some young ladies have the reputation of being intelligent because they can sigh cleverly; but your young lady can hold her own, and do it so well that she'll take you in hand also – well, and that's how it should be.' He slammed the lid of the trunk and got up from the floor. 'And now, in parting, let me repeat ... because there is no point in deceiving ourselves – we are parting for good, and you know that yourself ... you have acted sensibly: you were not made for our bitter, harsh, lonely existence. There's no audacity in you, no venom: you've the fire and energy of youth but that's not enough for our business. Your sort, the gentry, can never go farther than well-bred resignation or well-bred indignation, and that's futile. The likes of you, for instance, won't stand up and fight – and yet you think yourselves fine fellows – but we insist on fighting. Yes, that's the trouble! Our dust would corrode your eyes, our mud would sully you, but in actual fact you aren't up to our level yet, you unconsciously admire yourself, you enjoy finding fault with yourself; but we've had enough of all that – give us fresh victims! We must smash people! You are a nice lad; but you're too soft, a good little liberal gentleman – *eh volla-too*,* as my father would say.'

---

* *et voilà tout!*

'You are bidding me adieu for ever, Yevgeny,' said Arkady sadly, 'and this is all that you have to say to me?'

Bazarov scratched the back of his head.

'No, Arkady, there are other things I could say to you but I won't say them because it would be sentimental – mawkish. You hurry up and get married, start a nest of your own and beget plenty of offspring. They'll have the wit to be born in a better age, not like you and me. Aha! I see the horses are ready. It's time to be off. I have said good-bye to everyone ... Well, shall we embrace, do you think?'

Arkady flung himself on the neck of his former mentor and friend, and tears fairly streamed from his eyes.

'What it is to be young!' Bazarov said calmly. 'But I rely on Katerina Sergeyevna. She'll soon console you, you see!'

'Farewell, brother!' he called out to Arkady after climbing into the wagon, and pointing to a pair of jackdaws sitting side by side on the stable roof, he added, 'Look at that! There's an example for you!'

'What do you mean?' Arkady asked.

'What? Are you so weak in natural history, or have you forgotten that the jackdaw is the most respectable family bird? Learn from him! ... Farewell, *signor*!'

With a clatter the wagon rolled away.

Bazarov had spoken the truth. While talking that evening with Katya Arkady completely forgot about his former mentor. He was already beginning to surrender to her influence, and Katya sensed this and was not surprised. He was to set off next day for Maryino, to see his father. Anna Sergeyevna had no wish to hamper the young people and it was only for the sake of the proprieties that she did not leave them alone for too long. She considerately kept the princess out of their way – the news of the approaching wedding had reduced the old lady to a state of tearful rage. At first Anna Sergeyevna was afraid the sight of their happiness might prove somewhat painful to herself but it turned out to be quite the contrary: far from upsetting her, their happiness occupied her mind and finally won her over completely. This outcome brought her both relief and regret. 'Evidently Bazarov was right,' she thought. 'It was mere curiosity, and partiality for a quiet life, and egoism . . .'

'Children!' she exclaimed aloud, 'tell me, is love an imaginary feeling?'

But neither Katya nor Arkady even understood what she meant. They fought shy of her; they could not forget the conversation they had overheard. But Anna Sergeyevna soon set their minds at rest; and it was not difficult for her: she had set her own mind at rest.

27

Bazarov's old parents were all the more overjoyed at their son's arrival as they had not really expected him. Arina Vlassyevna got so excited and fussed to and fro in the house so much that her husband likened her to a 'little hen partridge': the abbreviated tail of her short jacket did indeed give her a bird-like appearance. He himself merely grunted and chewed the amber mouthpiece of his pipe; or clutching his neck with his fingers he would swivel his head round as though to make sure it was properly screwed on, and suddenly open his wide mouth and guffaw noiselessly.

'I have come to stay for six whole weeks, my old fellow,' Bazarov said to him. 'I want to work, so don't you disturb me.'

'You'll forget what my face looks like – that's how much I shall disturb you,' retorted Vassily Ivanych.

He was as good as his promise. After installing his son in the study as before, he not only kept out of his way but restrained his wife from all superfluous demonstrations of affection. 'Last time we got a bit on his nerves, my dear,' he said to her. 'We must be more sensible this time.' The old lady agreed with her husband but derived small benefit thereby, since she only saw her son at meals and was finally afraid to address him. 'My little Yevgeny,' she would begin, but before he had time to glance in her direction she was nervously fingering the tassels of her reticule and faltering, 'Oh nothing, nothing at all, just an exclamation.' And then she would go to her husband and, propping her cheek on her hand, say to him: 'My dear, how can I find out what our Yevgeny would like for dinner today? Sour cabbage or beetroot soup?' – 'But why didn't you ask him yourself?' – 'Oh, I'd only annoy him.' Bazarov, however, soon stopped shutting himself up; his fever for work abated and was succeeded by gloomy nostalgia and a vague restlessness. A strange weariness showed itself in all his movements; even his firm and impetuously resolute stride was different. He gave up his long solitary walks and began to seek company; he now took his tea in the parlour, strolled about the kitchen garden with his father and had 'quiet smokes' with him; once he even asked after Father Alexei. At first his father was delighted at this change, but his joy was short-lived. 'I'm worried about Yevgeny,' he confided dolefully to his wife. 'It's not that he is discontented or bad-tempered – that wouldn't matter: but he seems upset and sad – that is what's so dreadful. He never opens his mouth – if only he would rail against us. He's losing weight, and I don't at all like the colour of his face.'

'Lord have mercy on us!' whispered the old woman. 'I would hang an amulet round his neck but of course he wouldn't allow me to.'

Vassily Ivanych tried several times in the most circumspect manner to question Bazarov about his work, his health, and about Arkady. . . . But Bazarov's replies were reluctant and casual, and once, noticing that his father was gradually attempting to lead up to something in the conversation, he said irritably: 'Why are you for ever tiptoeing around me? It's worse than you were before.'

'There, there, I meant nothing!' the unhappy father hastily replied. Political allusions bore no fruit either. One day when they were discussing the approaching liberation of the serfs, hoping to win his son's sympathy, he started to talk about progress; but Bazarov only answered indifferently: 'Yesterday I was walking along by the fence and I heard some local lads bawling, not one of the good old ballads, but "The appointed time be here, Love comes welling to the heart . . ." There's progress for you.'

Sometimes Bazarov strolled to the village and in his usual bantering tone engaged some peasant in talk. 'Well, brother,' he would say to him, 'pray expound to me your views on life. For I am told the whole power and future of Russia lies in your hands, that with you a new epoch in history is about to begin – you are to give us a real language, and legislation.' The peasant either made no reply, or pronounced some such words as 'Oh – ah – maybe . . . we ain't always got no choice, you see . . .'

'Now you must explain to me what sort of a thing your village community is,' Bazarov would interrupt him. 'Is it the same world which we are told sits on three fishes?'

'It's the earth, master, that is stood on three fishes,' the peasant would explain soothingly in a good-natured, patriarchal sing-song, 'an' over an' above our world, our village community, I mean, we all know there's the master's will; on account of you bein' like our fathers. An' the more strict the master rules, the better it be for us peasants.'

After listening to such a reply one day Bazarov shrugged his shoulders contemptuously and turned his back on him, while the man went on his way.

'What was 'e a-talking about?' another peasant asked, a middle-aged, surly-looking man who had watched the conversation with Bazarov from the door of his hut. 'What 'e ain't bin paid, eh?'

'Not likely, brother!' the first peasant replied, and now there was no trace of any patriarchal sing-song note but, instead, a sort of careless asperity. ' 'E was just natterin' away about something. Wanted to wag 'is tongue a bit. 'Course 'e's gentry: they ain't got much understandin'.'

'Aye,' agreed the second peasant, and pushing back their caps and pulling down their belts they fell to deliberating on their own affairs and requirements. Alas for Bazarov, shrugging his shoulders contemptuously; Bazarov, who knew how to talk to the peasants (as he had boasted when arguing with Pavel Petrovich) – Bazarov the self-confident did not for a moment suspect that in their eyes he was after all nothing but a sort of buffoon.

However, at last he found himself an occupation. One day he saw his father binding up a peasant's injured leg, but the old man's hands shook so much that he had difficulty managing the bandage; his son came to his aid, and from that time Bazarov helped regularly with the patients, though he never ceased to mock both at the remedies he himself suggested and at his father who immediately applied them. But Bazarov's gibes caused no distress to his father: they even brought him some comfort. With two fingers holding his greasy dressing-gown over his stomach, and puffing away at his pipe, he listened to Bazarov with enjoyment, and the more malicious his son's sallies, the more good-humouredly did his delighted father chuckle, showing every one of his blackened teeth. He even went about repeating the witticisms, flat and pointless as they sometimes were – for instance, without rhyme or reason for several days on end he kept saying, 'That is a remote matter,' simply because his son, on hearing that he was going to matins had made that remark. 'Thank God he has got over his melancholy!' he whispered to his wife. 'It was marvellous, the dressing-down he gave me this morning!' Also, the idea of having his son as an assistant filled him to overflowing with ecstasy and pride. 'Yes, indeed,' he would say to some peasant woman wearing a man's coat and a head-dress like a horn, as he handed her a bottle of Goulard water or a pot of henbane ointment, 'you ought to be thanking

God every minute that my son is staying with me: you are being treated now by the most up-to-date scientific methods, do you realize that, my good woman? The Emperor of the French, Napoleon III himself, has no better doctor.' The peasant woman, who had come to complain that she was 'hoisted with the gripes' (though she was unable to explain what she meant by these words) only kept bowing and fumbling in her bosom where she had four eggs – the doctor's fee – wrapped up in the corner of a towel.

Bazarov once even pulled out a tooth for an itinerant pedlar of woven cloth, and although the tooth was quite an ordinary specimen Vassily Ivanych preserved it like some rare object, and repeated over and over again as he showed it to Father Alexei:

'Just look at those roots! To think of the strength Yevgeny must possess! That pedlar was lifted right up into the air ... I believe he could pull up an oak tree! ...'

'Admirable!' Father Alexei commented at last, not knowing what to answer or how to get rid of the rapturous old man.

One day a peasant from a neighbouring village brought his brother, who was stricken with typhus, over to Vassily Ivanych. Lying flat on a truss of straw, the unfortunate man was on the point of death: his body was covered with purple blotches and he had long ago lost consciousness. Vassily Ivanych expressed regret that it had occurred to no one to seek medical aid earlier, and declared there was no hope. And, in fact, the peasant never got his brother home again: he died as he was, lying in the cart.

Some three days later Bazarov walked into his father's room and asked if he had any silver nitrate.

'Yes, what do you want it for?'

'I need some ... to cauterize a cut.'

'Who for?'

'For myself.'

'What do you mean, for yourself? What's happened? What sort of cut? Where is it?'

'Here, on my finger. I drove over this morning to the village, you know, where they brought that peasant with the typhus from. They decided to open the body for some reason, and I've had no practice of that sort for a long while.'

'Well?'

'Well, I asked the district doctor if I could do it; and so, well, I cut myself.'

Vassily Ivanych suddenly went white to the lips and without a word rushed into his study, returning immediately with a piece of silver nitrate in his hand. Bazarov was about to take it and go off.

'For heaven's sake,' exclaimed Vassily Ivanych, 'let me see to it for you.'

Bazarov smiled. 'What a devoted practitioner you are!'

'Don't laugh, please. Show me your finger. It's not a big cut. Am I hurting you?'

'Press harder, don't be afraid.'

Vassily Ivanych paused.

'What do you think, Yevgeny? Wouldn't it be better to sear it with a hot iron?'

'That ought to have been done sooner. Actually, even the silver nitrate is no use now. If I've caught the infection, it's too late already.'

'How ... too late? ...' The old man could scarcely utter the words.

'Of course! It's over four hours since it happened.'

Vassily Ivanych burned the cut a little more.

'But hadn't the district doctor any caustic?'

'No.'

'Heavens above, how was that? A doctor, and without such an indispensable thing as that!'

'You should have seen his lancets,' observed Bazarov, and went out.

Till late that evening and all the following day Vassily

Ivanych seized on every possible pretext to go into his son's room and, though he not only made no reference to the cut but even attempted to chat about quite extraneous matters, he nevertheless stared so persistently into his son's eyes and watched him with so much anxiety that Bazarov lost patience and threatened to depart altogether. Vassily Ivanych promised not to worry, the more so as Arina Vlassyevna, from whom he had naturally kept it all secret, was beginning to badger him, asking why it was he did not sleep and what had come over him. For two whole days he held himself in check, though he did not at all like the look of his son, whom he kept watching on the sly . . . but on the third day, at dinner, he could bear it no longer. Bazarov was sitting with eyes lowered, and had not touched a single dish.

'Why don't you eat, Yevgeny?' he asked, assuming a casual expression. 'The food seems nicely cooked.'

'I don't feel hungry, so I don't eat.'

'You have no appetite? And your head,' he added timidly, 'does it ache?'

'Yes, it does. Why shouldn't it?'

Arina Vlassyevna sat up and was all ears.

'Please don't be angry, Yevgeny,' the old man went on, 'but won't you let me feel your pulse?'

Bazarov got up.

'I can tell you without your feeling it that I have a temperature.'

'Have you been shivery too?'

'Yes. I'll go and lie down, and you can send me some lime-flower tea. I must have caught a chill.'

'To be sure, I heard you coughing last night,' his mother murmured.

'I've caught a chill,' Bazarov repeated, and went out. Arina Vlassyevna busied herself preparing the lime-flower tea, while the old man went into the next room and clutched at his hair in silence.

Bazarov did not get up again that day and passed the whole

night in a state of half-conscious, heavy drowsiness. Some time after midnight he opened his eyes with an effort, saw in the glimmer from the little lamp before the ikon his father's pale face bent over him, and bade him go away. The old man obeyed but immediately returned on tiptoe, and partly concealing himself behind the doors of a wardrobe stood there, gazing at his son. Arina Vlassyevna did not go to bed either, and leaving the study door ajar kept coming up to it to listen 'how Yevgeny was breathing,' and to look at Vassily Ivanych. She could only see his still bent back but even that afforded her some faint consolation. In the morning Bazarov tried to get up; his head swam, his nose began to bleed; he lay down again. Vassily Ivanych tended him in silence; Arina Vlassyevna came in and asked him how he felt. He replied, 'Better,' and turned his face to the wall. Vassily Ivanych gesticulated at his wife with both hands; she bit her lip to stop herself from crying and left the room. Of a sudden darkness seemed to descend in the house; faces all looked drawn, and everything was strangely still. A raucous cock was removed from the yard and carried to the village, thoroughly perplexed at being treated in this fashion. Bazarov continued to lie with his face to the wall. Vassily Ivanych essayed various inquiries but they only wearied Bazarov, and the old man was reduced to huddling in his armchair, only now and then cracking the joints of his fingers. Occasionally he would go into the garden for a few seconds, stand there like a stone idol, as though stricken with unutterable bewilderment (this bewildered expression never left his face all through), and then return to his son's room, trying to avoid his wife's anxious questioning. At last she caught him by the arm and convulsively, almost menacingly asked: 'What is the matter with him?' Whereupon he pulled himself together and tried to manage a smile in reply; but to his own horror, instead of a smile, he found himself somehow seized with laughter. At daybreak he had sent for a doctor. He thought it necessary to warn his son about this, in case he should be angry.

Bazarov suddenly turned over on the sofa, fixed his father with dull eyes and asked for something to drink.

Vassily Ivanych gave him some water and as he did so felt his forehead. It was burning.

'I'm in a bad way, old chap,' Bazarov began in a slow, husky voice. 'I've caught the infection, and in a few days you will have to bury me.'

Vassily Ivanych staggered as though someone had knocked his legs from under him.

'Yevgeny!' he whispered. 'What are you saying? ... God forbid! You have got a chill ...'

'Don't go on,' Bazarov interrupted in the same slow, deliberate voice. 'A doctor has no right to talk like that. I've all the symptoms of the disease, you know that yourself.'

'Where are these symptoms ... of the disease, Yevgeny? ... I ask you.'

'What about this?' said Bazarov, and pulling up the sleeve of his night-shirt he showed his father the ominous red patches coming out on his arm.

Vassily Ivanych trembled and went cold with fear.

'Assuming,' he brought out at last, 'assuming ... that ... that this is something in the nature ... of an infection ...'

'Pyaemia,' his son prompted.

'Well, yes ... something like ... the epidemic ...'

'Of pyaemia,' Bazarov repeated sternly and distinctly. 'Have you forgotten your text-books?'

'All right, all right, as you wish. ... But we will cure you all the same!'

'Fiddlesticks! But that's not the point. I did not expect to die so soon: it's a fortuitous circumstance, and, to tell the truth, a very unpleasant one. You and mother must now fall back on your strong religious faith; here's an opportunity of putting it to the test.' He took a few more sips of water. 'But I want to ask you to do something for me ... while my brain's still under my control. Tomorrow or the day after, as you know, it will hand in its resignation. Even now I'm not quite sure whether I am making myself clear. While I have been lying here I have kept fancying red hounds were running round me, and you were making a point at me, as if I were a woodcock. Just as if I were drunk. Do you understand me all right?'

'Of course, Yevgeny. You are talking quite normally.'

'So much the better. You told me that you had sent for the doctor.... You did that for your own comfort.... Now comfort me too: send a messenger ...'

'To Arkady?' the old man picked him up.

'Who's Arkady?' Bazarov said doubtfully. 'Oh yes, that little fledgling! No, leave him in peace, he's turned into a jackdaw now. Don't look surprised, I'm not in a delirium yet. Will you send a messenger to Madame Odintsov, Anna Sergeyevna, she has an estate not far off.... Do you know?' (Vassily Ivanych nodded.) ' "Yevgeny Bazarov," he is to say, "sends his respects and told me to tell you he is dying." Will you do that?'

'I will.... Only is it a possible thing, that you should die, you, Yevgeny? ... Judge for yourself! Where would justice be after that?'

'I don't know about that; you just send the messenger.'

'This very minute. I will write her a line myself.'

'No, why? Say I sent my respects, nothing more is necessary. And now I shall return to my hounds again. How curious it is – I want to fix my thoughts on death, and nothing comes of it. I merely see a kind of blur ... and that's all.'

He turned painfully back to the wall again, while Vassily Ivanych left the study, and struggling as far as his wife's bedroom collapsed there on his knees before the ikons.

'Pray, Arina, pray,' he groaned. 'Our son is dying.'

The doctor, that same district practitioner who could produce no caustic when it was required, arrived and after examining the patient advised them to bide their time, and followed this up with a few words on the possibility of recovery.

'Have you ever seen people in my state *not* set off for the Elysian fields?' asked Bazarov, and suddenly catching hold of the leg of a heavy table which stood beside the sofa he swung it round and pushed it away.

'There's strength enough,' he muttered. 'It's all there still, and yet I must die ... An old man, at least, has had time to become disenchanted with life but I.... Yes, just try and set death aside. It sets you aside, and that's the end of it! Who is that crying there?' he went on after a while. 'Mother? Poor mother! Who will she feed now with her wonderful beetroot and cabbage soup? And you, father, whimpering too, I do believe! Well, if Christianity is no help, be a philosopher, a Stoic maybe! Surely you used to pride yourself on being a philosopher?'

'A fine philosopher I am!' sobbed Vassily Ivanych, and the tears streamed down his cheeks.

Bazarov grew worse with every hour; as generally happens in cases of surgical poisoning the infection spread rapidly. He had not yet lost consciousness and could understand what was said to him; he was still putting up a fight. 'I refuse to be delirious,' he whispered, clenching his fists. 'How absurd it all is!' And at once he would add: 'Now, take ten from eight, what remains?' Vassily Ivanych wandered about like a man out of his mind, suggesting first one remedy, then another, and ended up by doing nothing more than cover up his son's feet. 'We must wrap him in cold sheets ... give him an emetic ... a mustard-plaster on his stomach ... a little blood-letting,' he would exclaim with great intensity. The doctor, who had stayed on at his urgent entreaty, agreed with everything he said, gave the patient lemonade to drink, and for himself asked now for a pipe, now for something 'warm and strengthening' – to wit, vodka. Arina Vlassyevna sat on a low stool near the door and only went away at intervals to say her prayers; a few days previously a little looking-glass had slipped from her hands and smashed, and this she had always interpreted as a bad omen; even Anfisushka could find no words to console her. Timofeich had gone off with the message for Madame Odintsov.

Bazarov had a bad night.... He was racked by a high temperature. Towards morning he felt a little easier. He asked his mother to comb his hair, kissed her hand and swallowed a sip or two of tea. Vassily Ivanych took heart a fraction.

'Thank God!' he kept declaring. 'The crisis has come ... the crisis is over.'

'There, to think now!' muttered Bazarov. 'What a lot a word can do! He's found one – he said "crisis" and feels better. It's an astounding thing, the faith men still have in words. Tell a man he's a fool, for instance, and though you don't lay a finger on him he'll be miserable; call him a brainy chap and go off without paying him – and he'll be delighted.'

This little speech of Bazarov's, reminiscent of his old sallies, greatly moved his father.

'Bravo! Well said, excellent!' he cried, making as though he were clapping his hands.

Bazarov smiled wryly.

'So what do you think,' he said, 'is the crisis over or approaching?'

'You are better, that's what I see, that's what rejoices me.'

'That's first rate: there's never any harm in rejoicing. And *her*, do you remember? Did you send the message?'

'Of course I did.'

The turn for the better was short-lived. The disease resumed its onslaughts. Vassily Ivanych spent all his time at his son's bedside. He looked as if he were being tortured by some particular anguish. Several times he opened his mouth to speak – but the words stuck in his throat.

'Yevgeny!' he got out at last. 'My son, my dear beloved son!'

This unusual mode of address moved Bazarov. He turned

his head slightly and obviously trying to fight off the load of oblivion weighing him down he murmured:

'What is it, father?'

'Yevgeny,' Vassily Ivanych went on, sinking on his knees by the bed, although Bazarov had not opened his eyes and could not see him. 'Yevgeny, you are better now; please God, you will recover; but make good use of this moment, comfort your mother and me, perform your duty as a Christian! It's terrible for me to have to say this to you; but it would be still more terrible ... for ever and ever, Yevgeny ... just think what that means ...'

The old man's voice broke and a curious look came over his son's face, though he continued to lie there with eyes closed.

'I have no objection if it's any consolation to you,' he replied at last. 'But it seems to me there's no hurry yet. You say yourself that I am better.'

'You are better, Yevgeny, you are better; but who knows, it all lies in God's hands, but if you fulfil your duty ...'

'No, I will wait a bit,' interrupted Bazarov. 'I agree with you that the crisis has set in. But if we're mistaken, it won't matter! Even people who are unconscious can receive the last anointing.'

'Please, Yevgeny ...'

'I'll wait. And now I want to sleep. Don't disturb me.' And he laid his head back where it was before.

The old man rose from his knees, sat down in the armchair and holding his chin began to bite his fingers. ...

Suddenly his ears caught the rumble of a carriage on springs – a sound which so peculiarly strikes the ear in the depths of the country. Nearer and nearer rolled the light wheels; now he could hear the snorting of the horses. ... Vassily Ivanych jumped up and rushed to the window. A two-seated carriage, drawn by four horses, was driving into the courtyard of his little house. Without stopping to consider what this could mean he ran out on to the steps, in a burst of insensate joy. . . . A footman in livery was opening the carriage door; a lady in a black veil and a black mantle was getting out. . . .

'My name is Odintsov,' she said. 'Is Yevgeny Vassilyich still alive? Are you his father? I have brought my doctor with me.'

'Angel of mercy!' cried Vassily Ivanych, and seizing her hand he pressed it convulsively to his lips, while the doctor whom Anna Sergeyevna had brought, a squat man in spectacles, with a German cast of face, climbed slowly out of the carriage. 'He is still alive, my Yevgeny is alive, and now he will be saved! Wife! Wife! . . . An angel from heaven has come to us . . .'

'Merciful Lord, what is it?' stammered the old woman, running out of the sitting-room and, comprehending nothing, there in the passage she threw herself at Anna Sergeyevna's feet and began to kiss her dress like a mad woman.

'What are you doing, what are you doing?' protested Anna Sergeyevna; but Arina Vlassyevna paid no heed to her and Vassily Ivanych went on repeating: 'An angel! An angel!'

'*Wo ist der Kranke?* And the pashient where iss?' the doctor inquired at last, not without a touch of indignation.

Vassily Ivanych pulled himself together.

'Here, here, please follow me, *werthester Herr College*,' he added, remembering the old days.

'Ah!' the German said with a sour smile.

Vassily Ivanych led him into the study.

'A doctor from Anna Sergeyevna Odintsov,' he said, bending down close to his son's ear, 'and she is here herself.'

Bazarov suddenly opened his eyes.

'What did you say?'

'I said that Madame Odintsov is here and has brought this gentleman, a doctor, to see you.'

Bazarov looked round the room.

'She is here . . . I want to see her.'

'You shall see her, Yevgeny; but first you must have a talk

with the doctor. I will tell him the whole history of your illness, since Sidor Sidorin' (this was the district doctor's name) 'has gone, and we will have a little consultation.'

Bazarov glanced at the German.

'Well, talk away then quickly, only not in Latin; you see I know what *jam moritur** means.'

'Der Herr scheint des Deutschen mächtig zu sein'† began the newly-arrived disciple of Aesculapius, turning to Vassily Ivanych.

'*Ich . . . habe . . .* We had better speak Russian,' said the old man.

'Ah, zo zat iss how it iss . . . Please . . .' And the consultation began.

Half an hour later Anna Sergeyevna, accompanied by Vassily Ivanych, entered the study. Her doctor managed to whisper to her that it was no use even to hope for the patient's recovery.

Her eyes sought Bazarov . . . and she stopped short in the doorway, so taken aback was she by his feverish and at the same time deathly pale face, and by the dim eyes turned in her direction. She knew a feeling of sheer terror; a cold and oppressive terror; then the thought flashed instantly into her brain that she would not have felt like this if she had really loved him.

'Thank you,' he said with an effort. 'I did not expect this. It is a good deed. So we meet once more, as you said we would.'

'Madame Odintsov was so kind . . .' began Vassily Ivanych.

'Father, leave us. . . . Anna Sergeyevna, you don't mind, do you? Now that . . .'.

With a motion of his head he indicated his prostrate helpless body.

Vassily Ivanych went out.

* He's already dying.
† The gentleman knows German, it appears.

'Well, I must thank you,' Bazarov repeated. 'This is a royal gesture. They say emperors also visit the dying.'

'Yevgeny Vassilyich, I hope . . .'

'Ah, Anna Sergeyevna, let us speak the truth. It's all over with me. I've fallen under the wheel. So it turns out there was no point in thinking about the future. Death is an old jest but it comes new to everyone. Up to now I'm not afraid . . . and soon I shall lose consciousness, and then the end!' (He waved his hand feebly.) 'Well, what had I to say to you . . . That I loved you? That made no sense before, and makes less than ever now. Love is a form, and my particular form is already disintegrating. Better let me say – how lovely you are! And now there you stand, so beautiful . . .'

Anna Sergeyevna involuntarily shuddered.

'No, don't be alarmed. . . . Sit down over there. . . . Don't come near me – my malady is infectious, you know.'

Anna Sergeyevna quickly crossed the room and sat down in the armchair by the sofa on which Bazarov was lying.

'Noble-hearted one!' he whispered. 'Oh, how close you are, how young and fresh and pure . . . in this loathsome room! . . . Well, I must say my farewell! Live long, that's best of all, and make the most of it while there's time. Take a good look at this hideous spectacle: a worm, half crushed but writhing still. And yet there was a time when I, too, thought of all the things I would do, and never die, why should I? There were problems to solve, I said to myself, and I'm a giant. And now the only problem for this giant is how to die decently, though that makes no difference to anyone. . . . All the same, I'm not going to change now.'

Bazarov fell silent and began to grope for his glass. Without taking off her gloves, and breathing apprehensively, Anna Sergeyevna handed him the glass of water.

'You will forget me,' he began again. 'A dead man is no companion for the living. My father will tell you what a loss I shall be to Russia . . . That's bosh, but don't disillusion the old man. Whatever toy comforts a child . . . you know. And be kind to my mother. You won't find people like them in your great world even if you search for them in daylight and with the help of a lamp. . . . Russia needs me. . . . No, clearly she doesn't. And who is needed? The cobbler's needed, the tailor's needed, the butcher . . . sells meat . . . the butcher – wait a moment, I'm getting mixed up. . . . There's a forest here . . .'

Bazarov put his hand to his forehead.

Anna Sergeyevna bent over him. 'Yevgeny Vassilyich, I am here . . .'

He at once took her hand and raised himself.

'Farewell,' he said with sudden force, and his eyes flashed a last gleam. 'Farewell. . . . Listen. . . . You know, I never kissed you then. . . . Breathe on the dying flame and let it go out . . .'

Anna Sergeyevna touched his forehead with her lips.

'Enough!' he murmured, and sank back on the pillow. 'Now . . . darkness . . .'

Anna Sergeyevna went softly out of the room.

'Well?' Vassily Ivanych asked her in a whisper.

'He has fallen asleep,' she replied, almost inaudibly.

Bazarov was not destined to wake again. Towards evening he sank into complete unconsciousness, and on the following day he died. Father Alexei performed the last rites over him. When they were anointing him and the holy oil touched his breast one of his eyes opened, and it seemed as though, at the sight of the priest in his vestments, the smoking censer, and the candle burning before the ikon, something like a shudder of horror passed over the death-stricken face. And when he finally breathed his last sigh and the house was filled with general lamentation Vassily Ivanych was seized by a sudden frenzy. 'I said I would rebel,' he shouted hoarsely, his face inflamed and distorted, waving his clenched fist in the air as though threatening someone – 'And I will rebel, I will!' But Arina Vlassyevna, suffused in tears, hung her arms round his neck and both fell prone together. 'And so,' as

Anfisushka related afterwards in the servants' room, 'side by side they bowed their poor heads like lambs in the heat of noonday ...'

But the blaze of the noonday sun passes and is succeeded by dusk and nightfall, and then the night, with a return to the quiet fold where sleep, sweet sleep, waits for the tormented and the weary ...

28

Six months went by. White winter had set in with the cruel stillness of cloudless frosts, with its thick crunching snow, rosy hoar-rimed trees, pale emerald sky, smoke-capped chimneys, puffs of vapour from momentarily opened doors, of fresh faces stung by the cold, and the jerky trot of shivering horses. The January day was drawing to its close; the increasing chill of evening was nipping the still air and a blood-red sunset was rapidly dying away. Lights were burning in the windows of the house at Maryino; Prokofyich in a black tail-coat and white gloves was laying the table for seven with unwonted ceremony. A week earlier, in the small parish church two weddings had taken place quietly and almost without witnesses: Arkady's marriage to Katya, and that of Nikolai Petrovich to Fenichka; and on this day Nikolai Petrovich was giving a farewell dinner for his brother, who was going away to Moscow on some business. Anna Sergeyevna was already there: she had departed directly the wedding was over, after generously endowing the young couple.

Punctually at three o'clock the whole company gathered round the table. Mitya had his place too, and could now boast of a nanny wearing an embroidered head-band, and sat in state between Katya and Fenichka; the 'husbands' were beside their wives. A change had come over our friends of late: they all seemed to have grown handsomer and more virile; only Pavel Petrovich was thinner, and this, incidentally, still further enhanced the elegant '*grand seigneur*' air of his expressive features. . . . Fenichka, too, had altered. Wearing a crisp silk gown, a wide velvet bandeau round her hair and a gold chain round her neck, she was sitting with quiet dignity, self-respecting and respectful of everything about her, and smiling as much as to say: 'Excuse me, this isn't any of my doing.' And she was not the only person to smile – they all smiled, and they all looked apologetic; they all felt a little awkward, a little sad, and, at bottom, very happy. They attended to each other's wants with an amusing consideration, as though they had all agreed in advance to act a sort of artless comedy. Katya was the most at ease: she looked confidently about her, and it was evident that Nikolai Petrovich had already lost his heart to her. Towards the end of the meal he stood up, and holding his glass in his hand turned to Pavel Petrovich.

'You are leaving us . . . you are leaving us, dearest brother,' he began, 'not for long, of course; but still I cannot help telling you what I . . . what we . . . how much I . . . how much we. . . . But the trouble is, we don't know how to make speeches! Arkady, you try.'

'I can't, papa, I'm not prepared.'

'And I'm so well prepared! Well, brother, allow me then quite simply to embrace you, to wish you the best of good fortune, and do come back to us as soon as you can!'

Pavel Petrovich exchanged kisses with everyone, including Mitya, of course; in Fenichka's case he kissed her hand, too, which she had not yet learned to offer properly, and drinking off the glass that had been refilled with wine he said with a deep sigh: 'Be happy, my friends!' And then, in English, 'Farewell!' This English tail-piece passed unnoticed but everybody was moved.

'To Bazarov's memory,' whispered Katya in her husband's ear as she clinked glasses with him. Arkady squeezed her hand hard in response but did not venture to propose that toast aloud.

This would seem to be the end. But perhaps some of our readers would care to know what each of the characters we have introduced is doing now, at the present moment. We are ready to oblige.

Anna Sergeyevna has recently married again, not for love but out of conviction (that it was the reasonable thing to do) a man who promises to be one of the future leaders of Russia, a very able lawyer possessed of vigorous practical sense, a strong will and remarkable gifts of eloquence. He is quite young still, kind-hearted and as cold as ice. They live in the greatest harmony together, and may live to attain happiness ... or even love. The old princess is dead, forgotten the very day she died. The Kirsanovs, father and son, have settled down in Maryino. Their affairs have taken a turn for the better. Arkady has become passionately engrossed in the management of the estate, and the 'farm' now yields a fairly substantial income. Nikolai Petrovich has become an arbitrator in the land reforms and puts all his energy into the work; he is constantly driving about the district, delivers long speeches (he holds the opinion that the peasants must be taught to 'listen to reason', meaning they must be worn down by frequent repetition of one and the same phrase); and yet, to tell the truth, he fails to give complete satisfaction either to the cultured gentry, who talk sourly or with melancholy about the emancipation* (giving the final *on* a nasal sound), or to the ignorant ones who make no bones about cursing that damned ' 'muncipation'. He is too mild for both camps. Katya has given birth to a son, little Nikolai, while Mitya scampers all over the place and prattles away loquaciously. Next to her husband and Mitya Fenichka – Fedosya Nikolayevna – adores no one more than her daughter-in-law and when Katya sits down at the piano she would be only too delighted to spend the whole day at her side. We must say a word here about Piotr. He has grown quite rigid with stupidity and self-importance, pronounces all his *o*'s like *ou* and says

* The emancipation of the serfs in 1861.

'*Nou*' for '*No*', but he, too, is married and together with his bride has appropriated to himself quite a respectable dowry. His wife is the daughter of a market-gardener in the town: she had previously turned down two eligible suitors solely because they did not own watches, whereas Piotr not only had a watch – he even had a pair of patent leather boots.

In Dresden, on the Brühl terrace between two and four o'clock in the afternoon, the most fashionable time for promenading, you may come across a gentleman of some fifty years of age, already quite grey and apparently suffering from gout, but still handsome, elegantly attired and having that air of distinction which only comes to those who have been long accustomed to move in the higher ranks of society. He is Pavel Petrovich. From Moscow he had gone abroad for the sake of his health and then stayed on in Dresden, where he associates chiefly with English and Russian visitors. With the English he behaves simply, almost with modesty, but not without a touch of *hauteur*; they find him a trifle tedious but respect him for being, as they say, 'a perfect gentleman'. With Russians he is more free and easy, gives vent to his spleen, jests at his own expense and theirs; but it all comes very pleasantly from him, in a light-hearted, well-bred way. He is a Slavophil in outlook: as is well known, this is considered *très distingué* in the best society. He reads nothing Russian but on his writing-desk there is a silver ashtray in the shape of a peasant's bast shoe. He is much sought after by our tourists from Russia. Matvei Ilyich Kolyazin, happening to be 'temporarily in opposition', paid him a ceremonious visit when he was passing through Dresden on his way to the Bohemian watering-places; and the local inhabitants, with whom, however, he has little to do, treat him almost with veneration. No one is more successful than the *Herr Baron von Kirsanoff* in obtaining easily and expeditiously tickets for the Court choir, the theatre and so on. And within his capacity he continues to do good works; in a small way he still causes a stir; it was not for nothing that he had been a social lion once upon a time; but life weighs heavily on him ... more heavily than he himself suspects. One glance at him in the Russian Church is enough to confirm this, as he leans in some corner against the wall, motionless and lost in thought, with lips tightly compressed; then at long last he will suddenly recollect himself and begin almost imperceptibly to cross himself. ...

Madame Kukshin, too, has settled abroad. She is now in Heidelberg, no longer studying the natural sciences but architecture in which, so she declares, she has discovered some new laws. As before, she is hail-fellow-well-met with students, especially with young Russians doing physics and chemistry who crowd Heidelberg and at first flabbergast the simple-minded German professors by their sober outlook on things, and later on astound the same professors by their complete inertia and absolute sloth. In company with two or three such young students of chemistry, who cannot distinguish oxygen from hydrogen but are brimming over with destructive criticism and self-conceit, and, too, with the great Eliseyevich, Sitnikov, also preparing to be a great man, gads about Petersburg and, as he assures us, continues the 'work' of Bazarov. Rumour has it that someone recently boxed his ears but that he got his own back: in an obscure little article tucked away in an obscure little periodical he hinted that the person who had assaulted him was a coward. This he calls irony. His father sends him here, there and everywhere as before, and his wife regards him as a fool ... and a *littérateur*.

There is a small village graveyard in one of the remote corners of Russia. Like most of our graveyards it has a melancholy look; the ditches round it have long been overgrown; grey wooden crosses sag and rot beneath their once painted gables; the tomb-stones are all askew, as though someone were pushing them from below; two or three shabby trees barely afford some meagre shade; sheep wander at will over the graves. ... But there is one among the graves which no man molests and no animal tramples upon: only the birds perch on it and sing at dawn. An iron railing fences it in; two young fir-trees have been planted there, one at each end: Yevgeny Bazarov lies buried in this grave. Often from the little near-by village two frail old people, a husband and wife, make their way there. Supporting each other, they walk with heavy steps; they go up to the iron railing, fall on their knees and weep long and bitterly, and long and yearningly they gaze at the silent stone beneath which their son is lying; exchanging a brief word, they brush the dust from the stone, set a branch of a fir-tree right, and then resume their prayers, unable to tear themselves away from the place where they feel nearer to their son, to their memories of him. . . . But are those prayers of theirs, those tears, all fruitless? Is their love, their hallowed selfless love, not omnipotent? Oh yes! However passionate, sinful and rebellious the heart hidden in the tomb, the flowers growing over it peep at us serenely with their innocent eyes; they speak to us not only of eternal peace, of the vast repose of 'indifferent' nature: they tell us, too, of everlasting reconciliation and of life which has no end.

1861